Of Human Interest

To Tang

To Carole Chenk friend
with appreciation for your
interest.
     Lewis W. Green
     Jan. 22   2004

Of Human Interest

Lewis W. Green

iUniverse, Inc.
New York Lincoln Shanghai

Of Human Interest

iUniverse, Inc.

For information address:
iUniverse, Inc.
2021 Pine Lake Road, Suite 100
Lincoln, NE 68512
www.iuniverse.com

ISBN: 0-595-30544-X

Printed in the United States of America

In Appreciation

To Sandi Allison, who tirelessly and patiently did much of the computer work on this book as it involved arranging, pagination, etc. and who did it without pay. Her help was indispensible and most valuable. Much appreciation also goes to her husband Rex and her employer Mike Keleher, both of whom were highly supportive of our labors.

Thanks also to Buncombe County Sheriff Blobby Medford and his Chief Deputy George Stewart and former assistant Asheville Police Chief Gene Jarvis, all of whom relentlessly harped at me to do this book until I finally began it. We are old friends and those men knew me in the old days when much of this was happening. They insisted that some of the law enforcement experiences must be written, and that I was the only man present for most of it.

Contents

Dear Lord, Forgive Us Our Press Passes xi

The Man Who Sold The Great Smoky Mountains National Park 1

Ratting Out The Asheville Establishment 7

The Sheriff Who Couldn't Stand the Sight of Blood or Corpses 10

Curt Ratcliff, Mr. Chairman 12

Tom Donoho 16

Mamie Reynolds Redux 22

The Demonic Murders by The Foxes 31

A Freed Spirit Wandering Through The Bureaucracy 40

Bujie and Herman 58

Zeno 60

The Repentance and Redemption of Attorney Tom Garrison 62

Thad Bryson 65

One of The Martin Luther King Visits 67

Julian Bond and Lester Maddox 70

The Screaming Doomed Were In The Sky, Then They Were Dead
On The Ground, ... 72

Lannie Boy Briggs (Omar Shabazz) & Asheville Muslims 74

WNC Nazis—Frank Braswell 78

Carl Sandburg 83

About Thomas Wolfe & His brother Fred. 88

Older Men Watching: The Influence of MentorsWhen the student
    is ready, the teacher appears 101

The Pie Lady and Harold Thoms 107

Outward Bound School and the Code Three. 111

Zane Hill. 117

Colonel Paul Rockwell Of The French Foreign Legion 122

Doppelgangers, Wraiths, Spirits, etc. 126

The Recall Election of Clay County Sheriff Hartsell Moore. 131

Big Nell, For Whom The Bell Tolls. 134

Max Wilson and Gordon Greenwood 138

Typical Races In Buncombe County Circa 140

Sandy Fired 148

The Old Man's New Mule 150

Shoot Out at Curtis Creek. 154

The Return of The Mountain Lions 158

A Backwoods Snake Cult. 163

Time, A Robber Baron, Stole The Golden Years 165

83-Year Old Ex-Klondike Prospector's Shootout With Robbers In
    West Buncombe. 168

The Chief of Police Wore Diapers. 170

Asheville Police Corruption 177

Incident Report The Jailed Whore. 184

John F. Kennedy, The Plagiarist 185

Francis Stevens 186

Madison County Vote—1964. 190

An Essay by Lewis W. Green on Outlanders Moving into the
    Mountains 193

Buck Lyda, In Memory Of... 198

The Sheriff and Barbara 202

The Wop At The Top. 203

Surveillance of The Editor At All Souls 207

Nine Gays In Group Orgy In Public Park. 209

The Piss-ant Factor At Oral Souls Lesbyterian Cathedral 211

Literary Comments & Reviews Of The Books By Lewis W.
    Green. 217

Ghosts By The Wind Grieved. 219

The High-Pitched Laugh Of A Sainted Crazy. 227

Fred Chappell, Novelist and Poet Laureate of North Carolina, Here
    reviews Green's Collection of Short Stories, The High Pitched
    Laugh of A Painted Lady 236

Unsigned review 238

A Country Rag Rural Review 241

The Professional Background of Editor-publisher Lewis W.
    Green. 246

Dear Lord,
Forgive Us Our Press Passes

❖

(Become aware of everything, attached to nothing—the Jesuits)

First the apologia and disclaimers. Anything faintly approaching a memoir must of needs be laden with the first person singular, the irritating "me, myself or I". In the case of this work, there is also the need for high-powered name-dropping in some of the more interesting stories. Unless it is also laden with credible modesty, it will inevitably be labeled an ego trip. So be it, but let me, myself and I point out that after more than 40 years of newspapering and other investigative work, especially in Buncombe and other North Carolina mountain counties, almost anyone will have what is normally referred to as "ego" tattered and shattered. (However, following that baptism by fire, or initiation into the craft, the authentic ego emerges and grows stronger.)

This book is a compilation of both newspaper accounts and investigative experiences in law enforcement over a period of more than 40 years. As the years passed, one grows a bit jaded and as I put together this volume, I first decided to name it Asheville, The Theater of the Absurd. Many of these stories highlight the absurd in this town, but I determined to hold that title for my next book, which will chronicle my so-called excommunication from The Episcopal Church at All Souls Cathedral, which was truly fraught with absurdity enacted by absurd people as homosexual priests and parishioners began taking over. I was publishing The Independent Torch and as their political agenda grew, I began writing about them in highly offensive language, using pejoratives such as queer, faggots, dykes, etc.That drove them to extreme reactions, at last to a phony excommunication, and legal documents forbidding me from setting foot on church property, hiring off-duty undercover policemen keeping me under surveillance during services, and at last four police cruisers circling the church to bar my entrance. I have received some tentative inquiries about such a book from religious publishers.Some of those instances are in this book.

I became a reporter (I hesitate to use the highly pretentious term Journalist, which once meant people who wrote for real journals and now means anyone involved in any kind of newspaper writing) at The Asheville Citizen-Times in 1961 and remained there ten years. It was a highly rewarding experience for some time, then slowly the coziness of that ownership with an oppressive (and suppressive) local political machine began to take its toll. I quit the C-T and founded a weekly newspaper entitled The Native Stone, which went down in flames after three-and-a-half years. But it did win several N.C. Press Association awards. (They are listed in the resume I publish on a separate page herein.)

After a period of teaching at Warren-Wilson College, UNC-A, Haywood Tech and the Intentional Growth Center at Lake Junaluska, I founded a monthly political journal named Overtones, and after some years I started The Independent Torch, which I edited and managed for 16 years.

It was those years as an independent that proved the most productive for me as a novelist and freelance writer. Things occurred in that wild atmosphere that would not have if I was acting under the restraints of political and commercial supervision. It developed over a period of time into street or guerrilla theater, which many of my readers grew to expect and appreciate, others diagnosed as insanity. From time to time events would develop toward the ridiculous and it was not even appropriate to preserve dignity. Just accept the roles that fate scripted and ride with it. To hell with image. Journalistic street-preaching? As Asheville and the entire region began taking on the coloration of newcomers from other states, nations and cultures, and of the local new drug-ridden generations, the place gained a reputation for craziness and for The Independent Torch to stay apace, there came a requirement for a wilder, crazier approach. (Becoming aware but not attached, enjoying the many benefits of a growing and generally exaggerated local legend.)

Being also a novelist I extracted dialogue, situations, hypocrisy etc. from the daily rounds, which I have duly filed in my gigantic folder named "Notes & Observations." It should also be noted that some of the people who reacted strongly to come of the ephemeral news and feature material are going to find my coming historical writings galling. Ala Thomas Wolfe, don't you know?

But only a bit of that recent writing is included herein. This volume is from my older files and is a mixed collection of stories from those publications and is in no particular order because of the high state of disorder of my decades of filing.

I have chosen to lead off with the story of Clyde Leeson, an uninhibited friend whom I first met when I covered his trial in U.S.District Court in the mid-1960s on charges of selling much of The Great Smoky Mountains National Park, a wily scheme which rapidly spun out of his control and became of national interest: and for which he did not have to do a day in prison. A number of prominent and educated people bought some of the land and/or became involved in the scheme.

That story is followed by one in which I was leaked information by two of the most important men in Asheville who were disgusted with the conniving by the local city political structure. I could not use the names of those sources at that time, but now they are both dead and I do tell who they were in this edition.

After that, not in chronological order, comes stories of and interviews with such luminaries as Carl Sandburg, Martin Luther King Jr. during his visits here, Julian Bond, Thomas Wolfe's brother Fred and brother-in-law Ralph Wheaton, Dr. George Bonds of the Sealab project fame and many others

There is information on four of my mentors as my career developed. There are also stories of notorious local murders and other crimes, and the many pathetic human interest stories I covered as the subjects went toward their fates.

At the end of this volume I include some of the high-brow literary journal reviews of my books, with a rationale for doing so.

I have enough material like this in my files for at least two more books such as this (depending on time and circumstances) as well as the one planned on the excommunication from All Souls. Enjoy.

The Man Who Sold The Great Smoky Mountains National Park

❖

Swindles of the 1960s

In other days, the white man came and cheated the red man out of the land. Having set that precedent the white men have cheated each other out of the land under one pretext or another since then.

Let this be prelude to the most fascinating series of land swindles in the history of Western North Carolina. The private sale of much of The Great Smoky Mountains National Park in the mid-1960s.

Rather than label this as an interesting but ordinary small-town crime, one must look at it as a strange phenomena—a complex morality play. Destiny seems to have stepped in and directed the action thence.

These old mountains cast their spell, weave their history in the annals of commerce. Fortunes have been made in mining and minerals, lumber especially.

The century just past saw the administration of President Franklin Delano Roosevelt buy up much private WNC land for the government and dedicate it as the Great Smoky Mountains National Park. Tourism has turned it into a large commercial venture.

There! The great park. A jewel to be cut. Fate looked on to see who would come.

Ashevillian Clyde Leeson was charged and tried on several counts of mail fraud, and found guilty. Yet he never did a day in prison for it (though a lawyer, Fred Sigman, connected with the case did. He certified the titles).

A review of the trial transcript shows that only a befuddled case was brought in Federal Court against Leeson.

While the matter reached and maintained a local legendary status over the years, it only recently was revived when movie producer Karl Genus came here and showed interest in it. Nothing has come of that.

One of the important things revealed in the trial transcript was that Leeson never "sold" thousands of acres in the park and none of those who bought it testified that he had. He sold old land grant deeds more than one hundred years old, and intimated only that there may or may not have some undeeded property in them.

To add to the craziness and amazement surrounding the story, prominent figures were buying into the deal. Others not so prominent paid for their deeds with bad checks. Among those who got in were restaurant-motel mogul Howard Johnson, who bought the Nantahala Gorge to use it for a land-fill for cities throughout the eastern U.S. His plan was to "lop off mountain-tops to level off the gorge".after the canoe-kayak-tourist paradise was filled with garbage from cities throughout the south.

Another customer was a Superior Court Judge from Fayetteville who flew in to make his purchase, and a diamond dealer who arrived from New Orleans with two valises of diamonds with which to deal.

As it developed, we find Leeson renting a plane to fly customers (or marks) over the park so they might pick out the land they wanted. Local surveyor B.J. Lefler was in the plane to write a deed on the spot and notarize it even before they landed.

No poor and destitute people were defrauded—only con-artists in their own right. Some Mafiosa came to invest. As they flew over Fontana Dam, they asked what that was. It was explained to them that it was the only virgin lake left in the eastern United States, so they began negotiating for various amounts of front feet.

This comedy of errors began this way:

In 1965 Leeson was involved in some real estate deals in Jackson County with realtor Dick Parsons who happened to mention that a retired lawyer in Bryson City, John Randolph, had some historical old land-grant deeds he was interested in selling. Randolph was near 90 and had been retired for some time. He was also disposing of other such artifacts as he had picked up over the decades.

Leeson went to see him, found that Randolph was a jolly old gent sitting at an antique table in the exclusive Fryemont Inn and drinking Jack Daniels whiskey. They hit it off and talked about the deeds and their potential.

At that time Randolph said that there was land available—free and clear—in the old deed area, but it would take too much time and money to separate the wheat from the chaff by surveys.

He told Leeson he would accept any reasonable offer for them. Leeson's offer was $2,500 and four fifths of Jack Daniels. Randolph allowed Leeson to take the valises full of the old papers to his lawyer in Asheville, the late Henry Fisher. (As the affair progressed over the next couple of years, a number of prominent Asheville attorneys became involved in some form or fashion.)

Fisher took an overnight look at the deeds and the next day told Leeson there was potentially a fortune in those deeds. He had deeds ready in four days. Leeson took the deeds to Randolph, who signed them and sent them to Bennett's Pharmacy in downtown Bryson City. The pharmacist was a notary public and notarized them and the grand scheme was set in motion.

One minor glitch. Maggie Warren worked in the Swain County Register-of-Deeds office and she refused to register the deeds. She termed them invalid. Henry Fisher set in to raising hell and notified her that if she did not register them he would go straight to the state Attorney General's office. She registered them, but the registration meant nothing legally.

No one promised anyone any land. The understanding from Randolph to Leeson, and from Leeson to others later, was that there may or may nor be land free and clear under the deeds that the government had not bought and that it would likely take a surveyor to determine it. Let the buyer beware.

Some amazing figures were being mentioned in the Randolph documents. In the early days of transactions in the 19th century, upwards of 65,000 acres at fifty cents an acre was mentioned.

Randolph had been born and raised in Yancey County. He was descended from the Randolphs of the Famous Families of Virginia and had distinguished himself as a lawyer in North Carolina.

He practiced before the U.S. Supreme Court and had married well. At the time of the Leeson transaction he was disposing of most of his worldly goods and left his niece some valuable holdings, including an exclusive tourist inn, The Randolph House, in Bryson City. He was way too smart to make guarantees, nor did he even have to consider it. According to one of his nieces, he simply felt the documents were valuable as historical documents.

It didn't take long after the deeds were registered for destiny's river to rise.

The first action came when a builder in Mobile, Alabama, a friend of Leeson's, needed a loan to finish a project. Still innocent at this stage, Leeson told him he didn't have the millions the man needed but he did have the deeds which might be acceptable as collateral. Indeed (and in deed) they were.

It shifted into the most amazing and complex wheeling and dealing which saw Leeson indicted and convicted in U.S. District Court here on several counts of mail fraud.

Probably the only workable movie approach to what happened will be to explore the dramatic/ironic/-comedic twists, and also to show some of the characters in their most sympathetic light. It goes without saying that there is profound irony and some personal tragedy in the business strivings and life of Clyde Leeson, a good old boy whose ambitions exploded into a universal tale of greed and woe.

Getting to the point here, word got out that Leeson had this valuable land (which included most of the Great Smoky Mountains National Park, Fontana Dam, and the Nantahala Gorge, among other landmarks) and here came the customers. For the sake of a possible filming script it must be said that they were not innocents speculating their life savings, but rather (mostly) greedy sharps shooting for a deal, some investing ill-gotten gains from other deals.

For starters there was Howard Johnson of Florida, the founder of the Howard Johnson motel chain, who negotiated for the beautiful Nantahala Gorge so he could turn that into a garbage dump, where he could get concessions from most cities in the Southeastern United States to haul their garbage there by rail, level off the gorge and "make it flat and usable".

There came to the trough a Superior Court Judge from Fayetteville. There are several versions of him in the legend. One is that he brought his own plane and flew over the Smokies in company with Candler surveyor B.J. Lefler and from the air had suitable locations selected by Lefler. One version has it that as His Honor picked out his sites from the plane, Lefler wrote him a deed and notarized it. Lefler denies that part, but said the rest of the story is true.

Bring into the act two mafia henchmen, whom the legend says were brought here from Washington, D.C. by a restauranteur. Apparently they all bought some of the deeds Leeson was selling. That is testified to by Lefler, who says he was in the hotel room when that deal went down.

Lefler said the restauranteur would snap fingers in his left hand, and one of the mafiosa would put a cigarette in his mouth. Then he would snap the fingers on his other hand, and the other mafiosa would light the cigarette.

This part sounds faintly credible, since a version by former State Senator Herbert Hyde seems to back it up.

It seems that some of the land the mafiosa bought had legitimacy. Hyde said he later searched title in Swain County and found it to be good. Seeking the hoods, Hyde found they were by then serving time in a northern prison, so he went there and bought the land from them. He still owns it.

Here, pan the camera in on a New Orleans diamond merchant who had heard of the Leeson properties and flew here with two valises of diamonds handcuffed to his wrists. He began to swap diamonds for land.

Some of the land was paid for by bad checks. Now just how were they going to be prosecuted for buying non-existent land with non-existent bank accounts?

For sheer local laughs, we can see the many attorneys who got involved in one way or another, none illegally. What a script!

I have read the script that the producer Genus had prepared. He reveals Leeson as a solid, compassionate man whose lifetime has been spent here, educated in the Asheville public schools, held good jobs with local businesses, had friends and a great social life here. As his wife was dying from cancer in later years, Leeson refused to put her in a hostice, stayed by her bedside and was holding her hand when the end came. She stuck with him in those bad days when most of his old friends ostracized him, he made sure he was holding her hand when the dark angel came.

Yes, the elements are all there for a film production which could range from high satire, comedy, outrage at the greed of men, tragedy as a career seemed to be slipping away in Federal Court.

And shrewdness. Leeson's defense attorney was Lamar Gudger, who upon conviction of his client, gave notice of appeal, which put a new and more serious light upon the matter for the government. Lamar was going to ask that the government prove it owned the land, which would mean about 50 years of surveying and millions of dollars.

An insider told us the U.S. Attorney General sent word to this District Court to let Leeson walk. He got a long probationary sentence and was fined about $10,000, and with that the greatest scam that WNC had ever witnessed drew to a close.

As a sequel, however, and keeping with his sense of humor, Leeson has suggested that souvenir deeds to the Great Smokies be drawn up and he would be happy to autograph them. He revealed that he has already been asked to autograph last week's copy of The Independent Torch.

Very well, life continues on its track. Destiny made its hits and moved on.

A couple of years after the trial we saw Clyde on the street, asked him where he had been.

"In Federal prison," he said.

"What? I thought you walked…"

This was for a different matter, he said.

What?

"I sold some coal mines in Kentucky I didn't own…some that didn't even exist…"

Ah God. Marvelous.

His luck held. He said that he spent those few months of his sentence at an Air Force Base in Alabama, where his duties included, among other things, serving as a golf pro for the officers at the base golf course On these amazing factors, this legend was built, and grows. It would make one helluva movie.

Ratting Out The Asheville Establishment

◆

Federal Appeals Court Judge Braxton Craven & Chamber of Commerce Director Opie Shelton Saw Enough

As a testament to the civic corruption here, and the high level of disdain for the daily newspaper, within weeks of my opening of a weekly newspaper which I named The Native Stone, I developed some contacts whose credibility could not be doubted, but the disclosure of their names would have caused them much distress and probably career damage. Therefore I could not divulge the sources of the information then, but since thirty years or more have passed and both are dead now. Our primary contact was through emissaries I knew and trusted, and both approached without the knowledge of the other.

The first emissary was John Hennegar, a seasoned FBI agent who became a good friend when we worked together on some gambling and other racketeering going on here. (More stories on that elsewhere in this book.)

Hennegar showed up in my office with his usual deceptive smile and after the pleasantries said "I know someone who can supply you with inside information on some of these local government sleazes if you won't use his name."

"Well John, you know me."

"I don't know you this well. I have to be damn sure on this one."

"Come on, let's hear it."

He glared fiercely and said "Tell you what. You compromise this source and I'll see that you are found dead and your ashes are scattered to the four winds."

"How can they find me dead if my ashes are scattered to the four winds? Who the hell is it, J. Edgar Hoover?"

He leaned across my desk and said "Judge Craven wants to leak you some information from time to time. With no attribution."

Wow! J. Braxton Craven was one of the most distinguished Federal Fourth District Court of Appeals Judges, the last stop before the U.S. Supreme Court. On out past my field of gravity. Judge Craven had an office in Asheville's Federal Building.

"Why? What could he leak through me that he couldn't get someone in the government to give to the Citizen-Times?"

John snorted. "Ha. It's not national, it's local. It's something they wouldn't print."

We talked, it became clear. Judge Craven was truly a decent man. A conscientious citizen above all else. He belonged to the City Club and other organizations where the city's business, political and civic leaders gathered, and where they openly discussed most of the chicanery they planned. If they plotted something illegal he could do nothing officially because it wasn't federal. But he knew they discussed many things that affected the public, but that they didn't want the public to learn. Even though some of the top executives of The Citizen-Times were members and present, they weren't about to cover it because they were part of the power structure.

"It just burns Judge Craven up," Hennegar said.

"Why me?" I asked. The familiar answer.

"You're all there is," Hennegar said. "He knows they all read The Native Stone. When some of this supposedly secret or confidential stuff hits your paper prematurely, they will back off. A lot of this includes the Chamber of Commerce people and the Biltmore House people. The daily is their whore."

We set up a simple code word. If I got an anonymous tip in the mail it would contain that word. I never broke my promise.

At about the same time, the wife of a good friend came to me with a similar proposition. She said her boss would like to deal with me in strict secrecy. We went through essentially the same assurances I had made Hennegar. Then she picked up the phone and dialed, then said "I'm with Lewis. He says you can trust him. Here he is."

"Hello Lewis, this is Opie Shelton."

Good God! Another shocker. Opie was the relatively new executive director of the Asheville Area Chamber of Commerce.

"Glad to hear from you," I said. "What's up?"

"Lewis, I hear you've got several years of sobriety in AA. I also have several years. We both know we can't stay sober if we're not honest with the world."

"Right."

"Well, I've not been here long, but I'll tell you something you already know. This is the crookedest, most devious power structure I've ever been in. Some of the things discussed openly at meetings could conceivably get us all locked up."

Again, "Why me?"

"You're all there is. Some of the Citizen-Times executives are on the board. Everybody works together. I can send you some information, but you can't quote me. You'll have to check out the documentation yourself. Sometimes some of it will show up on the minutes, if you can get them. If you call me for confirmation I'll either have to deny it or have no comment."

That was suspicious, but after following his tips a few times I found them to be solid, as were Judge Craven's. Some establishment pillars were shitting bricks. They couldn't find out how the information was getting out.

The Sheriff Who Couldn't Stand the Sight of Blood or Corpses

❖

Coroner John Young & Sheriff Harry P. Clay

The youthful new Republican Sheriff Harry P. Clay could not stand the sight of blood. The old and politically seasoned Democratic coroner Dr. John Young knew that.

One Sunday morning at Deaverview a young wife had taken all she could from an abusive, estranged husband, and as he lunged up the steps to her home she shot him in the heart with a double-barreled shotgun. Investigating deputies removed the bodies to Ansers-Rice Funeral Home to await a coroner's ruling. Then they called Dr. John Young, then me. I arrived at the funeral home shortly after Dr. Young.

The body had already been stripped and was laying on a porcelain gurney, blood running down small channels, out a hole and dripping into a small bucket hung under it. In those days a coroner had the authority to order a sheriff to be present for an autopsy if he decided he needed such a witness. We all looked at the ragged, gaping wound in the man's chest and the blood draining down the table.

Dr. Young nodded sagely. "Uh huh, I think such a crime should be witnessed by the High Sheriff."

Present was the Chief Deputy Willis Mitchell, a seasoned retired ATF agent with a wry, subtle sense of irony. He said :"I knew he would do that. He knows the Sheriff can't stand the sight of blood, and the Sheriff was out drunk most of the night."

He turned and ordered a deputy to go get the Sheriff. Dr. Young, recognizing the potential of the situation, was in high good humor, exchanging wit and badinage with us. A patient man.

Finally the Sheriff came in, sweating and sick. He refused to look at the body. Dr. Young had a scalpel ready. He zipped the torso open, dipped in and brought forth a double handful of buckshot and clotted blood.

"Look here, Sheriff," he said. "I'm going to rule that this man died from a shotgun wound to the chest. Will you agree with my opinion?" He held the evidence out to the Sheriff, whose eyes rolled back and slowly slid down the wall, passed out.

The deputies were smothering grins and giggles. Dr. Young stared off to a mid-distance. His face held a faint smile, patiently waiting for the Sheriff to come to.

The Sheriff's eyes slowly opened and with the help of a couple of deputies he groped his way up the wall like a punchy prizefighter on the ropes. He was retching and sweating.

Finally he pointed his finger at the Coroner and gasped "All right, you Democrat son-of-a-bitch, I'm going to arrest you for defaming a dead body."

Willis shook his head, asked the smirking coroner if he was done, then respectfully led the heaving Sheriff out the door.

Curt Ratcliff, Mr. Chairman

Curt Ratcliff, a phenomenal politician in his time and setting, is gone. He died in such a quiet and unheralded manner that his friends did not get a chance to bid him farewell. He had been sick for all the years since he left office, so when he was hospitalized once again there was no alarm. He suddenly slipped away.

Congestive heart failure? Maybe. But perhaps it was partly heartbreak and disappointment.

Not of himself but for all the others he had witnessed fall short....

In a time for the obsequies, the neglected memories begin to pass again. Comparisons and similies must be sought to bespeak the man. We can seek elevated comparisons of the man's character from other times, decades, ages. But he was local, and of our time which alone illuminates him even clearer because this is a dark time for integrity.

Years ago, in Curt Ratcliff's time, I had a friend who was a Russian Rabbi, Schmeil Buchlender, dead himself these many years now, but then a judge of character and an observer of the human condition and of politics, in which some of the most interesting (and sordidly selfish) revelations of human nature are revealed. Though he had retired to Haywood County, He watched Curt, discussed him with me and others in the context of contemporary politics in the mountain area.

I remember this: Sam used an ancient Hebrew word, Aishim, which he interpreted as having the soul of a "justified" man, a proper man in the sense of being an upright, strong and intelligent person. When I look back on Curt, I now recognize all that. Intelligent and sensitive, and often unable to articulate his thoughts, but that was because he sensed when he was dealing with people who did not understand. That brings forth another quite grandiose comparison—the ancient Taoist priest whom fools took to be an even greater fool than themselves, but whom wise men recognized as an incomparable sage. Not because of the way he acted, but because of the way people reacted to him. Curt did not know about that, or care.

It was easy to misjudge him when he arrived on the scene. He was an Enka plant worker who had once operated a small country store. He knew the working people, which too many Republicans don't.

A young Harry P. Clay had won the Sheriff's office, and had such a remarkable record that he swept the whole Republican ticket into office the next election. One was Curt Ratcliff, a new Clerk of Court. In the second term, Clay became corrupt and crooked, consorting with the king-pin of Buncombe racketeers. Everyone involved in politics knew in the final year that Clay was doomed and those Republicans who had won because of him, ran like turkeys in the next campaign.

The subtle telling moments reveal a man's character. Ratcliff agreed to open his campaign headquarters up with the disgraced Clay. "I rode in on his coat-tails," Curt said. "I'll go down with him." He did.

But he had made an impression, and got a nice job with the housing authority. Then the time came to run again. He filed for Chairman of the County Commissioners. I can speak of that part of his career. I was there when he went in, and I was there when he went out.

I had founded The Native Stone and was wearing myself out with it. As Curt opened his early campaign, he could not get the gray whore of a daily newspaper to give him any coverage. Bob Long called me one Saturday morning and asked if I would provide photo coverage of Curt's first rally at Owen High School. I told Long I was too tired. "You're all we've got," he said. I went. Later, after he won, Curt said he owed me.

I told him "No, but remember if you follow Clay into corruption I'll be on your ass."

"I would be disappointed if you weren't," he said, and we closed that deal.

As a writer who has kept a personal journal for more than 40 years, and upon which to draw for writings other than The Independent Torch, I had a compelling interest in Curt and his effects. Comparisons between he and his successors? Those come away pallid.

He well reflected the larger community values. Though the easy label is conservative, that did not fit him snugly. Rather, his administration reflected common sense and tried to fit a practical approach into the constantly slipping structure of local politics.

Always the telling moments appeared. We knew he represented the people when he told The Chamber of Commerce pimps where to shove some of their schemes. With a deceptively soft smile, of course. It was that action, if no other, that revealed him in this way: In Miami years ago the 18-year old son of a very rich and wise mother implored her to buy him a yacht. She did. As owner that made him a ship's captain, so entitled him to join the Captain's Club, where merchant and military captains ate and drank.

Proudly he strutted to her. "Mama, I'm a captain now. I've joined the Captain's Club."

My son, my son, she said, patting him patiently. "I know you're a captain. You know you're a captain. But do the captain's know you're a captain?"

After some early encounters with Curt, the captains here knew he was a captain.

At The Native Stone, I unabashedly helped Curt in his reelection bids. Then TNS went down and I was without work—with a wife and three sons. Some time later I was sitting, quite depressed and defeated, on a boulder on my property in Fairview, when I saw (the now deceased) Lew Geddings, one of Curt's aides walking slowly through the trees toward me.

"Curt wants to know if you want a job? It's not much. It's one of these CETA grants. It's all we've got."

You betcha. It stretched into a couple of years, historical research at Southeastern Forest Research Station, teaching at Warren Wilson College, adjunct faculty at UNC-A (with the recommendation of Papa Doc Rainey, of all things. Rainey later beat Curt in an election).

Later I told Curt I owed him. "No, I still owe you for that Owen High School coverage," he said.

Some years later, as the Rainey/Ratcliff election drew to a close, I was at the Board of Elections. Curt was behind with three precincts still out. Margaret Shepherd softly, sadly, told me there would not be enough votes in those to pull it out. I was the one who went to Curt's office, where he waited alone in semidarkness.

"Curt, you're beat."

He slumped briefly, nodded, and said he was glad. He had been sick a year then.

As I left something occurred to me, less grandiose than all my earlier references. Something definitely Tar Heel. It was what once was said about Zeb Vance when he tried to deal with the state legislature a century ago. In local politics, Curt looked like a grain of polished rice in a barrel of rat turds.

The years went by. His heart condition worsened. Very few people went to see him. We had lunch a couple of time. Occasionally I would take someone there.

Morris Ratcliff, his cousin, called me early one morning last week and said "Curt died last night."

I went to the visitation. Most of the old crowd was there. A conventional wake of mountain people.

A couple of days later I walked through the woods to the boulder and sat awhile, thinking about it all. I pulled the memory file. Here was the telling moment…it came clear, hauntingly vivid. Here out of all those years slipped the ghost of Lew Geddings slowly, tentatively, through the poplars.

"Lewis, Curt wants to know if you want a job…It ain't much…"

And I shook for a moment. "By God, it was enough." I said to the poplars and brush.

And so, at the risk of a maudlin grandiosity, let me say farewell old friend. There is a warm wind at your back.

Tom Donoho

❖

A Man With High Personal Voltage

Big Tom Donoho died on election day in 2002, an entirely appropriate time for him considering his long and honorable involvement in politics, and we may safely assume that he had voted the morning he died. (At any rate, the candidates he was backing won.)

His influence, even on the day of his death, was felt among the city precincts. At lunchtime at a downtown restaurant, one politician had a call on his cellular phone. He turned to someone and said something incredibly brief, then that man turned to his lunch clique and said only "Damn, Tom Donaho has died."

We waited for the punch-line of this terribly gauche, and irreverent and political insiders joke, the lack of political correctness and sensitivity for which that lunch-bunch is noted. But it did not come. Everyone there slumped a bit and withdrew briefly into themselves and everyone present evaded each other's eyes.

Tom Donoho is dead?

Voting was heavier than usual that day, and the word spread among precinct workers at the polls. Always the first question was "How is Betty?"

There was the great sense of dread, because half of her had just been blown away. But Betty is Irish tough. People went by the house, but she was at the funeral home making arrangements. Then, in hushed reverence, all the nice things were sai—all true, of course, but not the whole truth. Here we enter some of the story of the Donohos and their long community service, not in any particular sequence or chronology, just some sketches that may help paint a clearer picture.

They were a pair, and in that combination we saw the virtues and a silent healing factor work out of their patience and great generosity, both in and out of the brutal political world.

We can go at length into all the good works which few people knew about, and for which the pair of them sought no public notice. But that was better done in eulogy at the funeral home.

I first knew Tom Donoho in the early 1960s when I was a reporter for the daily newspaper. He, Bill McCarter, Earl Myers, Bob Hill, J.D. Jackson, Bob Hill, the Henson boys and their step-father, D.O. Creasman (who piloted his private plane into a mountain in east Buncombe on a foggy morning) and others were active in the Optimist Club Santa Pal project. They requested that I write stories about that project to help raise money.

It did not take me long to fall in with this group of solid middle-class men, successful in their business endeavors, who met the harsh challenge of facing Asheville poverty and poor children in December. (Many of these guys had started life in poverty, had succeeded and remembered.)

I went with Tom and the others to the houses to investigate the applications of the poor parents, later to take the toys. Then they worked late on those cold nights to prepare the bundles.

These guys had small children of their own and perhaps should have been spending pre-Christmas nights with their families, but here they were, loud, boisterous, cursing and squabbling and packing toys and taking them down to poortown. And they would return to Santa Pal headquarters grim and chastened at some of the poverty they had witnessed.

I wrote graphic stories, my readers responded and the donations poured in.

Each year after the last packages were delivered, we would get our wives and meet at Buck's Restaurant for steaks and frivolity, telling funny and ribald stories about what we had seen this year. (One year they walked into an apartment with toys and the couple was making love. The guy looked around briefly, said only: "Put them in the corner there," and continued without missing a wiggle).

Big Tom was a part of that salty bunch. At the end of the feast, inevitably must come the memory of the small children whose sad faces brightened only once a year, and tears came to the eyes of the guys. Emotional beatings were part of this duty.

Tom Donoho was a big part of such charity. He stayed quietly generous in the years after all that. There will be no way to recall or recount the countless kindnesses he and Betty extended, the patience.

When I started The Independent Torch I saw Tom on the square. I hit Tom up for an ad. You had to know how things were with us.

"I don't need no advertising," he said. "My business is good."

"I don't care about all that," I said. "I need the money."

"Yes, well how much?"

"Five dollars a week."

"Jesus Christ! You can't make money that way."

"I'm not trying to make money."

"You sure as hell ain't."

Later we got into a hot Sheriff's race and The Torch was making some difference. Betty upped the ante to $25 a week. And anytime I wanted to publish a
large printing, they were among the friends I went to for the extra money.

God! The anecdotal material. At one point, early on, the rumor got out that
the Donohos were either owners of The Torch or had much influence. So I wrote
a story in which Betty was quoted, and I described her as a surly 350-pound per-
oxide blonde.

Here came the calls. One woman called her and asked her what she was going
to do about that. She said "Well, I'm going back to my diet. But what kind of
bleach I use is none of that editor's business."

Anecdotal material. Betty came from a poor Henderson County farm, where
she had to work. Finally, as an independent young lady whose beauty would rival
Marilyn Monroe, she came to Asheville and took a job as a waitress at a restaurant. Soon, who began to circle like a shark but Tom Donoho. Her boss, the
good Samaritan who looked out for his hired help, warned her (time and again)
to be careful about flirting with Tom.

"He does not mean well. You know what he's after."

But it wasn't too long until she led him to the altar. It lasted up until the day
of death. The local legend was constantly being updated by their friends.

Talking about it once. Tom said "We didn't go with her boss's opinion of me,
we went with the flow."

Patience? What good therapy they provided. When things gathered up on me
I would go to their kitchen table to get it out of my system. Loudly. They were
Irish, they knew, they knew.

Once I got cranked up began denouncing my foes. Tom looked at a blushing
Betty and grinned. "Have you ever heard that word before?"

"Once or twice from Lewis, and at a Civil Rights rally," she said.

They knew, they knew. In politics here they had come into their own share of
back-stabbing from a Democratic Party they had loved and served well—and
helped to finance.

The Donohos had been incorrigible Democrats, donating time, money and
services for years. They could be counted on. They never asked for much out of
the "party". But that "party" they knew was stumbling toward dissolution.

Then came the year one of their friends, Lt. Gov. Jimmy Green, wanted to run for Governor. In primary efforts, their faction of the Democratic Party was suddenly shunted aside by the Jim Hunt wing, which was pushing then Attorney General Rufus Edmiston.

The Donoho faction protested, were ostracized, humiliated in many large and small ways, rudely put in their place. Then Edmiston came with a criminal indictment of Jimmy Green (later dismissed). That did it.

At the time I was teaching and not publishing. They called me to a meeting. When I walked in I noticed some Democratic Party heavyweights were there in addition to the Donohos, police captain John Best, one of the most honorable officers this shitty Asheville Police Department ever had, Bill McCarter and a number of other staunch Democrats.

They told me, to my astonishment, that they wanted me to publish a tabloid sheet stating that they were turning away from the Democratic Party and backing Jim Martin, the Republican candidate for Governor.

I knew then that this was the early harbinger of disaster for the Democrats. I had seen these people operate too many times. So I wrote and printed the sheet by the thousands, and when it hit the precincts all hell broke loose.

A campaign train had been retained from Southern Railway and tooted across the state. The actor Jimmy Dean was aboard. I rode with it to Charlotte. People gathered at every stop. The Donoho money and influence had spread. I saw Democrats come to the train from every town and community. That's one of the big reasons Jim Martin became Governor.

Republicans were overjoyed. Sometime later I talked with Betty and Tom, who were being beseeched to join the Republican Party. They both said the same thing to the GOP here. "Hell, you don't have a party or even a decent chance of organizing one. We'll help you all we can, but we'll stay Democrats."

That was a matter of tradition. And that honesty made the Donohos stronger, especially among other honest Democrats who privately deplored what was going on in their party. As the years have passed, they were de facto political Independents, giving help to some Democratic partisans, but never like before.

Tom only ran for office once. City Council was not responsive to some issues. Time was growing tighter, filing deadline neared and no credible candidate had filed. In the last 15 minutes before deadline I persuaded him to file. He got there within minutes of deadline. He lost the election, when he saw the winners with whom he would have had to serve he was just as happy.

Tom grew older, richer, fatter. He worked many hours each day to the detriment of his health. Betty and his family worried but knew better than to lecture him too much. I had a close personal friend die and grew worried. What could I do? I went to their office one afternoon and demanded they get in my car. Reluctantly they did. I drove them to the mountain property I own in Fairview and asked Tom to put a camper up on it somewhere—without phone—and learn to relax. Politely, no. he can't do that. But thanks. Hell, I had to make some gesture to this man who did so much for everyone around him.

The years passed. We all mellowed somewhat. (Not much.)I grew to look upon him as a Shakespearean figure. Faustian in girth, Faustian in mirth. Relaxed, a man of the world, easy to get along with.

In recent years we sat together with other friends at Betty's lavish table and drank coffee and talked about all the other years. More recently Tom and I sat and chatted some about death. (We are both members of Masonic Lodges—Tom was a Shriner also and found that to be a great place to continue his charity toward crippled children. We talked about how meaningful Masonic burial rites are.)

In recent weeks his health got worse. He passed out in his bathtub. Betty finally got him to Park Ridge Hospital where a pacemaker was installed. He stubbornly returned to work.

Election day he went to one of his employes' home to pick up a list of material. She looked at his face, asked…he said he didn't feel good. She got him into a chair.

We had talked once about POWs willing themselves to die. Now in this chair death came. If he did not will it, then he agreed to it in the easy-going fashion he had. He slumped and was gone.

Gone? Only from his body, not from the environs, not from family, friends or sphere of influence. As he now travels the spaceways and timeways of eternity looking for his oldest buddy Quentin who had gone on before, we his friends all contemplated the sidetracks, spurs and spillways of memory.

Tom Donoho, bigger than life, bigger than death. Even the casket was extra large, and there was no way to count the mourners who came to the funeral home to see him off and to comfort Betty and the family. Sheriff Bobby Medford had been asked to say a few words, but he could not get them all said. The Sheriff apologized and began crying, as did many grown, tough men. Tom's fellow Freemason Randy Flack, a highly talented local singer and recording artist sang to his dead friend. A poem of devoted friendship, written by one friend to Tom many years ago was read. Yes, there is the streak of poesy hidden in these guys. Then the preacher and then that part was over.

There was a long convoy of mourners to a cemetery near Weaverville, where Tom and Betty Donoho had picked out their graves in the early 1970s.

There, under a bright blue sky the beautiful Masonic graveside ritual was performed. Then it was over, but those many mourners did not leave the grave. They stood about for a long time.

Sometimes I traffic in ghosts. Behind and at the edge of the crowd of mourners I saw the faces of a thousand poor and ragged Asheville children looking gratefully at the casket and flowers. And all the other needy, all the many others.

Time will pass, memory and pain will subside somewhat for the family and friends, but this is all recorded in the Masonic lore, across that bourne from which no man returns, in the temple in the heavens, not made with hands...

Then there followed the usual Donoho Irish feast at the house, with Betty, the gracious but tearful hostess seeing to everything. In keeping with the profound Irish sentimentality of the occasion, a friend slipped Betty the following poem of hope, poet unknown:

> *Do not stand at my grave and weep,*
> *I am not there, I do not sleep.*
> *I am a thousand winds that blow.*
> *I am a diamond glint on the snow.*
> *I am the sunshine on ripened grain,*
> *I am a gentle autumn rain.*
>
> *When you awaken in the morning hush,*
> *I am the swift uplifting rush*
> *of quiet winds in circling flight.*
> *I am the soft starshine at night.*
>
> *Do not stand by my grave and cry;*
> *I am not there,*
> > *I did not die.*

Mamie Reynolds Redux

◆

The legend revisited 40 years later.

Much of this information is taken from a story I published in The Asheville Citizen and numerous daily newspapers through the Associated Press wire in early August, 1962. More than 40 years have passed and I have not kept up with the subject, Mamie Spears Reynolds, in those passing decades except to hear occasionally that her life has turned out well, probably due to her simple and unaffected approach to life, despite being heiress to a large fortune, a jewel with a curse and close association with the biggest political, royalty and global social names of her childhood. The context of this will be constructed around her age, 19, at that time.

Mamie Spears Reynolds is the daughter of the late U.S. Senator Bob Reynolds of Buncombe County, whose tenure in Washington was in the 1930s-40s, and of the Hope Diamond heiress Evelyn Walsh McClean. Her mother died when she was a baby.

People here wondered, talked about her, loved her, envied her and sometimes spread gossip about her fabulous life—but she never knew much of that.. Her life was not one simple story, not a matter of stringing words across a page and easily hanging one paragraph under another until the story is finished. There is no ready made point of departure. Spun about her life is a vast, complex webbing with strands reaching many times about the earth in travels with her father; stretching into a time before her birth and touching high places and important people. A tale of fantastic and often dangerous situations, and of fabled jewels of a dark, tragic past and which carry a strange East Indian curse.

Inside this vast and confounding maze lies another enigma. Mamie herself—the tricky puzzle of any 19-year-old girl, baffling, contradictory and independent—typical enough to be atypical—much more than any male mind can cope with. It was well known that she was a rich girl, but her inheritance is larger than wealth. On both sides of her family tree are unusual and outstanding people, families who have been above the normal run of human activities. Taking a look at the boundaries of Mamie's life up to the early 1960s, there we find an astonishing scope.

During those old interviews with that young lady of the world, with topics ranging more or less on mundane matters was one thing—but opening her scrapbooks brought back the realization that here was more than an ordinary wealthy young girl with a cut and dried story.

Faded newspaper clippings show the place of her birth, "Friendship", in Washington, a home mistressed by Mrs. Evalyn Walsh McLean, heiress to a silver fortune and owner of the Hope Diamond There are photos of great glittering balls in full swing—a traditional gathering for Easter breakfasts, and bright, endless hospitality. Photos and clippings of political and society greats such as Vice President Alben Barkley, Gloria Swanson, Fredrick March and producer Alfred de Liagre, Jr. One photo of Mamie's grandmother shows the matron comfortably wearing both the Hope Diamond and the Star of the East.

There are snapshots of a little snaggle-toothed girl with a wide grin surrounded by dogs, a pony, a pet pig, a donkey and a horse.

A telegram dated 1949 from the Easter bunny, offering a reward for Mamie's good behavior, and behind that can be detected the puckish grin of an indulgent father. There are pictures of a the child with Santa Claus, and report cards with A's, B's and C's, friendly little personal notes from Harry S Truman inquiring as to her health; Frank Murphy of the U.S. Supreme Court, Gov.Earl Warren of California, a photo of Mamie and her father in Australia at the age of nine, with her note saying "When I grow up, all I want is to be a good housewife…"

Photos of Mamie with Zulus and Arabians, distant postmarks from Zanzibar, Durban, Port Said, Mombasa, Venice, Rome, a photo of Mamie in audience with Pope Pius in 1952. And Mamie and the Senator on board the last tramp steamer to leave Hong Kong as the Communists took control of China in 1949.

There is a friendly note from former Vice President John Nance Garner, and a pictorial account of a glittering and exciting six years of travel to places like Tasmania, Singapore, Nagoya and Tokyo. A personal note of concern about her health from exiled Romanian King Zog and Queen Geraldine in France.

Some pages are devoted to a very special friend, J. Edgar Hoover, head of the FBI, who was a close personal friend of the Senator. Hoover had known and loved Mamie since the day of her birth. Mamie had a silver bracelet presented to her when she was an infant. The FBI chief had taken her tiny fingerprint soon after her birth and transposed it onto silver for the bracelet. He later gave her his secret personal telephone number, which came in very handy later in her life.

Passed on to Mamie from her father's side was an urge for independence and a fierce honesty. Known to mountain people as "Our Bob", Senator Reynolds was acclaimed as one of the most colorful political mavericks ever to be picked by the people. As a young Buncombe County lawyer seeking his place in the sun, he won the prosecutor's race in Buncombe and Madison County in a race that still perplexes political observers. He campaigned some on horseback, filling his saddlebags with candy and rode into the mountain precincts with a brash honesty. He distributed the candy to school children and told them to remind their parents how to vote. But the one thing that stuck in the minds of voters was his fearless and utterly honest campaign.

"My opponent is a good, honest man," he would say. "But I need a job. I'm not doing this to serve you, it's for me. I need all the experience I can get, and I want to get it at your expense."

A simple, straightforward approach, the language of the mountain people. They laughed, went home and pondered this brazen barrister, nodded, then on election day they filed out of the coves and hollows, down off the ridges—and chuckling, voted him in.

With this honesty and uncanny perception of people, Mamie's father twice represented the state in the United States Senate. One of his opponents was the late Cameron Morrison, whose wife was an actress. Bob Reynolds favorite campaign ploy was telling the crowds that Morrison's wife was a thespian, and time and again forced Morrison into admitting it without further explanation. The inference was strong enough to win for Reynolds.

Thrown into the glamorous swirl of Washington, "Our Bob", the bachelor, cut a wide swath through the ranks of the ladies. He was a mountain swashbuckler with a winning way to feminine hearts. He met, courted and won Evalyn Washington McLean, daughter of Mrs. Evalyn Walsh McLean, who was famous as the greatest social hostess in the nation, and who was heiress to a large silver-mining fortune and who had also gained renown as a collector of jewels. In the McLean family at the time of the marriage was the Hope Diamond and the Star of the East, another huge jewel.

The Hope Diamond was a lodestone of tragedy, greed and violence, its tragic history dating back three centuries. About the size of a fifty-cent piece, this rare stone has been described as looking like "A tiny fragment of midnight sky, fallen to earth and still aglow with star-gleam."

The Hope Diamond is said to have been torn from the forehead of a Hindu idol and smuggled out of India by a Frenchman named Tavernier in 1642. Tavernier was later ripped apart and devoured by a pack of wild dogs. The legend followed—that ill-fortune would track the path of the stone, and history bears that out. Among subsequent owners: Nicholas Fouquet, a French official, was executed; Princess de Lamballe, fatally beaten by a French mob; King Louis XVI and Marie Antoinette were beheaded.

Henry Thomas Hope, an Irish banker, gave the stone his name and as far as is known came to a normal end. Hope's grandson, Lord Francis Pelham Clinton, died penniless. His music hall bride from America, May Yohe, left the diamond behind her when she went off in divorce. She wound up scrubbing floors. A subsequent owner Simon Montharides, was killed with his wife and child when he rode over a precipice. Sultan Abdul Hamid of Turkey lost his throne; Subaya, the Sultan's favorite son, wore the diamond and was slain.

The diamond was then placed on the market after the revolt of the Young Turks, and Mrs. McLean bought it. Some family tragedy followed, though the family does not lend credence to the legendary curse. Mamie was born to the Senator and the beautiful young socialite. The mother died when Mamie was a baby, the Senator thereafter dedicated his life to caring for their child.

(The grandmother died in 1947 and Mamie received a sizable inheritance. She could only draw interest from the fortune until she became 25, at which time the principal reverted to her.)

What was this young girl really like? Who was this young girl really? This young heiress about whom rumors and gossip abounded, but very little truth?

Indeed she was widely traveled. Her first global trip came at the age of five, and at the time of the interviews she had journeyed the breadth of the earth three times. Innumerable times she has gone abroad on short trips to get the unique edge of education that comes with travel. It was the desire of her father that she travel. He was afflicted with wanderlust in his youth, and as a native of a shut-in Appalachia knows that a wider knowledge of life comes from ranging across the world. So as a teenager she was at once a woman of the world (ah yes, Madrid, Paris…Cunard Liners…) and in the same instant a child of beautiful innocence, concerned only with her dogs.

At nineteen she was of a lively beauty—a healthy, ruddy complexion, frank blue eyes that cut away pretense so she could see to the heart of things, and secret joyous lights that played under the surface of her face. Not in the first interview did she reveal herself. She sat smiling, waiting, ever agreeable—but waiting and watching. It was in later conversation after she got to know us when she could turn loose a torrent of conversation that streams out from the river of her life. At that time she had strong opinions on the matters affecting her, but conceded that she knew those would change as she matured. And they did.

But some remained. "One thing I believe in," she said at that time, "is loyalty to my friends. I really need to say nice things about people, even those I don't like. I don't want to be guilty of loose gossip. I don't try to put on airs, and I don't think I'm better than anyone else. It's not who you are, but the way you act and think that's important."

At nineteen, what did she plan for her life? "I thought about training to be a model. I love pretty clothes, and I'm addicted to blue." Then in one of the paradoxes of a rich girl, "But I watch prices carefully when I'm shopping. I don't want to indulge myself in expensive things."

She was not much for movies, only one or two a year. "But I like the true artists of the theater, the ones who can throw themselves completely into their roles. I go to the plays when I am in New York, but I don't go there much now since I have attended all the debutante balls. But I am a TV bug and watch everything except westerns. They are all the same."

She readily admitted to theatrical ambitions, "But I still feel too shy in public. I don't think I could overcome stage fright."

But she read, mostly about her interests of the time—horses, racing or dog-shows. "I read a Mike Shane thriller occasionally, but I have no interest in classical literature. I love local history, or western civilization, or about ancient Europe, anything that pertains to travel."

A couple of years before this interview, she had developed an interest in drag racing, then at the time of these interviews it had revived. She had bought a 1961 Corvette and hired a driver to race in major stock-car races about the nation.

"I guess what I am most proud of are the prizes I have won racing I personally drove in and won several races. I could have had either a trophy or a five-dollar bill, and sometimes I took the money. I am proud of having earned the money with my own ability in rough competition with good drivers."

Her early schooling consisted of kindergarten and the first and second grades at Asheville Country Day School, through the seventh grade at St. Genevieve-of-the-Pines; further private schooling at The Academy-of-the-Assumption in Miami; and finally at Plonk School of Creative Arts in Asheville. Lastly, she was privately tutored by her nanny, Mimi Palmer, who was a school teacher and of all things, the president of a South Carolina bank before she heard Senator Reynolds was looking for someone for Mamie.

A conversation with her was uniquely stimulating, running along like a mountain stream: bubbling, fresh, clear, joyous, then whirling into an occasional pool of strange, dark silence. She would look at the interviewer, a fleeting troubled shadow crossing her brow, an ancient wisdom.

"My wealth? If you have money, you have many friends, but if you lose it you find out who is true. I never thought much about it, and don't care to. It's certainly not everything."

Again and again during our interviews it came, as if her mind had flashed a sonar signal under the surface of life, found a hidden reef and returned with a plaintive echo "…money's not everything". She didn't remember much about the Hope Diamond. Her grandmother sold it to a New York jeweler, Harry Winston, who later donated it to the Smithsonian. It is a lost memory to her, like the image of her mother.

"It's just a plain piece of rock as far as I'm concerned. I do know that it's very beautiful, but who on earth would want a great big stone like that. It's right where it should be, in the Smithsonian.

"I don't know its history, its weight or its value. I don't know who found it or where it came from. I'm not interested in it now or in the future." she said.

Perhaps her disinterest saved her from the old curse. That dark, brooding stone, the huge diamond in her past, the idol's eye whose path in history is strewn with the carnage of tragedy and death, the great black Oriental curse is lost and ineffective when confronted with her child's innocence. The curse is not what worries her. Old Appalachian superstitions…

"I'm very superstitious though. I won't walk under a ladder, and if I spill salt I throw some over my left shoulder. I hate to break a mirror, I won't put a hat on the bed, I won't leave for a trip on Friday, and I'm superstitious of the color green. I love the color to death, but I'm afraid of it." She voiced these fears, paltry in the face of the curse of the Hope Diamond.

Speaking of the fabled curse, then what were the most tragic things to befall a girl of her station? Again the paradox, the confounding contradictions. "Of course it was a tragic thing to me when my mother died, but I was so young I can't remember much about that. I remember she was a very beautiful woman, with poise and dignity. I understand that she was a most unselfish person, gracious and a wonderful hostess.

"She is buried in a mausoleum in Rock Creek in Washington, and when I'm there I go out and put two or three dozen roses on her grave.

"Another tragedy was when my brother (a son of Senator Reynolds by a previous marriage) was killed in an auto accident in Italy in 1950."

Then here, the maddening enigma. "But the biggest tragic (cq) of my life, the thing that has hurt me more than anything was the death of my dog. I was very close to it." At the time of the interviews, she still visited the grave of that dog and put roses on it.

The topic switched to music. She said she loved classics, soft dinner music, wild South Amerixcan beats and "Everything but rock-and-roll. I don't like the jizzy-jazzy crap they play."

She caught her own expression and laughed, then reverted to a mountain accent. "I come up saying ain't and things like that!" she said, and admitted to an occasion stronger expletive. "But it sounds crude to hear other people use it."

Then the talk drifted to heart interests—of course it would, the fabric of every young lady's life.

"Of course I want a husband. If I was really in love I would marry my man, no matter what his occupation. But he must be sweet, kind and understanding, and ambitious enough to get out into the swim of life. He must be a pleasing companion with compatible interests, and congenial with others. There must be life and virility about him, and he must be about the same age as me." (There, the faint echo of the note she had scribbled on the photo of she and the Senator in Australia at the age of nine.)

"When I grow up, all I want is to be a good housewife. The important thing is happiness…" and again came that far echo, "…money's not everything…"

"And have you ever been in love before, Mamie?"

She smiled. "Yes, but it was puppy love, Looking back it was foolish."

When asked how her name was spelled, she said "M-a-m-i-e, how else?"

Some women have spelled it _Mayme._ Her eyes brightened. She wrote it down. "Hm, sounds good. Maybe I'll use it that way."

Then abruptly a pensive sad silence. Slowly she said, in the language and tone of the very lonely: "But I've missed a great deal. Some people might think I'm too snobbish to go to high school proms, but I would have loved going to one, I really would have. But there was no sense in me trying to go incognito because there's always someone who knew me. It's something I wanted to do so much."

Mamie, the beautiful young debutante who attended the fashionable coming-out balls of the highest society had to endure the aching sadness of a teen-age girl alone. She missed the thing her generation had, the teen-age high school prom, and the prom passes through our lives but once.

Time passed and I lost contact with Mamie. Shortly after my story hit the Associated Press wires Senator Reynolds died, and following that Mamie met and married a New Yorker named Luigi Chinetti. Shortly after that they made the newspapers here when they were driving on Reynolds Mountain and came upon 19-year-old Billy Hendon.(Who later became our congressman.) Chinetti pulled a gun on him. Hendon took a warrant. It was a non-event but it did make the newspapers. Then she dropped from my screen.

However, rumors grew rife about Chinetti. Was he really mafia? Then there came word that Mamie was being held prisoner in a house in Connecticut until the mob could make arrangements to take over her fortune. But Mamie had two good-luck charms. The bracelet given her by J. Edgar Hoover those years ago, and his private phone number. She dropped the coin. Almost immediately the big house in Connecticut swarmed with agents, who roughed up everyone there and brought her home.

But the fates were still good to her. She had hired a dog-handler, fell in love with him and they got married, and still are, we think. The fortune reverted to her when she reached twenty-five.The curse of the Hope Diamond had passed her by and waved this beautiful blessing at her.

Mamie Reynolds (left) and Lewis Green (right)

The Demonic Murders
by The Foxes

❖

Starting on November 10, 1964

Police stopped a car careening along Patton Avenue in Asheville on three tires shortly before midnight that Tuesday (November 10, 1964), only to discover that a woman lay dying inside as her husband was trying to get her several miles to a hospital after she was shot during a burglary-murder at their home on Upper Hominy an hour before.

The criminals had flattened one of the tires on the car to prevent the couple from leaving, but the desperate farmer ran it anyway. The police rushed Mrs. Ovella Jean Lunsford to the emergency room, where she was pronounced dead.

This was the entry of a former petty criminal and some cohorts into the ranks of capital felony. The crime and its demonic mastermind remains a frightening legend in Buncombe County law enforcement to this day.

We take the following narrative from statements made to us by Mrs. Lunsford's husband, by investigators and court testimony: While the trial devolved into a bizarre circus despite Judge Hugh Campbell's best efforts (one of the defendants was prompted by his attorney into confessing on the witness stand). One of the killers continued into coming decades constructing an even wilder murderous legend, both in prisons and for a brief time of freedom.

The beginning: Dairy farmer Charles H. Lunsford had spent the day harvesting and selling hay, assisted by young Arrlie Fox, who noticed that the farmer had a large sum of money from which he made change.

The day ended and they went their way. The following day, Arrlie told his cousin Donald Fox and a friend, Carson McMahan, about the money he had seen. The robbery was planned. They got masks, guns and disguise coats and wrapped them in a burlap bag, which they concealed under the hood of a pick-up truck in case any law officers stopped them.

That night Lunsford and his wife had dinner, and shortly she went to bed upstairs. (He slept in a downstairs bed so he could rise early to feed and milk the cattle.) He watched television and at about 10 p.m., grew hungry and prepared himself a bowl of apple sauce. By then the young men had taken on Arrlie's older brother, Roy Lee Fox, a manipulator who held diabolical sway over the others in a number of previous small crimes. They drove up and down the road several times to make sure the way was clear. Arrlie donned his mask, and burst in through a front bedroom, while Donald lurked at the back door. (The other two, Roy Lee and Carson McMahan, drove the truck a short way up the road and parked.)

Lunsford threw the bowl at Arrlie, then rushed him and wrestled with him. Donald broke in and struck Lunsford's head with a .22 pistol, bending the trigger guard almost into the trigger, stunning the older man.

Lunsford grabbed an electric light pull-string, turned it on and began shouting to his wife "It's a holdup, it's a hold-up."

Mrs. Lunsford came down the stairwell, barefooted in her nightgown. By then Donald had extinguished the light, leaving only the kitchen light. Arrlie was attempting to hold her back while her husband, still dizzy, sat on the side of his bed holding his head. Donald fired one round into the wall. Mrs. Lunsford pushed toward a closet for a rifle. Arrlie had a small derringer in his pocket. He fired from his coat pocket and the bullet went into the floor beside Mrs. Lunsford. In the meantime, her husband had recovered himself and lunged into Donald, who knocked him down and began hitting him. Lunsford began shouting to her, "Shoot him, shoot him," She got to the kitchen door with the rifle, but became confused by the safety and could not fire.

Donald grabbed the end of the rifle and began to twist it out of her hands. Arrlie ran and grasped the stock of the rifle. Then Donald shot her and blood gushed from her mouth. The two young men rushed out of the house.

"I'm shot, get me a doctor," she said to her husband, then "…I'm dying."

The two robbers had ripped the telephone off the wall. Lunsford ran to lock the front door and to store his wallet in a dresser. When he reached his car, he found his wife sitting upright in the car, but as he backed down the driveway she slumped into him. Then he saw the tire was flat so he picked up enough speed so the car would roll on balance. As he rolled, the tire began to disintegrate. He drove about 20 miles in the effort to save her. They were near the hospital when the police stopped him.

The Investigation and Arrests

The young Republican Sheriff Harry P. Clay was now 32 and two years into that first term. It had been tough, an almost impossible two years since Democrats did not want to relinquish power or give Clay credit for anything—harrassment by lawyers of his deputies on the stand during various trials, phone calls, gossip in the communities about the reputations of deputies, etc. So far the toughest unsolved crime on the books was the robbery murder of William Lane Hyatt of Candler, who was shot and robbed as he worked in his pepper patch. Other tough unsolved crimes had built up, but they had occurred during the administration of the previous Sheriff, Democrat Laurence E. Brown, who had held the office for 32 years. Democrats were vocal in claiming that Clay should solve the Hyatt and other crimes. But before they left office, Brown's deputies had cleaned out evidence lockers and no leads, clues or interviews with suspects had been left.

But the dramatic Lunsford case had the possibility to elevate Clay's political career and the Democrats knew it. No one realized at the time that in his two years Clay had hired and built a savvy and loyal staff of deputies and investigators. They were largely inexperienced and did not look like much at first, but they owed no political favors and they were willing to work hard. During the subsequent trial, Judge Hugh B. Campbell commented for the record that it was the most thorough investigation ever brought before him. The Solicitor at that time was Democrat Bob Swain, and despite Democratic party pressures he brought his formidable professional abilities to bear. In addition, so that partisan balance might be present, Swain was assisted by the renowned Jim Baley, a Republican who had been U.S. District Attorney.

I was present for some of the conferences during the investigation. That investigation could have been, almost was, led into bottomless pits because a number of other crimes, previously mentioned, had happened in the Candler area and with these arrests, citizens were calling in leads to those. About 20 deputies were engaged trying to sift through these ideas. However, one informant had been present when Arrlie had assisted Lunsford in selling hay. At that time Arrlie had childishly exhibited a .22 pistol.

Jim Baley and Swain told the officers to now concentrate on working with this informer. This man presented enough pertinent information to warrant total concentration. He was Jackie Clyde Wilson, 19, of Grassy Branch Road, who told officers he saw pistols in the possession of the Foxes several times, and at one time he had to look down the barrel of a derringer the suspects had. He said the autumn before Roy Lee and Arrlie Fox and Donald McMahan had joined him at a restaurant, then they adjourned to a beer joint. Roy became involved in a fight and they were all ordered out of the place.

He said Roy then refused to take him home, instead drove to his own home beyond Weaverville. Roy ordered the car stopped at Lake Louise and fired a bullet through the car where he and McMahan were sitting. He said another of Roy's brothers took the gun, then they went on to the Fox home.

Wilson told the investigators that Roy made him mount a horse, then struck the horse, causing it to rear up and dump Wilson. Later Roy forced him to mount another horse and the others beat the horse and caused it to veer and gallop about. He said he didn't get off the horse until it ran into a barn and a beam hit his head and dislodged him. Investigators duly noted this, brought it to testimony at the trial. In light of later events in Roy's career, this sadistic behavior became important. Even Arrlie told officers, and later testified, that other robberies were directed by his older brother, although Roy never took risks in the holdups. He named several other robberies in which they had participated.

Investigators had enough. Swain and Baley sought and obtained warrants and indictments.

The Trial, The Circus

The Courtroom was packed downstairs and most of the balcony was filled. Not only for the spectacle of many lawyers, many defendants, but to see how this Sheriff's Department had performed and what would come out under oath. It took several days to choose a jury and right off some of the lawyers went off the beam, most notably Bob Riddle and Cecil Jackson. An air of surrealism arose The only way we could explain their behavior at the time was that they were trying for a mistrial.

At one point Judge Hugh Campbell ruled that none of the defendants had been threatened in any way, nor had anything been promised them. Then sparks were struck between the Judge and Riddle when Solicitor Bob Swain objected to Riddle coaching his client McMahan on the stand. Judge Campbell warned Riddle, and when Riddle replied to that the Judge had entered into the record that he had cautioned the defense attorney to keep quiet. Riddle objected to that and asked that the entire dialogue also be entered into the record, along with the Judge's "tone of voice".

As the trial continued, attorney Cecil Jackson, in cross-examination of Arrlie Fox introduced a note that Arrlie had purportedly written to Roy Lee in jail. When Jackson tried to get the note entered into the record, the Judge ruled it was not admissible at this time. He told Jackson he could enter it when he presented his case. But Jackson persisted in trying to get Arrlie to read parts of the note into the record.

The Judge admonished Jackson several times. Finally Jackson borrowed a match from Riddle, strode briskly across the floor and tried to hand the match and note to Arrlie. "Here Arrlie, do you want to burn this now?" An enraged Judge made Jackson return to the defense table.

Shortly the Judge took both Riddle and Jackson into his chambers. He allowed this reporter to accompany him. "Gentlemen, this is going to stop, and I mean now. Cecil is trying to burn the evidence and Riddle want the tone of my voice entered into the record.."

So it was haggle and argue day after day, then it was time for the old canny lawyer Don Young to present evidence. He put his client Arrlie on the stand, and after a few preliminaries softly asked, "Arrlie, did you boys kill Mrs. Lunsford?"

A matter of fact answer in a small voice. "Yessir."

A profound silence fell over the Courtroom. The trial was over.

Because of the deal made by his lawyer, Arrlie Fox got off with one life sentence. The jury showed mercy to the others and they received two life sentences. A couple of jurors later said that the lawyers had argued the men would never get out and so mercy was a good compromise and justice would be served. But that was not the case. In some months Carson McMahan went free in a new trial. Also in a few months, Don Fox was killed in the yard at Central Prison during a riot. Arrlie began doing his time at Craggy Prison, and Roy Lee Fox disappeared into the labyrinths of Central Prison to begin doing a double life sentence.

The public heard no more of Roy Lee Fox for years, then after about twenty years I received a call from one of my contacts who said that the day before a chartered private plane had landed at Hendersonville's small airport and unloaded Roy Lee Fox with more than $65,000 in cash. He also had a complete pardon signed by Governor Jim Hunt as his last official act before going out of office in that term. We began a slow and agonizing search for the official reason behind such a pardon. Though he was serving state time in Central, he had suddenly ingratiated himself to Federal authorities while serving time in a prison in another state.????

Letter to Gov. Hunt from a U.S. Attorney in San Antonio, Texas

"Dear Governor Hunt:

Upon the successful completion of the prosecution of those persons responsible for the murder of United States District Judge John H. Wood Jr., and the attempted murder of Assistant U.S. Attorney James W. Kerr, Jr., I would like to take this opportunity to bring to your attention the cooperation rendered to the Federal Bureau of Investigation and the United States government by an inmate in the North Carolina prison system. This inmate is Roy Lee Fox who is currently incarcerated in the federal prison system in the witness security program because of the danger he incurred by cooperating with the federal government.

"Mr. Fox first approached federal authorities in 1981 while incarcerated as a State prisoner at the Federal penitentiary in Marion, Illinois. Mr. Fox provided information to prisons authorities concerning a planned prison escape and acts of violence within the institution. He also provided information concerning admissions made by Jamiel Alexander Chagra in connection with Chagra's participation in the murder of Judge Wood and the attempted murder of Assistant United States Attorney James W. Kerr, Jr.

"In the summer of 1983, the United States was endeavoring to gather sufficient evidence to prosecute those individuals responsible for the attempted murder of Assistant U.S. Attorney Kerr. The United States was aware that Robert Piccolo, an inmate in the North Carolina prison system, had participated in that assault. In cooperation with Nathan Rice, warden of the central prison in Raleigh, the United States approached Mr. Fox and requested that he assist the United States in obtaining evidence against Mr. Piccolo concerning his involvement in connection with the Kerr assault in order to obtain Mr. Piccolo's cooperation. Although Mr. Fox was aware that if he were discovered recording conversations between Mr. Piccolo and him, he would be in personal danger, he agreed to assist the United States. We explained to Mr. Fox that we would be unable to commit the State of North Carolina to any particular reward for his endeavors but that we would communicate to officials of the state of North Carolina the extent of his co-peration as well as the danger to which he was subjected.

"Mr. Fox carried out his assignments in an admirable fashion, utilizing a concealed recording device and recording conversations between Mr. Piccolo and him. Although Mr. Piccolo was too paranoid to make direct admissions concerning his involvement, Mr. Fox endeavored to the best of his abilities to carry out his assignments.

"The United States was eventually able to make an agreement with Mr. Piccolo which resulted in an indictment of Jamiel Alexander Chagra and an individual by the name of James Kearns on the day before the statute of limitations expired. Mr. Fox has been willing since that date to testify on behalf of the United States concerning the admissions that Jimmy Chagra made to him while confined at the United States Penitentiary in Marion, Illinois. Although Jimmy Chagra's pleas of guilty nullified any need for Mr. Fox's testimony, he was always ready, willing and able to carry out this portion of the agreement.

"Mr. Fox has demonstrated a willingness to cooperate with the government and to abide by the rules and regulations established to regulate his conduct; he has also demonstrated a great sense of responsibility in executing his portion of the arrangement. All of this was done by Mr. Fox without a specific promise of reward and I do believe that your office should take this into consideration in determining if future incarceration of Mr. Fox is necessary.

"If I can be of any further assistance to you in this regard, please feel free to contact me.

"Very truly yours,
Helen Milburn Eversberg
United States Attorney

By W. Ray Jahn
Assistant United States Attorney"

So Roy Lee Fox was now recognized behind the walls as a prison "rat" (squealer) and behind the walls he was marked for death. Governor Hunt acted on the Federal request for clemency. He pardoned the killer. No one has yet addressed the source of the money or the chartered plane. He was once again seen around Buncombe and surrounding counties, but few people outside of investigators recalled him or his past. However, probation and parole officers strongly objected to Fox's release. Then the evil forces that were inherent in Roy Lee Fox emerged again rather quickly, and more bodies floated up in the wake of Hunt's pardon.

He was free for slightly more than a year when for no reason he shot and killed Morris Sams, 39, of Alexander. They were at an impromptu picnic at a French Broad River park with about three other people when Fox, for no reason, pulled a pistol, said that Sams had been saying bad things about Indians and that he was an Indian (he is not, of course) and shot him to death. He then coerced his companions into helping him dump the body in the river. After a night of thinking it over, he forced the others to help him retrieve the corpse, which was floating at a still eddy, then they took it to a side street in Swannanoa and placed it in a man-hole. With the help of informers, police found the body and arrested Fox on sec-ond-degree murder charges and first degree kidnapping. He was then sentenced to another life term plus 40 years. The others later testified that they had helped him because he told them that by virtue of their assistance they were now accom-plices and as guilty as he was. In that period of time, more murders occurred which were far from being solved. In particular, a couple of tourists from Ohio—a man and his wife—were murdered at a scenic site just north of Asheville called Buzzard Rock. Fox confessed to those killings, excerpts of which are in this story, but everyone involved, particularly law enforcement officers, doubted the veracity of the confession.

The questions remained. No one had ever heard of a newly pardoned mur-derer being flown home on a chartered flight. A former Federal law enforcement told us that he had heard from several reliable sources that Fox arrived here with between $60,000-100,000 dollars. See his confession, which states that he got $100,000 for the hit at Buzzard Rock. (Remember, most of that confession is dubious.)

Sheriff Buck Lyda had Fox brought home from Central Prison to verify that confession. Once again Fox showed that deep cunning of a genius. Acting on a tip, officers found a handcuff key secreted under his dentures, and later in jail he carved a realistic pistol from a bar of soap and tinfoil from a cigarette pack. He was on the verge of a jailbreak here when he got locked down.

Here is excerpted some telling details from that confession, obtained from law enforcement officers who were disgusted with Governor Jim Hunt's pardon of Fox.

"Detective Leroy Lunsford, APD, The Rev. Ralph Sexton Jr., SBI Agent Charles Hess and deputy sheriffs Randy Halford and Bobby Medford are present for the interview with Roy Fox at 10 a.m. on 3/8/90.

"Mr. Fox agreed that if certain conditions could be met between the D.A.'s office and himself he would assist in the investigation of the homicides of Bonnie and Wesley Mehaffey...

(Fox) "In regards to the Buzzard Rock incident, this was a contract murder. I was paid $100,000 to kill these two individuals on Buzzard Rock by Buncombe County (blacked out), who gave me a .38 revolver to do these murders at his sug-gestion, at his request. He did request me to return the weapon to him...this incident happened on May 20. I am only taking blacked out word that the reason of him hiring me to kill these people is that drug transaction went sour. The

Mehaffey's did have a kilo of coke. I was told that a kilo would be a bonus to me in addition to the $100,000...

"I had a clean system in regards to drugs when I stepped out of the penitentiary, but I was a very weak individual in regards to drugs, in regards to the lifestyle I had been living for the past 20 years. I made an effort to do right. When I stepped off that airplane, a charter flight, at Hendersonville airport, all my intentions was do right and what I mean as right is not being involved in no drugs...

"I was a very disturbed person. I just want to say theys no way in the world that I would have took this contract hit...as we all know I don't think I should have been out anyway the way that I got out I think that I should have had the counseling, the proper counseling...I think that Mr. Hunt signed my death warrant instead of turning me loose...he made a professional mistake when he turned me loose...

"I'm not saying that I was a good person in prison because I certainly wasn't. I was approached by the Federal Government to help solve the murder of Federal Judge Wood in San Antonio, Texas and a federal prosecutor from San Antonio. I had been sent from the North Carolina prison max section to the Federal penitentiary in Marion, Illinois..."

There was no trial in the Buzzard Rock murders and Fox went back to Central in Raleigh. I asked to interview Fox at the prison and was told that he was dying of brain cancer and was incoherent. I was getting different mumbles from prison sources. Then I heard he had died. But his family here had not been notified. Prison authorities told me the body had been cremated. It became too suspicious. I went to Central and asked for a copy of the death certificate. After fumbling around some, the person I was dealing with gave me one of the death certificate forms filled out in handwriting. I had never heard of a document in such a bureaucracy being filled out hastily by hand. (Some time later I was sent one properly filled out by computer.)

And so I find myself in agreement with most local law enforcement personnel who doubt that Fox is dead and perhaps he is somewhere, either in prison or out, doing some work for the Federal Government.

A Freed Spirit Wandering
Through The Bureaucracy

The Native Stone died its death in 1974. There sits the editor with a wife and three small sons, earning a scant living with cameras and some free-lance investigations. Curt Ratcliff, the Chairman of the Buncombe County Board of Commissioners, saw my predicament and sent someone to see me. There were some CETA grants available. Salaries were quite low ($9,000) more or less, but he thought they might tide me over.

The U.S. Forest Service's Southeastern Forest Experiment Station needed a researcher to write a history of the station. I went for the interview. I had known the station director, J.B., for several years. He was a Ph.D and savvy about the federal bureaucracy.

We had coffee in his office. He said he knew my work would do but he had doubts about whether or not I could stand some of his staff for long. Or they me. I told him I had to, at least for a while. He laughed, said he was going to watch this with great interest.

Right off I began to see what he meant. They had openings for a historical researcher and a public relations man. I had more than two decades in journalism; a recently graduated Ph.D. in history was given the public relations job.???

My immediate supervisor in publications was a Yankee who had a master's degree in something and was a frustrated wannabe writer. Hereafter I shall call him Supe. Shortly after our initial interview he told me the word was out that I was crazy. I asked him if he knew what that meant. "Well, not exactly," he said.

"You'll find out in due time," I said. But what he said was a cue for what was to come. In conversation I revealed that my great-grandmother was a full-blooded Cherokee from the Snowbird section of the reservation. It was so entered into the records because there was a need for minority representation there.

Work in Publications was quiet, scholarly. Old records and early correspondence detailed how the experiment station was formed and how it evolved into a major component of the U.S. Forest Service. Most of the workers went to their daily grind, very little of which required innovative skills.

40

I was assigned to a small office in the sub-basement of the Federal Building, from which I would wander forth to seek records. I maintained contact with Supe by telephone. (His extension number was 0 ((zero)), and when I talked to him I would say "Zero, this is extension 7…" Finally he asked me not to call him Zero. "That sounds like I'm nothing," he said. "No, no," I said. "You are very important in the Publications hierarchy. Zero comes even before number one." That mollified him for a time.))

The day came, of course, when boredom became excruciating. Supe's office was across a hallway where several office workers busied themselves. Frequently, by chance, several would gather about the water fountain near Supe's doorway. There had evolved in them a subtle air of sarcastic satire about Supe—not disrespect or insolence, rather sly shots past his ability to discern. One day the gathering happened and without warning the dumb Indian emerged in me. Supe was holding forth on some incredibly personal problem when suddenly I blurted "All right, Zero. Where is my hat?"

Supe intuited that something crazy was in the air. He cut his eyes about cautiously. The others smiled and averted their eyes.

"What hat?" Supe asked.

"The Forest Service hat. The Smoky Bear hat."

"What are you talking about?"

"Is this the Forest Service or not? The Rangers get hats."

When Supe got frustrated he would gasp and wheeze. "We are not a field unit. We don't get hats. We get clothing allowances."

"Aha! I see. Well, even better. Where is my clothing allowance?"

"Gasp, gasp. You don't get one. You're not a regular employe."

"This is patent discrimination. Where do I file a complaint? What kind of deal is this?"

At that point, J.B., the station director, appeared on the scene, grinning faintly. "What's the matter, Lewis?"

"He won't get me my Smoky Bear hat."

Gasp, gasp, exhale, snort. "Sir, I've tried to explain to him…we don't get hats."

J.B. stared at him for a moment. "I got one," he said, and sauntered off.

Then, the badges and powers of arrest.

As research progressed I discovered that all Forest Service employes once had the power of arrest on Forest Service property. I mentioned this in conversation with

Frank Plyler, another savvy, long-time USFS department head. Years earlier I had established a friendly, relaxed connection with him. He had been at Pearl Harbor when the Japanese bombed on December 7, 1941, and I had interviewed him about it. When I mentioned the powers of arrest, he said "Oh yes, for years we carried badges. I've still got them in the safe."

In a couple of days I was in Supe's office. The dumb Indian flared up. "All right, Zero, where is my badge?"

Gasp, gasp. "Oh God, now what? What badge." (He is trying to be patient with this breed Indian.)

I became quite serious. "My badge. What do you mean what badge? I'm not going to arrest anyone without a badge."

Gasp. Inhalation, teeth clack, gasp. Then, "We don't have badges. I'm sorry."

"Well then, I'm not going to arrest anyone," I said.

"Yes, please don't try to arrest anyone," he wheezed as I went out the door.

Then I went to Frank Plyler's office and asked him. He grinned, divined something going on. "There in the safe," he said. I got four bronze badges and pinned them on my shirt. Then I returned to Supe's office. He was on the phone to New Orleans. His eyes widened when I pointed to the badges. "You said we didn't have badges," I accused, turned quickly and went to Frank's office and returned the badges to the safe. Then I stepped into the next room. In minutes Supe burst through the door. "Where did he get those badges?" he asked.

Frank stared blankly at him. "What badges?"

"Oh Christ, the FBI will be here," Zero sputtered

A visit from strange suits

Within a few weeks of my being hired, two men in suits came to my office. They were dressed in suits which I recognized as investigators or intelligence. These were intelligence, full of false heartiness.

"Lewis, we've been checking out your records," one said.

"Uh oh! Well, am I going to jail or what?"

"No, no, no. Puh…leeze. How would you like to go to Bolivia?"

"I'm listening. What for?"

"Well, our government is helping with some experimental tree plantations near La Paz. We'd like for you to make some photos of the trees."

"I see. Are you part of the Forest Service?"

"Not exactly."

"I thought not. What do you need with photos of the trees?"

"We'll figure that out. Now, you've got the perfect background for this. If you wander into the villages you can get touristy photos of the people there."

"Especially the ones with ammo bandeleros and grenades around their shoulders. La Paz is near where they killed Che Guevera, no? Are the guerrillas still active there?"

"Lewis, Lewis….what has that got to do with tree plantations?"

"Yes, I wonder. How much is the pay?"

"The same thing you're getting here. And expenses. That program…"

"Are you kidding? I've got a wife and three sons. We're just barely getting by."

"We can work other methods of payment."

We haggled and kidded awhile. I assured them I wasn't interested. Their smiles had grown thin. "Call us after you consider it awhile. You've got the perfect credentials."

No, no, no and again no.

Impersonating A Journalist For J.B.

I was getting anxious to leave SEFES. Dr. Frank Hulme, a distinguished professor at Cornell University had retired years earlier and was teaching at Warren Wilson College. He had written critical art, book and theater reviews for The Native Stone, and had asked me for several years to consider teaching a class at WWC. Then he called to see if I could get the CETA grant transferred. I began pondering. But first…

The PR man at SEFES had proven ineffective. Word came from Washington that the assistant director there was coming to Asheville for a ceremony, to be accompanied by other VIPs. One was an astronaut who had taken some seed to the moon and he, accompanied by Governor Jim Holshouser's wife and another NASA official, were going to plant the seed at UNC-A's botanical garden. This was a major coup for SEFES. J.B. called a press conference at the cafeteria in Asheville Mall. I went there just to see it. Five minutes before the time, no reporters had shown up. J.B. started getting panicky.

"Lewis, what are we going to do?"

"You know how the so-called Asheville media is. Do you want me to impersonate a reporter."

"God yes. You think we can get away with it? How will I introduce you?"

"I am the president of the Western Carolina Regional News Council, and this is so important that I have decided to come myself instead of sending someone."

I ran to Woolworth's and got a legal pad. Then J.B. escorted me into the big room where the dignitaries awaited. He put me in a solitary chair out in front of the dias and introduced me.

"This is Mr. Lewis Green. He is president of the Western Carolina Regional News Council and a prize-winning journalist. He has decided this is important enough for him to cover himself without sending any of his reporters." Then he embellished some himself. "Mr. Green also files his material with all the big news organizations in the state, including all the daily newspapers, television stations and wire services." (God, I wondered what the big wheels would say later when clipping services brought in nothing for their scrapbooks. What the hell?)

Adding to the plausibility was Mrs. Holshouser nodding to me and smiling. I had met her at many political gatherings so she knew me as a journalist. So I began getting statements and posing what I hoped were relevant and some skeptical questions. One or two of the SEFES employes had dropped by, very curious about what was happening and my role in it. Then J.B. decided it was enough. He arose, said "Mr. Green, I'm sorry but we now have to go to UNC-A and plant the seed."

I suddenly grew very stern just to mess with J.B.

"I'm not through yet. I have more questions. All the readers west of Charlotte are quite interested in this."

He gritted his teeth and glared. Just as I was pulling this Supe walked in. He knew nothing of this charade. Here was his CETA man haranguing the dignitaries. Then with a certain grandiose authority I dismissed them. Mrs. Holshouser and the assistant Director from Washington came to me for a moment to chat, to butter up to this media wheel and thank me for my time and interest. Supe seemed at a loss. I strode up to him and asked

"You don't know who I really am, do you?"

He gasped, cut his eyes about. "No sir, exactly who are you?"

"I'm in charge of this whole operation," I said and strutted out the door. I had decided to take Frank Hulme's offer at Warren Wilson.

Warren Wilson College

CETA agreed to transfer my grant to Warren Wilson College in Swannanoa. Here a false note was struck from the beginning.. President Ben Holden welcomed me in his office. We both chatted a moment about military experience, then he said "Welcome. Your credentials are in order."

I winced. I didn't have any teaching credentials nor did I pretend to have any, but I had a lot of experience and I didn't cost the college any money. I taught the first journalism and creative writing courses at WWC. (The program has developed over the intervening years to a nationally-recognized course.)

The head of the English Department was Jed Bierhaus, an effeminate and scrawny Episcopal Priest who was a dead ringer for some of Washington Irving's creations. As we talked for the first time in his office, I noticed a copy of Kraft-Ebbing in a prominent place on his bookshelf. (So! An interest in strange sexual practices, eh?)

He suggested we get the editor of the school newspaper in to do a story on me.

"Why?" I asked.

"So they'll know who you are."

"Why not let them find me out at their own speed as the days go by?"

That caused him some discomfort, but all right, he said.

The first course in Journalism was team-taught by Dr. Jack Boozer and myself. (Frank Hulme laughed when he talked to me. "We have thrown you into a beerhouse with a heavy boozer," he said.)Very soon the students found Boozer out. He knew nothing of journalism, rather continued to try to concentrate on English, spelling, syntax, etc. But they weathered that class with a certain savvy that students develop about teachers.

Someone at the top had decided quickly that the J class should have nothing to do with the production of the school newspaper. I was the problem. Some of the power structure in Asheville were on the board of directors and my investigative and expose work at The Native Stone had shaken them. They would have vetoed my hiring if it had gone through regular channels, but the CETA program was merely an administrative matter involving red tape. Nor did I want to mess with the campus newspaper. Yet, there were interesting developments.

A young, bright-eyed Californian named Bob came into my office one day and announced that he wanted to be an investigative reporter. He said he was already doing a project on his own but the campus newspaper wouldn't consider even his letters to the editor. He asked me to direct him. He said he had overheard conversations in the kitchen where he did his student labors intimating that the school was being cheated. It was paying for top-quality meat but an inferior grade was being delivered. How could he prove it? he asked.

We conferred and connived. He had shown enough initiative to copy the stamped code off the sides of beef in the refrigerator, but he didn't know what to do next. I told him to go to the Oteen Ingles grocery and talk to a friend of mine in the butcher shop. He did. Good God. The college was paying top prices for low-grade meat. Somehow Bob got access to the invoices and found out that the man in charge had signed off on top-grade meat. Why? He asked me. I explained the law of kick-back. Then he talked again to the campus editor, who wouldn't touch the story. "How can we get it out?" he asked, getting more and more discouraged. I showed him where a mimeograph machine was in a side office. We talked with a woman there who showed Bob how to operate it.

I told him the Warren Wilson board of directors were to meet there on the coming weekend, and their custom was to spend the night in dorm rooms. Bob wrote the story and mimeographed it. I told him that to wait until after midnight Saturday and slip it under their doors.

The food service manager was soon gone. At the end of the term young Bob headed home to California to seek a newspaper job. I wrote him a letter of high recommendation.

Orientation of foreign students in basic journalism and ethics

One class I taught by myself was made up of about 12 students, all foreigners but three. Generally Africans and middle-eastern Muslims. That first hour was taken up with introductions and getting acquainted. The second hour was taken up with free-wheeling criticism of the United States and its moral shortcomings by most of the foreign students. The criticism was unanimous: You Americans have very little moral strength or convictions. This is a land of deals—wheeling and dealing no matter the consequences; a high degree of infidelity to honor and principle. You make deals, deals, deals, no matter what.

Then the lessons began. Because of their shortcomings in the language, I told them I would make classes simple and easy on them. It would be mostly a familiarization course—the makeup of a newsroom, what assignments to what reporters, what editor handled what news, how it was routed or channeled to the proper editor's desk, the decisions made there (what typeface and headlines would be most appropriate for what stories, etc.)

As the days passed, long periods were taken up with discussion and argument about current affairs as reported in the media, both local and national, and how important that was to our imaginary readers. Inevitably the discussions drifted toward the shortcomings and hypocrisy of the American political and business systems, and the overweening greed and grasping exhibited by most Americans. If a point was made intelligently and backed up by fact, I agreed. Much of the time I did not comment or disagree, choosing instead to let the flow go uninterrupted.

By this method I learned much about the thinking embedded in them by their own cultures.

My relationship with them was relaxed and easy. We ribbed each other, talked of personal matters. I learned their handicaps and limitations. But duty is duty. It came time for mid-terms. I told them I would make it as easy on them as possible. Most were in financial straits and I knew that it was imperative for them to make passing grades to stay in school. I had to test them for the records, but I would go over the answers several times so they would know what was coming. Almost joking, I said there would only be one way to fail, and that would be to break the teacher-student covenant and cheat. "But why cheat when I'm going to give you all the answers but one? I do think you should go to the library and look up one answer, which is easy to find in a reference book on printing. And here are the questions and answers. The managing editor manages the newsroom; the city editor manages the city news; the state editor manages the state or regional news; the telegraph editor handles the wire news from the wire services such as the Associated Press or United Press International etc.

"The answer you must seek in the reference room is the definition of Ben Day." (Ben Day is a print process named after its originator, and is made up of gray dots to use either as background or borders to boxes on the pages, usually with boldface type. It was only two short paragraphs in that reference book.)

They took the test and passed it, except that all but one did not get Ben Day. Only an American girl and a Japanese boy had gone to the library. But the Japanese boy misunderstood it to be a color process. Several had written it as a color process used with photos. One had written that Ben Day was the president of the American Civil War Confederacy and had invented a color process of dots; another that Ben Day had also invented the kite and got his electricity for the printing press from lightning.

After checking their papers I confronted them. "All but Jayne have failed. Now who else went to look it up." A Japanese boy raised his hand. "You told all the others, didn't you?"

"How did you know that?"

They mostly had the same information, which resulted in the failing grade. "You cheated. For God's sake, you cheated. You could have gotten that one wrong and still passed with a high grade. But you cheated."

The atmosphere had changed. Eyes were averted in guilt and embarrassment. I called them into my office one at a time. I notified them, each and all, that they had failed. But, I said, knowing their strained resources and circumstances, and generally good work and attitude, Let's see what we can do. "What do you think your grade should be?"

Invariably, "An A sir."

"No, you cheated and failed, but I'm going to give you a C, barely passing, but it'll get you through."

"But sir…"

To each and all such a conference. Class resumed, strained. But up toward the end of the term I let them see that my stance had softened a bit. They brightened. One day in open class I let them state, among their peers, what they thought they deserved. An A or B, one and all. I nodded in contemplation, which seemed to cheer them.

Nearer the end, I once again took them into my office individually. "Sir, I deserve more than a C."

"You absolutely must have more than a C, right? But you cheated. All right, I don't think you're worth it but I'm going to give you a B."

"Oh, thank you, sir, thank you, thank you, thank you…"

On the last day when I formally announced their grades, I was cold and grim. "I have one last thing to say to you."

They waited, passing grades in hand, but apprehensive nonetheless.

"I want to say this to you. When we first started, most of you were highly critical of this country, the land of deals. Well, you failed this class on the moral grounds of cheating. But I made you a deal."

Silence.

"You took the deal. Now get your asses out of my classroom and don't look back."

Only the beautiful, brilliant Jayne lingered, a small smile on her face.

"You ought to be ashamed of yourself."

"Why?"

"You made naturalized Americans out of these pure souls."

Ken on Idi Amin's Death List in Uganda

Ken had one of those complex African last names where vowels and consonants do not mesh. He was a tall light-skinned boy from Uganda, utterly polite and pleasant at every turn, anxious to please.

He had a compelling naïvete and innocence. He came to my office one morning astonished by an experience he had the night before. One of the female professors, edging into spinsterhood, had dressed in an outdated fashion and taken

Ken out on the town (Black Mountain) the night before. "Meestor Green," Ken said, "she took me to her apartment and tried to kiss me. I was so embarrassed for her I ran to my dorm. I can't face her now."

Shortly thereafter he came to my office with an even greater problem. It was summer and most of the students and faculty were gone. Like many foreign students at Warren Wilson, Ken worked at several on-campus maintenance jobs to help pay his tuition. But it was not going to be enough, he said, and he was going to have to return to Uganda. However, he said, his family was on the death list of Uganda dictator Idi Amin, as was he. "He's going to kill me if I return there," Ken said and began to weep softly. The Warren Wilson administration could do nothing, he said.

"The hell they can't," I said and immediately left my office for the office of Ben Holden. He said he knew of the situation and was trying to work with it, then admitted they could do nothing because of visa rules etc.

"Well, you'd better," I said. "If this school don't do anything to help that kid, I'm going to the offices of the Federal Wage and Price people and turn you in for working these kids long hours for next to nothing."

Then came one of the telling moments in my work at academia. We understood each other. Ben had been an Infantry battalion commander in World War II's China-Burma-India campaign, had a Ph.D from Yale, a man of great accomplishment and prestige, looked at me sadly and admitted "Lewis, I'm only a gray-headed figurehead here. I can't make decisions. The board does all that."

In some astonishment, I returned to my office and contemplated at length. At last I got out my private phone book and called the guys in suits who had visited me at Southeastern Forest Experiment Station.

"Lewis, great to hear from you at last. Are you ready to go to Bolivia?"

"That is big negative, but I've got something you might want."

"What?"

"There's an Ugandan boy here who must be important because he says he's on Idi Amin's death list."

"Will he cooperate?"

"I'm sure of that. He'll have to. These bastards are going to ship him back."

I introduced them at lunch the next day at the school cafeteria and got out of their way. Then I lost contact with Ken. Years later I was in the Asheville Federal Building and Ken shouted at me. He was dressed in an expensive blue pin-stripe suit and was carrying a briefcase.

"Meestor Green, sor. How great to see you again. Guess what job I have."

"What?"

"I'm working for your government."

Drugs Appeared At Warren Wilson

One of my students was Donk, an alias for these uses. He was a good enough student who generally went his own way in a lackadaisical manner. His mane was a golden toss, as were his brows, and though a handsome boy he and the girls were slow and cool toward each other. One day I noticed some marijuana plants sprouting in the widow box of his dorm window. I pointed that out one day as I walked past the dorm. He grinned, said yes, he often got by with a little help from his friends. What the hell? I was by now affecting the kindly and tolerant professor pose.

Some time later, several of the faculty noticed that Donk's popularity had increased and many more visitors were in and out of his dorm. When I asked him, he had a most cheery laugh. Donk was always open and candid. He had gone to Florida on the break. Wandering along the beach early one morning alone he received a gift from the gods. A large bale of marijuana had washed ashore and was bobbing in the tide.

Donk dashed to get his car and loaded it up. The bale was so big he couldn't quite get the trunk closed. Nonetheless, he got his belongings out of his motel room and drove straight to Warren Wilson. His luck held. No law-enforcement officers stopped him. But when break ended, he had friends, friends, friends and money, money, money. (He said he sold it to some fellow students at discount rates, and often gave it away.)

The administration at WWC tried to pretend there were no drugs there. True enough, compared to other campuses drug use was slight. Then I had a call one day from a friend who was a deputy sheriff. He wanted to know what was going on at Warren Wilson. An informer had called him to say that a foreign student had gone crazy and was running about the campus and into neighborhoods screaming and singing, laughing and cursing in crude English.

The answer came soon enough. A South American student had received two kilos of cocaine in the mail. He was supposed to sell it but communications had gotten garbled, so he did some experimenting. He began to sniff and eat it. That came to an end when he ran alongside a passing freight train and tried to hobo it, fell under it and both of his feet were cut off.

Faculty and administration tried to blame me for calling the cops. I assured them I would have but the cops had called me first. The ostracism began. That was all right with me. I was contemptuous of most of the faculty anyway.

Then payback came for me. Let us go back a few years. I founded The Native Stone in 1971, the year Jim Hunt first ran for Lieutenant Governor. He was to make his opening announcement in Western North Carolina at Waynesville Country Club and called a press conference there. I was the only newsman to attend. I gave him two full pages of text and photos. Fast forward now. He won, later ran for Governor and won that.

Back to Warren Wilson. It was announced that Governor Hunt was coming to check on something, so the kiss-ass administrators and faculty and most of the student body came out to the parking area to greet him. This black sheep was standing more or less alone. In comes the governor's limosine. In the back seat with the governor was State Senator Zeb Alley of Waynesville, an old friend. As they entered the area, Zeb spotted me and nudged the governor, who immediately ordered the driver to stop. Before going on to the big wheels on campus, Zeb and the Governor came to me, began shaking hands, slapping me on the back and inquiring loudly as to my health, etc. Then they pulled me along to where sulky administrators awaited.

The following day I was summoned to the president's office. "Lewis, we were just wondering...we need a few things done in Raleigh. Could you speak to your friend the Governor?"

The Liberals Sex Ploy

There was no end to the dumb little lies the faculty told on each other. One of those with whom I got along explained it this way when I asked why such educated people, who had access to the wisdom of the ages, did some of the things they did. He said one reason was that the stakes were so small—they never had been involved in high-stakes principles. Another was that they all posed as great intellectuals. The fact that I had one novel published (And Scatter The Proud) and John Blair was in the process of preparing my collection of short stories (The High Pitched Laugh of A Painted Lady) for publication caused some ill-hidden jealousy. That friend told me that the cautious little mediocrities on the faculty would never forgive me for that. They feared they needed to publish or perish and they couldn't publish.

This is all leading to the grand finale of my stay at Warren Wilson. In addition to teaching journalism and creative writing, I had agreed to do an independent studies course on wilderness survival. My sole student for that was a pudgy little girl named Beth. At this time the feminist movement was gathering some interest among the females on the campus, and Beth was fully into the rhetoric.

She had been raised in Japan by Presbyterian Missionary parents, and her resources were very limited. We interviewed in the cafeteria where most of our later meetings were held. I explained to her that I would provide her with some gear at my expense, and the lessons would take place on my time. For that, I told her that the feminist attitude would not go far with me. In order that I would teach her, she must not use any of that rhetoric with me. In order to prove that she had the right attitude toward the teacher, when we were meeting in the cafeteria, I would tell her to go get me some coffee and she must immediately oblige with respect. Or else no class. (She had to struggle with that, but she did it.) I bought her some polyethylene for use as shelter in the mountains, a small cooking kit, etc., and basic survival food.

I own part of a mountain in Fairview and I would take her there and show her how to construct a lean-to, build a fire and cook on it, and make observations of the land and creatures, particularly the rattlesnakes. She began developing self-reliance, discipline and confidence. But she had a little friend who bore a startling resemblance to a small wet duck, either Huey, Dewey or Louie Duck (comic strip associates of Donald Duck). Her name was Jana and one day she invited herself to join us at the lunch table. As I explained to Beth some technique or the other, my coffee ran low and I said abruptly "Go get me some coffee, Beth."

"Yessir," she said and jumped to do it. Jana went red and screamed "Beth, why are you obeying this pig's orders. Let him get his own damn coffee." But Beth had learned. She scurried on to get the coffee. Then I said to Jana "She owes that obedience in payment for the course. If she don't do that, she's out."

"What does the college say about that?"

"I don't give a shit what they say. Sweetie, I've developed a bad attitude about some of these things that go on here."

She pouted on, but did not leave. After Beth and I finished talking, Jana asked if she could take the course. I said no. Then she asked if she could sit in on some of it, and I agreed to that. As time passed it became therapy for her, and then she confessed to me that she was a lesbian. (The first ever to come out of the closet at WWC.) I asked if Beth was one and she said no, they were only friends. For some reason I asked Jana exactly what lesbians did. She said she didn't know, but she was going to find out. Some weeks later she said some girls had begun knocking on her dorm door after hours.)

Jana was also paranoid. She had once looked in my office window and saw Beth, Bierhaus and me conferring. She thought we were planning to deprive her of her student teaching certificate. Then she brought a porn publication to my office once that a male student had given her. Some time later she told me she was afraid of me. Why? "I think you're dangerous and somebody is going to get hurt."

"Well, that could be a possibility when some of these smart asses run their mouths. But I'll tell you what to do to set your mind at ease. Go down to the administration offices and tell them of your fears."

"But why?"

"So that when dead bodies start showing up around campus, they'll know who to come after."

Ah God! Academia.

But she did go to the campus preacher, a poseur name Fred something who considered himself a psychoanalyst. She told me later that he had decided in a Jungian fashion that what I had said to be a sexual hint.

My grant was coming to a close. Some of the foreign students wanted me to stay on and teach an advanced course. I felt I could get an extension from CETA. I went to Bierhaus's office and asked. It was one of those dark and brooding days in the mountains, a perfect setting because Bierhouse was the very archetype for a Washington Irving character, especially in this setting. His face grew long and grim.

"We can't do that, Lewis. A female student has accused you of making sexual advances to her."

I am thinking. Which one of these chickies has been talking. But I am learning about the liberals. My long experience in interviewing and interrogation conditioned my intuition to spot a con job when I saw it.

"Who?" I asked.

"Well, I just can't tell you."

"Yes, goddam it, you aren't getting away with this. Who?"

He grew frightened in the face of the Drill Instructor.

"Jana," he stammered.

Aha. I'm on safe ground. I grinned at him and asked if he knew she was a self-proclaimed lesbian. That threw him off and he sent me to administration, where I set in raising hell. The old gray-headed Ben only shook his head. "I can do nothing."

"I'm suing your asses," I announced.

The next day I took Jana to the law offices of Bob Long, where she said in a deposition that she had made no such accusation. A bit later, the Dean, a neurotic by the name of Sam Scoville, came to me and said I couldn't beat them in a lawsuit since they had much more money than me. "Yes, and you're going to have to spend it on lawyers," I said.

Then panic set in. A bit later he came to me and said the real reason for not renewing me was that no one could get along with me. Frank Hulme laughed and said "Don't let them get away with that. I told them before they accepted you that nobody in the English Department would be able to get along with you."

Scoville changed his rationale again, to one much more ridiculous. He said the real reason they were letting me go was that they had been informed that I had been sent to Warren Wilson to "foment revolution". When I finally stopped laughing in his face, I told him he couldn't make a campus radical out of me because I had voted for Barry Goldwater.

It did put me in trouble with my favorite Jayne. Our relationship was not sexual, but rather mutual adoration. When she heard the rumor she came to me with tears in her eyes, and I had to spend some time convincing her that if I ever had any sexual designs on a student it would, of course, be her. I told her I was much too high principled to do anything but admire and love her from a distance. All right, then, she said, and we did kiss at last.

But it was coming down to its end. Shortly before my time was up, CETA had informed me that the Political Science Department at UNC-A had asked for me through Dr. Gene Rainey, an old political friend/enemy. He had recommended me to the new department head there, Dr. Tom Scism.

So shortly before I left WWC, I walked into the faculty lounge one day. Three bloodless professors were sitting there. Separate from them was the premier professor of the music department. He was one of my rare supporters. He was sly, subtle about the ways of the faculty. He saw me, and to set the stage shouted "Lewis, what's going on now."

I took the cue. The old dumb country boy said "They have put upon me again. They know no shame. They have accused me of making sexual advances to a female student." (This professor was not an innocent man, but he later married his mark. Some of the students had told me that some of the professors were known for "an A for a lay").

"Oh no! You're right. There is no end to perfidy here. Not you, of all people. You didn't do that, did you?"

"No, no, no. The only thing I've done here like that is go to bed with three faculty wives."

We both turned and momentarily stared knowingly at the three professors, who in turn stared meekly at the floor.

Onward To UNC-A

A CETA administrator had called to tell me that Dr. Gene Rainey had heard I was a free agent and had talked the head of the Political Science Department into placing me as faculty adjunct. I met with them for the interview. Since it was CETA, Scism did not have to clear my employment and he had already hired two more from the program. At that time the Political Science Department consisted of Scism, Gene Rainey and Bob Farzanagan, who was the son of the Shah of Iran's top general. I was welcomed warmly by them, but I was given little to do, and it was six weeks before I was assigned an office. My business was conducted at a table in the snack shop.

Most poly sci departments are known for causing problems with the administration, experimenting with internal and external power struggle being the nature of the courses. The UNC-A poly sci professors were quite familiar with the uncontrolled political coverage of The Native Stone. They were interested in my experience. But Dr. Scism told me later that when Dean Riggs heard he had placed me he called him about it. "You hired Lewis Green? You goddamned fool. You had a powder keg down there and now you've thrown a lit match into it."

Ah God! My reputation always precedes me. I have to live up to it as soon as the students hear of it. But while UNC-A was as strange as Warren Wilson, it was a vastly different strangeness. There was a freedom among the student body. The potheads were out in the open with it, student sexuality was blatant, the younger faculty members constantly demonstrated overweening ambition and treachery toward each other and their department heads. Most of the older, more mature faculty kept enough of an even keel that stability was maintained and the school functioned properly.

The Chancellor was Dr. Bill Highsmith whom I had known as a reporter. Pete Gilpin had been a colleague at the daily newspaper, and was now Dr. Highsmith's public relations officer. Highsmith was generally on a balanced course (except when it came to poly sci, at whose mention he sometimes frothed). Those times Highsmith and I met on campus we stopped to talk, anticipate and predict possibilities in local and state politics. More on some conversations with Highsmith later.

In a short time, Scism revealed himself as an active alcoholic. When in the throes of it he became irrational and vindicative. At departmental meetings the discussions would often grow heated, and when a disagreement arose between me and a full professor, he would agree with the professor. However, often at night, after he began drinking, he would call me at home to say I had been right in that day's discussion, but that he had to support the regulars over a CETA employe. When I brought this up at a subsequent meeting, he would deny it.

Finally I reached my limit and began taping the night conversations, then I played him one. Shortly he began spreading the story that I was taping the sexual fantasies of coeds. (don't I often wish they would confide all that in me?) I jumped him one day on the sidewalk and he ran through the halls of one building screaming that I was trying to murder him.

Then I was transferred to archives, where my job was to print archival quality prints from hundreds of old 8x10 negatives given the university by Ewart Ball III. They were of Asheville from about 1915 through the twenties and had been made by his grandfather, the premier photographer of that time.

Archives was in the library basement at the time, and often some students would drop in to chat or talk about photography. One day as I walked through the library, my supervisor, Bruce Greenwalt, approached me to inform me that the campus police had told him to lean on me and make me pay a couple of parking tickets. Bruce was a cautious, meek professor and spoke in low tones. Following my form I loudly said "Once again I am being put upon by the powers that be, persecuted. They know no shame. My enemies are legion. They are everywhere. Demonic Liberal Democrats. They put upon me at every turn..." and on and on in loud rhetoric, encouraged by the laughs and applause of students. Bruce was chagrined, trying to quieten me down. The students were snickering.

Bruce said "I know its not the money, it's the principle. I protest the parking situation here too."

"Really? How?"

"I put my bumper sticker on upside down."

"Bad, Bruce, bad. These cops will turn your car upside down so they can read it."

Finally Highsmith had to call me in about the two tickets. "You have to pay this," he said.

"I'm not going to." He grew livid. Then I laughed and said "Bill, there's a way out of this. I'm quitting in a couple of weeks."

He brightened. "I'll take it. Forget the tickets. It's been a privilege to have you here for this time." We grew silent for a moment, then he asked slyly "What do you hear out of Political Science?"

"They're trying to get you, Bill."

He went red again. "Goddam it, I knew it. They don't let up." He took pen and pad out.

"Who?"

"Everybody but Farzanagan. He's the only friend you've got."

"Yes, bless him. He's been good. I've always trusted him." He was writing names down.

"They're not the only ones, bill."

"Aha. I don't doubt that. Who else?"

I sat contemplating all the slights and cuts I had suffered.

"Well, everyone in psychology is always belittling you.

"Aha!Aha! Who else?"

"Social Science."

He scribbled away. "Thanks, thanks. Those bastards, I gave them their jobs."

We arose and shook hands. "Good luck to you." he said. "If anyone needs luck it's you."

Bujie and Herman

How the lawyers Bujie Pegram and Herman Stevens came to consort is one of the mysteries of nature's chemistry. Bujie was a slick, polished lawyer from Winston-Salem who came to Asheville and opened a lucrative practice. Herman was one of Buncombe County's back country lawyers whose poor clients often paid him with bags of potatoes or turnips, sides of pork, jars of moonshine and much good will which he could translate into small political clout.

The friendship grew out of Bujie's eagerness to learn mountain ways and recognition of and appreciation for Herman's sly mountain wit, which many of the city lawyers didn't quite catch. Herman accepted him despite the slick little jibes Bujie took at him from time to time. Herman awaited his time.

The criminal trial lawyers were a salty bunch. At lunch and between breaks at court, they met for coffee and lunch at the Courthouse snack bar and a couple of nearby small cafes. There they would swap ribald stories, embellish them, play practical jokes, etc. It was from these stories (and murder trials he attended) that Bujie learned to fear Madison and Haywood counties.

More than likely it was in that environment that Bujie and Herman developed a friendship, where Bujie revealed his eagerness to learn mountain ways and his ignorance thereof. As time passed they began to hunt ruffed grouse together and the friendship deepened. Bujie took certain liberties in his jibes at Herman's hillbilly ways.

One day Bujie asked Herman if he knew any place where they could hunt the next Saturday. Herman said he would make inquiry. That night he called an old friend, a Madison County farmer, and asked if he could bring a friend there to hunt.

"Yes.. While you're down here, Herman, stop by the house. I need for you to do me a favor."

Saturday they drove to the farm in Bujie's car and spent the morning hunting the upper acres. At noon they returned to the car and drove toward the other acres, between which stood the house and barn. As they neared the house, Herman said "Pull in here, Bujie. I need to talk to him a minute." Bujie got nervous.

"You mean you haven't asked him if we can hunt yet?" Herman shrugged, went to the house. The farmer asked if he had any deer loads for his shotgun. Yeah.

"Well then, Herman, I need for you to do me a favor. My old mule is sick and about to die. I've had him so long I ain't got the heart to put him out of his misery. Will you do that for me? He's down there in the barnyard."

Herman got back in the car and pointed down the road to the barnyard, where the mule was swaying against the fence near some cattle. "Pull in there, Bujie," he said. He did and Herman loaded some deer loads in his shotgun, got out and leaned across the fence, put the muzzle under the mule's jaw and blew his brains out. Then he turned and stared at Bujie and said "To hell with him. If he ain't gonna let us hunt, I'll kill his goddamned livestock."

Bujie took off, the open door banging. He went straight on to Winston-Salem and called his wife from there, telling her not to answer the phone or door.

The farmer came down to look at the dead mule and Herman. He saw the car was gone. "What in hell?" he asked.

"I need a ride home," Herman said.

Zeno

Zeno Ponder was one of two brothers who dominated the Madison County Democratic Party for many years, and Madison was and is one of the mountain counties populated by fierce, independent and difficult people who took their politics very seriously. One reason being that in that time there was very little industry or other employment there. The state government provided much of the employment opportunities as well as the few vital services. The Ponder brothers had been instrumental decades earlier in wresting control from Republicans, and they kept control, ruling with iron hands. Their methods met with stern disapproval by the editorial commentator Arthur Whitesides of WLOS in Asheville. Whitesides was the quintessential flatland outsider with no understanding of mountain politics and whose approach was that of the idealist newsman.

One of Zeno's aides and allies called me at The Native Stone one morning and said Zeno would like to make a statement, but only if I would assure him that I would put down exactly what he said. He told me that WLOS's gadfly commentator Arthur Whiteside had been giving Zeno hell about mismanaging the poverty program in Madison County

"If it's not lies I will," I said.

The next day I met the aide in Marshall and he led me to Zeno's farm. Zeno was in a field working and the aide waved him up. Zeno stood stiff and formal, not looking at me. That aide introduced us (I had known Zeno about 15 years then, on both friendly and hostile terms.)

Zeno stuck out his hand, bowed slightly and said respectfully "How are you, Mr. Green?"

I shook hands with him and asked "Zeno, what is this Mr. Green stuff? What in hell are you up to?" He ignored that.

The aide said, "Now Zeno, Mr. Green here publishes The Native Stone, which you read. He has assured me he'll quote you accurately. He'll put down exactly what you say."

Zeno looked at me, "Is that right, Mr. Green?"

I nodded, got my pad and pen out. Zeno drew himself up to a formal stance and said:

"All right. I'd like to state that Mr. Arthur Whiteside is a goddamned lying son-of-a-bitch."

I was scribbling it down. The aide went white in the face. "Watch out, Zeno, he's writing that down."

Zeno looked at him in puzzlement., "Well, that's what I thought we had him down here for."

The aide said "That ain't going to look too good, is it, Lewis?"

I said, "I'm not here to exercise censorship. This is a free country. Mr. Zeno Ponder is one of the most important Democrat politicians in Western North Carolina. People value his viewpoint. They want to hear what he's got to say." Zeno nodded in solemn agreement.

"Now Zeno, what about those lying bastards at The Citizen-Times?"

"Right. How much space can I have?"

"You can have all of the front page and most of page 3 and we'll continue it next week if need be."

The aide had jumped between us. "Jesus Christ, Zeno, just shut up."

The Repentance and Redemption of Attorney Tom Garrison

◆

Reclaiming Lost Honor

Tom Garrison now lies in his grave, and for all the paradoxes of his life the greatest is this—that his respect among friends and colleagues in the Bar Association was returned and at last raised to its highest.

Tom truly was selected by those higher powers beyond our understanding to stand the tests of spirit and soul. Somewhere last week, as he made his crossing to stand before whatever bench of justice is over there, surely the saints stood to applaud.

Here are a few words for a friend, but they will not suffice. Tom's life must be examined under another light and from a different perspective than which most other men are judged. Mere words will not explain what he endured, nor why. We had to be there and see it as the years passed. We often had to wonder when he would break. His was one of those perplexing lives into which we could not enter to comfort or counsel him. Only this thought comes from the preacher in Melville's Moby Dick: "Woe to the man who pours oil on the waters that God has troubled"

We will not know why God put that upon him. Many years ago trouble descended upon Tom, and it was that kind of Biblical woe from which no man can flee. Why review it all here? Let it be said that personal, family and financial problems came upon a gentleman who had been raised in a certain school of thought and who did not want to abandon that conscience in the end. He stood to his duty once a dark veil had been lifted. He could not ever have been prepared for those problems, and those problems brought financial ruin.

As he faced into his storm, he began to spin his life around helping others, perhaps instinctively seeing that to be the only spiritual escape from those demons besetting him. Many years ago when I was a younger reporter covering the Courthouse Tom was the County Attorney. We guardedly made our way toward a trusting friendship. I was at the beginning of a career and he guided me along in the complexities of county legalities..

One day he called and asked if I would be interested in meeting and writing a story on a nationally prominent luminary who was not making himself available to reporters. Certainly I would. "You camp a bit, do you not?" he asked. Yes. Very well.

A few weekends later I met Tom and the local realtor Bill Johnson and we went to a cabin near Bat Cave on Broad River. Tom, ever the strangely shy and formal, yet curiously relaxed gentleman, introduced me to a man I had heard much about. He was Dr. George Bond, who was heading up the government's first Sea lab experiments in the Caribbean, much of which was top secret. He was directing experiments under the sea, which were to prove the first step toward weightlessness and other conditions anticipated in later space travel. Tom had told Dr. Bond some of my background, and that eminent scientist felt free to discuss some of the classified aspects of what he was doing so I could better understand the story. He trusted me because Tom Garrison vouched for me. I marveled at that because I hadn't known that Tom knew that much about me. As we talked Tom nodded and smiled. The last day together the importance of this meeting dawned on me and I pulled Tom aside and thanked him for this opportunity. He smiled, said "I wanted the best man around to do this interview"

That story went on the Associated Press wire nationwide and it was one of my early boosts. (And if you are yet within hearing distance, my friend Tom, thank you so much, thank you, thank you...)He did those things so often for the people around him. He was like that even when his world began caving in around him. Suffice to say we are talking about wife and children and his own career. And a huge but well-hidden drinking problem. There were sudden expenses. This man of the old school went forward against adversity, uncomplaining. Then suddenly it broke into the open. He had stumbled and the wolves moved in.

A mutual friend, attorney Bob Long, came to me one day and told me Tom had been indicted for embezzling a client's money. "I'm representing him. Will you be a character witness in Federal Court?"

Don't ask, just tell me Tom needs it. It was not a pleasure but it was a deep privilege. Tom, Bob and I walked to court together, then came back down the street together. Tom had a lot of restitution to make. He did not yet stop drinking, but some of the facts were out and he was not harshly condemned for it. He lost his law license. In a while Tom sought help from Alcoholics Anonymous. His sponsor said that Tom had begun to grapple with the truth of himself.

But the Jobian trial was just beginning. Years went by. Tom had to work as a paralegal for other lawyers. He did not make much money, but under stern self-discipline he made restitution. Slowly, slowly, slowly…A vindictive lawyer successfully fought the restoration of his license for too many years. By then those people in the legal profession dimly recognized that some higher test of character had been placed on him. Yet he did not lose that incredible sensitivity and gentlemanly conduct.

He was at the Courthouse each business day, courteously doing his work, mending himself, patiently waiting. At last in that welter of slow fast years, a new wife who believed in him. Then the powers relented and his license to practice law was restored. This man who had been so proud of his professional status, so shamed during the bad years, was at last restored. He could practice before the bench.

The daily newspaper here, even when it prints the facts it lies. It is a dingy gray whore. After eighteen years of shame and ignominy and at last vindication, they printed an almost total recap of the entire shameful incident—in detail. Why? Tom was not a political force. He posed no threat to the order and well being of the community. That story, even if almost factual, no longer was based in reality. But Tom, the gentle man, did not bend under that load either. It was worth noting that members of the Buncombe County Bar Association, normally a stoic and blasé lot, were highly incensed. "Who wrote that?" they asked. They knew that reporter. Jay Hensley. His judgment, never good, was assumed to be distorted by pills. One could assume that these people who deal daily with public records will be watching for any daily reporter or editor to show up on the records.

I felt some need to apologize to Tom that day for the sins of the writing craft. He smiled, said "Everybody gets what's coming to them. Now I've had all mine."

I noticed, if you will pardon this conceit on my part, this attempt at clairvoyance, that he was truly and at last a free man that day. All the prices had been paid, all the tests had been taken and passed. He stayed here with us a while, just to practice a bit of law. Perhaps it is redundant to say that Tom pretty soon grew old and died, and died if you please, with a wisdom and dignity that most of us will not attain. There! One of the lessons out of the tests. Suffering…

I went to the funeral at the Methodist Church in Weaverville that afternoon. I have stood at many biers, over many graves. Unlike so many, at this one I felt that something vast had passed through the sky toward completion. A man had gone through here in the fire of this valley. There was lightning, thunderheads in the western skies, and some distant rumbling. The greetings of old friends, and if you please, some far applause.

Thad Bryson

✦

Lest ye be judged

Thad Bryson was a lawyer from Bryson City, one of the old-timers whose roots went back here in the mountains for several generations. He was quite versed in the nuances that made him effective in the practice of law in the old mountain courtrooms. It follows, then, that he was also well-versed in the various nuances of politics. Thad was getting along in years and had gotten as far as he was ever going.

But an opening came for the appointment of a special Superior Court Judge for a limited term and it was offered to Thad, who took it. In a few weeks he was assigned to a term in Buncombe County and immediately showed some of the lawyers in Asheville who was running the Courtroom. Many became uneasy because the way things were done in the back mountain courts was different. I had known him for years and had no trouble understanding what the man was about.

Courts were part of my beat at the time. A lady schoolteacher had shot and killed her husband in North Buncombe and Thad was the judge. It was uncomplicated so a jury was quickly picked and testimony began on the first day. As the day ended the defense counsel approached the bench and asked Thad something. Before he banged the gavel he instructed the jury not to discuss the matter among themselves, and curiously added, "Now I don't want any of this to be printed in the paper." (He could get away with that in the back counties.)

Knowing him, I assumed he was trying to accommodate the defense in some pro forma way he knew couldn't be done. I went to the newsroom and wrote the story and turned it in without saying anything, as I would any story..

The next day I headed for the Courthouse at 2 p.m. and met Tom Lipsey on the street. Tom was involved in the case. He was shaking his head. "That mean judge is going to get you."

"For what?"

"He told you not to print that."

"Tom, you're a lawyer, you know damn well he can't do that."

"I wouldn't mess with him for a split second."

I walked into the Courtroom and Thad glared fiercely at me. Everyone in the Courtroom looked on with interest.

"Mr. Green, you come up here," he snarled, thumping the bench. I too am familiar with the subtleties. Thad had to save face. He leaned over, still frowning fiercely, and said soto voce "Listen Lewis, I know where DeSoto's gold mines are supposed to be in Swain County."

I nodded, chastened. "Where are they?" I whispered.

"You come over there in a week or two and we'll go to them and you can do a good story. You interested?"

I know the drill. "Yessir," I said, nodding solemnly.

"Now, do you understand?" he bellowed. I nodded.

"That'll be all."

I turned around. Everyone in the Courtroom seemed satisfied that he had tempered justice with mercy. But he left off the admonition about not printing it when he adjourned for that day.

About two weeks later an older woman reporter named Mary Cowles was filling in for me and Thad pulled that on her. She didn't know what prior restraint was and Thad's admonition scared her. She didn't write the story but she did tell the editor, who apparently also did not know about prior restraint. The next day's paper had no story about the trial but there was a furious editorial about this ignorant backwoods dictatorial judge. That editorial was filed on the Associated Press wire, and Thad was denounced editorially by every major newspaper in the country.

The following week I was in the hallway outside the Judge's chambers, where he was talking with some lawyers. He saw me and bade me enter.

"All right, Mr. Staff Reporter Lewis Green. Why weren't you up here covering court last week like you are supposed to do?"

"They had me doing something else…"

"God damn, I've never seen such a mess. I'd have ordered you not to print it and you'd have printed it and that would have been all there was to it."

One of The Martin Luther King Visits

❖

mid-1960s

In the years following the assassination of Martin Luther King Jr. in Memphis, a considerable body of opinion has arisen that King's star was falling in Civil Rights affairs at the time of his slaying, and that more militant blacks were surging forward (much in the manner of the present Jesse Jackson/Al Sharpton fiasco.)

There was a little publicized incident where both King and Malcolm X were addressing a meeting of white leaders. One of the more prominent whites had said that they just didn't want to deal with King. Malcolm X then replied in uncharacteristic calmness "If you don't deal with him today, you'll deal with me tomorrow." Subsequent events nationally showed that Malcolm X was again prophetic.

The years have solved some of the problems, have not solved others.

King appeared at various functions in and around Asheville in those days, and as a reporter for the daily newspaper here I was assigned to cover him. My beat was normally the police/courts beat, and since there were heavy security considerations about King's visits, that came under my beat.

Normally he would fly in to the Asheville Airport, where he was met by functionaries from whatever institution he was to address i.e..Montreat-Anderson College, Blue Ridge Assembly, and a couple more. Harry P. Clay was Sheriff at that time, and he provided several deputies to escort King's convoys to the destination and back to the airport. One black officer he always assigned personally to MLK was the late Bruce Steele of West Asheville. I generally rode in one of the escort cruisers.

At that time, King was hotly controversial and in keeping with its policy, the newspaper management did not want very much written. Strangely, I do not remember any advance publicity on King's last visit here, though I was tipped off that he was due to fly in here. It was this visit's silence and lack of enthusiasm that later led me to believe the reports that King was on the downhill skid.

I was in the newsroom when I got a tip that someone had called in a bomb threat on King's plane. I arrived at the airport just as two inexperienced deputies arrived. King was inside the terminal with his wife, but Bruce Steele was at the plane with the two deputies. While Steele didn't know who I was, he had seen me around the Sheriff's Department. I learned later that he thought I was an FBI agent. So did the airport manager. I went to the plane and he handed me a flash-light and asked if I could station a man at the gate and "keep the public out, especially the press."

Of course. I turned to Bruce and instructed him to get to the gate and keep people away, especially the press. He saluted and said "Yes sir."

I got on the plane with the deputies, one of whom asked "How do you search for a bomb?"

"Nothing to it," I said. "just look under everything. If you see something suspicious, let me know immediately."

"Why, what will we do then?"

"I don't know about you, but I'll get out of here."

We really didn't believe there was a bomb. We searched, then I went to the airport manager and handed him the flashlight. "I've got to get out of here," I said.

"Why?"

"I've got to file my story." He wheeled all about. "Jesus Christ," he said..

Bruce Steele had all the broadcast media lined up at the gate, refusing to let them in. When they saw me they were incensed.

"What are you doing in there?" one screamed.

I turned to Bruce and said "This is a very dangerous situation about national security. If those bastards say anything else, put every one of them in jail."

He saluted and said "Yes sir," turned and glowered at them. They grew apprehensive. This was an entirely unforeseen development. A Citizen-Times reporter with obvious authority ordering them jailed. They shut up.

Inside I found MLK and his wife. While she was relaxed, he was fuming about the delay. I introduced myself, then started a short interview. But he got on his topic.

"Now, as a middle-class white man, what are you doing for Civil Rights?"

"Listen," I said. "You're on the wrong track."

"What do you mean?" he demanded.

"I'm not exactly middle-class. I don't make but about $75 a week." He pondered that.

"Do you have black friends?"

"Some. Ford Hennessee is one."

"Does he visit in your home?"

"No."

"See!" he was triumphant.

"He just won't visit. He's afraid of the rattlesnakes in my yard. But his wife Juanita and their children do. We go camping."

His wife began giggling and he frowned at her.

"You ought to be doing something for the movement," he said.

"What are you doing about the alcoholic problem in the country," I abruptly asked.

That stopped him for a moment. "Exactly what are you getting at?"

"I am active in programs on alcoholism. I just can't save the whole world. You take care of the black problem and I'll handle what drunks I can, black or white," I said.

Julian Bond and Lester Maddox

❖

In the mid-1960s

The Civil Rights movement was gathering momentum and the nation was in the grips of fear and paranoia. However, outside of news media, people in the mountain area were untouched except for certain local episodes of blacks crossing their centuries-old lines. It was inevitable that wider exposure to those realities would come, and the more open-minded and curious moved toward that light.

The "outside agitators" who came here on invitation to speak sparked a certain resentment. Those included Martin Luther King Jr., the young and polished Julian Bond of Georgia and North Carolina's Golden Frinks, now forgotten, but who led Murphy to Manteo freedom marches among other things.

It was resented, yet, it had to come.

I was working at the daily newspaper at the time, and was assigned to cover a visit to Western Carolina University by Julian Bond. The speech was filled with the usual rhetoric, but the telling moment had already come in a pre-speech interview. I had heard that Bond had made a statement to an Atlanta newspaper reporter that then Governor Lester Maddox was somehow more amenable and acceptable to the black movement than the previous Georgia Governor Sanders, a white liberal.

Maddox had risen to political power by standing in the door of his restaurant in Atlanta with an axe-handle, a symbol of white resistance. (He served blacks at the back door of the restaurant.)

I asked Bond about that statement and he verified it. He said Maddox had done several things that blacks had appreciated. He said that he and other black leaders had gone to the white liberal Sanders when he was Governor and asked that blacks be put on draft boards and other commissions and boards. Bond said Sanders had oozed out of it by telling them that he would do something as soon as he could but the voters would crucify him if he moved too fast.

Then when Lester Maddox was elected, they had no hope but went to Maddox anyway and said "Governor, we'd like to have some blacks named to draft boards."

Maddox's action was simple and straight. "You all serve in the wars, don't you?"

Yes. This hard-core Klan sympathizer turned to an aide and said "Put 'em on the draft boards."

At that interview, Bond revealed another facet of Maddox's thinking.

The Governor held People's Day frequently at the State House, where people could voice their complaints. Two blacks who had just escaped from one of the state's chain-gangs (and who had been regular patrons at his restaurant and knew him) showed up in the line, told the Governor that they had just escaped and needed to talk to him about conditions in the chain-gangs.

"Just stand over there until I'm though with this line," he said.

After everyone had gone, the two described conditions, food, treatment, etc. at their chain-gang. The Governor explained to them about the budget the legislature had given him which didn't allow for improvements, then he had one of his simple inspirations. He had the power to pardon.

Bond said Maddox later visited most of the chaingangs and prison-camps and set up a card table and chairs. Then, with the records of the less dangerous black felons and misdemeanants, he would ask: "Boy, if I turn you loose will you promise me that you won't steal anymore?" Or whatever.

With that assurance, he would order them pardoned.

The Screaming Doomed Were In The Sky, Then They Were Dead On The Ground,

❖

Then The Casket Salesmen Came To The Makeshift Morgue

For the moment the sky over east Hendersonville was filled with the screaming doomed, then they grew silent when they hit the ground. An airliner had taken off from the Asheville Airport, but it had not reached altitude when it collided with a single-engine aircraft. I got the tip at my home in Fairview and quickly drove there. In the median strip of the new I-26 was what appeared to be a strangely smiling stewardess up to her hips in a hole. But there was no hole. She had been killed when she landed on her feet. Her legs were jammed upward into her torso.

That was the first of many horrors I encountered. I park on the perimeter of where about 80 people had fallen to their deaths. Bodies were mangled, some torn into pieces. Rescue people were arriving from every nearby town. A C-T photographer, Bert Shipman had arrived and we stumbled about through the carnage. Then I got a tip from a cop—I think it was then Sgt. Gene Jarvis of t he Asheville Police Department. He suggested we go immediately to the makeshift morgue set up in the National Guard Armory not far away. He said some undertakers were crowding in trying to make a profit on the disaster. We went there.

We were stopped at the doors by a National Guard master sergeant. I explained to him that we were newspapermen. He wouldn't budge. I told him we were within our rights. He still refused. I asked to speak to someone in authority. "I'm in authority here," he said. By then I was getting pissed. I told him I didn't know anyone with any less authority than a master sergeant in the National Guard. "I said 'you've got a Captain, haven't you? Get him.'"

The Captain was equally as obdurate. I told him I knew something was going on in there and I wanted to see it. About that time an SBI agent named Satterfield walked up, flashed his badge and asked "Is this enough authority for you?"

"Are you a cop? Why don't you get outside and direct traffic or something. There's no law being broken in here."

At this time a solemn looking man in an expensive business suit strode up. "I am the coroner and I'm the final authority you need to speak to. Now I want you out of here."

I recognized him as a Hendersonville funeral director. I asked him to step out of earshot of the others. There I lied to him. I told him I was in charge of obituaries at the Asheville newspaper, that I had a right to be there and if he didn't allow that, I would see to it that his obits got screwed up for the next ten years. He stared at me a moment, then underwent a sea change. "Of course, of course," he said. "Feel free to move about. If I can help you in any way…"

I saw Weaverville undertaker Buster West sitting at a desk, grinning. He was part of the state's emergency team and hastened to the morgue and set up operations immediately upon hearing about the crash on his radio. When I got with him, he motioned to some other men in suits, all of whom seemed to be seething at Buster.

He introduced me as an investigative reporter who was looking into complaints of their profiteering on the families by trying to sell them caskets, and he suggested they give me their names. But they immediately left. I thanked Buster for his assistance.

It was only about 40 years later, as I was working on this book, that one of Buster's former sons-in-law told me that when the first emergency call came in to Buster, he was sitting at his desk talking to a salesman from the Batesville Casket Company, and he took the salesman to the morgue, where he and the salesman sold distraught airline officials caskets for all of the dead.

Lannie Boy Briggs (Omar Shabazz) & Asheville Muslims

It is time to unfold some of the possibilities of domestic terrorism at the local level, and with the right conditions various groups and individuals could have a deleterious effect on stability. If it deteriorates enough here, and then nationwide, the mid-Eastern terrorists are well on the way to succeeding. One problem is avoiding panic among the people, who have been living in a fantasy world about such possibilities for decades, and thereby becoming more and more vulnerable when this big one occurred on 9/11.

As a starter, let us go back to 1971, when this editor founded a weekly newspaper here called The Native Stone. (It is not to be confused with the later editions published by the late Claude DeBruhl, who bought the paper in 1974 and turned it into his own political propaganda rag.)

My office was in the Jackson Building Annex, one block from The Block, which then was a market-bazaar-dope den etc. for the black community.

One day early on my secretary left our bank bag and our entire funds ($600) on her desk while she was in another room. The bag was stolen by a young black boy who headed for The Block, where he gave it to the late Lannie Boy Briggs.

Lannie Boy was a black in constant trouble with the cops for various things, including petty thievery. It was a surprise when he came to my office shortly and handed over the bag and money with the threatening scowl he used on honkies.

"You ain't much, man, but you all we got," he said.

In no little astonishment, I asked "Lannie Boy, You ain't got me mixed up with any of your white liberal brothers, have you?"

"I'd never be that weak," he said.

Why this?

"We like your paper, such as it is, and my name ain't the slave name Lannie Boy no more. It's now Omar Shabazz and I got the Muslim faith. I have changed my ways."

My last $600 was in that bag and Lannie Boy/Omar Shabazz had returned it. I do believe he had found his spiritual path. We grew to nod to each other warily on the street, and sometimes speak.

A few weeks later the cops arrested him for stealing a purse from a lady's desk in the Buncombe County courthouse. Instinctively I found that hard to believe. I went to then Chief of Police J.C. Hall and told him I didn't believe Omar Shabazz had done that.

"Don't get conned by Lannie Boy," the Chief said.

As it turned out, they had no evidence at the time, but they convicted him and sent him to prison.

A year or so later I ran into Omar on Pack Square and we went to a restaurant for coffee. He insisted he was innocent.

"Are you still a Muslim?" I asked.

Then he told me something which is the thrust of this piece of writing, and subsequent events, both locally and nationally, have proven his prophetic voice.

"Stronger than ever," he said, and told me the Black Muslims were operating in prison systems across the nation, and that no black entering the prison system, especially the young, could escape the powerful recruiting efforts of the Black Muslims. The solidarity of it offered them stability, protection and security in the jungle of prison.

He had begun calling me Mr. Green and I asked why. "We are being courteous, and we are being honest and all of that."

Suddenly I recognized a new sense of personal power in Omar.

"And Mr. Green, we are being quiet about it."

Knowing the inclinations and propensities of my fellow honkies to doze on, I suddenly recognized the implied and powerful threat of violence in silence.

This was the time the when events of the 1960s were being digested. Malcolm X was now emerging as a balancing factor, if not a totally new and frightening element, in the black push for equality. One could hear the faint echoes of a prophecy he had made at a conference in the north, which featured both he and Martin Luther King Jr.

Some of the white politicians were complaining about King's methods and Malcolm X said: "If you don't deal with him today, you'll deal with me tomorrow."

Time passed. Malcolm X was assassinated, as was King, and chaos reigned among militant blacks until other forces evolved, not the least of which was Louis Farrakhan. Among the militants (and now many moderate blacks) Jesse Jackson was not recognized as a leader even then but as a self-serving opportunist.

Back to Lannie Boy Briggs/Omar Shabazz. His wife had taken the Muslim name of Nefertitti, and I got to know her when I taught a free-university type class in journalism for blacks at Hillcrest Housing Project later in the 1970s at the request of the black Buddha of Hillcrest, the late Carl Johnson.

Lannie Boy was still being hounded, but she was able to tell me something about the Black Muslims locally. But not much. They were still here and they were still quiet.

I lost touch with Lannie Boy/Omar Shabazz until I read his obituary several months ago.But out of those conversations thirty years ago, I recall that Lannie Boy had said a great impetus to the growth of the prison Muslims was the threatening growth of the KKK and other white supremist groups in the prisons. From other sources I have learned that Latino gangs have since evolved into a power bloc in prisons, particularly in the southwest.

The matrix or ground for internal terrorism has been here for decades. This nation was founded on revolution and a form of terrorism, and the tatters of that attitude have come on down in a distorted or perverted form, particularly in the Southern Appalachian mountains. There are latent and possibly explosive groups in our midst. We have more examples from personal experience.

In the 1980s then Governor Jim Martin formed a statewide defense militia in response to certain waters which were stirring. The militia was to serve more as emergency units than anything. It was mainly to supplant or reinforce the N.C. National Guard in times of emergency. Traffic control, emergency medical matters, things like that. It was not to be an armed unit.

I was commissioned a Major to serve as intelligence officer to the 83d Highlander Regiment under Col. Thad Bryson Jr. My early duties included running background checks on those applying. Some thought it was the sort of militia that had sprung up all about the country and came in ready to go up against subversives, etc. They were turned away, but we had the feeling they would either form or find a militia more suitable to their aspirations.

In the course of my duties, I saw the potential for future danger.

At about that time I received an undercover assignment from a Federal office to infiltrate an Aryan Nations guerrilla training camp at Topton in the Andrews/Robbinsville area. The camp was operated by the late Nord Davis and was to train "'patriots". Some of those who came were members of The Army of God, and if you think the present terrorists are fanatics, you should meet some of the Army of God. (There were hints that Nord Davis's camp had links to the Branch Davidians in Texas.)

Some years earlier, a Spruce Pine man named Frank Braswell somehow became head of the American Nazi Party and that swelled into something that frightened many people. Braswell was one of the leaders in the notorious march in Skokie Illinois.

The ATF sent an undercover agent named Mike Sweat to nail Braswell, which ultimately happened. At about the same time, some Jewish doctors in Greensboro who called themselves Communists decided to hold a "Death to the Klan" rally. Members of the Klan went to it. When the doctors pulled guns, the Klan shot them to death..

And so a big Federal investigation began, with indictments issued. Braswell and the Nazis requested an attorney and Federal Judge Woodrow Jones appointed Ashevillian Billy Parker. Then they requested an investigator, so Judge Jones appointed me and I worked closely with Braswell and the Klansman Caudle, who had participated in killing the doctors. See another story on Nazis in this volume.

Go to Eric Rudolph, the more recent instance, not so much for what he is accused of doing but what the government became suspected of doing. This is not the place for an examination of the Rudolph case. After months of investigation and combing the Cherokee County mountains, no Rudolph. (He was finally taken into custody early in 2003 at a dumpster in Murphy.) But the suspicion among many natives there was that the black helicopters and all were merely to send a message and warning to those in the mountains which are suspected of being a hot-bed of potential terrorists. And the cavalier attitudes of some of the old mountain boys emerged as the anthrax situation developed.

"Man, that ain't nothing but bad cocaine,. You sniff some of that and you come down the same way. Those ragheads ought to try some of this good old mountain moonshine or some of the high-grade marijuana raised on the ridges. Everyone could be happy and love each other."

And so, if the anthrax and other developments panic the nation, one can prophesy that all the disparate groups, none of whom are beholden to the pledge of allegiance or any other loyalty to this government—indeed, they have all said for years that the government of the United States is their enemy—may well turn to massive outlawry and/or their particular revenge…then, true chaos in the old Biblical sense.

WNC Nazis—Frank Braswell

(These events occurred during a time when I was not working at journalism, rather working on a special Federal investigative assignment. Therefore I did not develop any files that I could keep because of the strictures of classified governmental confidentiality. As these events transpired, and after the assignment was completed, it was hard to see it as a whole. I am not yet aware of all that happened in the investigation, particularly as it concerns the Ku Klux Klan But it was indeed of a unique, baffling and strangely entertaining whole, and in the end, infinitely sad. Most of this is taken from uncertain memory, assisted in part by some of the participants.)

Frank Braswell of Spruce Pine was thought to be chief Nazi in the Southeast during the late 1970s and early '80s. On first glance that is not to be taken lightly. Frank had led the notorious Nazi march in the Jewish Community of Skokie, Illinois and terrorized most of those residents. He and his crew were in full Nazi regalia, banners, arm bands, uniforms and all. Frank and his wife Patsy also strode about Asheville from time to time with khaki uniforms, swastika armbands and jackboots. That had gained the Nazis considerable notoriety and prestige among right-wing zealots. It also placed him under scrutiny by the FBI and other Federal agencies. Some right-wing activity on a minor scale was developing in Asheville.. The Secretary of State had granted articles of incorporation to a group chartered as The Universal Equality For All White Americans who had set up headquarters at 6 Biltmore Plaza. Also a man named Charles White was working toward establishing a group called The National Association For The Advancement of White People. Police were keeping a wary eye out, but later described the activities of those groups as merely nuisant..

In the right-wing circles at that time, there was much insider scheming about weapons, explosives and plans, and of course that aroused much interest among agents. Sometime after the Skokie march, the Klan had a rally in a field at an Indian reservation in Eastern North Carolina. The Indians had not been intimidated, rather rushed the group and had put those Klansmen to rout. That was enough, sometime later, to encourage some Jewish doctors in Greensboro, who called themselves Communists, most of whom actually carried Communist party membership cards. There had been a little Klan activity in Guilford County which had been publicized, so the Jewish doctors held what they called a "Death to the Klan" rally, and brought guns which they waved around while they chanted loudly. Then some Klansmen showed up—not the kind that had been intimidated by the Indians earlier. They pulled their rifles from their cars and shot some of the doctors to death. (That incident was taped by television crews, and the tapes showed the doctors had pulled guns first and juries later found the Klansmen innocent on grounds of self-defense.)

This seemed like a rising tide of ultra—right-wing activity, and undercover Federal agents began to infiltrate. One agent who seemed to hit upon a live one was ATF Mike Sweat, who gained the confidence of Frank Braswell of Mitchell County. Frank was purportedly part of a conspiracy to blow up a farm of oil tanks located between Winston-Salem and Greensboro. He told agent Sweat that his group had many tractor-trailer loads of high explosive hidden in a secret warehouse in the Mitchell County mountains, and a plan to move it en masse on tractor-trailers at the ordained day and set off massive explosions which would destroy the oil tanks.

Sweat alleged in his investigative reports that Braswell and other Nazis had stashed several tractor-trailer loads of dynamite, TNT, C-4 and other explosives in a big warehouse on a certain road in Mitchell County, and would transport it all out on the day appointed to blow the oil storage tanks. I later went there and found only a 12X20 foot hut on a dirt road that would barely support a jeep.

Sweat tendered his reports to his superiors, who authorized him to fly Braswell all about the United States at government expense to meet with fictional co-conspirators who always failed to show up; and to check on caches of weapons and explosives which always seemed to be moved shortly before Braswell and Sweat arrived. Braswell later told me that he knew Sweat was an agent and that he decided to play him along and live high on the hog at government expense. That was later verified by some of Sweat's colleagues and superiors.

I was never certain at what point the Klan was supposed to have entered this situation, but when Frank Braswell finally conned himself into a Federal indictment, some local Klansmen were also indicted, even some of those who had killed the doctors. Following their indictments they asked for an attorney to be appointed, and Federal Judge Woodrow Jones gave them Asheville attorney Billy Parker. In a little while, they also asked that an investigator be appointed. Billy recommended me, I suspect, since he felt I would be able to communicate more clearly with these mountain defendants.

Judge Jones, whom I knew slightly, did appoint me, with the understanding that my time and expenses would run no more than $1,000. My orders included running background checks on those on the jury list and possible witnesses and as thorough a background check as I could do on Mike Sweat and other government witnesses, then any other information that I could develop which would be of assistance to the defense. But when money for my time and expenses ran out, things had gotten far too intriguing for me to quit, so I stayed to the end.

But before Braswell and other Nazis, which included his wife Patsy, and the Klansmen would accept me as their investigator, they tendered some questions to Billy Parker about my own background and qualifications. Braswell knew me slightly by reputation as a reporter, and after they found I was not a Jew, a Catholic, a Mason etc., and had a background as an undercover investigator for various Federal and State agencies, they accepted me.

But I also made some inquiry as to Frank Braswell through unofficial channels. He was relatively undistinguished in the Penland-Mitchell County area.though I had some suspicious experience with the name Braswell in that area in this Nazi context. Once I had gone with the attorney Bob Long to Bakersville about something and we had driven out to a farm owned by a dentist named Braswell. Parked on a sloping pasture was a World War II Nazi Stuka fighter plane. All I can recall from my conversation with him was that the pilot had to take off rapidly downhill and land coming in at a low stall uphill.

In keeping with this motif, the Braswells were employed at a bar named The Bavarian Cellar at Innsbruck Mall which was also heavily suggestive of German influence. I have no doubt, given the notoriety of their Nazi activities, that the owner was aware of the couple's political leanings. I would go there from time to time to have coffee with them and discuss my investigative findings. I recall nothing else about that period of the investigation.

In the course of my inquiry about Frank, I heard that once he and his wife Patsy had engaged in an all night gunbattle with law-enforcement at their home, but it had nothing to do with politics. As best as I can recall, Patsy was a relative of one of the Spruce Pine officers and he did not approve of her marriage to Frank. He had gone to their home in a fit of resentment accompanied by a couple of other officers. Frank opened fire and the night was taken up in a shoot-out, with Frank going from window to window firing and Patsy loading and handing him the weapons. I think that situation got worked out as a local matter. No one was injured, indicted or fired.

After my appointment was accepted by the Nazis, we had our first conference in Billy's office. The attorney was nervous, considering the first mix of this clientele. No sooner had we been seated than one of the Klansmen stared at Braswell and said: "Braswell, do you know what us Klansmen think about the Nazis?"

"What?"

"You're a bunch of left-wing pinkos."

Tension was high, Billy stirred nervously. The Klansman turned to me. "What do you have to say, Mr. Green?"

I thought a moment, evaluated what was getting settled here. "I'll tell you something before we get too far down bad-ass lane here. You boys shot the doctors, but Frank and Patsy had an all night shoot-out with the Spruce Pine police department."

Chairs were shuffled, caps pushed back and we swam in tension, then Billy Parker said "Gentlemen what we're going to talk about here is the defense in this case." He held them to that.

My investigation began. I got the Court to authorize me to get Mike Sweat's military record from the Army. I went to the local Army recruiting station, presented my credentials and by the next day I had the records. If I had gone through channels, it would have taken a couple of weeks.

Sweat had been telling people that he had been in Special Forces in Viet Nam. The Army records bore that out. There were some top-secret and classified flags in his record, so I knew he had been in the hot zones—Special Operations Group—although the records only said SOG. At that time Special Operations Groups were not officially recognized, instead the initials were disguised as Studies and Observation Groups.

Then I began discreet inquiry into potential jurors and witnesses covered by the Western District Federal Court to see who would likely be sympathetic or hostile to the Nazis. I also took a long look at Agent Sweat, who had worked as a policeman in a Florida town after he got out of the Army. I went there and got some almost irrelevant, yet valuable in its own way, information. Neighbors who remembered the agent said he had kept more than 15 Dobermans in his small yard in a housing development, and that he mowed his grass while wearing Bermuda shorts with his service pistol strapped to his side.

Patsy participated in the defense. Her accent was certainly back country Appalachian, and her education was scant, but all that belied an incredibly sharp mind. I worked with her some to get some of the glitches straightened out before trial, and at times as Sweat testified. I suggested that she question Sweat as to his military background, and more particularly the SOG material. She asked him what SOG meant and he candidly said Special Operations Groups. She turned to me. I whispered "That's classified and he's not supposed to let that out."

What then? She asked. I told her to ask him if that is not a top-secret designation and what does it really mean?

She asked him and that discombobulated him. How did she know that? Finally he answered "Studies and Observation Groups". Her astuteness, and Sweat's discomfort, was not lost on that jury.

On another occasion, in conference, I asked her why she didn't read Mien Kampf, Hitler's jail manifesto written in prison before he rose to power. She smiled. "I have," she said.

I was then taken aback. "Has Frank read it?" I asked.

She waited a long moment, said only no.

During the trial, Frank and the Klansmen displayed boredom, nervousness, impatience, disinterest. But I'll always remember Patsy, dressed as best she could, neatly groomed to a T, fighting it out when Billy Parker let her go at it. My impression was that she cared very little for Nazi politics, but Frank was her man and she was giving him her best.

There was a lot of public interest. Out-of-town media were playing it for all it was worth. This powerful Nazi ogre. I was torn between laughing at the media and the government, and crying for Patsy and their two kids.

(The defendants were convicted and all went to prison but Patsy. The judge considered her kids. I thought of the time before the trial when one of my sons had to accompany me to Spruce Pine on a different matter. On the way back, I told him we had to stop to see someone for a moment. I drive us down a ragged dirt road a few yards to an old battered trailer in the bushes. That was where the Braswells lived.

We went in and I introduced my son to Frank and we chatted a moment. I asked Frank how he was doing and he shrugged. I could see. The children were thin and unenergetic. I had $12 which I "loaned" him and asked my son, who had a few dollars. "Give it to me and I'll give it back to you when we get home." He did and I "loaned" that to Frank also.

As we drove toward Burnsville, my son asked me who that man was. "He's the most powerful and feared Nazi in the eastern United States," I said.

"Oh," he said, then "What exactly is a Nazi?"

Some months after the trial I ran into Judge Jones in a cafeteria, who took me aside and asked what had been my opinion of Frank Braswell.

"Sir, I think if someone had let him join the Spruce Pine volunteer fire department, he never would have joined the Nazi Party."

Carl Sandburg

Generally a reporter for a daily newspaper in a small dumpy city is not notable in and of himself or herself. But Asheville and environs (especially the mountains) for decades had its attractions for the famous and powerful, most of whom were willing to go along with interview requests, and that allows the local journalist to rub elbows with the mighty and thereby perhaps light and some enlightenment reflects upon them in some small manner.

In my career as a reporter for this daily here, back before it got so bad (it has always been bad, but not this bad) the foregoing statement held true. However, the acquaintance with poet Carl Sandburg evolved in a quite different manner.

Sandburg was held in high esteem by Ralph McGill, who in those days was recognized as a "progressive" voice as editor of the Atlanta Constitution. McGill was also a friend of Robert Bunnelle, the publisher of the Asheville Citizen. So each year on Sandburg's birthday, McGill would send a magnum of champagne to Asheville for Bunnelle to see that it got delivered to the poet.

Bunnelle began dispatching me to take it to Sandburg's Flat Rock residence. (I always assumed that was because I was about the only member of the staff who was staying sober and could be trusted with booze.) At the same time I was assigned to cover Sandburg's annual press conference and birthday celebration, which was only a courtesy on his part because he did not like a fuss on the occasion. (Sandburg had been a newspaperman in Illinois before he gained fame as a poet and biographer of Abraham Lincoln.)

On the first occasion I made it a private matter to give him the champagne after everyone was gone. He offered me a drink and I told him I didn't drink. He grinned, said he didn't either and put the bottle aside. We had a brief, inconsequential conversation that day. He asked about my family life and I told him I had a baby son. "I'd like to meet him," he said. "It's been so long since I held a tyke…"

And there it began. Many visits with my wife and first-born son, the only one we had at that time. Though Sandburg did not especially like photos, he was willing to pose with my family. I have some gems, so valuable at this remove in time.

We talked some of writing, but not much. He was very kind about it. He said one cannot learn poetry or even writing from study. He said that one merely "does" poetry and quoted some source I've since forgotten. Write only of the great things from your highest vision. "To write an epic poem, you must live an epic life."

So we talked of Lincoln and the Illinois ways and people and so forth.

I suppose if any one thing cemented our friendship it was an incident at one of his last birthday celebrations. Plenty of reporters and television people were now making the obligatory pilgrimage. They always asked him about Presidential politics. He told me once he didn't keep up with that. He had only been interested in Lincoln. I noticed a time or two at those occasions that he would appear to be senile. In later conversations he grinned, said he faked it because today's newsmen bored him stiff. Wearing his trademark green eye-shade, the poet-philosopher-historian-biographer-newspaperman lumbered into his study for the interview.

Then, that incident. UNC president Friday came for the occasion. That old anvil had laughed at many broken hammers. It was his 87th birthday and he watched the hammer of another year break off and join the others on the slag-heap of his life. Reporters jostled about, got in each other's way. One cat from Channel 4 kept standing in my way. I finally reached and pulled his camera plug. He wheeled about and swung at me. I laid him out. Consternation everywhere, then everyone nervously grew solicitous about the poet. He was grinning widely. "Great," he said. "This is the old days in Chicago."

About 15 newsmen had set up various cameras. Sandburg looked at the television rigs. "These cameras look more dangerous than newspaper cameras," he said.

No sooner was he seated than Dr. William Friday, president of The University of North Carolina, and UNC Chancellor Paul Sharpe formally presented him with a momento from President Lyndon Johnson.

Dr. Friday read "…and a happy 87th birthday to Carl Sandburg, a legend in American literature…from his friend, Lyndon B. Johnson." Then he presented Sandburg with an autographed photo of he and the President. "Well, that's a very nice thing for him to do after the election," Sandburg said in a congenial midwestern accent, smiling with pride. He slowly read aloud the notation, then mused in a low voice, almost to himself, "It's not often you get a presidential autograph." Then he looked up and smiled and said "I wonder how much I can get for this?"

Henderson County's most imminent goat-farmer ranged near and far with observations, mostly satiric. Newsmen began to ply him with questions. What does he think of President Johnson?

"We've had worse. So far he hasn't muffed anything."

Did he think JFK would be judged as "great" by historians?

"I don't know. For his age and what he stood for in his brief time…it's hard to say."

Then a glint came in his eyes. "I do think he surpasses Calvin Coolidge," he said.

What did he think of contemporary poets and poetry? Would they measure up to the likes of T.S. Eliot, Robert Frost or Sandburg?

"No," he answered quickly with an emphatic nod of his head, then chortled.

Is he planning any new volumes of poetry?

"I've got some done. When I'm ready I'll release them. I ain't afraid of launching a new one.'

A newsman asked him something about an autobiography.

"Well, I'm not about to write it seated in a chair in front of a bunch of wise-guys."

What about the Beatles? Asked an impudent newsman.

"Those Englishmen? I don't know."

Why did he take it upon himself to write Lincoln's biography?

"I was dissatisfied with all the writing about him that had been done up until that time, so I decided to do a good job of it myself."

One lady asked a totally irrelevant question, if it was not true that Sandburg "was a very softhearted gentleman".

"Mushy," said Sandburg, then he turned to the television people and said "You look like a very menacing lot."

Has any President in the last century reached the stature of Lincoln?

"I won't answer that," he said.

Then he gave a brief, biting appraisal of reporters.

"Reporters who are good interviewers are rare these days. If they are interviewing an author, more than half the time they haven't read his work."

At that point, several defensive newsmen hastened to ask him about various passages in his poetry. He continued for a few more minutes, then signaled that he was tired. The din, gabble and roar of the interview faded. The newsmen gathered their equipment and left.

Sandburg autographed a book for Dr. Friday. Then he chatted briefly with his wife. "It is a good many good years for us," he said. Then she slowly led him from the room.

One of his books had been opened to the poem ***Four Preludes on Playthings of The Wind***. The opening lines caught the eye.

"The past is a bucket of ashes."

His health began failing. I think it was diverticulosis. I had things to do and didn't go see him much. I grew very busy on the Asheville police beat. But one evening, with nothing else to do, and presentiment upon me, I sat and wrote a long piece about him from my experience and the files. Then I put it in the "can", where we filed away pieces for future reference.

A couple of weeks later, on a Saturday night I found myself weary, weary, weary. There had been two downtown murders and I had to stand around the scenes for a while.

I was on a committee at the new Outward Bound School at Table Rock Mountain so I called my wife. I needed to get away, I told her. I'll go up there and camp. "Very good, but call the newsroom. They're looking for you."

I waited until I got to Morganton, then called them. "Bad news," the editor said. "Sandburg passed on. I know you would want to write the obituary."

Once again a great weariness came over me. "I already did—a couple of weeks ago. It's in the can. You can update it," I said. I drove on to Outward Bound. Nobody up. I unrolled a sleeping bag, laid down beside a known rattlesnake den and wondered how the hell do you live an epic life around Asheville?

Carl Sandburg with Lewis Green and son, Brennan Green

About Thomas Wolfe & His brother Fred

The following material on Thomas Wolfe and his family and local memories of them is reprinted in part from a story I published in The Asheville Citizen-Times in 1964 and which was subsequently filed with The Associated Press. The story won the first place press award in features competition that year. Included following that story is a subsequent story I did on Wolfe's brother Fred and his brother-in-law Ralph Wheaton, both of whom Wolfe assigned large roles in his acclaimed first novel, Look Homeward, Angel. Following that section are comments made to me by the late Garth Cate, a celebrated man in his own right and who was working at the old Brooklyn Eagle when Wolfe was in New York, and who knew the novelist personally. Garth had retired to Tryon from New York and I became acquainted with him after my Wolfe story appeared locally. Garth contacted me about his material and following that a long and fruitful friendship developed with him. More on Garth Cate in another section of this book All this material has been placed in the archives of the Thomas Wolfe Memorial.

Here begins some of the reprint of my 1964 story:

No person can now dispute Thomas Wolfe's claim to greatness, and the years have proven him North Carolina's leading novelist. The old hurts, both real and imagined, which his writing caused have long since been healed in the townspeople.

Literary critics, with the passing of time, have adjudged Wolfe to be one of the nation's greatest writers, and place his work alongside some of the best of all time. The Wolfe legend feeds and grows on Time—Time which was of such essence and importance. Time which was of such urgency. Time which he shaped into great rushing rivers to sweep him onward to far countries in his search.

Those great visions in Wolfe's brain seemed to swim in those far, unseen spheres that sang to Shakespeare, Milton (from whose "Lycidas" the name Look

Homeward, Angel, was taken), Sir Francis Bacon, Goethe and select others. Like Herman Melville, Wolfe seemed to proclaim "Give me a condor's quill for a pen! Give me Vesuvius for an inkstand! To produce a mighty book you must choose a mighty theme."

So Thomas Wolfe, an improbable North Carolina mountain boy, chose to immortalize the citizens of Asheville as unlikely subjects for a mighty theme. The legend of Thomas Wolfe is romantic, and it seems difficult to reduce him now into the human realm of flesh, blood, dream, hope and agony. Time has passed, and those who knew him grow fewer.

An evaluation of the author, the family and Asheville of that time was made by talking with all number of persons with whom had made contact of varying duration. Several were interviewed, none of whom claimed a long or intimate friendship with the author, but most of whom had not previously been interviewed by researchers.

These were like small ships which passed in the night—rocking briefly in the turbulent wake of that huge argosy which was Thomas Wolfe, freighted with the heavy riches of genius and bound for strange, far ports.

Wolfe had written "I am a part of all that I have touched and that has touched me…", so a part of the Wolfe story must come from those who touched his life in small ways, those who noticed the many facets of the author and his family. They do not shed a strong and revealing new light, but rather small gleams and glimmers which came through personal observation, and which even at this writing faded and shifted in deceptive memory.

Dr. Roy Roberts (who was the Buncombe County physician at that 1964 interview) considered Wolfe the greatest writer America has ever produced, and felt that the author had a tremendous concern for mankind. He said that Wolfe had yet to be recognized for being the great philosopher that he was.

"He has written prose that will endure as long as Shakespeare. I was a country boy and didn't know those people he wrote about. But I was at the University with him when he was beginning to come out of an awkward adolescence. He was a big old fellow. I don't know if he deliberately played the 'unwashed genius', but he certainly acted as if he enjoyed his Bohemian existence. In a way he could be compared to the beatniks of the fifties, except that he was a bona-fide intellectual.

"The last time I saw him was in a restaurant on Broadway in Asheville about midnight one night. He came in and ordered a bowl of cereal and didn't speak to anyone. Knowing what I know now, I would say he was extremely depressed. I would say also that he had been drinking. I had one of his books outside in my car that I wanted him to autograph, but I decided this wasn't the time to ask. He ate his cereal and lunged out the door. I understood that he was living in a cabin at Oteen at that time."

It was no secret that Wolfe frequently looked too long upon the ripe grape. He was known to get roaring drunk if the occasion demanded it. Or as one lady closely connected with the family said "Oh, he'd get roaring drunk whether the occasion demanded it or not."

Miss Louise Watson formerly of Burnsville recalled when Wolfe was subpoenaed to appear as a witness in a murder that happened there. At that time she was a secretary in the Yancey County Courthouse. She remembered seeing him hulking up and down the corridors waiting for the trial. "He was very friendly and pleasant, not stuck up. Folksy is a good word for him,"she said.

But she said he appeared to be afraid of mountain folks vendettas and feuding. He was afraid someone would shoot him. "They couldn't have missed him if they aimed anywhere near him, he was such an immense man," she said.

The man who allegedly did the killing warned Wolfe "This better not show up in any of your books."

Alas, the complete experience is duly inscribed in "The Return of the Prodigal."

So that very folksy, friendly manner described by Miss Watson was denounced by Wolfe's non-literary critics. They accused him of acting in such a manner as to lull them off guard so they would relax and be themselves. Then, they insinuated, he would hasten to his digs and ruthlessly scribble out everything they said and did.

Mrs. Fannie Gross had a passing encounter with the author. With some friends she went to his cabin at Oteen one evening to take him to dinner. "He had a few drinks, but he didn't talk much," she said. "His speech was nowhere as grandiloquent as his writing."

Mrs. Gross knew the family, particularly the sisters, quite well. She owned an antique shop at the time, and Tom himself would drop by from time to time to talk with her. She said the sister Mabel (Wheaton) often complained of people pointing her out as Thomas Wolfe's sister and said she was tired of it. "But I think she really loved it."

She had a Wolfe book autographed thusly by Mabel: "To Fannie Gross, who understands my brother and has from the first."

She said "Oh, they flocked to him when he became famous. He was a literary lion. But I think he was secretly weary and skeptical of all the adulation after all the scorn he had faced.

Two Asheville attorneys were at Chapel Hill with Wolfe, and they recalled his rise to campus prominence. They were Irwin Monk and Carl Greene. Greene had the memory of going to a dance in Hendersonville one night with Wolfe when they were blades. "I always thought he had a brain," he said. "It seemed inevitable that he would reach fame. A lot of his work was pure fiction, but a lot of it was experience garnished with imagination. He was the newspaper editor at Chapel Hill. I well remember the humorous editorials he wrote.

Monk knew Wolfe as a boy. He is portrayed in Look Homeward, Angel as Lewis Monk. He recalls the aut hor when a child as "tall, stooped, with a large head and plenty of hair."

He continued "I didn't think he was particularly brilliant as a child, but he did well in college. I remember once he put a masthead on the campus newspaper, calling it "The Nuisance & Disturber", a lampoon on the Raleigh News & Observer. By then it was easy to predict his coming eminence."

Asheville attorney (who later retired as a judge) Bill Styles remembered seeing Wolfe often as the author walked from the cabin he had rented at Oteen. "He walked in any kind of weather, and he strode along like an ape, a hulking giant of a man swinging his arms."

E.C. Goldberg who ran a newsstand on Patton Avenue for, remembered well the extravagant, exuberant, lusty, querulous, high strung and nervous Wolfe family. In his early years his family and the Wolfe's were neighbors. "We lived two doors below them. I remember some of the boys stealing cherries from the tree in the Wolfe backyard. Mrs. Wolfe caught us and gave us a switching. The next day she sent Tom to our house with some baskets and said she would go halfers with us if we'd pick some more.

"Fred sold The Saturday Evening Post and I thought he would be the smartest. He'd come down the street carrying the magazine, flipping the pages and muttering and stuttering his own marvelous spiel of words. Yes, I knew them all. Ben drank a lot, so did Frank. The old man got well-soused from time to time.

"After he finally returned home Tom came into my place for a shoe-shine. He had a deep, bass voice and just stood there grinning for a minute. He was afraid someone would do him in. He asked me how the people had taken Look Homeward, Angel. I don't think people were quite so hurt and insulted as has been pictured. Everybody said those things in the book were true."

Lelia Smith wrote down her impression of an introduction to Wolfe for the Wolfe collection at Pack Memorial Librar y.

"A friend called and asked if I would like to meet Mr. Wolfe. We went in a car to pick him up at an Asheland Avenue address. He was to talk to a group dedicating a new auditorium. When introduced, I could only stare at him. It appeared to me that I had never seen such a large man. He towered above us all, and his dark, unruly hair and deep penetrating eyes were quite a shock at first glance. His hands were huge and seemed out of proportion, even with his dark stature. He was dressed in a dark suit and spoke very seldom. He seemed so ill at ease we were all at a loss for words. I remember saying to my friend later that Mr. Thomas Wolfe could only be a great genius.

An Episcopal priest who had retired and come to Asheville for his health in 1933 became one of Wolfe's best friends as far as translating the spiritual and artistic depths of his writing is concerned. He was the Rev. Norvin Duncan and later earned for himself a sympathetic role in the author's pages.

"I was anxious to meet the family after I read Look Homeward, Angel. I was so fascinated by Mrs. Wolfe that I went to see her again and again," he said. "Tom was much more different than what the community thought of him. I began to see a religious side to his writings.. I went to the public library for a copy of his book. I met a rather cold stare and an icy 'That book is not allowed here.'

(Editor's note: The library wouldn't let Look Homeward, Angel in until F. Scott Fitzgerald, staying at Grove Park Inn while his wife Zelda was hospitalized, went to Pack Memorial to check it out and was told they didn't keep it. Fitzgerald went to a book store and bought a copy and raised enough hell until they put it on the shelf. Wolfe's brother Fred told me later that, true to form in Asheville, the biggest reason they wouldn't put it in at first was "Mama was on the wrong side of politics here.")

"The first sight I had of Wolfe awed me. He filled the door when he came in and I envied this giant his fine health. Strange! He's gone now and I'm still hanging on.

"I don't think Wolfe recognized his own religious depth. In 'You Can't Go Home Again' he writes of the City of Lost Men—not in the heaven or hell sense—but that they had lost all moral perspective...buy and sell and buy again...

"You would almost think one of the old prophets had written it. I see Isaiah in there. Wolfe understood that these men had lost all sight of moral and spiritual values. Tom heard the sermons on Sunday, but he knew how these men lived here through the week. Some of the things in Look Homeward Angel are pretty raw—well, by George, that's what he saw right here in Asheville. Oh, there was a religiosity to him.

"He was eccentric, but any genius the world has known has been that way. His mind was out of the normal run of things—to me it was on a much higher plane than he was given credit for. Emerson said to be great was to be misunderstood."

Mrs. Helen J. Motley never knew the author, but she was good friends with his mother near the end of the Wolfe furore in Asheville. "She carried herself like a true patriot. I remember her blinking her eyes a lot and pursing her lips thoughtfully," Mrs. Motley said. "She told me that the last words Tom said were to the doctors and nurses at Johns Hopkins hospital. He looked up from the operating table and cautioned 'Don't bore too deeply' before his brain operation. Then he laughed."

Then he died. This great genius was maligned and berated. He expressed his loneliness best in a short story when he returned to the land he loved and found only sorrow there at old, tired midnight. It was a land where he saw, heard, knew and understood every one—but not one could see him or understand him.

Great rivers of time had surged out of his brain and spilled across his pages—and in 1938 the great weary river ran to its death in the sea. He lay dead, he who had stroked out such beauteous, stirring passages of death in his own family, he who had given form, shape and strange merit to the dark intruder in our lives. They brought him to Asheville from Baltimore to bury him.

Mrs. Motley went alone to the funeral home and sat awhile, alone with the oversized casket. "He looked so handsome in death…like a marble statue," she said.

And she saw a small symbol of Wolfe's sad futility about his family. It rendered meaningless all the family's protests about the portraiture of smallness in the book. She said it had been placed there by his mother, the peculiar, irrational, illogical and tormented mother. It was a small handwritten sign on a piece of cardboard placed on the casket which read "Don't Touch."

Some Interviews by Lewis W. Green With The Author's Brother Fred

Facts about the Wolfe family were lost to fiction, truth to legend and fidelity to myth. Sadly there was only one left of that boisterous band of originals—Fred Wolfe—and who could set the record straight if not he? And in trying to recount how things really were for them, perhaps he pursued a lost cause. Many things had been written about the Wolfe family, wild gossip bruited about and genuine "authorities" quoted at length. However, Fred Wolfe felt that nobody asked him, and he was a part of the events and experiences that his brother Thomas Wolfe later shaped into works of literary genius.

Fred Wolfe's own personality was lifted entire and transposed onto the pages of the great Wolfean works. (He was portrayed as the stuttering brother Luke.) In the wake of my recent feature which the Associated Press spread through many large newspapers and which aroused much debate and discussion, Fred contacted me and said family pride requires him to speak out when the family was subjected to wrongful interpretation at the hands of so many who knew nothing at all about them.

He spent his declining years in Spartanburg and came to Asheville on one of his many trips. He asked to address some of the issues which people had raised in my quotes on Thomas Wolfe. Our free-wheeling interview started on the porch of The Old Kentucky Home on Spruce Street. Before it ended, this writer, Fred and Ralph Wheaton, Fred's brother-in-law (the late Mabel Wolfe's husband) had journeyed about to a good part of Asheville.

"I'm not saying that anybody told you a lie in that story you wrote, but I feel that they didn't tell the complete truth and they didn't tell it because they didn't know it, I guess.

"Now there was the part of the story where an Asheville woman said Mama had put a sign on Tom's casket after it arrived at the funeral home."

(An Asheville woman was quoted in my story as saying the eccentric mother, Mrs. Wolfe, had placed a sign on the author's coffin which said "Don't Touch".)

Fred continued. "I want to tell you some things about Tom's final illness and death, which has never been written. By this example you may see how everything else about our family has been so twisted and distorted.

"Tom got sick in Seattle and Mabel went out there. She stayed with Tom and the nurse, a Mrs. Crawford, at Kings County Hospital, until it was decided to bring him east. They had to load Tom on the train through a window. That's how tall he was. Mama met them at Chicago and rode on to Baltimore with them. I met them at Baltimore about 12 to 14 hours after they arrived. We stayed at the hospital while they ran some tests. The doctors said there was a tremendous buildup of pressure inside Tom's skull.

"Tom looked at Dr. Dendy and smiled as he shaved a spot on his head and applied a local anesthetic. Dr. Dendy said 'Tom, I'm going to relieve some of that pressure.' And Tom said 'You're not going all the way through, are you?'

"At that time they drilled a hole through his skull and the infection spurted all the way across the operating room. The big operation came later. The doctor told me that Tom only had five chances in a hundred to survive if the tubercles were massed in the back of his head. He said if they were multiple and spread all about the brain then there would be no chance.

"They were multiple and spread. Now this next is important to understand about the casket and 'Don't Touch' sign. They had to shave Tom's head for the surgery, and remember that he died three and a half days later. So he was totally bald. An expert wig-maker was called and he hurriedly made a wig from Tom's own hair. Also at the funeral home in Baltimore they didn't have a casket long enough for Tom, so they made a long one on special order that night.

"I stayed with the casket on the train all the way down the country until it went into the funeral home right across the street from the house. It only stayed over there an hour and forty-five minutes, and no one was to be allowed in there during that time. I don't know how that woman you quoted got in there.

"Anyway, Mama didn't go near the funeral home. She stayed back in the kitchen to herself until they brought Tom home. Now it couldn't have been Mama who put that sign up. Don't it seem logical that if there was such a sign saying 'Don't Touch' that the undertaker would have put it there—in the event that someone might have walked in there and inadvertently disarranged the wig? But mama got the blame for it, as far as that woman goes. It is just one of the many things I have had to contend with. People are bad about embellishing things. I can't get everything that's been told straightened out. But I get as much of it as I can," Fred said.

At that moment some tourists came up the walkway to the Wolfe home, and Fred leaped up and walked to them. "Welcome, welcome," he said and introduced himself.

"Well, we've wanted to meet you," the tourists said.

'You honor me," Fred said, "I'm still Luke and I still stutter."

While he stood talking to the visitors and showing them the house with a wide wave of his forefinger, Ralph Wheaton smiled wryly, fondly, at his extraverted brother-in-law. Ralph a retired executive and salesman with National Cash Register Co. is portrayed in most of Thomas Wolfe's works as Hugh Barton.

He remembered the family well. "There was something going on every last minute..oh, they were a real bunch. I was accepted from the start after Mabel brought me to meet them,. I melted right into the family and was never made to feel like an outsider. I personally never had any arguments with any of them, although they had plenty of arguments among themselves," Ralph said.

In those days, Ralph, was around the Wolfe Memorial about every day, and has posed for countless tourist pictures In his home on Evelyn Place he kept many Wolfean momentoes, little household articles belonging to Mabel before she died in 1956. Fred was still with the tourists and Ralph grinned again and nodded toward him. "Why, he stands and talks like that to everyone who comes," he said.

"Many people have come to me first and asked if I thought they could get Fred to talk. I tell them that isn't the problem, the problem is to get him to stop," Ralph said.

Fred heard that, returned to us grinning. He said he is dedicated to helping around the old family house that has become a shrine to his brother, and fills many speaking engagements at colleges, universities, high schools, public meetings and "...any bunch which is misguided and foolish enough to ask me."

The two old men were the diminishing remnants of a generation of stability, of family ties, a generation whose houses lasted a lifetime and family life rotated around the old "homeplace". They remembered Asheville in an epochal time, and of being of that family with its foxfire glow of fame.

Even after death, the family remains unbroken as far as that generation is concerned. They keep well the family graves. "The cemetery is an interesting place," Fred said. "We come to them in the end, so why fear them in life?" We had moved from the house to Riverside Cemetery where all the Wolfe's are buried.

Fred waxed, gesturing about with his hand. "Here you can see the inexorable toll of time, how it moves among us."

And here too, as he gestured about, one could see how W.O. Gant-Wolfe did truly bestow upon his offspring a love of drama, rhetoric and feeling. He pointed a finger among the gravestones...Ben Wolfe, died 1918; W.O. Wolfe, 1922; Thomas Wolfe, a Beloved American Author, 1938; Mrs. Julia Westall Wolfe, Dec. 7, 1945 ("Mama died at a miserable hospital on Park Avenue in New York, Fred said bitterly).Leslie, a sister, nine months of age...Angels call our beloved sibling...Mabel's grave, and Grover's grave. Grover was Ben's twin brother who did in infancy. "They were born during a Presidential campaign," Fred said, "and Papa, feeling good, I guess, had said let's name them after the candidates, and so we had Grover Cleveland Wolfe and Benjamin Harrison Wolfe."

Frank's grave is there, but one is missing. A Wolfe sister, Effie, is buried in Silverbrook Cemetery in Anderson, S.C. And a sign of family harmony at the Wolfe plot. W.O.'s first wife, Cynthia Hill, who was buried there with the full approval of Julia Westall Wolfe. "Mama never cared," Fred said. "There was never any kind of hard feelings."

He said "The morning Ben died I came out here with Papa and Captain Haywood Parker and picked out this lot. Later I had the bodies of the ones who had died earlier moved here from Newton Academy, and the family monument was moved here too. It is of great granite dignity. "It is the finest of Barre granite," Fred said. Papa bought it a long time ago. All the gravestones here are Barre except the two footstones on Mabel's and Tom's graves. They came from a granite quarry at Elberton, Georgia, and they're a fine grade of stone too."

He said most of the immediate Westall family, his mother's people, are buried in the plot adjoining. Fred took flowers to the graves each time he came up from Spartanburg. Often he found that Ralph has been there before him with a bouquet. They kept the plot clean and well-tended. Then the mobile interview moved out of the cemetery to Ralph's home. On the porch they relaxed.

"Haw," exulted Fred, "Let me tell you one time that I embarrassed Ralph, and I could tell you of many other times.

"In 1918 I was a Navy enlisted man at City Park Barracks in the Brooklyn Navy Yard. Ralph was a top man in his business organization, and he came to town and put up at the old Waldorf-Astoria, the old one where the Empire State Building is now. Those cash register people were having a big convention. Ah, if you could only have seen that old brownstone building.

"I was on duty and a guard came up and told me I was wanted on the phone. It was Ralph. He wanted me to have supper with him. We met at the restaurant. I have never seen such grandeur and opulence, chandeliers and thick silver. Ralph picked up the menu in that grave, dignified fashion he has. It was in French. Ralph studied it, preparing to order.

"That damned bird they called the headwaiter was smirking and hovering about. Oh hell, I said, I can't read this. Can you bring me some ham and eggs? Haw, well, they did, brought it in a casserole."

This interview was again in motion. Fred drove up Charlotte Street and thence to Woodfin Street where the house/memorial was. He is never in the vicinity of the house but that he stops to putter a moment. He sees not the house as it is now, a museum to perpetuate his brother's fame, but he sees it as it was in those lost days when the family was coming and going. It is part of a memory of days and nights that were wonderfully loud, friendly, boisterous, argumentative and secure, something that has been amputated from his life by the blade of time.

He sat wearily upon the porch and picked up the issue of the paper that had my story. He had marked those things to which he wanted to take exception. He read briefly from a paragraph, then shook a stern finger:

"Now you have described my family as '…extravagant, exuberant, lusty, querelous, high-strung and nervous…' I guess some of those adjectives are all right, but extravagant, no! You can't say that in all honesty."

"Well, could I say emotionally extravagant, Fred?"

. He thought for a moment, rubbed a thumb over this chin and grinned hugely.

"Wy, wy, wy, why, I guess that wouldn't be too far wrong," said the only Wolfe we had remaining.

Garth's material

The following was written by Mrs. X, who in the 1930s worked for Thomas Wolfe for several months in Brooklyn as a typist and secretary, Wolfe had asked Garth Cate to recommend someone. This woman had done work for Garth at The Brooklyn Eagle. Wolfe wasted no time in hitting on her.

"Dear Garth, your letter as always was a delight and a boost…even the part that that gives me fits for being too young and inexperienced to recognize and/or realize what I missed by not devouring Tom Wolfe at his invitation, putting aside whatever personal revulsion I might have felt at the time. The simple basis of my antipathy for the man was his disregard of fundamental cleanliness. The absence of this little item is enough to make me flob my gob (vomit to you) and the months I worked for Tom were New York blisterers, enhancing and magnifying the assault on all five senses. If another reason is needed, I flinched at the thought of being "copy" for any future public diary. Please try to forgive me for not having the clairvoyance to see his future greatness, but make it easy on your magnaminity (cq) by rejoicing in my own personal integrity, which was perhaps, only then beginning to assert itself.

Really Garth, it isn't that I'm "just not interested", but let's be objective. Tom courteously suggested that we have an affair; just as courteously I declined. I was not ungracious, I was not outraged, I was not flattered. It was just a run-of-the-mill question, and he didn't press—nor did I give him a chance to. My little old button nose probably took a retrousse turn, and if it did, it was involuntary (see above) and not meant to offend. But with Tom's perception, he undoubtedly didn't miss it. Beyond that half-hearted attempt to "know me better'; my shopping for him and cooking for him a couple of decent meals; my discouraging attempt to clean up his dismal living quarters—even to making curtains for the room in which I worked—his complete indifference to the whole matter and his utter disregard for the amenities which put us poles apart—THERE JUST ISN'T ANYTHING TO TELL! So stop being mad at me. You wouldn't want me to invent something, would you? And what price glory if I did?"

Garth wrote the following note to me on 10 July, 1970.

Lewis, you may want to publish my comments on the character of Tom Wolfe concerning the Dorman matter. An example of his lack of conscience, of any sense of gratitude or compassion for those with trying family problems, in his willingness to work up his personal experiences into salable copy is seen in the Dorman affair. (The Dormans lived at 40 Veranda Place, Brooklyn when Tom roomed there in June 1941, if my notes are correct.), This was covered, but never completely, in some of the "bigs" (publications) Marjorie Dorman was a brilliant Eagle reporter whom we all admired. Her father was an impecunious erratic inventor, a sister was not right mentally. The mother was a fine normal mother. When Wolfe was broke they took him, fed him, mended his socks, etc. Later he wrote a story, published in Scribner's Magazine, poking mean fun at the father and the sister. They sued for libel and defamation and collected $2,500 from Scribner's.

Scribner's lawyer called on Eagle people to see if he could find witnesses whose testimony would help Tom if they went to trial. Saw a friend of mine, Harriet Hoppe, secretary to the publisher of The Eagle. They asked if she would testify if they went to court. She told them she would but for the Dormans. So they settled. And Tom was mad at Scribner's and wrote and talked about their "ignorantly, dishonestly selling him out." Harriet Hoppe knew Tom well, and like all of us, she liked him but being an honest woman of character took her position. Tom's wonderful face, his engaging stutter, his casual disarray, his sprawling form, his kaleidoscopic talk and unbounded appetite made him a fascinating human.

Tom would not admit Scribners's was right, said they took the easy way out, not caring for his reputation. If they'd gone to trial the verdict would have surely gone against him Tom was 30 or 40 years ahead of his time in his desire to be free to use all the four-letter Anglo-Saxon words which grace much of today's writing. And so often he talked of "They", an abstraction that at different times meant different people, social forces, editors, jealous or selfish friends or hangers-on. (They won't let me use these good strong old words that come so naturally to all honest writers of colloquial dialogue," he'd lament.)

He not only had to capture the essence of every scene that opened to him, but he must capture every person's interest and approval—even if he didn't care a darn for them, and to prove his valor and irresistibility, lead every acceptable woman to bed. Compulsion, but no compunction or compassion. You'd be interested in Wolfe's letter to the New York Herald Tribune which ran in 1935, re his reading. A print is attached here for you. Your guess as to its correctness is as good as mine. Most of us err a little at times, esp. In younger days when telling of our favorite books. When we have lunch again or you visit us I'll have more stuff. **G Cate, 10 July 1970**

Older Men Watching: The Influence of Mentors

When the student is ready,
the teacher appears

Dr. Roy Roberts
Rabbi Sam Buchlender
Col. Paul Rockwell
Garth Cate

Dr. Roy Roberts, a native of Asheville who returned to Asheville in the early 1960s after retiring from the Army, was distinguished in military medical circles. He became county physician with an office in the Buncombe County Courthouse. I became acquainted with him when my newsbeat with The Citizen-Times included the courthouse.

Jim Burnette operated the first floor coffee shop, a den (and din) of political chit-chat where most of us involved in courthouse business drifted at various times during the workday. Dr. Roberts had his own coffee shop adjacent to his office where he received various visitors. I had published something about the Korean War which had impressed him, so he came to the downstairs coffee shop and introduced himself as a Korean War veteran too. (It came out much later in our friendship that he had been personal physician to Syngman Rhee, the president of South Korea. I then did a feature story on Dr. Roberts and Rhee which was picked up by the Associated Press.)

Dr. Roberts, whose family line was deep in Buncombe, was brilliant and well-versed on just about everything concerning local history, families, businesses, but most importantly to me, an Oriental approach to learning. (I had written my first book, "The Year of The Swan", a Chinese fable/morality play but had not published it at that time.)

That and some of my writing for the newspaper led him to discretely inquire as to my interests, then he suggested that I study Brynner's translation of Lao

Tzu's "The Way of Life", a small Chinese classic. "You will be able to understand it more than most," Dr. Roberts said, and that flattery drove me to it. (Paradoxically, a couple of years later another of the men whom I have listed as a mentor, Garth Cate, the retired editor of the old Brooklyn Eagle who had retired to Tryon, not only recommended that study but gave me a copy of The Way of Life autographed by the translator.)

Once one got hooked on conversations and studies with Dr. Roberts, one stayed hooked. He was a staunch Democrat and most of the top local politicians sought out his advice. Another thing revealed to me by Dr. Roberts was the machinations of The Chamber-of-Commerce in keeping too much control over the local media.

Dr. Roberts lived on past the turn of the century, into his 90s, and was an influence almost until his last days. He served on various boards and commissions, and many younger members complained of his drowsiness, etc. The older ones knew Dr. Roberts easily had experience and information past their understanding at hand. Anytime his ease and drowsiness was discussed with me, I could only smile and think of the effortless ways of Lao Tzu.

Rabbi Sam Buchlender

A Jewish lady called the newsroom one day and asked me to come to Lake Junaluska where she was having an art exhibition and cover it. I told her there was some art I could appreciate, but that I would generally be unable to comment intelligently on it. But she insisted, saying my shortcomings would not count; that I absolutely must come. I cleared it with my boss, whose father was an artist. "Go," he said, "you're as good as we've got. Fake your way through it."

At Junaluska I met Mrs. Schmeil Buchlender. Her work was truly beautiful, but I had not the background for apt review. I suggested that instead of me doing a lot of writing, I have the photographer make several photos and let the readers do their own judging. Fine with her, then she shyly (and slyly) said the real reason she wanted me to come was that her husband, a retired Rabbi and world-renowned forestry expert, had read much of my writing and wanted to meet me.

Highly flattered, I went to their home. Sam was short and stout, but a power emanated from the man that anyone with any sensitivity could immediately divine. He was jovial, gracious, buttered me up only for a moment, then dived into discussion. I remained for about three hours caught up in talk that ranged from music to war to Jewish theology. (Sam said at that time, and often reiterated it as the years went by, that there were few Jews in America, but "...plenty of people who in their hearts were clerks and shoe salesmen...". He stayed away from the temples and synagogues, he said, because they mostly held to a disappointingly low level of profundity.

He said he had once called one of Asheville's Rabbis, and talked to the wife about coming to use the library. He hung up angrily, he said, when she kept talking possessively about "his library". Sam said it was not "his" library, rather belonged to the congregation and the use of the possessive indicated something he wanted no part of.

There was no doubt about his snobbery, but his life's experience had forced him to a high level from whence he could make such contemptuous utterances. He had paid the price for his Jewishness. He was born in Poland and was accepted into the most prestigious Rabbinical school in Russia. It was while he was there that the Nazis came and purged the Warsaw ghetto of Jews. Sam's parents were among the first to be executed.

Sam joined the British Army during World War II and participated in the Exodus to Israel in 1948. He did much writing of those tactical and strategic experiences and anytime in later years he went to Israel, he was warmly welcomed.

Sam said that the Rabbinical school from whence he graduated taught that its graduates could not be paid for their services in preaching, et al, but must earn their daily bread in some other field, so that their message would not be influenced, even slightly, by considerations of money. So Sam Buchlender went into forestry. In that he also distinguished himself. As his life progressed he became the principal forestry adviser to such important people as the President of Mexico and former Cuban dictator Batista. Among other things he was able to show them how to turn formerly trash brush into highly profitable products, and worked with various medical and scientific authorities to develop medicines.

Sam also became affiliated with the scientific and theological figures at Princeton University and most of his papers are now in archives at Princeton. He also made available to me numerous copies of that work.

How do you describe the teachings of such a mentor to an interested protégé? Mostly by the give-and-take processes of observation and example, by explanation and interpretation of the subtle nuances falling into place in our daily lives.

For some reason, Sam would not talk much about the Hebrew mysticism of The Kabbalah. He knew something about it but never revealed how much. The word itself means "received teachings" and knew the implication of knowing that teachings had been received rather than merely taught. However, Sam said that part of the Kabbalah that deals with The Void or The Abyss frightened him he said. (In there, that deep unconscious holds forces and images that are almost impossible for a mind not trained for years in Kabbalah to grasp and deal with. Insanity is the usual result.)

Sam and his wife separated. She had been in Hitler's death camps and as her years increased so did her demands on him and those close to her. Sam moved into the Clayton Apartments in Waynesville and held forth for a small number of friends.

I didn't hear from him for a time. I tried to contact him and got no answer. His apartment was locked. Then I heard he had suffered a severe stroke and was immobilized in the Haywood County hospital. I went there, walked into his room as a nurse tried to spoon feed him. He merely muttered, refused the food. She had a heavy silver spoon. I took it from her and struck him in the eyebrow and told him to eat. He rolled his eyes, said "Lewis, where in hell have you been? These bastards are trying to kill me."

The nurse later whispered that I should tell Sam she was no bastard. He apologized.

He was later transferred to a nursing home in Asheville and a bit later he died. He was buried in the Jewish cemetery at Riverside. The only Jew in attendance was a bored man, someone on the cemetery committee who was in a hurry and who had no idea of Sam's background. The only others were myself and three Gentile mountain ladies who had been his neighbors years before on Hyder Mountain in Haywood County. They remembered him as a good, kind man and wept for him at his graveside.

Col. Paul Rockwell

In another section of this work is a much more definitive piece on Col. Paul Rockwell, easily the most distinguished and cosmopolitan man in Asheville among intellectuals and civic-minded peers.

I became acquainted with him when he asked that I cover meetings of the old English Speaking Union, a prestigious world-wide organization of intellectuals committed to sharing information among their group. Most of them were involved in journalism in one form or the other. Colonel Rockwell himself was a journalist who had written several books and held a measure of recognition among European circles.

He was a brother to Kiffin Rockwell, the Asheville pilot who had joined the French Layfayette Esquadrille early in World War II and was the first of that group shot down and killed by the Germans. A historical marker honoring Kiffin was erected on Merrimon Avenue near Hillside Street, where the Rockwell family home was located. It still stands.

Colonel Rockwell had his own marks of military distinction. He had gone to France himself early in World War I and served in battle with the tough French Foreign Legion. He won some honors with that elite group, and later in life when he visited France that government required he be greeted at seaports and airports with honors and artillery salutes. In World War II, the American Army made Paul a full Colonel where again he served with distinction.

When I worked at UNCA I took several groups of students to that home for interviews. Even the most callow and cynical of those students were impressed at the depth of experience and knowledge of Colonel Rockwell, who was well along in years at that time, and at his ability to communicate it in terms they could relate to.

Many times I sat in his parlor with he and his wife Frue and listened to the stories of his and their lives. Their approach to this lifetime on earth was almost that of a wise and enlightened civility, certainly as civility would be understood in Asheville as the curtains of their lives descended in those fading years of the 1960s. Despite that, there was no raised eyebrows, no condescension, always an open-minded acceptance of other viewpoints, other ways. Even as the city and society took a turn toward what must have seemed to them the barbaric.

Garth Cate

There is more definitive information on Garth Cate in the section of this book on Thomas Wolfe, but due to his influence on the author at the right time, he must be noted as a mentor in the true sense of the word. He entered my life shortly after I published a long feature on Thomas Wolfe in the daily newspaper.

Garth called from Tryon (he insisted I call him Garth), said he had been following my writings for some time, and with publication of my piece on the author Thomas Wolfe felt he should at last get to know me.

He had retired years before from the old Brooklyn Eagle, and had extensive other newspaper experience in New York City. He said he had several experiences with Wolfe and knew various other things about him which could be of historical value to Asheville readers. Garth made that information available to me, and recently while going through my files I found it and donated copies to the Wolfe Memorial here.

Garth and I met at the old restaurant in Battery Park Hotel, and he brought along papers to prove the authenticity of his claims. But after that we spend several luncheons and dinners at his home, where he assisted in educating me to the ways of big city professional journalism and the absolute need for accuracy and, as the case might be, in proving it with evidence. (Generally, I have ever since reproduced the public record to back up many of the hot stories I have written.)

More importantly, and almost with serendipidity, he reiterated what Dr. Roberts had said: he led me to Lao Tzu's "The Way of Life", and as importantly guided me into some of the nuances of that. (Somehow, coincidentally and strangely, I was in a used book store in Asheville and found the same Brynner translation, inscribed in front with this "Lewis Green, Miami, 1943". Garth did not know Dr. Roberts.)

There is a broader picture of Garth in the story herein of Thomas Wolfe.

The Pie Lady and Harold Thoms

The old Pie Lady? I never knew her or anything about her until she had been dead for some time. She was old and impoverished and made her way for years by selling homebaked pies in various neighborhoods and to select clients. For all practical purposes she was not important in the community but her death and subsequent events propelled she and I into one of the biggest, if not the biggest, letters-to-the-editor controversies during my time at the daily newspaper in Asheville.It also brought forward, in the fullness of time, some amazing revelations about the author Thomas Wolfe and his luck in getting information about the land scandal and the bankrupting of the City of Asheville for his novel You Can't Go Home Again.

As the situation developed I was subjected to high levels of denunciation from some of the most prominent people in the community, including one of the richest (at the time) and most influential men in Asheville. He was Harold Thoms, founder of Thoms Rehabilitation Center. (In the end, which took several years, we became friends as a result of the story on the Pie Lady, and he was one of the people who helped open my eyes to some of the then recent history of the city and much of the system of corruption which existed up until then, and which is still in play here in various guises.)

The Pie Lady story, one which evolved from a sweet little human interest story by the late Gertrude Ramsey into something that involved the Welfare Department, county leaders and attorneys and Thoms Rehabilitation Center, and a number of self-appointed local spokesmen of the public mind and mood..

Mrs. Ellen Roberts, in her 80s then, for years had gone from door to door selling home-baked pies. She lived at a ramshackle house at 276 Hazel Mill Road that had neither electricity nor plumbing. She had accrued a clientele, but most importantly she had saved up the money she took in from the pies. Then she died, but before she died she became slightly befuddled, then telling only a few, and in increments, she made several donations amounting overall to several thousand dollars to Thoms Rehabilitation Center. She had asked that no mention be made of that while she lived. After she had been dead a decent time, Gertrude

Ramsey wrote the story which brought tears to the eyes of many of our readers and a few maudlin letters to the editor.

Very well, God is in his heaven and all is well.

Then, enter el Diablo, this reporter, called by some The Crown Prince of Chaos.

Several days later I was in the Courthouse when one of the employes of the Welfare Department hailed me. "You know that story about the old Pie Lady? It's a hot potato in the inner sanctum both here, with the County Commissioners and the county attorney. They're afraid it's going to come out."

What? Well, the Health Department is belatedly concerned about the pies, and there were other concerns. For instance, Mrs. Roberts lived with an aged sister who baked the pies. Half that money was hers. She didn't know Mrs. Roberts had given away their life savings. Not only that, Mrs. Roberts had been drawing a welfare check in the amount of $35 a month and had signed a document with the county which was a lien on any real or personal property she owned, so the county could foreclose. The then county attorney, Tom Garrison, refused to auction off the house, on which was owed $4,450, because the elderly sister still lived there.

I wrote the story. The Citizen published it. All hell broke loose. Among the many outraged letters to the editor, two are worth mentioning. First was one from a Mrs. Millicent Printz, prominent wife of a wealthy doctor and active in school-board politics. Among other of her suggestions was one that said now that I had done this, why not now expose Santa Claus.

I dropped her a note in which I suggested that now she had revealed herself to be on the side of the Angels, and was wealthy herself, she should now hie herself over to the hovel where the old surviving sister lived and give her some food to live on until the Welfare Department could move.

A couple of days later Dick Wynn, the executive editor, called me in. He said that Mrs. Printz had an ulcer that had been dormant for eighteen years.

"Yes?" I asked.

"She received your letter and the ulcer broke loose and she's in the hospital about to bleed to death."

"Um, sorry!"

"No you're not. For your information and for the record, I now again remind you that company policy forbids us from replying to their letters," he said.

"Ah hah. Well, I'm not familiar with company policy."

"The hell you're not. The hell you're not. You know more about company policy than anyone here. You have broken and bent company policy. You have let light into dark corners of company policy that have hitherto gone unexamined."

And on and on.

"Very well, then. I'll just write the dear soul a letter of apology".

"No, no, no. I beg of you not to further stir this…"

During this public furore, Harold Thoms expressed his disapproval with a statement that made the newspaper. He accused me of being a young unknown reporter out to make a name for myself. After that, whenever I saw him at some public function he would scowl, frown and stomp about.

Now, fast forward a few years. I had left The Citizen and founded a weekly newspaper, **The Native Stone,** in June of 1971. More than a year went by, It was hard going. Advertisers were afraid of it. Christmas was looming and money was low. About dusk one evening my advertising man and I sat pondering when suddenly in the doorway loomed the imposing figure of Harold Thoms. He was a big man physically and wealthy. He wore an expensive Hamborg hat and topcoat. He glared at me a moment, then softened and grinned slightly and strolled to my desk. He lay down a one-hundred dollar bill and said "Lewis, don't pretend you don't need that because I know damn well you do. Thirty years ago I published a weekly newspaper in this damned town and they ran me broke. I've been watching you ever since your coverage of the Pie Lady to see if you would be as honest with these politicians as you were about her. You have been, as I was in my time."

We became friends. In an avuncular fashion he told me about his time. He had graduated from college in Ohio and he and his wife came here and founded a newspaper.

He said they nearly starved, and many nights all they had for dinner was popcorn. He had to keep a shotgun in his car to ward off angry political ward-heelers who didn't like what he wrote.

Asheville went bankrupt at that time. Harold Thoms covered that scandalous trial. The daily newspaper was weak in its coverage, and soon after the trial the court records disappeared. It was as if it had never happened..

Then the author Thomas Wolfe came to him and said he had heard Harold Thoms had kept copies of his newspapers and some files. He told Thoms he wanted to include something about the scandals in his next novel.

Thoms was a businessman. "Are you going to make some money out of this?" he asked Wolfe.

"Yes."

"I want some of it."

"A deal."

You can find that in that section of ***You Can't Go Home Again*** about the real estate deals in Asheville in the twenties.

Though he persevered, he never made a living at newspapering. Later he founded radio station WISE and some other stations in Virginia and got rich. But he kept a home base in Asheville and his experience with the scandal trials kept him vitally interested in the workings of the city.

He told me that he had watched the city pay its way out of bankruptcy over the forty-year life of the Sinking Fund Commission under the direction of the long-time City Manager J. Weldon Weir. Then in the sixties Weir began losing power and in 1972 new forces took over City Council when Dick Wood became Mayor. Harold Thoms told me then that Dick Wood & Co. were taking the city right back down the old track toward bankruptcy.

Sometime later I was covering the annual Democratic fundraising wing-ding at Grove Park Inn, the Vance-Aycock. As I walked in Harold waved me to his table. The only person with him was Harry Blomberg and we fell to talking about the city. I asked Blomberg if he agreed with Harold's assessment that Asheville was heading back into trouble.He laughed loudly.

"It's a matter of time," he said. And here it is. Most of the city's property, including City Hall, has been mortgaged.

Outward Bound School and the Code Three

The North Carolina Outward Bound School opened at Table Rock Mountain near the Linville Gorge early in the 1960s. Since my beat was the entire WNC region I was assigned to cover it. Pop Hollandsworth, the former headmaster at Asheville School For Boys had been named as director at Outward Bound. Named as assistant was George Greene. Both men had long experience as outdoorsmen, to say the least. Greene was a retired Marine Sergeant Major. I had been introduced to the two at their office for only a short time when Sergeant Greene excused himself. Later as I prepared to leave, he took me aside and presented me with a pair of new rock climbing boots, thereby proving himself a Marine Staff NCO in the finest tradition. He learned that I was also a Marine and his sharp eyes grew sharper. (More than 30 years later I still have those boots.)

Each class at Outward Bound lasted a month and I covered them as they happened. Both men were well aware of how important newspaper coverage of their new school would be, and shortly I got drafted.

Sgt. Major Greene asked if I would be interested in serving as chairman of the scholarship committee. The school was well known for serving boys and young men from wealthy families, so I asked why they would need a scholarship committee. Pop Hollandsworth told me there was a compelling need to try to attract the less fortunate, and also that there be publicity concerning an effort to reach out. I asked who else was to serve on such a committee and both grinned and said pick your own. There would be little for them to do. Those duties would be taken care of at other echelons, but it could provide some publicity for whomever I chose.

I appointed a young Asheville lawyer named Bob Riddle; a drive-in theater operator named Joe Pless; and a woman active in civic affairs, Helen Reed. An older Waynesville freelance television cameraman named Jimmy Reed kept in close contact. I told them there would be nothing for them to do except pose for one newspaper photo. Indeed that was true for a time.

But the good Sergeant Major Greene and I huddled in the finest manner of conniving Marines operating on short budgets. We were getting needy students, but they could not afford outdoor gear or little else. We agreed used military surplus would be ideal, but Sergeant Major Greene had been out too long and had lost his contacts at Camp Lejeune.

Then I told him I had a good friend who was the Commanding General of the18th Airborne Corps at Fort Bragg, Lt. Gen. Bob York who had Asheville connections and I saw him often. Ah God, it is a grand experience to see a Marine Corps Sergeant Major's eyes take on such a light.

"Can you handle him for such a clandestine transfer of property?" He asked.

"Let me see. I think so."

General York was a brother to Arthur York, who was a distinguished Asheville businessman and whom I knew through my work. I met him covering local civic club meetings and he often complimented me on my work. He knew of my military experience and told me of his brother Bob, who was commanding general of the 18th Airborne Corps, which meant he was over all the paratroop forces in the U.S. Army. That was certainly impressive and I suggested doing a story on him. Arthur okayed that and invited me to his home the next time the General visited.

The General was lukewarm to the idea of a story but we enjoyed getting to know each other and chatted, both then and at later meetings, of the military. He had begun his military as a private in the Alabama National Guard. I had begun at 16 as a private in the 120th Infantry, North Carolina National Guard in Waynesville. General York later received an appointment to West Point and volunteered for the paratroops early in World War II. We became friends through the offices of Arthur, and the General invited me several times to come to Fort Bragg for a visit. My schedule always worked against that until I got involved with Outward Bound and the good Sergeant Major Greene.

I called General York and told him I could arrange a visit and at the same time I told him about Outward Bound and that we needed some surplus foul weather gear, such as ponchos, boots, sleeping bag, waterproof bags, etc. He was taken with the idea that Outward Bound was somewhat equivalent to basic Army Ranger training.

He said he didn't know anything about post surplus sales but he felt it would be no problem, being as how that he was the Commanding General. He asked if I wanted to bring anyone else and I said I felt like the scholarship committee would enjoy it. He set a date. All the members of the committee except Mrs. Reed agreed to the trip.The cameraman Jimmy Reed wanted to accompany us.

In a week we left before dawn one morning in two station wagons and arrived at Fort Bragg's main gate. At that point the situation became unbelievable. The MP came to my car window. I told him that General York was expecting us. He asked if my name was Green. Yes, then he signaled and a staff car with a flag with three stars came immediately and escorted us to the Carrendon House, which was the house on base that top VIPs stayed at, whose most recent guest was President Lyndon Johnson.

General York could not be there to meet us. A younger relative had been killed in Vietnam and his funeral was to be held this very day in Cabbarus County. But he had left word that I was to be accorded all the privileges of the rank of three star general. But he had told them nothing else. So here appears a mysterious Code Three, apparently with three members of his staff. An officer assigned as our escort made a phone call and told someone that a Code Three whose name was Lewis Green, and staff, would be at the top-secret mission briefing room in the next few minutes, While the Fort Bragg intelligence people didn't know exactly who I was, procedure required that all Code Three visitors be briefed on current Airborne and Special Forces operations throughout the world.

At that time, secret operations were going on in the Congo and a couple of other African nations. I saw the significance and signaled my escort that none of my group was cleared to hear this. He nodded, made a signal to the briefing officer who then subtly shifted into information that was not hot. Then the escort radioed someone that the Code Three and staff would be at a helicopter landing pad in a few minutes.

We rode there in two staff cars with three star flags flapping. The escort told us that part of the Code Three treatment was a tour of the newly formed top secret Raider school for Ranger and Special Forces graduates, and following that the Code Three and entourage would be treated on a drop zone to a special exhibition parachute drop by the world famous Golden Knights parachute team. As our cars speeded toward the helicopter landing pad, both Pless and Reed said they would go only to the pad, that they were afraid of flying and that Riddle and I would have to make the rest of the tour alone.

The helicopter was late, and a big and very impatient black Lieutenant Colonel was waiting, quite apologetic to the Code Three. When the chopper arrived, the Colonel jumped into the chopper and bellowed "You people are late and this is a Code Three mission. I'll tell you what you'll be flying after this. You'll be flying jeeps out of the goddamned lower echelon motor pool."

Then he turned with a great sardonic and courteous grin, bowed and said "All right, sirs, get in the aircraft."

Both Pless and Reed nodded and meekly boarded. The chopper took us deep into the woods on post. The Raider School was experimental, a forerunner for some of the training later to be incorporated into covert Special Operations and Special Forces. We walked about the area. At the place where rappelling was taught, one of the NCOs tested me out. "Sir, do you want to rappel down the wall?" Certainly. I could have done much better, I later protested, if I had not been wearing slick-soled civilian slippers.I got halfway down the wall and my slippers betrayed me. (This day's entire action was being recorded by Reed on a Super-Eight home movie camera I had brought along.I still have the film.)

We were then flown to a drop-zone, where our escort said a special drop by the Army's elite parachute team, the Golden Knights were to make a demonstration jump for the Code Three guest. We alone were in the bleachers as they jumped and went through their paces.

Ah, God. The surprises in store for Code Three Green. The master-of-ceremonies then announced that I would inspect the Golden Knights. If you saw the movie The Dirty Dozen you know the next scene. Here is the disheveled Code Three, tired after the long drive and other activities, trooping the ranks of some uneasy elite parachutists. Who in hell is this General in civvies? He's got to be near the top in the CIA or another clandestine operation.

To each one I moved, did a left face and muttered. "At ease, trooper."

"Thank you, sir." Ramrod straight.

"You men have well earned your reputation. I am proud to have the honor of inspecting you."

"Thank you, sir. Thank you very much. It is our privilege and honor, I'm sure, sir, to have such a distinguished warrior as you here with us." Then on to the next one. Everyone was highly pleased that the Code Three had found them worthy.

It is necessary to note here that on several occasions as we started this adventure from Asheville I told the committee members that we were going to have to jump with the airborne here to show them we were worthy of their company. As I returned to the bleachers, the master-of-ceremonies announced on the loud-speaker that the guest of honor and his staff would be taken up in the chopper to 5,200 feet and be with the top jumpers as they made a very complicated jump. I arose. Jimmy Reed ran under the bleachers bleating and shaking his head. Joe Pless ran behind a concession stand, also shaking his head.

"All right, Riddle, let's get aboard."

We followed the jumpers onto the craft. Riddle was quite uncertain, his voice weak. The chopper lifted off. "Are we going to jump?" he squeaked.

"Yes indeed."

"Where are our parachutes?"

"We don't get any. What we are going to do is wait until these guys open their chutes, then we jump out and land on their canopies. I told them we were tough bastards."

Riddle searched my face, saw at last that I was putting him on.

The later flight back to the main base was uneventful, except for one thing. One of the chopper crew asked Jimmy Reed, by now caught up in all the pageantry, just exactly who is this Code Three. Reed was exhuberant. "He's the greatest writer in North Carolina and is the head of a chain of Outward Bound schools." That pilot nodded in awe. However, the look on Pless's face showed he had all he could stand. That night we ate at the officers club with our escort, a very bright first lieutenant. They all had a few drinks, grew mellow.

The young officer finally got his nerve up in this relaxed atmosphere, inquired discreetly almost out of my earshot, "Just who and what is Lewis Green?"

Pless could not contain himself. He had enough of Code Three Lt. Gen. Lewis Green. "He's nothing. He's a nobody. He's a reporter for the worst newspaper in the state. Riddle here is a hack lawyer. I run a drive-in theater and I'm not sure what this guy with the TV camera does."

We all grinned except the Lieutenant, who finally nodded and said. "That's good. That's real good. That's the best CIA cover story I've heard and I've been escorting guys like you around for quite a while."

A bit later as we drove back to the Carrendon House I asked Pless "While you were being so candid with the Lieutenant I must ask why you didn't add in your part that the drive-in theater you ran is sleazy?"

General York was delayed in Cabbarus County for another day but he had a member of his staff trying to round up surplus gear for us, with little success. At that level they did not know how to operate. I inquired quietly of a Staff Sergeant on the administrative staff of the Carrendon House where the Staff NCO club was located. "I see, sir. You want to talk to the zebras with all the stripes."

"Roger. And I need for you to get me a couple of fifths of Old Smuggler scotch."

In the late afternoon I went to the Zebra Club, seated myself and sat the two bottles in plain view on the table. Vibes went out. Soon one of the waiters came and I told him I was open for negotiations with someone in supply or quartermaster. I looked around the tables at those grizzled Sergeants and their overseas service patches, spotted some with Korean War patches, entered conversation, gave them the booze, told them what I needed and that it was for some students at what amounted to a civilian Ranger training school.

A few drinks. "All right," said one Zebra with a Korean War era 187th Airborne patch, "where are you parked?"

"Where do you need for us to be parked?"

He told me, said "Leave the doors unlocked."

Everything went as it should. General York was back the next day and Code Three and staff met with him in his office. Chit-chat and introductions. Finally he asked "Did you get what you needed?"

Yes, damn plenty.

He grinned. "I heard you got fixed up quite well."

We drove home, unloaded the station wagons on my front porch on Rocky Fork. A day later I delivered the gear to a pleased Sgt. Major Greene. As students unloaded and stored the gear, Sgt. Greene and I exchanged brief nods and grins, very little conversation. Wise to the ways of Zebra Clubs, he said he didn't need to know anything.

Zane Hill

❖

The Unaccountable Murder of His Son

From his first appearance on the public record many years ago, it was obvious that he was a troubled young man causing problems for the people around him. But despite the accumulation of an arrest record that boded ill, most court officials found him almost inconsequential compared to the average run of criminal. He could be seen as a typical low-level Jekyl-Hyde, a punk with some delusions of grandeur and overblown sense of importance in that low world of beer joints and common laborers.

My first brush with him came at a brawl one Saturday night at the Candler Amvets Club. My new wife was a nurse on the night shift at the hospital and I was a police beat reporter. I usually spent Saturday nights riding with one of the Sheriff's Department cruisers. If the action got hot, sometimes the night chief deputy would deputize me, as he was authorized to do in cases of emergency. This Saturday night it got hot. I was riding with Captain Howard Martin on a call to Woodfin when he got a priority call to go to a brawl at the club. The brawl didn't start until we got there.

Sheriff Harry P. Clay, a newly elected 30-year old Republican had defeated a Democrat who had been in office for 32 years. Buncombe County Democrats were outraged about that and had made it hard on Clay's department from the start. So lurking at the Candler Amvets Club were some former Democratic deputies jagged up on moonshine and beer. They were inciting other troublemaking hangers-on.

No sooner had Clay's deputies asserted control than it started. First bottles and fists, then chairs. Martin turned to me and said "You're deputized." One guy had jerked a deputy's club off his belt and ran at me with it. I grabbed him and wrestled him to the ground and we got handcuffs on him. In the confusion he got up and ran off with the cuffs.

Deputy Richard Ledbetter edged a cruiser into the crowd and we handcuffed and loaded three guys into the back seat and locked the doors. Martin told me to accompany Richard to the jail with the prisoners. By then that section of the Candler highway was swarming with people choosing up sides. (Witnesses for the Democratic defense, one cynical deputy called them.) Richard bulled the car through the crowd, siren and lights going. We were going 70 or 80 down the Enka straight when Zane Hill slid forward in the back seat and began kicking Richard in the back of the head, forcing him up over the steering wheel and against the windshield. The cruiser began running other vehicles off the road and bouncing in and out of the ditches. Richard handed me his slapstick and told me to quieten Zane down. I pushed Zane's legs off the seat and told him to get back. He kicked at me and I let him have it twice in the forehead. Blood flew.

Police radios were busy, and in those days many people had police scanners. When we reached the alley to the jail behind the Courthouse, a crowd of jeering Democrats had gathered. I began pulling the prisoners out of the back seat. Zane Hill observed the crowd of Democrats and in a most pitiful voice, raised his cuffed hands to his head and bleated "Police brutality". I slung him toward the Courthouse door and said "Hell Zane, I'm no cop. I'm just your average citizen like you out for a good time on Saturday night," then I flipped a bird to the gathered crowd.

Zane hired lawyer Billy Styles to defend him. I learned that Zane had a lengthy criminal record so I went to the ID Bureau and got a copy. The rule is that if a defendant does not take the stand during trial, his record may not be offered against him.

I had been getting telephone death threats from Zane ever since the incident so I wanted to see what kind of crook this was. It looked bad. Dangerous. In Haywood County in my Marine-on-liberty days I had built a small record myself. I was going to have to testify so I knew Styles would bring that up. I called the Waynesville Chief of Police, Arthur Paul Evans, an old Marine friend of mine, and asked him to send me a copy of my record. Then I folded it up and put it in my coat pocket with Zane Hill's.

The trial was held in General County Court with a relaxed old Judge, Burgin Pennell, presiding. No jury. I took the stand and testified before a courtroom full of hostile, smirking Democrats. They knew the trap had been set for me. Then Styles began cross-examination. "Now Mr. Green," he said in his trademark high nasal tone, "I believe you've been charged with assault in Asheville yourself, haven't you?"

"Yes sir, but I wasn't convicted."

"Well, what else have you been tried and convicted of in North Carolina?"

Ah well, he had me there, did he?

"Well, I've got my record here in my pocket if you want to read it to the court," I said.

"You just go ahead and read it to us," he said, smiling slyly.

I took out some folded sheets of paper and began reading. "Burglary, attempted rape, breaking and entering. pointing a gun, wife beating (several counts), drunk driving, arson, assault with a deadly weapon…" and on and on. The eyes of the courtroom spectators were wide. They had heard I was wild in those other days, but this? I read on. Billy Styles began to fidget as he realized what was happening. Judge Pennell was looking at me in surprise, then I said "Your honor, I'm sorry. I've made a mistake. That was the defendant's rather lengthy, scandalous and outrageous police record, if you noticed."

The Judge looked out the window a moment then let out a brief cackle. Styles was saying "Objection, objection…" while the Judge was restoring order. Then the Judge said, "Sustained. Now go ahead and read us your record, Mr. Green."

"Drunk and disorderly, affray, resisting arrest (several charges) assaulting an officer, one charge of VPL for which I paid a $14 fine…"

"What is VPL?" the Judge asked.

"I don't know, but I surmise it's either vulgar and profane language or violation of the prohibition laws, both of which I was guilty of numerous times but I only got charged once, your honor. I don't really know. In Haywood County they sometimes made up their own laws as they went. But you can say that I am an expert witness on resisting arrest."

Prosecutor Bob Swain's eyes were staring off into the distance, smiling.

"You can come down," said Styles.

Outside of some anonymous threatening phone calls in the middle of nights, I lost track of Zane Hill for several years. Then one day, a grim headline.

Candler Man Charged With Murdering Son

So his violent bent came down to killing his own son. Investigators said he had once again gone to his estranged wife and began assaulting her. A grown son was present. He had gone to the telephone to call the Sheriff's Department and his father shot him in the back three times while he was on the telephone. The 911 tape recorded the son's last words. With this, Zane Hill's slow but inevitable slippage toward death in the gas chamber began.

The slow legal process was heart-rending for the family, neighbors and other observers. As evidence and past records were introduced at the trial, it became painfully obvious that this was the destiny the man was following. He had slipped through the net of society. If he had ever sought, or been directed toward, psychiatric help, it is not on record. Even as the process moved, Hill fully revealed at last his psychopathic turn, his long-muffled inner secret. He had a death wish. He was offered a plea—guilty of murder in the second degree with at most 14 years in prison. Hell no, he wanted to plead not guilty. The death penalty was inevitable after he was found guilty.

There was the glacial movement through the appeals process. None of it went his way. As the date approached, he was moved from his cell on the death row block to what is called the Death Watch area. Some observers at the time said that Hill seemed unable in the last few weeks to accept what was coming. But then it was time. There were chairs for 16 witnesses, four of those were deputies from the Buncombe County Sheriff's Department. They were Captain Pat Hefner, Mike Wright, Jim Medford and Sam Constance. From the District Attorney's office was Ron Moore and Kate Dreher.

Captain Hefner was a detective when Hill murdered his son. He said "It's nothing I take any pride in, but it is an integral part of our justice system. The jury spoke in 1990. I support the death penalty, and I wouldn't do that if I'm not ready to witness the result."

Hill was given the chance to speak and pray with a chaplain, and to record a final statement for the public. Then his gurney was taken into the death chamber and the curtain was drawn. Specially trained personnel then entered behind the curtain and connected the cardiac monitor leads, the injection devices and the stethoscope to the appropriate leads. The warden informed witnesses that the execution was about to begin. Then he returned to the chamber and gave the order to proceed. Harmless saline intravenous lines were turned off and thiopental sodium was turned on, putting Hill into a deep sleep. Then the lethal solution—procurium bromide, a total muscle relaxer—was injected and Hill entered into death. He was the first man from Buncombe County to be executed since World War II. Captain Hefner said Hill seemed ready in the last couple of days, and went calmly.

The warden pronounced him dead, and a physician certified that death had occurred. The witnesses were then taken to elevators and Zane Hill's body was released to the medical examiner.

And then the days to come. Everyone involved in the long demonic trek Zane Hill had made from his boyhood on down to that antiseptic chamber pondered. What was he all about?

Colonel Paul Rockwell Of The French Foreign Legion

1960s

Turning in the direction of local history, the editor of The Independent Torch will use many sources, many taken from old interviews and conversations in more than 40 years as a newsman and writer here. One of the richest sources of information was the late Col. Paul Rockwell, an authentic aristocrat, cosmopolitan and world traveler who spent most of his life—from 1906—at the family home at 142 Hillside Street in Asheville, and who died several years ago, well into his nineties.

He was a journalist with an international reputation and a soldier, having fought in World War I with the French Foreign Legion. He joined FFL early in the war before the United States entered, was wounded and was invalided out. He then became a war correspondent for the Chicago Daily News for the remainder of World War I, and following the war remained in Paris in the expatriate colony with Ernest Hemingway, Gertrude Stein, et al, and knew James Joyce, Thomas Wolfe and other literary figures of the time, as well as many famous governmental and military men.

He returned to Asheville in the mid-1930s. The Colonel kept his credentials as a journalist and won some major recognition as a historian.

(A historical marker is on Merrimon Avenue for his brother Kiffin, who also had gone to the French forces early. He was in the legendary Layfayette Esquadrille and was the first American to get killed in WWI.)

In addition, Colonel Rockwell was a world traveler, historian and raconteur. He had a phenomenal memory and consorted with the highly placed in world affairs. He was a legend in France, was awarded the Legion of Honor for his actions in FFL, and anytime he visited there, the French government ordered a 19 gun salute upon his arrival each visit in honor of his valorous service in the Legion.

Col. Rockwell also fought the in the United States Army in World War II, and retired as a Colonel. In his day he brought much prestige and honor to Asheville in a quiet and unassuming manner.

Both before and after his stints in Europe, he was steeped in Asheville's cultural and political life and had observed the doings here with a practiced, but never jaundiced, eye.

I first met the Colonel when I became a reporter at the daily newspaper here in 1961. In those days they had what was called a public service beat, a maiden cruise for new reporters. It was a hodgepodge of small offices such as the Red Cross, YMCA, Employment Security Commission and some general assignments. I was assigned to that for a couple of months.

A part of that beat, which every ambitious reporter shunned, included covering the English Speaking Union meetings held at Col. Rockwell's house on occasion. Very few locals recognized the profound importance of those small and generally unpublicized meetings. Not only did various world figures come to speak, but they traveled to Asheville from other places to hear each other speak and confer with peers.

It turned out to be one of the most interesting assignments I ever had, and I cultivated a long-time friendship with Colonel Rockwell and his wife Prue. Even after I was assigned to other beats Colonel Rockwell insisted I cover his cultural affairs. Later when I was teaching I took students there to talk to this imposing elder statesman with white walrus mustache.

Inevitably the talk would turn to local affairs, usually politics and the course of events here, and Colonel Rockwell would offer information from that amazing bin of experience and memory.

He will be used a source in many of the planned articles of memoir and history planned for The Independent Torch. His accumulation of knowlege ranged far back in time. ("This was the first territory the whites actually stole from the Indians," he said.)

"Actually the most solid and industrious early settlers did not settle in and around what is now Asheville. They set up in the Far Western counties—Clay, Graham, Cherokee, Macon—and none of the real leaders of that time in Asheville's development came from here. They came out of East Tennessee and other states. Rankin, I believe came from Newport, Tennessee. One of the first mayors I recall, was one of the Stikeleathers, who also came from somewhere else," Col. Rockwell recalled.

He was able to outline the processes and people that set the tone for strong, almost dictatorial, leadership in Asheville and Buncombe County.

Rankin first. "He held various offices and he always wielded incredible power, but people respected him. I thought he was the biggest man on earth before I grew up," Colonel Rockwell said.

The Colonel was well versed in the old methods of ruling a population. He said he felt that the community rulers (not leaders) of that time held the classical political attitude in that they sought to make the entire community a harmonious whole.

"That was their first consideration. They had good university educations, generally, and they were sensitive enough to know that the only long-term workable political methods would have to take care of the people before they took care of the business interests," he said.

In most instances of hardship among the lower classes, the astute rulers would know of it quickly and see that they were fed and sheltered—and the children encouraged to become educated as situations warranted. This included a small black community, most of whom immigrated here with wealthy white families from South Carolina who summered here. Patronizing? You bet, as it would be seen in this day and time. It worked quite well. The poor were taken care of without humiliation, and they responded in kind—with respect for their employers and employment.

Col. Rockwell revealed that the first taint of commercial corruption came to Asheville as a false Reputation was floated that it would be an ideal resort area for tuberculars.

"They put big money in here," Colonel Rockwell said, "but there was a peculiar split in their reasoning. First, they began to advertise it as the ideal resort with a healthful climate. But only the undertakers prospered. Those with tuberculosis were dying off rapidly instead of regaining their health. The air here was not conducive to helping lung ailments."

One sanitorium near his home, which later served for decades as the Shangri La Apartments, had a bizarre ambience.

He said "You could hear the 'lungers' coughing in the night. That wasn't all you could hear in the night. You could also hear the coffins being nailed shut after they died. They didn't do it in daytime hours because they feared someone would find out and that would hurt the town's image."

Local ordinances and regulations held firm for some time, but the people putting money into the sanitoriums needed some convenient shunts around the law, so they began putting money into the campaigns of unethical and greedy small-time opportunists—some of whose old portraits grace the walls of public buildings like real leaders—and that was the beginning of the slide downward to what we have today. That new kind of official had no compunction about changing laws, ordinances, rules and regulations for the benefit of their wealthy sponsors.

Col. Rockwell said that first influx of big money took political power out of the hands of the politicians and put it into the hands of business leaders (from other places). The situation remains basically unchanged, except for some particulars. Whatever Asheville is now, for good or ill, it had its genesis at that point.

He said that a local law was passed by the legislature which would allow but not mandate the Asheville city and Buncombe County governments to give the old Board of Trade $4,000 annually for operations to benefit the area. The Board of Trade evolved into the Chamber of Commerce and now receives more than $150,000 a year from each of the governments. (Nobody knows for sure just how much goes there from hidden funds.)

"Practically speaking, we do not have politicians now," he said. "We have a strange mutants who win political power but whose attitude in undeniably greedy. They do not even have a good business philosophy, or they would understand that business and politics function best when in balance."

His quiet activities continued well into his last years. When he died some of the most accomplished people came to mourn or send condolences, mostly without notice of the general run of the power structure here.

Doppelgangers, Wraiths, Spirits, etc.

◆

The incident at Wildcat, etc.

One of the million memories of my childhood homeplace, not well imprinted at the time, was of myself at the age of 11 or 12, sitting on a boulder in our front yard. There had been some heavy rain. We lived back in the mountains, reachable only by a dirt road which could be almost impassable in bad weather, which made the incident even weirder. A strange car pulled into the rough cul-de-sac we used as a driveway, separated from the house by a strip of pasture. As I stared, a strange man and two women got out and walked to the fence. Then they all stared at me and as I looked at the man, an eerie electrical current passed from his eyes into mine. Unsettled, I leaped from the boulder, looked back at them but they had disappeared. I ran into the house and told my mother someone was there. It took less than a minute for her to come out, but they were gone. She chided me, told me she hadn't heard a car, that a car could probably not get up the road in that weather, nor had the dogs barked. It was only momentarily puzzling, filed away and noted only for the strange electric current that had passed between the man and I, and then forgotten. Time passed. Family tragedies occurred and my father died, my mother moved away, I went into military service as did my brother. My sister finished college, got married. The house of our childhood burned to the ground, leaving only stone walls beside the boulder. The old driveway roughened, eroded some by rains.

Then years later I was working at The Citizen-Times. One slow afternoon several of us were caught up on our work. The boss told us to take the rest of the day off. Someone asked what I intended to do and on impulse I said I might drive to Haywood County. Mary Gilpin was the librarian and Gertrude Ramsey was the society editor. Both said they would enjoy such a drive, so we went drifting. During the course of the afternoon, again on impulse, I asked if they would like to drive to old Wildcat, where I was raised. So we went up that rocky old road and parked at the cul-de-sac, We got out and stared at the old rock walls, then suddenly there appeared on the boulder a small boy. We all gaped and as I looked that eerie current passed between the eyes of the boy and me. Then he leaped from the boulder, disappearing in mid-air.

We all stood there a moment. Finally Gertrude Ramsey asked "Do you know that boy? Where did he go?"

There was a long silence. "He went to tell his mother…"

"His mother? Where is she?"

Silence again, then a numb answer from me. "She's gone."

Both women recognized something weird was going on.

I had recognized the way the boy wore his gallus-straps, one twisted in a certain way, as I had always worn mine.

"Who was that kid?" Mary Gilpin asked.

A period of silence, then

"Me. Myself."

We drove down that old road in silence.

A Visitation of a spirit at California Creek in 1980

In early January, a very cold day in 1980, I left Asheville in mid-afternoon heading for Washington County, Tennessee, where I had been involved in an investigation in Johnson City. The temperature was about five degrees. It was clear but there had been some snow a couple of days earlier. On US 19-33 about three miles north of Mars Hill I suddenly hit a patch of ice. My car spun off the road, clipped down a power pole, hit the side of a bridge and pitched, upside down, into California Creek. The ditch was about fifteen feet deep there. I was knocked unconscious. The creek was up and I was under the water. My first thought was that I was bleeding to death through my ears since I could hear the strong rush of blood. Then I realized it was a cold flow so I knew it was water. My seat belt was proving dangerous since it held me under. I got it loose, then had to finish busting the shattered window on my side with my head to get free. (Don't ask me the rationale for that.)

I stood stunned in the creek, staring at my upside down car which was still running. My head was quite bloody. I thought I was still in Korea wondering bemusedly where that strange red car had come from. At that time I could feel a presence standing beside me directing me to get out of that ravine. It was just getting dark and the wind was howling. I crawled up the bank and got onto the shoulder of the road, trying to flag traffic. Nobody stopped. I was wearing a reversible coat, and the side out was fake wolf skin, and it was iced over. With a child's stunned thinking, I figured that the reason no cars were stopping was that they thought I was a bear and they had been warned not to feed the bears. But I knew I was freezing to death and shaking fiercely.

Then suddenly a car stopped and a man helped me get into it. A woman appeared out of the dark and told me an ambulance had been called and was on the way. As we waited I asked the man what his name was. It was Cody. Then I said "Well man, I can't tell you how much I appreciate this. You've saved my life."

He shook his head, smiled strangely and said "You're welcome. I know how it is."

By then I was losing blood and coming and going into consciousness. I remember being loaded into the ambulance and hearing the siren. As we drove away I began cursing the state, the weather, my luck in general. The ambulance attendant was a bit elderly and was in work clothes. He was scowling at me. There was no heat in there. I asked him to turn the heat up. "Not until you quit taking the name of the Lord in vain. I'll have you know I'm a preacher and I won't put up with that cussing."

I set in to cussing even more, and shook and shivered at the way to Mission Hospital, coming and going into consciousness all the way. They wheeled me in and nurses began cutting my icy clothes off. One nurse, probably to comfort me and distract me, said I had nice eyes. To return the compliment, I told her she had a very nice body, what part of it I could see.

She knew this had happened in Madison County and made one of those amazing leaps to conclusion.

A piece of glass had pierced my chest and she exclaimed, "Here's where the bullet went in."

I revived, raised up, screamed, "Who shot me? Where is that damn preacher."

By then she had extracted the fragment of glass. They wheeled me to the X-ray room. In time they wheeled me into the hallway and left me. Then the nurse came to me and said "We need more X-rays. You've got big spots on your lungs."

Good God! Now I find I have lung cancer. But it turned out to be some muddy water which had gotten into my lungs from the high water of California Creek. Still, I'm having trouble getting it together. She brought the report in for me to see, and it was quite poetic. She had written that I had gone into the"rushing and tumbling water of a beautiful and scenic mountain stream."

Poetry everywhere. She then told me I was to contact Trooper Cooper of the Highway Patrol.

At least that had a ring to it.

Home that very cold night, so sore I had to sleep on the floor so I could spread out. Then in a week. I went to the garage on Burnsville Highway where my totally wrecked car had been towed. Among other items I needed to recover were two pistols, one of which was pertinent to the Tennessee investigation.

They knew me at that garage. One man I knew asked who had finally stopped to help me.I mentioned Cody's name.

Several people there stood about and stared.

"Lewis, Cody got killed in a wreck at the same place a year ago."

A week or so later I went to the Madison County Register of Deeds and got his death certificate, which is still somewhere among my papers.

There is a weird preamble and postscript to elements of this story—one of the pistols. I was teaching a writing class at Haywood. The December previous to the wreck I had a dream that I was being led up a flight of winding stairs to be executed. A few days later one of the girls in the class, who had been absent for some time came in late, acting strange, asked if I would drop by her apartment after class. I did and upon arriving she asked me to come upstairs to her bedroom. I did, with some reservations. At the head of the stairs she got a pistol there, wheeled and pointed it at me. "You've turned against me," she said.

"What's this about?" I asked.

"You've put something in my dope."

I started buying time. "Honey, I didn't know you could put something in dope. I thought dope was what you put in something. What kind of dope did you have and what did I put in it?"

"You put angel dust in my pot." Then I rushed her and took the pistol away. By then she was hysterical so I took her immediately to a clinic in Franklin. I still had the pistol later when I wrecked in California Creek. Trooper Cooper called me later and asked if I was an investigator. I said I was, and he told me he had to charge me with carrying two weapons unless I took credentials to a magistrate in Mars Hill. Which I did and got the pistols back. The point here is that the girl's gun was in the hands of the State Highway Patrol for several days. Then she called me and asked me to return her pistol, which I did.

I did not hear from her or the pistol for some time. Then I read in the newspaper that she had testified in the trial of her boyfriend. He was up for shooting to death a State Highway Patrolman near Hot Springs. She testified that she had loaned him the .25 automatic that both myself and the Trooper had in our custody shortly before she loaned it to her boyfriend, who had then shot another State Trooper to death.

The Recall Election of Clay County Sheriff Hartsell Moore

❖

1980

He had been the Clay County Sheriff for several terms in addition to being the Tax Collector. For both jobs he was paid $200 a month, which he had to collect himself, and out of that he had to buy his gas. There is a story that he once got a call from the Shooting Creek community that a gunfight was imminent. "Well, tell the winner to come on in so I can arrest him.

Hartsell had won the 1978 election, but a great deal of controversy ensued and for reason not clear (after a noisy meeting, during which about 75 guns were also in attendance, according to one attorney there,) Governor Jim Hunt called for a new election. In view of the risk, the governor sent about 18 State Highway Patrolmen and 18 SBI agents to go to Clay County to oversee the election.

United Press International in Raleigh hired me to provide wire service coverage. Hartsell had hired Asheville attorneys Bob Long and Jeff Hunt to protect his interests. I went out for a while the day before the election on a scouting expedition. Tension was high and most people anticipated someone would likely get shot.

That someone was almost me, but in a different county and on a different matter. It was after dark when I drove homeward. I stopped in Franklin to find a restaurant. Going the wrong way on a one-way street, I got stopped. I got out and gave the officer my driver's license. He looked at it, whereupon he pulled his pistol, stuck it in my face and said "Green, I'm going to blow your goddamned brains out."

I thought he must be joking, but immediately saw that he wasn't. I was alarmed but not yet frightened. I told him I had worked at law enforcement and that I understood stress and that we ought to go get a cup of coffee. But he was still enraged, waving that magnum about. "If it was just you, I'd kill you right now. But she's been screwing all of you."

"Man, who in hell are you talking about?" I asked. His wife, he said. Not me, I said.

Yes, at the Cowee Hydrological Lab operated by Southeastern Forest Experimental Station. You visited there some. Yes indeed, but…

This was his last night at Franklin Police Department, he said, and he didn't want to spoil it by killing me. "You get out of town right now," he said.

I got in my car and drove off, but he followed me. Okay, so he's going to get me out in the country. On the highway I pulled into the parking lot of a restaurant. He came right behind me. I realized he was still in rage. "I told you to leave," he shouted.

But I had my pistol by then and got out of the car. "I got one now," I said. He hurriedly drove off.

When I got back to Asheville about 10 p.m. I called FBI agent John Quigley and told him of the threat. What is the Federal angle? he asked. What was he after you about?

He said I was screwing his wife. There was a moment of muffled sound. What's so funny, John. Stop laughing.

I'm sorry. I'm not laughing, I just have the hiccups.

Well, I thought I ought to report this threat.

Very wise. If you turn up missing or dead, this will give us one starting point. Shit! I hung up.

To Hayesville the next morning, Election Day. I found Hartsell at the new justice center and jail and t old him I had to get some sleep. He waved back the hallway at the new cells. Go sleep in the jail. There's no one there.

I went in the first cell, eased the door shut. In a couple of hours I sensed someone standing outside the bars. It was Jay Hensley with whom I had worked at the Citizen-Times years earlier. No fan of mine. Some woman reporter was with him. He barely concealed his glee. What have they got you for? he asked. Another frame up by Democrats, I said. I really didn't rob that bank. Oh? their eyes widened, hidden joy. This is another frame up by the Democrats. The women reporter's lips were twitching in joy. We hadn't heard about it, she said. I sat up put my shoes on, stood, then pushed the cell door open. They stumbled back. Get out of the way, I said. I'm breaking out of this hick jail. They huddled against the wall.

I drove around the precincts that day with Hartsell and various others. There were enough people with guns and threats to justify all the troopers and agents.

Hartsell was worried, but some of the troopers and agents told me they thought Hartsell had won.

The polls closed and the Sheriff and I went to his small office to wait on the count. I put my tape recorder on his desk. Soon enough someone came and told Hartsell he had won big. We laughed and joked while the troopers and agents gathered in the outer office, relaxed, laughing and talking.

Then a Republican precinct worker ran in and told us that the Democratic poll workers had taken the ballot boxes home with them. Hartsell had one chew of tobacco in his jaw, but his eyes narrowed and he took another chew. Then he told me he was going to arrest the troopers and agents, put them in jail, swear in some of his backers and go to those houses and get the boxes. He yelled at them to get in there, then he said, "Boys, I'm going to put your god dam democrat assess in jail and I'm going to go get those boxes."

They crowded in and one asked what boxes but agent Maxey was already unsnapping his pistol. Hartsell, you ain't putting me in jail, he said. The others nodded grimly. I was in the crossfire cone of this upcoming massacre. I reached quickly and turned on the tape recorder, hoping someone would find it and know what had happened.

After an interminable time, Hartsell slumped and asked me what he should do. I told him the boxes had all been sealed and if they were tampered with that would be a big problem for the Clay County Democrats. Another long pause, then the tension drained away. All right, Hartsell said. State Trooper Charlie Long looked at me, said damn, I'm glad you were here.

They all went back to being brother cops. Somebody brought coffee and donuts. Everyone congratulated Hartsell. I gathered my gear and began shaking hands of cops and politicians. Then Hartsell asked if I was going back to Asheville that night would I take something to Bob Long his lawyer. Sure, what? He brought in four fruit jars of white lightning. All the State Troopers looked on with interest.

Hell no, Hartsel, I said, and ran out the door.

Big Nell, For Whom
The Bell Tolls

◆

1970s

A bell was ringing briefly somewhere early that morning as cold dawn came on, one man said. He said he heard it clearly and the old woman sitting on the window ledge heard it too and she quit crying for a moment. It seemed like a burglar alarm in one of the buildings above Asheville's Lexington Avenue had gone off, or a loud telephone. It didn't ring but in that clear moment, but that hung in his mind, and upon later reflection it seemed appropriate that there should be a bell ringing, however briefly.

A bell and a chill wind, loneliness and darkness.

Now if you are ever on Lexington Avenue in winter, you will notice that the wind slashes raw and unbridled out of the mountains of Madison County and North Buncombe and as it goes up that street in December it is as sharp and bright as a bayonet.

Lexington is a community of its own, even as Beaver Lake and Kenilworth, even as Malvern Hills or Bent Creek. The people who come there know each other and they weave, knit and stitch the fabric of the street's life out of their own. There are several low taverns with loud jukeboxes and a rich mixture of good citizens, hookers, drunks, transients and the workingman. They all come to Lexington, but nobody much stays there.

Nell Austin Reed stayed there. She had no other place. For the full dimensions of her life, we must consider several things.

First, the record. Born 1908 in Yancey County. Nell Austin Reed, alias Big Nell and/or "The Shuffler".

Education—none.

Next of kin—none.

Address? Weaverville, Fairview, 33 Orange Street, the Flynn Christian Fellowship Home, and finally (and mostly) the Buncombe County Jail.

Yes, The Shuffler called jail home.

At times on the record there is a shaky signature, other times there is a policeman's scribbled notation beside the line for signature "…not able…"

Here follows the nature of The Shuffler's offenses against society: drunk, trespassing, disorderly conduct, drunk, drunk, drunk…

Then here follows the ignoble prices she paid for her ignoble violations: twenty days, $18, $20, nol prosse with leave, $14, ten days, $14, $14, ten days, five days, thirty days…

Here and there are indications of small mercies. "Released by order of magistrate…judge ordered release…judge said release…"

But to fill out the dim penciled outlines of The Shuffler's life, you must go to those misbegotten friends on Lexington. They all knew her, thought well of her. She was part of the life on the street, and when she could not go out and bum for herself, some of the bums went out to make a score for her and when the bums show such charity there is a big sign of humanity.

She once worked at the Enka plant years ago, one said, and had a husband but maybe not a family. But that is in the dim past and nobody knew for sure. Sometimes she blubbered drunkenly about it. Nobody knew when she had lost her way. She had just always seemed to be there on the street.

The Shuffler. Will nobody speak for her? Yes, only if someone will help tell Big Nell's tale. They didn't call her The Shuffler much in recent years because she didn't shuffle. She sat, she lurched and heaved, but she had gotten too fat to shuffle. She weighed so much it took six men to load her into an ambulance, one man said. In recent years she had ridden the ambulance a lot. Nell had made a select list—the chronic drunks that county officials ruled she could not be taken to jail because she might die there and they would be liable. She had been sickly for a long time, but they would not treat her at hospitals.

Wine and beer, booze and paint thinner, sterno and anything else.

She was a good old woman," one lady of the night said. "She tried to help and encourage people and always had a good word."

The last few months had been particularly hard on her, one man reported. Taxis wouldn't haul her. They wouldn't have her in her home at the jail. Nobody would rent to her. Her bladder leaked and she had little control over her bowels. So she sat out on the street and bummed money when her Social Security check had been spent and sent her friends for wine.

This had gone on for two or three years, a man said. She sat and slept all night in doorways. Sometimes if she could get to her feet she would get in an abandoned car and sleep; but most nights she slept in doorways or alleys. Some people would get coffee and sandwiches for her—or wine. She was at Broughton Hospital here while back, but even that mental hospital wouldn't keep her.

"She never hurt a soul but herself," that man said. "Sometimes she'd cuss the cops because they wouldn't lock her up. One cold night a cop called Judge Allen and told him Nell didn't have any place to go and he ordered them to put her in jail on some trumped up charge, rules or no rules."

A cold day last week one bartender said to hell with it and let her come in and sit in a booth all day so she wouldn't freeze, but he had to close at eight o'clock. She left her old suitcase and a canvas traveling bag on his shelf.

That night Big Nell, The Shuffler, began hurting deeply as she sat on a window ledge in front of the bar. The temperature fell below freezing. Before dawn the next morning, one man said, he stopped to speak to her and they both heard the bell ring. Hark, the bell. Then she began crying again. Another man on his way to work said she was still crying a few minutes later and told him she was dying. He said he and another man went to the police station and asked them to put her somewhere, but a cop laughed and told them to take her home with them if they wanted her to have a place, they had worried with her enough.

The next time anyone checked about a half-hour later and Big Nell was not crying. The massive body was sitting there a child's hurt face and a frozen tear. Big Nell had made her last hard passage, cut to death by the quick bright blades of December.

And there was an accounting of Nell's estate—two bags, an old nightgown, a couple of ragged dresses and half a pack of Rolaids. Did The Shuffler have trouble with her stomach recently?

Yes, The Shuffler. Damn, will nobody speak for Nell Reed of Lexington Avenue?

All right, a few words. It is better then, is it, for them to die on the cold street than in jail?

No politician or hospital or the community at large can be blamed for people dying of natural causes at home. Who was to know?

She was a citizen in her own way. She had her place in our town. She lived along in the same time with us, and she was one of us. She paid no taxes, but taxes are a sometime thing, and will last only as long as mankind lasts.

She spoke ill of no person and treated none shabbily. She had a good spirit, and such spirit will endure long after the last taxes have been collected and spent. Therefore, send not to see for whom the bell tolls. It tolls for thee and me.

So on Lexington before dawn one day in December, with a half-life behind her and a full death before her. A drunk died.

Yes, therefore, send not to see for whom the bell tolls...

Max Wilson and Gordon Greenwood

✦

Press Assistance In A Chairman's Campaign

In those days of the 60s there was an understanding at the daily newspaper that reporters could help political candidates shape their press releases for a fee—as much for the convenience of copy editors as anything. The rule that reporters could not influence the content, they would only take content from the candidate, stylize it and return it to them. The candidate would then take it to the editor who would make the decision to okay it and send it to the composing room.

That was the year Republican Max Wilson challenged Gordon Greenwood, the Democratic incumbent Chairman of the Board of County Commissioners. Max called and asked me to write his press releases (with the understanding that I was to only develop his information into journalese style).

But before the campaign got underway, Gordon sent his top henchman, E.B. DeBruhl to ask if I would do his releases. I told him about my deal with Max. He got with Gordon and called back and said he didn't care as long as I would do his also. I called Max, who said he didn't care either. Thereupon, almost immediately, the rules were discarded.

Max called, ready to go. "All right, Lewis, what am I going to say."

I thought for a moment, then said "Accuse him of favoritism in the ambulance situation. Say that Gordon makes sure that the big Democrat Buster West at West Funeral Home gets most of the business. (This was before the county took over emergency management.)

"Damn right. That sounds right. Put it in there."

I wrote it and gave it to him and he took it to the editor. It was to come out the next day. I called Gordon and said "Good God, Gordon. There's a story coming out that Max is accusing you of conflict of interest by showing favoritism toward West Funeral Home in the ambulance business."

Gordon thought for a minute, asked "How is that conflict of interest.?"

"I don't know but it sounds mean."

"What am I going to say?"

"Well, naturally it's not true. It's your normal Republican lie."

"Put it in there."

I called Max and told him Gordon said it wasn't true. "What am I going to say about that?" Max asked.

"Wait a couple of days then say that you are getting up the records and statistics."

"But I don't have anything."

"Not yet, but you are getting them."

"All right, I'll take your word for it. Put it in there."

I called Gordon. "Max said he's got the records to prove it."

"Damn it, I told them to get rid of those. What am I going to say now?"

"There's just one thing left."

"What?"

"The Republican mudslinging has started early. I'm checking with my lawyers about suing them."

"Right. Hell yes. Put it in there."

(For the record, the Democrats won that election.)

Typical Races In Buncombe County Circa

◆

1950–60

There are faint but eerie parallels (or at least reminders) of the 1962 Sheriff's race in Buncombe County and the present repercussions of this year's elections both locally and nationally.

In that year, a 30-year-old unknown Republican beat a Democratic Sheriff who had held the office for 32 years. If memory serves., he was the sole Republican elected that year and was at the mercy of Democratic county commissioners and other Dem office holders who refused to cooperate with him in any way.

Harry P. Clay won by an official margin of 146 votes. But it turns out the margin of victory was much higher after Sheriff Laurence Brown called for a recount. More on this later in this story.

Perhaps history can be a guide. Clay was so publicly thwarted by Dems after he won that he became a martyr, and in the next election he carried every Republican on the ticket.

(Let it be said that Clay became so corrupt in his second term that he was subjected to numerous Federal investigations and was soundly beaten in the next election. He was also defeated several years later when he ran again as a Democrat.)

This crop of Democrats are much smarter that those of that time, so Ramsey may be fairly safe, except from the usual whispers, evil hints and gossip.

The 1962 election was the first Democratic loss in decades, and the campaign suddenly became tough and tight in the late summer and early autumn.

Young lions were coming on, howling for a place in the Democratic heirarchy, but had been effectively suppressed for a decade or two.

But even party members were growing tired of Brown. Some of his deputies were as arrogant as storm troopers, corruption was growing, bag men were in place.

Fate turned slowly against them. Jimmy Rogers was the managing editor of The Times (there were two daily papers in those days) unaccountably and for reasons not clear yet, he sent a reporter out to do an expose on gambling operations here.

That reporter bought lottery and baseball tickets at various bookie joints and ran a story.

When that story broke (to the astonishment of everyone everywhere since the newspapers were in the pockets of Democratic party leaders), the General County Court Judge remarked that he would like to talk to that reporter. Two deputies then went to the reporter's house, pulled his phone off the wall, slung his mother-in-law down on a couch and took the reporter in.

There began the slow slide. While nothing was ever done in court, that incident was a beginning.

Bear in mind that Claude Ramsey was the executive editor of The Citizen-Times. His brother Gordon was Sheriff Brown's chief deputy. The incident simmered. Longtime Democrats were beginning to think…

Yet it seemed to die down. Than some members of the Asheville Jaycees offered a critical opinion on that and several things.

In a few weeks, the state Jaycee organization held its annual convention at City Auditorium, and as usual, served cocktails. Suddenly deputy sheriffs barged in to raid and arrested Jaycees on liquor charges It was harassment without doubt and while the court action was meaningless, the political reaction was reaching critical mass.

The police reporter at The Citizen was Bob Matthews, an ageing wimp who was frightened. Someone at the Sheriff's Department made out a phony warrant and showed it to Bob, who added it to his list. Then the warrant was destroyed and that guy sued the newspaper later and won a settlement.

So on two occasions that year, the brass at the newspaper backed down. The reporter who had been manhandled, and the libel lawsuit. The cowardice at the newspaper was laughable. The wimpy reporter, a Democrat, did not sue for false arrest, etc.

Then there was one more incident, in which this editor (who was then a police reporter at C-T) played a part.

I was checking reports at Memorial Mission Hospital one Friday night and found one just taken on Tate Lyda, one of Brown's deputies (and the father of Buck Lyda, who later became Sheriff here).

The report noted that Lyda had suffered a scalp laceration as result of being hit with a pistol. I knew that Lyda was supposed to be on vacation.

Beef Capps, the night chief deputy was there, so I asked him what had happened.

"Nothing. We don't want this in the paper," he said. I got pissed. This was my first confrontation with the department. I asked again. He said again that "we don't want this in the paper."

I blew up. "Who the hell is we, Beef? Are you pregnant or something."

Chastened, he directed me to the Courthouse basement, where a suspect was being questioned by Chief Investigator Flake Moffitt. I burst in on them, The Department had gotten an ineffective lawyer to sit in. I asked the suspect what had happened.

"What the hell, man. You don't think you're going to get this in the paper, do you?" he asked, savvy.

"I'm going to try," I answered.

The man had recently gotten out of prison and rented a house in Beaverdam neighboring one Lyda had rented. They shared a mountain spring. On vacation, Lyda got on a drunk and pulled the ex-con's pipe out of the spring. The man went up the hill and put it back. Lyda then went up there with his pistol to intimidate the man.

But the man took the pistol away from Lyda and beat him up with it.

I called the story in to the city editor and went home. For God's sake! They printed several paragraphs of it. Then the most revealing thing occurred. I went to work Saturday afternoon and here came Mrs. Clyde Bradley to my desk. "Did you write this?"

"Yes indeed," a bit riled because she was the wife of the Chairman of the Board of Elections and a big Democrat. I thought she was going to raise hell.

She hugged me, said "It's about time this newspaper did something about that mess over there."

Wow! Something dawned on me. Someone from the machine saw the importance, benefit and political significance in that story. Other Democrats weighed in quietly. I got some threatening phone calls from deputies, but time was nigh. The election was soon.

Election day was a classic. The county turned out in large numbers. There were reports of threats, fights, bribes, etc.

After the polls closed, we at the newsroom had gotten returns from all but two precincts—No. 10, all black and Democratic; and No. 4, all wealthy white and Republican.

Claude Ramsey, the executive editor, sent me to No. 10 to get the returns, which were being tampered with. I brought them in, then No. 4 came in. Ramsey, incorrigible but knowledgable Democrat that he was, looked at it and said, sadly:

"Gentlemen, Laurence has lost by 150 votes."

He had it so close. Brown lost by 146 votes, then called for a recount. I went to the basement of the Courthouse, where Brown had retained some lawyers. One was a young lawyer, who went behind the curtains of a couple of machines, came out to confer with colleagues a moment, then said: "We don't want a recount."

People in the know told me later that Clay had won by a couple of thousand votes. The Democrats stole all they could and still lost.

They did not take it in stride. On the day Clay was sworn in, he found cruiser battery and radio cables cut, uniforms piled up and pissed on by outgoing deputies, anti-freeze drained. I made photos. They allowed me to print nothing at C-T.

Later I talked to Paul Pitillo, clerk of the old Police Court about it and told him derisively about Claude's reaction. He reported me to Claude, who then called me into his office. I thought he would give me hell. No, he hung his head, shook it and said "Lewis, the chief deputy is my brother. Family gets in the way of principle…"

Years have gone by.. I grew older. Time has proven Claude right on that one point.

When young Republican Harry P. Clay won the Buncombe County Sheriff's office in 1962, it signaled a sea-change in Buncombe County politics. The office had been held by Democratic Party godfather Laurence E. Brown, Sheriff for 32 years. Brown was one of two big bosses and a few lesser stalwarts who kept the political scene here in solid control..

When Brown fell to the voters, it seemed that the most power in the Democratic party flowed to J. Weldon Weir, the city manager who had risen through the ranks of an even older machine years before and had taken charge.

Other office holders—powers to a lesser extent—were Coke Candler, chairman of the Board of Commissioners; Winky Digges, the Register-of-Deeds who had taken that office after his father had held it for years; and Zeb Weaver, the

Clerk of Superior Court. While highly influential inside the Democratic Party, these three could not really wield the big power.

There were some others who remained loyal to the party, but who did not hold office and were not trusted by Weir. But one maverick had began emerging with his own power base, and he was such a wild card in the deck that Brown, Wier and all others treated him with kid gloves, though he had risen with their help.

He was Bob Swain, at that time the Solicitor—or District Attorney—for the district comprised of both Buncombe and Madison counties. Through the judicious use of his official prosecutorial power in both counties, Swain had knitted an alliance with the Ponder clan in Madison. There was a amorphous reservoir of Democratic votes along the borders of Buncombe and Madison. These remained free of any political obligations to the Weir machine, but they were seldom taken into account until the invisible war later began between Swain and the Weir machine.

At that time it was said that with the fall of Laurence Brown, Weldon Weir saw an opportunity to take over county politics and made his move.

Swain was up for reelection. During the 1962 race he had been a good Democrat and fiercely fought the Republican Clay. But being the prosecutor, he had to work with the Sheriff's Department on a daily basis and an uneasy truce settled between the Sheriff and the prosecutor. In addition, Weir felt that Clay was a weak and naïve young man whose purpose had been only to knock Brown out, and then be dropped between the cracks. The Republicans seemed to have no future here.

Swain was a drinking man, as was Clay, and they began to hold after-hours conferences over bourbon. A bond was formed. Swain's behavior was becoming scandalous and rebellious to the city boss and certain other Democrats. It was decided that he must go. Among other things, Swain had been arrested for drunk driving by a young politically naive State Highway Partrolman. (That patrolman shortly found himself transferred to some backwater district in eastern North Carolina.)

Weir was backing former Public Safety director Charlie Dermid_against Clay, then selected young Dem lawyer Bill Moore to run against Swain in the Democratic primary. Moore was an up-and-coming young attorney with a future in the party, it seemed, During those years, very few younger aspirants were able to get the backing of the machine.With such backing Moore handily defeated Swain in the primary.

(There were other Democratic politicians lurking in the underbrush, ready to play a role. They were attorney Bruce Elmore, who had a considerable following but who was hamstrung because of his loyalty to the Democratic Party, as was Claude DeBruhl, an activist from an old political family.)

Both had fought Weir within the confines of party discipline and had never helped Republicans. Neither played any visible role in what was to become the explosive charge to destroy Weir and others in his machine, but they were later suspected. They did not show more than nominal support for Weir.

A vital part of Weir's strength flowed from the black precincts, which were under his influence, if not control. But Elmore also had much influence in those precincts, while DeBruhl's strength was in other areas. Again, no one familiar with the events of that time has ever blamed either for direct involvement for what was to come.

Shortly following the primary that defeated Swain, the Board of Elections office in the Courthouse was broken into and the registration books of some black precincts were spirited away, never to be seen again except by the thieves.

An angry hue and cry went up from the Weir faction—and of course the newspaper, which was in Weir's pocket. I was working the police beat at the time, but more and more the police and court beat was merging with the political beat. I had covered Swain's activities as Solicitor for several years, so I went to him.

Grinning like a Cheshire cat, he set up a howl of indignation, borrowing appropriate outraged thetoric from Shakespeare, the Bible and other works of highly elevated prose.

"Right here in this Courthouse, thieves have been at work. Perhaps the Republican Sheriff's Department is not sufficiently aware and on the ball enough to keep such fearful and awful scalawags and scoundrels from trying to tilt elections and thwart the will of the innocent and good people, the trusting voters...."

Etc. etc. etc.

"Are you blaming the Sheriff's Department for this?"

"No, only for indifference to the welfare of the voters and negligence in allowing people to roam about the Courthouse in the middle of the night and..."

Etc.

A couple of nights later I went into the Sheriff's office and found Clay and Swain toasting each other from of a fifth of Jack Daniels. They turned and looked at me suspiciously, then began their alibi.

Clay, slurring his words: "Lewis, this is the worst thing that can happen. We are launching an investigation...the FBI and SBI will find the criminals..."

Swain belched, looked out the window.

"Why," said I solemnly, "the Solicitor here told me you were in on this."

"No, no, no," Swain said, "I think you probably misunderstood me. This is awful…"

Etc.

The significant thing about the theft was that those books contained numerous black people who were dead, who had moved away or didn't even vote. Yet they had voted each election. Now they would have to be reregistered in a looseleaf notebook under strict supervision. That would obliterate much of the vote the city machine needed.

I was on good terms with the Sheriff and Solicitor, and I could read sign. They knew something. I investigated. Now begins strict speculation, verified only by a few who said they were in on it.

Swain and Clay had one or more deputy sheriffs break in and take the books. One of those had a key to West Funeral Home in Weaverville, and possibly as a temporary measure hid the books at the foot of the corpse in a casket containing the remains of a fairly prominent Democrat, whose visitation was to be held the following night. (An interesting point of speculation: the funeral home owner was north-end Democratic ward-heeler Buster West, who only smiled when asked about it, shook his head and said nothing.)

The deceased Democrat was a member of a fraternal lodge, and thereby rated an honor guard at the visitation. One of the culprits was a member of the same lodge and happily volunteered to serve as one of the honor guard. He told me some time later he could not resist a smirk as Weir and other Democratic leaders filed past the casket which held the very books they desperately sought.

As it was, circumstances prevented the deputies from returning that night to retrieve the books and hide them elsewhere. So off to the funeral and a North Buncombe graveyard the next day, where it is said in the lore of the time, the books still repose at the feet of the corpse.

Under the tutelege of Swain, Clay learned fast. When the election came, to the chagrin of the Weir faction, who had sadly underestimated the political prowess of the two, every office up for election went to the Republicans, riding in on Clay's shirttails. The Solicitor's office went to Clyde Roberts, and that was the year that a Republican strong man emerged. Curt Ratcliff, an Enka plant worker won the office of Clerk of Superior Court. (The only office not challenged was that of General County Court, and so Bob "Whip" Wilson was the only Democrat in office for the next four years.)

Time passed. That was Weldon Weir's last hurrah. A new Asheville City Council "retired him" and replaced him with an out-of-towner, Phin Horton.

Then Sheriff Clay went crooked and began consorting with local racketeers, and grew quite wealthy for a time. When the next election came, the voters kicked all the GOP shirttail riders out. The Democrats resumed control.

Outside of the rise of Curt Ratcliff a few years later as Chairman of the Board of Commissioners, the local GOP blindly resumed shooting themselves in the foot or feet, and even so, in a few years some of them turned on Ratcliff.

With the help of some leading Republicans, Democrat Gene Rainey took over as Chairman. After a couple of terms, Rainey stepped down and Tom Sobol won the Chairmanship. After a couple of terms, a young naïve Republican won the office. He had no coattails in that election.

There was a popular protest song in the sixties, ***Where have all the flowers gone?*** Some of the Democrats who went with Swain would get around Weldon with a soft paraphrased refrain, but if he ever got it he didn't let on.

Where has all the power gone, long time passing. Where have all the poll books gone, long time ago?

Gone to graveyards, every one. When will they ever learn?

Sandy Fired

She came to the daily newspaper in Asheville from a newspaper in Tennessee. She was very ambitious and anxious to make a name as a hard charger, but also very inexperienced. Arriving here as she did, she knew nothing of The Independent Torch. Reading a couple of editions, she apparently decided to expose both The Torch and its apparent insider knowledge (and tolerance) of widespread corruption and insanity among local officials.

The Torch had a front page satirical piece about a hot race for the Chairmanship of the Board of County Commissioners. The story was that the (fictional) local chapter of The Convicts Association were endorsing one of the candidates who was for the construction of a new jail, while his opponent was for new schools.

In this satire, the leader of The Convicts Association, one Chester The Molester, had pointed out to a writer for The Independent Torch that the candidate backing a new jail had promised more television, coffee in the cells and some beer and marijuana for cellblock parties, conjugal visits by girl friends, privacy for those to take place, and on and on.

This girl reporter saw immediately the potential to outrage the conservative elements of the community, make a name for herself and probably win a promotion at that old gray whore of a daily newspaper. Early one morning she called the editor of The Torch and with no little grandiosity said archly:

"I notice you have quoted members of the Convicts Association in this story."

"Yes. So?"

"I would like to know how you got access to the convicts. Who let you into the jail to interview them?"

"Well, actually I didn't have to go to the cells. Members of The Convicts Association are down on the streets passing out brochures for their man and collecting campaign contributions. It is outrageous. Some of them can be found in the taverns and beer joints spending those campaign contributions."

"What? Who let them out? Who authorized that? Do any of them skip town?"

"I suppose the Sheriff did. He's got the keys to the jail and he's a member of the same party as that candidate. I don't know why they would skip out. They've got it made in the jail here. They come and go as they please if they have the right political connections, and free marijuana is provided to the right ones."

"What? What? What? I think you're in on this somehow. I heard this is a crazy county. Some kind of coverup on your part, eh? You didn't bring that out in your story."

"Hell, I'm the one who brought this much out."

"Yes, in a limited circulation. My god..."

"May I ask, how much experience do you have?"

"Well, I've not been working very long, but I am a graduate of journalism school."

Ah, a moment of light.

"Very impressive. Sandy, do you know what satire is?"

"I think so."

"Ah, very interesting. Do any of the editors at The Citizen-Times know you called me?"

"No."

Aha. Another moment of light. They will. There is a policy of education here at The Independent Torch.

My next week's headline said **"Citizen-Times Reporter Tries To Intimidate The Independent Torch."**

She got fired. I trust she went to the dictionary to find out the meaning of satire.

The Old Man's New Mule

A February 1966 story

Unheard go the small stories in the depth of a small city's life…ribald laughs, feeble cries, of small tragedies and the unyielding will to keep going despite all. The little people struggling against the rising, gaining tides of change in their lives. Occasionally such a story turns in the surf, then sinks again into the murky ebb of our draining days.

Here is the story of George Holmes, a 79-year old black man who lived in an old weathered house at the end of Jersey Street, a muddy steep lane in Stumptown within sight of Riverside Cemetery. He has spent his years close to the soil, farming when he could, then gardening when city restrictions were passed.

His wants are simple, his manner is humble and religious. He has a great love for nature. Always in his life there were chickens, rabbits, dogs, cats, some food for the birds in the winter. From his earliest days George owned a mule, that most unlovable, stubborn and deceitful of God's creatures. But George Holmes had rather have one mule than a hundred horses. He got along well with them.

For many years people in the Montford section watched George and the mule. More than once pictures of the two have appeared in the newspaper. That gentle old man, calling out cheery greetings from his wagon seat behind the mule. Twice a week he would hitch up his mule to the wagon, then drive to a supermarket on Lexington Avenue where he would load up on scraps to feed his fowl, rabbits and other animals.

When he was not gardening, George worked as a plumber's helper for various firms about Asheville in years gone by, but when plowing time came he and the mule went about plowing the small gardens for those people who depended on him for it.

A few years earlier he was admitted to a hospital for an operation and had to give up the heavy work. Yet he and the mule made their appointed rounds, and you could set your watch by his wagon trips to pick up the feed and scraps.

But abrasive time sanded down the boundaries of George Holmes' life. His wife died that year and George watched in quiet resignation as she was laid to rest. Now all he had was his old friend the mule.

They continued on their way, making as much of a living as an old man can with a mule.

Before his wife died, the couple had drawn $35 a month from the welfare department. After her death, he was cut to $13 a month. George had a neighbor write to the department about it, and it was raised to $21 monthly. But that was not much help. He paid $23 a month on the house he rents. George also drew a small amount of Social Security, but even then the months are long and the money is short.

George and his mule persevered, heads held high. They were working, not begging. He kept a small garden behind his house, and rented other little patches of ground from his neighbors. He sold a few chickens and eggs, and in that way made up the difference in the months that went by.

George and the mule had grown old together in their various allotments of time and life. Then a severe cold spell descended in January. George held close to his fire. Neither man nor mule can work in weather like that.

On February 14 of that year, the winter eased some. George harnessed the mule and they went out to work. On a path near his house, the mule faltered, then fell sideways into a ditch. George returned home, got a hatchet and mattock and returned to the mule. He dug out the ditch banks and cut bushes until he freed the old mule, but it stumbled about from weakness then pitched into a ditch on the other side of the path. This one was full of cold water. George got a friend and the two of the tried to extricate the mule.

It was getting late. They gave it up and called the fire department. Firemen came, looked, told George they couldn't do anything. He let them call the Buncombe county Rescue Squad, which came and worked, but they couldn't get the mule up. One member of the squad looked at the animal laying in cold water in mute agony, then gently told George the mule wouldn't be able to walk if they did get it out. They asked him what he wanted them to do. They all knew what had to be done.

George studied a moment, then bent and looked sadly into the eyes of his mule. He walked away as the animal was put to death. Then the word went out among his friends in the Courtland Avenue-Montford section. It was as if a person had died. White and Negro together began to talk about doing something for George Holmes.

Though his years were many and he'd outlived a lot of mules in his time, George felt that he had enough time left to wear out one more strong mule. His neighbors were not wealthy and had no idea what a mule cost. But they arranged a committee to help the old man get one more mule. The Rev. Wesley Grant, pastor of the World-Wide Missionary Baptist Tabernacle at 97 Choctaw Street agreed to serve as a recipient of donations, but word of mouth did not bring in much money. One of his friends said "We're not going to stop until we get him a mule. Without a mule there's no telling what might be come of him."

A mule is not much to ask of this world, when you're old and the days keep draining away and you want to earn your keep right up to the end.

Nothing changes in this little city but that it somehow remains the same. With great faith the neighbors insisted they would once again see…plodding along up Montford Street toward Lexington Avenue, George Holmes and his mule…like it always was.

Then, this writer published the story in the newspaper and the response came. Here is the follow-up story.

"People Care And George Holmes Has A Mule

"Out of a seemingly cold, distant and indifferent public, and into the bleakness of an old man's waning life, it came like the warm winds of springtime. A poverty program welling from the hearts of concerned citizens, lavishly bestowed on an old man of the soil who wanted only one more mule to help him make his way through the remaining days.

"Now George Holmes has his mule, a strong, sprightly and headstrong creature delivered in mid-week by his pastor. The old man handles his new mule, "Ol' Frank" with a firmness that keeps the obstinate, sad-eyed and willful beast about its tasks.

"White and Negro neighbors joined forces to raise enough money to buy the mule. Nobody had a clear idea what a mule might cost. The Rev. Wesley Grant, pastor of the World-Wide Baptist Tabernacle agreed to serve as a collector for the drive. Letters to the editor poured in and by the end of that week more than enough money had accumulated. The Rev. Grant and George went to Riceville Road and paid $100 for the mule.

"Not only did he get a mule, but all the latest accessories. The Rev. Grant purchased horseshoe nails, paid back feed bills and bought more feed for the animal, then wire for a fence. There was still a surplus of $226.55 with which The Rev.

Grant bought a good light wagon for the mule to pull, some coal for George's stove and to pay his rent up for some time in advance.

"The list of donors totaled 48 persons—some sending as little as $1, some sending much larger sums. It came from all over Western North Carolina. One summer resident here from St. Petersburg, Florida, sent in a sizable sum. Some signed their names, some signed "a friend" and some sent money without a covering letter.

"George said simply "The Lord bless them all. I don't know what else to say. I wish I could say something more…"

Shoot Out at Curtis Creek

Clouding up and those clouds moved slowly in from the west on a cold wind and began stacking up. Saturday night was coming on, with nothing much to consider as news. Then the phone rang. A deputy sheriff said curtly, "Hey, get out here to Curtis Creek. Old man Smith is holed up at his house and has started a shootout. We may have to kill him. This is going to get hot politically and we need a reliable witness."

Curtis Creek was about 12 miles out in Hominy. The wind rose and the frequent gusts almost blew my car off the road. Mr. Smith's long, stony and twisting driveway led off Curtis Creek Road. A Sheriff's Department cruiser blocked it off, and despite the building storm a number of neighbors had gathered nearby. The Sheriff had ordered them evacuated and all nearby house lights extinguished. I asked that deputy what was happening.

"We don't know. One of our boys went to serve a mental warrant. We've been getting complaints about him pointing a gun. He threatened the Postmaster for sending him used mail. He broke into wild laughter for no reason A neighbor said Smith had fired 57 rounds before we started to return the fire."

He said neighbors had described Smith as a good and kind man until recently. Smith was a 68-year old widower whose mental health had been deteriorating over the past past few weeks. Someone called us but he had barricaded himself in his house. "One of our boys went to the door and almost got shot. We've got this house surrounded. The Sheriff and Chief Deputy have tried to talk to him but he shoots at them."

"Where are they?

"They're both laying on that bank right behind the house. The Sheriff wants to talk to you."

I scrambled up the brushy bank to where Sheriff Clay and Chief Deputy Willis Mitchell were huddled behind a tree. They could look into the back windows. The wind grew higher. Willis said "Listen, I must assure you that I'm too old for this. See if you can't use your clout here with the Sheriff and get him to send me home. My bones are aching and my inner soul keeps telling me to quit this job right now and go home and sit by the television with a good drink. Yas, yas..."

"Well, why aren't you?" I asked the Chief Deputy.

The Sheriff glared at me. "Because I want him here. I want everybody here, including you. I may deputize you. The Democrats will swear that we murdered this old man."

"You can't deputize me. You don't need me that bad." This was not an emergency. Besides, that could definitely be a conflict of interest in this case.

I was hunkered down beside them. Mr. Smith fired a couple of rounds at us, then directed his fire to the front yard.

"Now sir," Willis said. "This is a dangerous situation. What we need is for those Democrat County Commissioners to bring us a drink and consider such situations as this for a raise when the budget comes up. Put that in the newspaper."

"Don't even think about it," Clay said and began pointing out to me where the various armed deputies were stationed. Then I slipped off the bank and crept and circled around the yard to where Harold Crisp was crouched beside a shed. Smith turned off the lights and a heavy gloom descended. Clouds now blotted out what moonlight there had been and treacherous shadows around the house increased the danger. The enclosed porches shielded Smith's movements from view and the officers found it impossible to trace him. He was at one window and then another, firing into the deputies positions. We whispered for a moment then Mr. Smith fired, the bullet hitting within six inches of Harold's head.

I crawled across the front yard to another deputy while the old man was firing in the Sheriff's direction. That deputy said "Mr. Smith has got an arsenal in there. So far he's fired from a .30–.30, some .22 rifles, at least two shotguns, two different pistols and a .30–06."

While the officers fired back from time to time, they seemed intent only on driving him from window to window. On the Sheriff's instructions Captain Howard Martin and Captain Robert Hutchins did fire several bursts from Thompson sub-machineguns at the eaves of the house and the roof and tops of windows to move the old man. One time Robert Hutchins rushed the door with a shotgun, but Mr. Smith hit it with a rifle round and destroyed it. Hutchins had to go to a cruiser for another weapon. The Sheriff and Chief Deputy grew hoarse from shouting instructions to the men. I went back to that position and the Sheriff said "The last thing we want to do is kill that old man. I'm ordering tear gas."

By now some snow was falling. They fired tear gas into several windows, filling the house. It was in there for hours and the old man didn't even sneeze, but kept firing. They all tried to engage him in conversation to no avail. Once he shouted that he had two broken legs.

"All right," Clay answered. "You throw those guns out and we'll come in and help you to the hospital." No answer. Time passed. At this point Captain Bill Green, who had been walking among the men's positions, crouched and ran toward the porch. Crisp said Smith raised his gun to shoot Green. Crisp shouted, "Don't do that, Mr. Smith."

The battle-clatter raised again over the scene. They had three tear gas canisters left. They fired them into the house. Everyone on the scene but Smith coughed. Finally he shouted to them in a clear, calm and lucid voice. "Boys, I want Groce Funeral Home to handle my arrangements." Quiet reigned for a time, then the voice, the sad voice, floated in the dark, tragic little cove. "You hear me? I want Groce Funeral home..."

Then we saw a flash inside. A small glow reflected into the front yard and flickered. The end seemed near. Deputies murmured, stood upright. Smith fired into them again. Then the dancing light of bigger flames leaped into the yard. Apparently Smith fed the flames with kerosene Shortly the tear gas ignited and the house burned down around him and in that inferno he died with no further comment.

All the deputies gathered about, shivering and sad.. The Coroner Dr. John Young made a tentative ruling. He said he found signs of one bullet wound in Smith's abdomen.

The Sheriff counted his men. There was he, Mitchell, Crisp, Green, L. Sutphin, Jim Harrison, J.C. Laws, Doug Seay, Jim Lindsey, Clint Burleson, Martin, Hutchins, assistant Chief Deputy Gray Burleson and special deputy Hubert Stockton. All present and accounted for. Finally I stumbled down that rocky road in the dark and away from the frozen, stinking cove that was suddenly so bleak. An ambulance was parked there, disquieting in the dark. I could barely make out the silver sign in the window.

Groce Funeral Home.

It was too late for a Sunday story so I wrote it Sunday night for Monday's paper. The boss, Dick Wynn, called me in. "Several reliable people have called to tell me that Sheriff Clay was in Daytona at the races Saturday night."

"No, that's shit. I was with him all night."

Later at the Coroner'inquest, Dr. Young tried every way to shake my story. "Did someone not shoot him up there that night? Did the Sheriff not tell them to kill him?"

"No sir, the Sheriff was there on that hill. I heard him tell the deputies several times not to kill Mr. Smith."

Exoneration.

Sometime later I checked the death certificate. Death from smoke inhalation.

The Return of The Mountain Lions

The big cats had not been heard nor seen in many a moon. They lived only in legend and campfire and lamplight tales told by the old folks, and those stories were not verifiable. But I heard one in the early 1970s, and I saw it and tracked it, and called Buncombe County Deputy Sheriffs who were with me when it screamed at my home in the mountains. But even so, we told very few people about it because they did not seem to believe it.But more reports came in. I reluctantly published a story about it in my newspaper, The Native Stone, along with photos of its tracks in the mud. There was query from readers who wanted to believe it, and reliable reports of sightings and experiences came in from farmers about stock being killed and mutilated, and then some hunting dogs killed one—a most rare young black panther—at the edge of The Great Smoky Mountains National Park near Cosby, Tennessee. Some wildlife people there, who read The Native Stone, made a photo and called me and The Cocke County (Tennessee) Banner and the Sevierville (Tenn.) News-Record, a Cosby weekly newspaper, and invited us for photos.

We now lead into this with excerpts from our initial story in January 4, 1973 edition of The Native Stone:

A mountain lion had been seen and/or heard in the mountains of Fairview in recent weeks, then one night it carried off a calf from one man's pasture. Several residents of the area, all known to be of good witness, reported various contacts with the big cat. (There was some opinion that the beast may actually be a wolf—one high school girl said she sighted two wolf-like animals a few days ago on Old Fort Road below Sheets' grocery.

My first experience came on a warm late summer night. My family had retired for the night and I had a small fire burning at the edge of the yard. We were living in a mobile home way back on a forested mountain we owned, where we were in the process of building a house. The power company had not yet installed power so we were using kerosene lamps and candles. I had worked late and built the fire to heat coffee and enjoy the night. Then suddenly our dogs began barking and raced out the driveway. In seconds they raced back whining and cowered under the mobile home.

I went in and got a .22 rifle and took it to the end of the house, squatted down and waited.

In a couple of minutes I could dimly see something moving silently in the drive. The flickering fire gleamed in its eyes. I waited until it was hovering over me about five feet away, then I fired once straight up over its head. Whatever it was wheeled, bounded soundlessly twice and faded into the woods.

My wife came out and I told her I thought a deer had come into the yard. But I thought then that a deer's hooves would click on the gravel. The incident was not enough to mention, except to a couple of employes.

Later in the autumn I took two of my sons hunting. We killed a fat ground-hog, took it home and skinned it out. Having little time and wanting only the skin, I threw the carcass into the woods below our home. I was up late that night writing (we had power by then), and in the late hours an eerie wail rose from the woods. Curiously enough, I took it for a wolf. I had never heard a wolf, save in the movies, but I had heard coyotes and wild dogs. It was not one of them.

My wife had expressed a desire from time to time in things occult, so I awakened her and said "You always wanted to hear a ghost. Well, there's one out there in the woods raising hell. Why don't you go out there and interview him for me?" All she did was turn on all the lights and load guns. The eerie wail continued. I had a hound at the time named Underdog, who had an unusual howl of his own. I opened the door and told Underdog to sound off and show the beast up. Underdog bolted into the house and got under the bed.

The following night the sound changed from a wolf-like howl to the throaty wail of a big cat. Again I awakened the wife and bade her listen. The scream went on for a couple of hours as the dogs huddled under the house. I worked late the third night. As I arrived home the animal began screaming again. I loaded a shotgun with buckshot and went out after it. It was a canny animal, screaming from time to time, drawing me ever deeper into the woods. Then it stopped for a few minutes. The next time it sounded it was between me and the house. I went in and called the Sheriff's Department and told the dispatcher there was a critter out there disturbing the peace, and would probably commit more crimes if it hadn't already. As soon as I hung up I heard what seemed to be a cow bawling as the beast screamed.

Shortly deputies Ed Whitaker, Bruce Black and Walt Robinson arrived. As soon as they dismounted their vehicles the screaming began again. Four men with shotguns went into the woods. Robinson, a black man, said he was a city boy and was going to remain one. Whitaker, a mountain boy from Fairview, said he was sure it was a panther and that he had heard it near Reynolds High School a week ago.

Walt Robinson said he had been called to a farm near the school earlier and a woman there told him she had some horses in a barn and they were going wild. He said the woman said the animal had screamed like a banshee. "I'm scared," she told him.

"Not half as scared as I am," Robinson told her, and since there was no law being violated in his eye—sight he hastened away. The night they were at my house I urged them to be careful in the brush since the place was loaded with rattlesnakes. All the deputies then said they could see no violations of the law or U.S. Constitution and got into their cruisers and left. "Rattlesnakes and panthers. To hell with this," Whitaker said.

As the word spread, neighbor Bob Sheets of Rocky Fork Road and his son, Bud, went out one night to hunt it, but found no track nor sign. Bob said he had found some panther tracks years earlier in the snow above nearby Craigtown.

Wade Wright, then a 19-year-old, told us he and his uncle were coon hunting a year earlier in the Fairview mountains when they heard what they thought was a beagle. "Then it sounded like a woman screaming. I didn't see it or look for it. We came out of the woods right then. It scared our dogs worse than us."

Lewis Miller of Old Fort Road said he had heard something like "a loud kid crying" on Rock Quarry Mountain a few days previously. He said he didn't know what it as. "I heard one time they had turned some cougars loose near Chimney Rock to kill off some diseased deer, but you'll have to ask the Forest Service about that. Or it could be something loose from a zoo. For awhile I thought maybe some of the boys who go out west hunting might have brought something back and turned it loose to have a little fun."

Mr. and Mrs. Gary Sales of Taylor Road in Fairview said they had been awakened about three months previously by the screaming. Mrs. Sales said the beast was "crying loudly" on the slope behind their house.

"It's been a pretty good little while since we heard it, but one of our neighbors heard it as late as Saturday morning," she said.

Eighteen-year-old Harriet Shields of Rocky Fork, then a freshman at N.C. State University, said she saw what she thought were wolves on Old Fort Road a few days previously, but she wasn't sure what they were. Their eyes reflected an eerie yellow before they wheeled and ran.

Buster Brown, who lived then on Harris Road in Fairview, said he had been aware of the presence of what he took to be panthers for five or six years. He said he found tracks where it and/or cubs came to drink from a stream near his home "The first track was about as big as a silver dollar, and I thought it was just a big bobcat that had come to drink. Then later I heard screaming and found tracks about four and a half or five inches long. It's a mountain lion, and I think it's a blackish one. I don't think it ought to be killed, but I do want to see it. Bernice Rogers saw it and shot at it about two months ago when he saw its eyes flash," Brown said. He said some dogs had been brought to hunt it but the dogs immediately came off the mountain and wouldn't go back.

Fairview Fire Chief Johnny Henderson told us that he and his wife had both heard it "back when it was warm weather". He said he had been listening the night the dogs had been brought. "Whatever it was got to within 250 feet of my house and pitched a loud fit and walked back and forth, clawing the ground. It was about 11:15 at night. The next day I saw his tracks and they were bigger than any dog I've ever seen. I believe it was a mountain lion," Henderson said.

Rumors spread that something had killed a calf belonging to Howard Franklin of Webb Cove Road. We checked. "Let's put it this way," Franklin told The Native Stone. "I had a calf killed and carried off by something."

He said all he found were smears of blood and the left hind leg from the knee joint down. Something had taken the rest of it."

"Whatever it was came back the next night," Franklin said. "I was harrowing my field after dark and my tractor lights hit it over on the hill. It wasn't afraid of me. The light was too bad to use a rifle, so I got a shotgun with buckshot and pumpkin balls. When I started walking toward it it turned its head and walked sideways away, slowly. I just saw the bulk of it and know that it had yellow eyes, but I can't say that it was a panther. I saw a track, a big round track which didn't resemble a dog or bear track. But I don't know...I never have seen a panther track."

He said the calf had been killed below his barn and carried away, not dragged. "A bobcat can't kill a calf or carry one. A dog won't carry one. I don't know what the thing was, but it was as big as a lion," he said.

Then community interest lessened and the production of The Native Stone took precedence. One Sunday I took my wife and sons hiking in the Fairview mountains. Suddenly we came to a muddy ford in a brook and saw big tracks with noticibly extended claw marks. The tracks seemed to be of one adult cat—about five inches or more—and of two cubs, about the size of silver dollars. I laid down a match book and a cigarette lighter for comparison, made photos and published them in the next edition, then time went on and all again grew quiet.

So we had all these tales and experiences, but the only real evidence were tracks and the utterly convincing stories. Then a call from a deputy sheriff in Cocke County, Tennessee.

"My dogs have killed a painter," he said. "You want to see it?" Damn right. I made haste. The narrative is best now carried by quoting a story in the July 5, 1973 edition of the Sevier County News-Record under the headline

Panther Killed Near Cosby.

"A baby black panther was killed by dogs last week at a home near the Cosby Campground of the Great Smoky Mountains National Park.

"Though some people there suspected the young cat-like creature to be a panther because of its size and weight, no one had ever seen one of these creatures before and its actual identity was a mystery. Its body, packed in ice, was taken to the curator of the Knoxville zoo for positive identification.

"The curator identified the animal, which had such glossy black fur that it almost sparkled in the light, as a baby panther. He said it was quite young and had not cut its entire set of teeth. It measured 34 and ½ inches long and weighed between 35 and 40 pounds.

"Mike Myers, assistant chief ranger of Smoky Park, said 'We have had occasional reports of long-tailed cats, but we have never before had any proof positive that such an animal was living in the park. The possibility had been considered, but all reports have been third, fourth or fifth hand. We could not put much stock in them and we haven't had any reports of livestock missing from farms around the park.

"Identification of this animal is proof enough that panthers are living in the park. Anyhow, there has to be at least one male and one female," Myers chuckled."

That was in 1973. I still live on the mountain. There are now pesky bears. In the snow around my cliffs I can find bobcat tracks. Wild turkey has been transplanted, and there are some wild boar. Several outlanders have moved in with their noises. Often I write late at night, and sometimes I go outside after midnight and cock my ear. Nothing. Yet, I wait and hope and listen…

A Backwoods Snake Cult

Most of the snake cults in the mountains had gone underground, but in the late 1960s and early 1970s they again emerged into public view. In Cocke County, Tennessee, bordering Madison County, a congregation became quite active in various ways until one drank some poison and died. Immediately after the funeral a judge served a restraining order, but the minister, the Rev. Liston Pack, served notice back that they intended to go on with their services.

At the time I was editor/publisher of The Native Stone, a weekly newspaper I had founded here. The Raleigh office of United Press International assigned me to file a story and photos of the next service. At the time I had employed two northern girls fresh out of college, who were willing to work for low pay in order to get newspaper experience. I took them along to Cocke County.

As we wound up the brushy trail to the church, one asked if I thought there was any danger in getting bitten at the services. I walked along warily, replied we would be lucky if we didn't get bitten before we got there.

I introduced myself to the preacher and we chatted about what he did. He was without doubt a religious man. Among other things he told me the members had to be "anointed" by Christ and The Holy Spirit before they would even attempt to pick up snakes.

As the services began, the congregation got danced up to drum, guitar and tamborine music. The Reverend then took rattlesnakes and copperheads out of boxes and in the atmosphere of strange, mystical rhythm began handing out the snakes. (Our photos were later published in a number of religious and Appalachian culture magazines.)

Later I talked more with the Reverend about his abilities. He told me he had only seen one snake he was truly frightened of. He said a man had given him a water moccasin in Knoxville only days before and he had it in a low pen in his yard.

"Something's wrong with it," he said. "It gets to swelling."

I went to take a look. There lay a Queen Cobra about six feet long. I backed away.

"Reverend, don't get so annointed you pick that one up. That's not your everyday fundamentalist Cocke County Christian rattlesnake. That's a sophisticated Hindu royal temple snake. She won't understand what you're doing."

I saw the preacher a couple of years later in Cosby, Tennessee and inquired as to the state of the Cobra. He told me he got more and more uneasy and finally one day he went out the blew it in two with a shotgun.

"I don't know if that was right or not," he said.

Reverend, I believe you did the right thing, I told him.

Much later in Johnson City I chatted with the judge who had restrained them. To hell with it, he said. One of these days I'm going to jail the whole bunch.

Time, A Robber Baron, Stole The Golden Years

They were old then, faintly puzzled about where their lives had gone; perplexed by Time, the robber baron. A retired mountain farmer and his wife, parents of a friend of this writer. The son and daughter-in-law had talked them into leaving their old homeplace in the cove and moving into town with them. They were puzzled about that too, but were too old to put up much of a fight.

And one day in the late 1960s, the writer visited with them. Retirement had closed in about them and I suggested a ride through the country for fresh air and some scenery. As we drove about, we talked about the things that old folks discuss with a younger man and enjoyed the camaraderie. Somehow—none of us later remembered just how, we drove up the road to their old home in the cove.

They had never wanted to leave, really. The cove and its green slopes and tree-topped ridges was their life. Here is where it had all started.

His ancestors had settled here long ago. Here is where his father and his father's father had been born. That ancestor was a stubborn Welshman, and passed a heritage of thrift and industry to his descendants.,

In this one's time he married the daughter of a Yankee, a schoolteacher when she was young and single. She lived with an uncle of her future husband. She thought him a reluctant and frightened suitor and that nothing could come of it. She went off to summer school to further her teaching education. When she returned on the train she found him nervously pacing the station floor with a wedding license in his perspiring hand. While she had been gone, something bigger than his shyness had overwhelmed him.

He won her consent. Before the wedding the honest young man had awkwardly tried to explain to her that sometimes it would be a hard life. The saucy little schoomarm smiled. She knew that better than he did.

Here in this cove is where they started their lives together—a strapping young mountain man and his happy, blushing bride: the girl who said she would be happy to share life with him and had marched staunchly down through the good years and the bad to prove it.

We parked the car below the old cabin and slowly made our way up to it. They were not strong then, enfeebled. Time, the despoiler.

They didn't quite seem to belong her as fully as they once had. A baffling thing, something had broken the skein of their lives. We went into the abandoned house that time had stolen from their lives and I saw them as they had been.

He was a strong man of sterling character, a man who had loved his cove even as he had cursed it and extracted the substance of their lives from the soil of it. His stock had grazed the slopesll and watered at its clear, pullsing streams. He had picked the hard way to make a living, and when he had retired and looked back he begrudged not a whit his choice.

On that afternoon we sauntered into the old house and through the empty rooms.

"Here," she said, "this was our boy's room. In here is where he was born and in here is where he slept. Yessir, up here in this cove is where that boy come up—with plenty of hard work to keep him out of trouble."

In her tender reverie was the proud meaning of her marriage and motherhood.

"Yessir," said the old gentleman," he come outta that bed a'fore sun-up and and he was back in it by dark, and glad to get in it, too."

Time, that great and merciless robber. The son that was born into that room was even then loping into middle age at fast clip.

Then suddenly I was out of the picture. They weren't aware that I was there. They walked from room to room, the old man holding her arm, talking in low tones, plundering about in memory's vineyard.

"Here in this room is where we used to have the dances. We'd have fiddlers and banjo-pickers, and move all the furniture out so we'd have room."

As the thought of one dance paraded across his mind, he smiled a little. His wife remonstrated with a frown. She knew his thoughts. He quit thinking it. It was their secret, not mine.

They walked out into the yard, where there had been grapevines and purple plum trees which furnished them ripe, exploding fruit. Here was the little apple orchard and the cherry groves, the time-lost peaches and pears. Here under these trees they sat and sang their songs in the gloaming. They looked into the musty old cellar, loaded in those days with apples and potatoes, pumpkins and salted meat from slaughtered stock. It was dank and dim now, the shelves rotted and broken.

Here in the yard the fowl had run—chickens and guineas, pea-fowl and ring-neck pheasants which ran tame on the lawn. The old man stopped and stared up at the ridges. Up there is where his foxhounds ran in trumpet-throated baying through crisp autumn nights—of another day when he could chase with them—before Time, the pirate, had taken his youth.

Holding hands they looked at the ridge-tops, at the trees swaying in the suddenly high, howling wind. It was the same song they had heard in the trees through the good times and the bad, the rich seasons and the barren—the life given them then taken way by Time, the thief.

But for this moment they had triumphed—they were pilfering their golden treasures back from Time's vast vault, picking among the shining memories and discarding the dreams that hadn't come true, and carefully fondling small precious incidents long since forgotten.

There, the barn, corn-huskings and mountain friendliness. The building was now an old and sad thing.

Yes, tragedy had drifted over their lives in a dark fog. Over there on a hill, shining like a new coin in the golden afternoon sun, was the church they attended; and the marble-studded ground that held their dead.

But Time purloins all things. The thief had favored them, with stealthy fingers had taken the grief.

They looked at each other and at their past collapsed around them and considered all that had been. You can't go home again? Ah, perhaps one time is allowed.

I looked at my watch. The relentless rogue had stolen the hour. I reluctantly cleared my throat and reminded them it was getting late. It was a sacrilegious thing I did. The spell was broken. They had to return from those distant meadows of reminiscence.

We walked slowly back to the car in the lengthening shadows. They were hushed and reverent, as if they had seen something others would not see and they would never see again. Behind us the dreams returned to their own time. There was only the sagging old house, empty and waiting for the great thief's covetous touch.

The ghosts were gone, gone, gone with the full grapes and bursting plums, the time-lost fiddle skirls and the baying hounds, gone with all the things of other, brighter years. The old man and woman and I got into the car. To the west slipped the sun—brother of Time, the great Thief—taking another of our days and skulking silently away from us all.

83-Year Old Ex-Klondike Prospector's Shootout With Robbers In West Buncombe

✦

The early 1960s

Three would-be robbers in their early 20s saw their plot to rob an 83-year-old ex-Klondike sourdough go awry Thursday night when they entered his rude cabin in Leicester under the pretext of seeking water for their car. Tony Lunsford had gone to bed about 8 p.m. when he was awakened by a banging on his door and a man's voice saying he was from the nearby Sandy Mush community and his radiator had gone dry.

The old prospector arose, lit a kerosene lamp, slipped a pistol into his pocket and opened the door. The three men rushed him and shoved him onto the floor in a corner. He then began shooting and they fled on through the shack and dove out a back window, leaving a trail of blood. He said one of them was right up against him when he began firing. Lunsford said he felt he was still alive because of his lifelong habit of keeping a pistol handy in his isolated cabin.

(Lunsford, who had gone to the Klondike to mine gold from 1903-1916, was not the average naïve farmer. He had those years of developing a strong frontier intuition in Alaska's backland goldfields, and here a week or so earlier a neighbor, William Lane Hyatt, 68, had been shot and robbed as he worked in his garden and was now in a hospital, where he died a few days earlier; and also a few days earlier a nearby shopkeeper, Mrs E.C. Harris had been robbed of some $2,000 by a masked gunman as she got out of her car in her driveway.)

He was struck above the eye by some object, but he did not know what it was. He had only a bruise. In addition to the man he knew was wounded, Lunsford said he was sure his bullets hit at least one other. A pool of blood was found in that room and other bloodstains beside his bed.

He could not tell what kind of car the men were driving. When they drove away, he went to the house of Mr. and Mrs. James Reeves, who called the Sheriff's Department. A deputy called me and I went to the scene. Roadblocks were already being set up by the department and the State Highway Patrol.

At the scene, Chief Investigator Flake Moffit and Deputy C.O. Capps were gathering evidence. When the suspects dove out a back window, they left behind a cap, a package of cigarettes and a .22 calibre target pistol. Moffit said their wounds must have been serious because of the amount of blood on the ground. A fingerprint specialist was called and an all-points bulletin was broadcast. Asheville city police were brought into the area for roadblocks as far as jurisdiction would permit.

I drove to the Sheriff's Department and called the editor and told him this was going to be an all-night search. Inside an hour two calls came in from hospitals in the Piedmont. Wounded men were checking in. I rode first to Maiden with deputy Herb Deweese and a couple of others. The suspect there was seriously wounded and that Police Department posted a guard. We found the other in another town and followed the same procedure. This suspect told us where to find the third man.

He was a young man whose home was in a nearby community. We found him trembling in bed, and he began crying. Without further ado he made a confession sitting on his bed, being hugged by his mother, and right there wrapped the case up for these officers. It was in the days before Miranda.

The one ironic statement he said that remains in memory. "I'm glad we didn't hurt that old man."

Herb shook his head and laughed. "Son, just be glad that old man didn't kill all of you."

The Chief of Police Wore Diapers

✦

2002

The Woodfin Chief of Police, highly glorified in the local media for a week, turns out to have admitted in an SBI investigation that he is queer and had engaged in "diaper"parties with some other officers in out-of-town motels, where they dressed in diapers and gave each other enemas while they masturbated.

Chief Peter Bradley, a resident of Biltmore Forest and a member of—wouldn't you know it?—All Souls Episcopal Cathedral (Better known as Oral Souls Lesbyterian Church), raised controversy that week of glory when he made several accusations against newly elected Woodfin Mayor Homer Hunni-cutt of various types of malfeasance, including fixing traffic tickets and encourag-ing citizens to assault members of the Woodfin Police Department.

Hunnicutt, who admitted to this editor that he was rendered almost speech-less by the sudden blasts in that high yellow whore of a daily newspaper and the gaudy whore of journalism, WLOS-TV.

They slashed at Hunnicutt, and lauded Mr. Clean, Chief Bradley, without ever checking him or his references out. As it turned out, Bradley's so-called expe-rience with some local law-enforcement agencies was not as "glowing" as that jerk who writes for the Citizen-Times, John Boyle, made it out to be.

The admission about his "bi-sexuality" as he called it, surfaced during a State Bureau of Investigation inquiry into some criminal allegations at the local Department of Motor Vehicle in the year 2000,which involved Bradley, who was employed there at the time.

(An anonymous letter to Bradley a couple of years ago was curiously entered in the SBI investigation, and reports were made, including his admission. That letter to Bradley and a couple of SBI reports signed by the bureau's assistant director, are found on pages 4-5 of that week's Independent Torch)

Coincidentally, they also grew out of a friend's domestic court case involving child-custody, at which time allegations of the diaper caper were raised. At that time rumors about Bradley's involvement in those perverted activities were fairly widespread, When they reached our desk that year the political aspects were minimal so we left it alone. However, Bradley's political activities became blatant and his own behavior threw the matter into the public arena.

In the course of that domestic case, and another involving some Asheville police matters, a journal purportedly kept by one of the participants was obtained by one of the wives. One person involved in that earlier civil trial said that the journal indicated that the participants would order diapers from some company, then go out of town—even as far as a Georgia city—where they would don the diapers and give enemas to each other. Police officers were involved.

The keeper of the journal then duly noted how the tube was inserted into a rectum, the fluid entering and how long it took for that participant to "get a hard-on". There is also said to be descriptions of how the fecal material emerged and smeared into the diaper.

Bradley, although reputedly wealthy and living in the swank Biltmore Forest area, has long been known as a "wannabe cop". One Biltmore Forest resident remembers that as a boy of seven or eight, his parents bought him small police uniforms and let him "direct traffic" on the town streets.

Bradley's application for the job included a long list of glowing law-enforcement experience, most of which local lawmen have scoffed at A friend of this editor, a long-time member of Alcoholics Anonymous, recalls making calls on Bradley's father, a wealthy psychiatrist before his death. He recalls the father as being "far gone" and observed that it was no wonder Peter Bradley grew up into such a sad state.

His membership in Oral Souls Lesbyterian Church certainly could not have helped him grow in a different direction. After the priest Todd Donatelli (The Wop-at-the-Top) came there, I was writing extensively about the perversions said to be practiced by the sodomites there. One in particular I mentioned was what they called the "Golden Shower", where they urinated in each other's faces. At coffee hour a smirking Donatelli said "Why Lewis, even straight people do that."

I said "That ain't straight, your holiness."

After Bradley was hired Mayor Hunnicutt was made aware of the new chief's rumored twisted sex proclivities. He told The Independent Torch that the hair stood up on the back of his neck.

"I could just see him arresting some young boy and patting him down in a search and lingering too long on his genitals. That would be one hell of a lawsuit for Woodfin, and we're broke now" Mayor Hunnicutt said.

Hunnicutt was accused of being one of the "good old boys" and telling a cop he could fix tickets as fast as he could write them.

Homer Hunnicutt is not one of the "good old boys". Woodfin is not sophisticated enough to develop any good old boys. But he does participate in the town's politics, where they sometimes tell lies on each other, curse the opposing party etc. But some of them said they never lied like the new Chief of Police.

The Mayor couldn't fix traffic tickets if he wanted to. Every ticket written must have a copy sent to the court system, and only the office of the District Attorney can dispose of them.

As for encouraging citizens to assault officers, he had to giggle. "We got some pretty tough lads in the police department," he said. "I wouldn't encourage anybody to mess with them." He said he did not feel it was the Woodfin Police Department's job to get on the bridge over the interstate and try to clock speeders.

"We promised the citizens here protection in their homes, and we ought to be patrolling regularly. I don't want to engage in any other debate with the Chief."

. Before we add perspective on the Woodfin Police Chief matter, let us try to clear up some inaccuracies the local media here has propounded, which has resulted in major confusion. Then later in this piece, we shall note how far afield that dumb little twit at WLOS and the pretentious jerk at the daily newspaper have gone.

To begin, District Attorney Ron Moore was not my source for the supposedly classified State Bureau of Investigation files on Pete Bradley. I was the first to release the documents, which myself and several others had since some time in the year 2000. That material had its beginnings after a intra-agency fight at the local Department of Motor Vehicles, where Bradley worked at the time.

If you will refer to the anonymous letter to Bradley, and if you have any familiarity with bureaucratic politics and jealousies, you should be able to detect the stab in the back to Bradley. (So you'll know, there is some ongoing state interest in this matter. Everyone concerned, including state investigators, have voiced the desire to let this inconsequential matter at DMV dwindle away.)

Those documents were made available to me then but since it was such a picayune matter and involved only bureaucratic politics and I let it go. My thrust then, as it is this year, is partisan political tactics at the local level and at most that material then concerned only the normal bureaucratic pettiness.

The Independent Torch was the first channel into public consciousness of the bad history of the suspended Woodfin Police Chief Bradley. Let us reiterate here that District Attorney Ron Moore did not leak anything to us. We had those documents, and some others, for a couple of years. Others have also been in possession of the same documents for that length of time, but we did receive three different copies in the mail from other sources as this controversy developed. We assume none were from Ron Moore, since he and I have been at odds for several years over his light treatment of Democratic political activist Bill Oglesby, who had been charged with pulling a pistol on some deputy sheriffs. Those in the know found the information amusing and only of minimal interest until Pete Bradley, in his own bumbling fashion, blew it out into the open.

We reiterate, the genesis of the Woodfin controversy is found in that SBI investigation into allegations of wrong-doing at the local office of the Department of Motor Vehicles a couple of years ago where Pete Bradley was then employed, and it spun out of that low-level bureaucratic backstabbing hinted at in the anonymous letter to Bradley which was in the SBI files, and whose author—a fellow DMV employe—is suspected, if not actually known.

We shall get to some of this later in this story. The accusation against the DA which was presented by that dumb twit at WLOS, and which had most people with an investigative background groaning in embarrassment for her. (She and Boyle were doing their best to uncover the source of the leak when they should know that their very profession demands they protect sources in such matters, and actually exploit them. It is probably because Bradley is queer—both news outlets have for years tried to protect and encourage the encroachment of queers into Asheville's public and civic life.

She was buttressed by that dumb shit at The Asheville Citizen Times, John Boyle, who seems to be operating under the same professional fantasy (but nobody can figure out what the delusion is for either of them Neither is from here, have no background in the situation or people involved, so they go on with their feeble scripts which they apparently learned from sit-coms).

Ron Moore is up for reelection this year, and by the nature of the approach of these media geniuses, we assume it to be political and directed against the DA. Whatever else Moore has to answer for—and we assume it is plenty—he does not have to answer for leaking this report to us. We think he is working under professional ethical constraints which would forbid it. Nor do we suspect his staff.)

We suggested last week that we would have more names of queer law enforcement personnel. However, our source with an out-of-town journal has not come through, so we are reasonably certain of only one name, a man who was fired by Sheriff Bobby Medford, probably for such activities. That man then went to work at Asheville Police Department, where he presumably coupled up with Pete

Bradley, then employed as an officer by APD. Our reliable informants identify him as James Gajdik, who now lives at 1126 Hardy Circle in Dallas, Georgia.

We must now grow a bit vague, but we did learn that Bradley brought his perversions with him from DMV and somehow these two—and other officers, we presume, began doing the diaper number, among other variations.

Bear in mind that what we are now talking about is not connected with the DMV fight.

This new officer was the one who kept the journal with the graphic descriptions of enema tube insertions and baby-like cries and moans as the diapers were changed. An informant tells us that notations in the journals also indicated—in an almost clinical fashion—whether or not the insertee achieved an erection, or in the language of the journal, "a hard-on".

Gadjik was married to a woman cop at APD. For reasons not known to us—but suspected—that marriage came down to a bitter end and wound up in court. (Do not confuse this domestic case with one we have published in this edition where Bradley took his wife to court on a domestic violence charge for threatening to kill him with a pair of scissors and a loaded pistol).

Back to the original domestic case. Testimony revealed the perversions of these officers in some detail, including Bradley's major role. The first hint came to me that year as I was having lunch with one of the female lawyers in the case and her husband, a former Captain who was my supervisor when I was a narcotics officer with former Sheriff Buck Lyda's first dope squad. I mention this simply to say I trust their veracity.

But all it was good for then was the normal irreverent and cynical laughter we often affected. However, there were documents that Ron Moore would have no knowledge of, since this all came out in civil court. Documents from that matter as well as the DMV case were fanned all about and there was much gossip and ribald laughter in law enforcement circles. (The Pete Bradley history is known widely among cops in WNC.) We go into this to show how inept these news people are in "investigating" such matters.

We will go aside here for the moment. Bradley revealed at the last Woodfin meeting that many of the cops at Asheville Police Department are queer. In our files we have incidents which will bear that out. In some stories we published more than a year ago we noted some incidents.

An Asheville attorney was arrested in a prostitution sting on Lexington Avenue after he solicited an undercover policewoman for oral sex. A female cop of our acquaintence told us he would have better luck trying to get a blow-job off some of the male officers who would have accommodated him regularly.

In that story we related many instances from a court record of a civil trial of some police officers who had been fired for some slight offenses when such sexual escapades were going on with officers who had not been fired.

In one instance two drunk lesbian cops were at a party of the Fraternal Order of Police and were busy going down on each other on the hood of a cruiser., but other lodge members were so drunk they didn't know or care.

Other more interesting sidelights: a Baptist minister was arrested in a prostitution sting at the same time ten cops took a whore to the FOP lodge and went about gang-banging a pathetic drug-ridden whore on the pool table. No disciplinary action was taken against them. Still another top officer's wife, a cop herself, grew so tired of his infidelities that she began trying to screw every officer on the force, as well as any civilian who wanted it.(That officer went to a friend of mine and asked if he had been screwing his wife. "Not yet,", he answered We also published the lengthy criminal record of Asheville Police Chief Will Annarino's lesbian sister.

In this atmosphere, and out of the queer atmosphere of All Souls Cathedral, emerges the very unstable wanna-be cop Pete Bradley, one of the quality white folks who live in the swanky Biltmore Forest suburb.

Apparently he felt right at home because the diaper-enema parties proceeded apace and officers went to various out-of-town motels and hotels.

(We should probably note that many people who just have to have something to say insist that what people do in the their own little private universe (or universe of privates, if you will) should not concern other people. The hell it shouldn't. We've had a world-wide epidemic of AIDS spread in this fashion. The exact number of those affected is kept secret, but why? Because it's nobody business?

That leads us back to Pete Bradley, whose defense consists of pointing his finger at Mayor Homer Hunnicutt and so far as the media is concerned, has been successful at making the Mayor out to be an uneducated dummy.

Now is a good time to point out Bradley's education. His resume points out that he is a graduate of Newfound School. That's another thing he shouldn't have confessed to. The Newfound School was a so-called private, progressive school on Grove Street founded in the 1970s by a couple of uppity women, if memory serves. I lectured on writing there several times.

It was a formless "school" of wealthy junior and senior high school age children,. One of the teachers was, if memory serves, John Agar, a fuzzy-liberal son-in-law of the late Congressman Jamie Clarke whose wealth came from converting Farmer's Federation (a co-op) funds to his own use.

All I could see at Newfound School was unruly, spoiled children who were constantly pumped up with condescending flattery by fawning teachers. That fits in perfectly with the rest of Bradley's biography.

In this edition we have published the felony law, Crime Against Nature, which might apply here. At least in view of the confessions Bradley has already made about the diaper caper, he should be asked if there was any penetration by a penis as well as having an enema nozzle shoved up their anus. If so, felony.

For the nonce, let us go to the sophomoric situation which got Mayor Homer Hunnicutt involved. It began as a matter of hasslement between Hunnicut who had not yet assumed office and one of the Woodfin officers, who also knew better.

Apparently the cop had been guilty of overzealousness with town motorists. Hunnicut, of the old populist breed was on the side of the citizen and told the cop he could fix more tickets than the cop could write.

The cop knew that nobody in town government can "fix' tickets, and Hunnicutt knew that too. They were merely engaged in a squabble between boars. The only people who apparently did not know it was a fake threat was those two dimwits in the media, and from coverage since the meeting, they still don't realize it—or they are keeping it alive to favor Bradley.

But Bradley is dead as far as a law-enforcement career is concerned. He was suspended but still makes statements indicating the people of Woodfin will be tolerant of this mess.

But it is like that old Cherokee saying. Bradley is snakebit and going to die.

Small game get struck by a rattlesnake and continue hurriedly on down the trail. Then they grow drowsy and fall. And here comes the rattler, ready to dine.

Asheville Police Corruption

The Asheville Police Department is perhaps the most critical department in local government, but for decades interested and knowledgable citizens have looked on with despair, knowing it to be a laughing stock.

The Asheville Police Department has had a terrible reputation for years for corruption of all sorts, now finds itself slipping even further in public esteem—and ridicule—with one more dumb proposal of its incompetent and stupid Chief of Police Will Annarino, whose latest rationale about police pay verges on retardation.

For those not familiar, Annarino recently proposed paying new recruits with college degrees more than veteran cops with the same degrees. Those officers appealed to the city manager, Westbrook, who upheld Annarino, as everyone expected, then appealed to the Civil Service Board, which also upheld Annarino. The next move will likely be appealed to the court.

I have covered and otherwise been associated with APD for 40 years this year. I went to work for The Asheville Citizen-Times in 1961, and after a few weeks on what was called the public service beat, I was assigned to police and courts.

In the ten years I was at the newspaper, I covered mostly police and courts and politics in Buncombe and other WNC counties. I know whereof I speak. Having had a wild youth which resulted in fights with cops, I had more than a passing familiarity with their attitudes, aptitudes and propensities.

However, experience with APD, which was then and is now a laughing stock among other law enforcement agencies in WNC, gave me a view of such dimension that I lost much respect for them, at least those at the top.

That is not to say there has not been some remarkably honest officers, whose outrage at what they witnessed day to day was dampened by the need to stay on locally in their chosen profession. I knew many fine officers, some who stayed on until retirement; many who got disgusted and left, many who were crooked bagmen, some brutal ones and some unethical men who had no business wearing the badge

(An amusing aside. The Chief of Police in my early time was A.R. "Pitt" Sluder. He had assigned a new recruit to a veteran officer to take out and break

177

in. I was in the Chief's office one day a couple of months later when he summoned the veteran in.

"Does the new man know anything?" he asked.

'Hell chief, he don't even suspect anything," the officer said.

Chief Sluder was himself a master of malaproppery. One day I crossed Pack Square on my way to the Courthouse and saw a crowd gathered about a disturbance involving several policemen in front of Peterson's Grill on Pack Square. I went on to the Courthouse, and returning stopped by Pitt's office to ask about it.

"Oh, we first thought he had gone berkshire but it turned out he was having an Appalachian fit.")

That was the man at the top then In the early days I was privy to conversations and memories of the older officers who told me corruption was rife and it had always been that way in this century. Much of the small time corruption and bribery was not only condoned by the political leaders, but encouraged and put to use for political purposes.

. Speaking of advanced college degrees in reference to the progress and tradition of corruption in the Asheville Police Department, we will refer you to some research done by a candidate for a masters degree in the early 1970s.

The following excerpts were lifted from a thesis presented to the faculty of the Department of Political Science at the University of North Carolina at Chapel Hill in partial fulfillment of the requirements for the degree of Master of Public Administration.

The thesis was presented by Julian Branson Prosser Jr. in July of 1972 and was entitled "Two City Managers In Asheville, N.C.: Politics, Administration and Policy Formulation."

:Page 27: "In addition to the influence of city employees during election times, traditional methods of granting favors were utilized by the Machine. Ticket fixing and favors by police for loyal supporters of the Party were routine. Charges have been made that gambling, prostitution and bootlegging activities were allowed to exist if payoffs were made to the proper persons. The police court, manned by Machine supporters, became known as a place where drunk driving charges would be easily hidden for the proper price. As do most political machines, the Asheville Democratic Machine relied heavily on ethnic and racial groups for its core support. Four black wards could be delivered almost 9 to 1 for administration candidates. This support combined with the influence of municipal employees provided an almost unstoppable combination. Administration forces are said to have entered each election with 5,000 votes."

In talking with older and retired cops in the years following the replacement of the old Asheville Police Court by the District Court system, I was told that some fixing could be done at that level, but some cops had wised up and began making their own deals for bribes either on the spot or later. That is said to still exist somewhat.

One deal became legendary. A cop wrote a ticket then accepted a $25 bribe. God! He took a check. The canceled check was then presented to authorities, and the officer was fired. Savvy cops, some of them on the take themselves, laughed at the idea of taking a check.

To go back further, at one time almost everyone on APD belonged to the Ku Klux Klan. In some of our editions we reproduced two photos of Asheville cops serving as honor guard and pallbearers at a Klan funeral for a Klansman who was also a cop.

APD was feared by black citizens, as were most police departments in other days. One of the earliest local incidents on record was the lynching of a black named Will Harris, the story of whom was featured in one of Tom Wolfe's short stories Child By Tiger. Harris came here to work at odd jobs and was a veteran of a war, probably World War I. He had been shoved around some by policemen, but his breaking point came over a woman, so I was told by the late Jesse Ray, a black undertaker.

Harris got a high-powered rifle and walked up Biltmore Avenue shooting. One of the people he shot was a cop who had taken cover behind a power pole. The bullet went through the pole and killed the officer.

Harris escaped and a manhunt began culminating in his shooting death in the south end of the county. His mutilated body was put on display in the window of a funeral home on Pack Square. While Harris was held to have deserved what he got, the black community seethed for years.

In my own time, I walked into the police station in the early 1960s and went to where Detective H.F. "Blondie" Holland was interrogating a black for some small crime. Holland slapped the black out of his chair several times until he got a confession. I reported that to my editor at the time. He told me to leave it alone, lest we endanger our relations with the police. In those days such incidents were fairly commonplace and were generally overlooked.

Some black areas lived in uneasy truce with the police. In those years Water Street was a hive of gambling joints, prostitution, bootleggers, shot-houses etc.

I once asked Pitt Sluder, since it was so visible there, why the police didn't do anything about it. His answer was imminently practical: "That's the biggest part of their economy," he said. "If we come down too hard, they'll steal the town blind." I learned later that members of the so-called vice squad received weekly payoffs from the black operators..

A few years ago I was doing some undercover work for a federal law enforcement agency here. One of the APD detectives was allegedly stationed on The Block at the corner of Eagle and Market streets every Friday. Gamblers would drive up and hand him their payoff, which he would tuck into his sock.

The Federal team had parked a van on Biltmore Avenue, from where we could shoot photos of the action a block away. Federal interest came from a racketeering standpoint. However, so many dope deals went down in front of us that the bag man was blocked from the lens. Those local dope deals were not under Federal jurisdiction, so we made the photos available to the police and state DA at the time. Nothing was ever done. A couple of those Federal agents retired here, and are still around in case anyone needs to verify.

There is the sleazy case of former Police Chief Gerald Beavers, who held the job before Annarino. Beavers was the Police Chief in Louisville when the former city manager hired him. Craziness soon set in. He reportedly began an affair with a female officer. Our sources are good. It happened that they were shacked up in a Tunnel Road motel on the night that the city's dope squad had set up surveillance there with a video camera. They did not know the Chief was there, and as far as can be told, got no footage of him. But a private eye hired by Beaver's wife did.

But he learned of them being there and disbanded the dope squad. The guilty flee when no man pursueth.

All the while Beavers was beating his wife with some regularity;. The Independent Torch got hold of his separation records and printed them. That got him fired. From here he went to Kansas as a police chief. More information was coming out by then.

It was toikd by officers here that Beaver's dope squad in Louisville had all been indicted for dealing, etc.

I had a call from Kansas detectives who wanted to see my files. I agreed. and they came all the way from Wichita to copy my investigative files and copies of The Torch.

There's enough recent anecdotal material to confirm suspicions of Asheville Police Department being out of control. One joke among officers was that the department has hired more queers and dykes than go to Oral Souls Lesbyterian Church.

Not too long ago an Asheville lawyer was arrested in two separate prostitute stings. The last one was comic opera. The lawyer pulled up to an undercover hooker on the street and asked for the price of a blow job. Then he saw the trap and fled, but he was caught, televised, tried and got fined etc.

But the amusing and most telling thing was said to us by a female officer. "Hell, he can get some of the male officers over here for that," she said.

Speaking of which: I had a small print shop on Pritchard Park in the early 1980s. As I left late one night, a police car was parked behind me and the officer's head was in another car giving a babe a long kiss and caress of the breasts. The officer was female. Later her female companion was shot and killed in their bedroom after a party. It was ruled accidental during a suicide attempt.

Then in a Federal suit filed and later dismissed, one deposition stated that at a drunken party at the Fraternal Order of Police Lodge, two lesbian officers were on the hood of a car doing their dyke number.

Speaking of the lodge, only a few years ago some publicity accrued from ten officers gangbanging one of the local prostitutes on a pool table at the FOP lodge. While Annarino likes to say that no cover-ups are condoned at APD, those names were never released. But some wives later got them anyway and fanned them around.

Another hilarious script of poetic justice came about that time. One cop had been running around on his beautiful wife, who was also a cop. Then, officers said, she retaliated by screwing anybody who wanted it. That officer went berserk (or berkshire, as Pitt Sluder would say) and went around trying to find out who had accommodated her. A guy I know told me the officer had approached him in rage and asked if he had screwed the darling. Unintimidated, my friend replied "Not yet..I'm waiting on my time."

Another guy (as if feeding a cue later to Bill Clinton) said that while he "did not have sex with that woman", or intercourse, he got what he needed anyway.

Even more to Annarino's discredit, recently an officer allegedly beat up a broken down homeless man. There may or may not have been an investigation. Then a teen-age girl and her boyfriend get drunk at a party at an officer's house, and the girl is killed in an accident later that night.

I can point out some experiences with some of the cops still there. At the little print shop on Pritchard Park I printed a monthly political journal called Overtones, and in one edition I called the public's attention to some gambling operations.

Either stupid or naïve, a young cop named Jon Kirkpatrick wrote a letter to me saying that was a fabrication and that there was no gambling here.

I went to a bookmaker I knew on the block, then to one I knew on South Lexington and one on Flint Street and got them to give me some old lottery and baseball tickets, which I reprinted the following week in Overtones. I heard no more from Kirkpatrick about that. Later he somehow got promoted.

Following that incident, I parked my car on the street near my shop with the right rear wheel about 2 inches on the curb. Patrolman David Shroat gave me a $5 ticket. I took it to then Chief Fred Hensley and said "Damn, man. Is this all this clown can get me for?" Fred called Shroat in. The ticket was cancelled. (I don't mind fixing one when it favors me.)

In my time here in recent years, I've been subjected to all kinds of petty harassment from this kind of shithead on APD. One of the most telling ones: I returned from eating one night and found that some of the street people had urinated in my doorway. They were across the street. I went to them and asked who had done it. One big guy said "For the sake of argument, I did. What do you want to do about it?"

I busted his nose for it and the brawl began. One got me from behind with a 2X4 and laid me out. They beat and kicked and ran. When I came to I staggered to the police station and reported it to Captain Bob Branson, who also was no big fan of mine. He smiled and said they could do nothing. (Later Lt. Hoot Gibson, who was a friend of mine, identified the guy with the board.)

I saw the DA of the time, Ron Brown, at a restaurant in a day or so and told him about it. He was with his blonde girlfriend, whom his wife didn't know about, so I presume for the blonde's benefit he said "Well, if you kill the guy I'll try you for murder."

No kidding? I printed that exchange in Overtones.I understand his wife read it. Shortly the DA suffered a heart attack.. A friend in the ambulance service called me to say they were on the way to the hospital with him A bit later, that he was dead.

"Do you hear these tears falling?" I asked. "I will put on a black armband and go into mourning immediately." (His wife was a lady to the core. At the funeral, she invited the slut to sit with the family.")

And shortly the guy who had hit me with the 2X4 died of natural causes also. Again I wept.

Safe and secure in downtown Asheville in the sure and certain knowledge that APD is going to be watching out for me. Or watching me. More recently, as I wrote about the queers and dykes at Oral Souls Lesbyterian Church, the Wop-at-the-Top, Rev. Donatelli felt extreme danger from this notorious terrorist Lewis Green,. who had donned a latex glove and gave the finger to one of the more pathetic queers who had been bugging me. Donatelli went to Annarino, who agreed to let Detective Ross Dillingham stake me out at services. I spotted him the first day, followed him off the grounds and jumped his dumb ass. (His father had been in APD also but he got fired for stealing all the money in the FOP treasury. Just another one of those occurrences which make life so amusing at APD. Ross Dillingham is no longer with APD. He is selling real estate, we are told.)

Then Donatelli signed a year's contract with the emotional wreck of a female cop to keep me under surveillance during services. Smart! I knew her. Besides, some insiders at the church had told me about the church's deal with the cops. Once I thought that I should suggest to her, knowing her domestic and emotional problems, that she go up to the altar or rail and pray. Then I thought better. Not here. She doesn't deserve what comes from the accursed and wicked spiritual life at Oral Souls.).

A bit later that dumb shit Donatelli excommunicated me (not in actuality), had the council to ban me from the church grounds, and had four police cruisers down there to head me off in case I came.

(Four cruisers for little old me? I glowed. This was something like the old days when it took that many...

This is all street theater for Donatelli and Annarino. A big show. Annarino knows me better than that.. He also knows I'm a special deputy on the Sheriff's Department anti-terrorism squad.

Oral Souls will answer later for that piece of shit.

As I understand it, Annarino will become an issue in the upcoming City Council election. That was cinched recently when he was caught allowing certain evidence to be destroyed, and drew harsh publicity for that.

"We don't cover things up here," Annarino said, to laughter echoing all about the city.

Incident Report
The Jailed Whore

Sheriff Buck Lyda was in the throes of paranoia again. He had hired the former U.S. Marshal Max Wilson as his chief deputy, mainly because Max was a lifelong Republican and helped to shore up Republican support in the election. Now he began to see Max as a threat: he told several people that Max was going to run against him in the next election, which was more than three years away.

Buck met me for dinner one evening and told me that he had a statement from a whore in jail that in exchange for sex she had received money and drugs from Max for years when he was Marshal. I knew this to be a lie. I had done undercover work for the Marshal's service during the time Max was it and knew there was no way for that to be true. I had also known Max on a personal level for many years and the accusation was out of the question. You could always tell when Buck was crazy by his voice and eyes.

He told me we were going to set Max up that night by taking the girl from jail and having her call Max to meet her. I was to be part of the ambush by taking photos of the transaction. The meeting was to take place in the parking lot of the Deaverview Housing Project. I was later briefed by another deputy, who also told me that Max kept his pistol in an ankle holster. "If he bends over, Lewis, shoot him."

Wow! I kept my cool but I was busy thinking of what I would testify at any inquest. I would say that I always got nervous in shoot-outs and had accidentally shot the wrong man.

So we got the girl and went to the parking lot. She was set free so she could go to some apartment and call Max. (That was in the 1980s and she's not back yet.)

After a couple of hours, the lead deputy gave it up and we drove around for a couple of hours. Finally he asked me "Lewis, what are we going to do about the girl?"

"The whore is not my responsibility," I said. "My job is to kill the Chief Deputy."

John F. Kennedy, The Plagiarist

The following was written by Lewis W. Green and published in The Asheville Times on December 7, 1965. It has been republished in The Independent Torch. While the mainstream media has been highly critical of the plagiarisms of Sen. Joe Biden and others in Washington in recent years, none have disclosed this blatant theft of the work of an obscure Lebanese poet who later achieved fame as the author of The Prophet.

There are two chief voices which rise above the clamor to guide the affairs of men. One sounds from the beauty of the soul; the other from earthier considerations.

Poets and politicians—from the pen of one may spring the purpose of the other. The hand that lights the torch may not be the one that slings it burning down the darkened pathways of human endeavors.

And flaming words of an article written in Arabic fifty years ago by a Lebanese poet glow along the paths of our time.

Kahlil Gibran, now famous for his **The Prophet**, a forty-year perennial best selling collection of poetry and essays, wrote an article for an obscure publication when his people were struggling to break free of an oppressive political and religious feudal system.

Writing for the Middle East of that time, he couldn't have known he was also writing for a particularly poignant time of change in the United States.

In part he said, "There are in the Middle East today two challenging ideas, old the new. The old ideas will vanish because they are weak and exhausted...

Addressing himself to his people of that time, Gibran advised "Ask not what your country can do for you, but what you can do for y our country..."

In that obscure publication, the article was entitled "The New Frontier".

From the midnight reflections of a young poet, an idea was flung down the decades and stolen in high-noon urgency by a young Massachusetts politician in his first State of the Union message in 1960.

Francis Stevens

About Francis Stevens for a reading at All Souls Episcopal Church in 1991. Francis was a tattered and inarticulate old man who came for the services for many years, and who was struck and killed by a car at Oteen.

The title of this piece on Francis Stevens shall come at the end. Some kind of explanation of Francis shall come at the end. Forgiveness shall come at the end. But before we go to those invisible spiritual paradoxes, let us take up the visible.

Francis always stood just without the gates, in the Baptistery usually, entering to take communion. It is a fact that sometimes he did not smell good. Some people accepted him anyway, some faked acceptance and others did not. Many seemed oblivious. Yet there he was.

What to make of Francis? We made him whatever we needed. Perhaps some had made the wrong thing of him, busy contriving easy symbols, using them to leap to easy conclusions, from whence he may be dismissed. Some made him a homeless ragamuffin. Other made him a wino and derelict. He was made out to be retarded or brain damaged. To all he seemed to be a pitiful wreck, an old, broken tatterdemalion.

He was none of the above. When he finally passed, he had a genuine funeral in a socially acceptable grave in a reputable cemetery. There were authentic, substantial mourners. He had a respectable obituary in which survivors were listed, if you please. He had a home in Oteen. A church membership was named. Did you notice that it was not All Souls Episcopal? It was a Catholic church. Had they failed some test? Was he ours after all?

I have seen Francis about for a long time. I have seen Francis at the flea market. I have seen him on Lexington Avenue doddering about. I have seen Francis at the library reading. Francis reading?

Yes, what can be made of Francis? Not how we come to understand and explain Francis, that strange symbolic figure tottering among us. We could say piously there but for the grace of God…(Well, isn't that a precious little conceit? Perhaps God can yet arrange that.)

Despite all, he was not a practical problem. He posed no problems except for the conscience. The visible Frances caused no trouble. It is simple to make people what they are not. Yet in the privacy of our own spiritual understanding they become what we say they are. I make much of Francis even as I argue with myself. Going to the altar each Sunday I passed Francis back there and nodded to him. He didn't need my compassion. He was not taking, he was giving. He gave his weekly dime to the usher's plate He offered guarded, shy friendship to those who would take it and return it.. Did we not need him?

Let us now move to the invisible spiritual realms. I have long been a student of weird and heretical theologies, pondering over many an ancient and outlandish tome. Through many a long and curious trek, I have arrived at one definite and immutable spiritual truth.

Whatever goes around comes around. (Usually at the most inconvenient times and with a thousand fold increase in mass and velocity.) But how to determine at any given moment whether it is going around or coming around? Is this a consequence? Or will it bring consequences? Or if you must, here in this Christian setting, do unto others as you would have them do unto you. Which arouses a mystical premise…will you pardon my restless, midnight questions about the likes of Francis. That mystical premise suggests that spiritual truths are in direct contradiction to conscious perceptions. It is like the printing business—all backward, upside down and reversed, making no sense at all until the final impression is laid, at which point it all takes shape and we may read with understanding.

Now we see through the glass darkly, then we shall see…or more to the point, the last shall come first and vice versa and you may add many etceteras here.

In the ancient Hebrew mystical and magical works called Kabbalah, some interesting scriptural concepts are advanced. For instance, it was once believed that Satan was an agent of God and was said to be sent by God to tempt or test the human soul. That belief changed as the centuries went by, but most poets and seers are still in agreement that God uses certain abstracts as agents for his will. Here are some:

Death and time and old October.

What strange shadowy symbols must I employ to make something of Francis? I will go for this moment to that great book of Negro poetry, *God's Trombones*, to the line where God tells Death, "Go down, Death…"

Now this paraphrase: "Go down Death and bring Francis home. It is October. I may give them a hard winter. Francis is eighty-five years old. He's had enough."

So, in a recent week in old October, fragile, tottering Francis was knocked off the far edge of this life and spun away by these winds.

October? I know about the portents of October. I came to All Souls in October. I took one of the folding chairs in back beside Francis. He was quite tolerant. As the Sundays came and went I watched him, perhaps made too much of him. He did Mudras with his fingers, which are a form of silent Mantra, a communication with finger gestures to the deep unconscious, or as Dr. Jung has intimated, God's Country. (That ancient Chinese text, the I Ching, calls it the Devil's Country, but the devils in their theology are not as frightful as ours.) These finger signals were developed centuries ago in the Far East, raised to high prayer by Japanese Ninja mercenaries. Francis made secret hand gestures to himself. Did he know something we do not?

I have looked here and there in the holy books—the sacred and the profane—for Francis. His eyes were at times as wise as those of the chief Yogims of Tibet. They were as deep and ancient as the wells of Egypt, focused on distant scenes, as set as the eyes of the Sphinx.

Eighty-five years old? What contradictions. An old man? No, he was an ancient boy. A hurt boy?

Retarded? Brain damaged? That chief prophet of the Age of Aquarius, C.G. Jung, has noted that what often appears to be mental illness is actually a manifestation of superior intellect.

Or spirituality.

Good God! Is it possible? Francis could be one of the most dangerous entities in Christendom, a threat to the ordered, complacent mind. We have ample warning about the likes of Francis. That embroidered warning was once posted on the wall in the Northrop room.

Be careful lest ye entertain Angels unaware…

Or Christ knocks but once…

Yet this is, after all, the Age of Aquarius. The Scripture is being revised frequently. Old images and symbols lose meaning. The parallels and metaphors fade.

I have old memories. Yes, I know the sorcery of old October. There are farewells in old October. I heard hidden flutes in one October, Buddhist flutes upon the wind, Taoist gongs in chilly nights along the ridgelines, bringing death in late November when Chinese ambushes began…pardon me, I digress here. But Francis was a veteran, his obituary said. Does that explain his eyes?

Yes, we come ever again to old October. The fey mind roams in this October. Disconnected, feverish thoughts at old midnight as the hours slip toward dawn. I hear farewells in old October as the year turns toward its death. I dimly sense those strange little spins that God puts on death and time, strange dark time.

Restless midnight visions. I saw Francis broken, twisted and neglected, lying dead upon the street. Old dark time, sent by God, came and made the hit and swirled away.

God sends these agents to test us. Have I again failed one of these miserable tests?

What to make of Francis Stevens? Have I made too much? Who was he? The scriptures evolve into new interpretations. In the autumn wind we hear those unbelligerent epiphanies, those naïve, trustful symphonies of the New Age. We look at the symbol and gentle metaphor, the hopeful theologies.

Now here at the end, rising with the wind, some understanding. A perspective, a title, the whole story.

E.T. went home.

Madison County Vote—1964

Madison County lived up to its reputation for violent and hardball politics in an election on June 1, 1964, at Mars Hill and all precedents were broken during a primary campaign which saw one of the county's Democratic Party strongmen pitted against a strong contender from McDowell County in a race for a seat in the State Senate, and which resulted in a wild, free-swinging brawl.

Zeno Ponder of Madison was running against Clyde Norton of Old Fort. Ponder was a long-time activist, but this was the first time he had risked his power and reputation before the voters as a candidate. Before the vote counting was done at midnight a Highway Patrol Captain, district commander in Asheville, had dispatched 20 troopers to the school on a stand-by capacity where the voting was held, but Captain Johnson said his men had no authority to enter the fray unless he was ordered to do so by the Governor. A big brawl broke out in the evening as the vote was tallied, and the State Troopers could only stand by and watch.

(Even later an SBI investigation was held, but the confusion was so great that no clear ruling was entered in the weeks following.)

Rumors had been called in to the newspaper all week about potential problems at Mars Hill, but no one in authority had bothered to look into the potential for a wild brawl. On election night the donnybrook began and injuries mounted, but Madison Sheriff E.Y. Ponder, (a brother to Zeno and of equal if not greater power) described that by saying "…they just had some skin knocked off."

I had reported the rumors to the state editor all week, but state and city editors had little to do with policy and avoided thinking about the potential problem, and did not care much for Madison County anyway. So election returns from all the counties in our circulation area were coming in to the newsroom at nightfall.

Then executive editor Dick Wynn called me into his office to tell me half of the State Highway Patrol west of Charlotte were enroute to Mars Hill and there was big trouble. He told me he wanted me to not take a gun or camera, but go to Mars Hill. "Be polite and call everyone sir, but find out what the hell is going on."

I went by my desk and got my camera (my pistol was in the car), and as I left the building a young cub—a part-time sportswriter was getting off work.

"Hey, are you going out on something? How about letting me come along."

I agreed. It was in the days before the Interstates. We got past Weaverville before he asked where we were going. When I told him Madison County, he got quiet for several minutes, then asked "This is election day, isn't it?" He had heard about Madison County politics.

We got to the polling place just as a deputy sheriff knocked some man out the door and stomped him. The cub retreated across the road and hid behind a power pole. Just then the beautiful young wife of the Republican Mars Hill Mayor, Bill Powell. Half-drunk and crying, she ran up to me and asked "Whose side are you on?"

"Why madam, I'm on the side of truth and justice," I said.

"Well, you're in the wrong goddamned county," she said and staggered away.

(The tension had further risen at about 10 p.m. over a ballot box found in a closet at the precinct, then it grew more volatile as a poll book was missing for a time and a charge that the final count showed a total of 595 Democrats had voted despite a registration of 477.

(At that time the vice mayor of Mars Hill said the fighting climaxed a day of hot politicking which saw a group of Democrats with a duplicate voter list set up a check-in table at the gate to the school grounds to enable them to keep what they described as a "correct tally".

(At the end of the day's voting, that group had tallied 470 Democrats and 54 Republicans who had entered to vote. That group then entered to watch the paper ballots being counted.

(According to one of the voting officials at the time, precinct officials took a dinner recess and the doors to the polling place were locked. Later the boxes were opened for counting. Zeno got 412 and Norton got only 183. The citizens asked to see the official poll book and were informed by the registrar, John Robert Anderson, that it was missing. As the heat grew, the book was produced from a closet, as well as a fourth ballot box stuffed with ballots.

(At that time, Mars Hill police chief R.J. Ammos was asked by precinct officials to serve as a precinct official and it was at that time Captain Johnson of the State Highway Patrol was called.)

It was at that time, when I had arrived, that three deputies arrived to take the ballot boxes away. Chief Ammons refused to let the deputies take the boxes. Then Roy Freeman, chairman of the Madison County Board of Elections, arrived with four men who had been deputized by Sheriff Ponder to get the boxes. Then fighting between the deputies and citizens ensued in and about the school doorway. Freeman and the deputies prevailed and spirited the boxes through a shouting, jeering, cursing crowd, away where they were taken to Marshall.

I had gone to use a phone and when I returned the cub told me the deputies had taken the boxes away in a cruiser. I told him to come on. We got in my car and headed for Marshall, a few miles away. I just couldn't resist it. I asked "When we get there, do you want to operate the camera or the gun?"

He grew silent, then said, "Just let me out here. I'll walk or hitchhike back to Asheville. I just want to be a sports-writer. I'm not interested in this kind of dangerous shit."

I kept going. The deputies had about a ten or 15 minute head start on us, but when we got to Marshall the Sheriff was alone in front of a big blackboard, putting up the totals of hundreds of votes.

"Well, E.Y., how did you all do?"

He smiled slyly."Looks like we won big."

"Congratulations." I used his phone to call the results in.

On the way back to the newspaper, the cub asked "Where were the ballot boxes, any way?"

"Don't you know anything? They're in the French Broad River half-way to Tennessee by now."

An Essay by Lewis W. Green on Outlanders Moving into the Mountains

✦

Published in The Appalachian Journal In 1976

Now the strangers came and tried to teach us their ways,
And they scorned us for being what we are.
But they'd just as well be chasing moonbeams,
Or lighting penny candles from a star.
                    —An old Irish song of Rebellion Against The British

Strangers on the land. They have little respect for the land. They are killing it, said a voice whose faded eyes watched a long, steep driveway being cut and improperly ditched. He whose ancestors took the land from the Indian by force and guile now watched helplessly as rich outlanders took the old homeplace for a big summer home.

In truth, many of the old homeplaces are bought up by natives, too. And in some cases the outlanders have shown more consideration for the lay of the land than the natives. But those outlanders who do not show consideration may feel the sharpness of rebellion.

In North Carolina, the true mountaineer—a dwindling tribe—shares one characteristic with his fellow Tar Heels, and shares it vigorously.

Violence.

Recently Senator McNeill Smith of Guilford County, chairman of the state's crime study commission, spoke on the state's high incidence of aggravated assault. "It appears that since Colonial days, North Carolinians have been a straight-forward, hand-at-the-plow and hand-at-the-gun group of people. We settle our grievances directly and personally."

Violence is not now and was never all there is to the mountain man, nor his exclusively. But it was more important that some would like to admit. Violence was generally effective for the moment, and often the moment was all that concerned him.

And in the mountain man is a residual identification with that old American Revolution against power and privilege. The people most often moving in on him have smothering amounts of money and no sensitivity all for his independence. As a result, there are strong and deep undercurrents of resentment against strangers, who do not know the code.

(Yes, there was a code of the hills, and though it was rarely articulated—it did not have to be—its latitude was such that it could accommodate dutiful hospitality as well as murder. Andrew Jackson one said that there are some offenses and insults against the person which cannot be remedied in a court of law.)

Tough, tenacious, the old spirit of this region lives on in the people, despite the fact that identity has been raked to pieces over the snags of a thousand sharp intrusions. The way of life is tied necessarily to the past.

Who are the mountaineers? Argue all day: if you aren't one, you can't tell. Those poor, hard-core dullards in Dickey's *Deliverance* no more represent the Appalachian mountaineer than do the citified middle class. And that citified group calling themselves mountaineer is a like a fat quartermaster calling himself a soldier: the infantrymen chortle.

Explain the mountaineer in ancestral terms. The faint recollection of the old folks, the family cemeteries. He is yet held to the ground by those old bones.

Family reunions and homecomings on the grounds.

People have been coming in for decades, but they came in apologetically, and though the tourists swarmed in summer, they were merely irritants. Their numbers were so small they posed no threat. Once the strangers were considered stupid, ignorant buffoons. Yes, for every denigrating hillbilly joke told on him, the mountain man had one or two he told on the flatlanders. Example: car full of tourists trying to find out which highway they were on, stopped to ask a mountaineer, "Is this 19-23?" He fixed them with a feigned, fierce eye. "No, h'it h'aint. Ye damn fool, this is 1943."

Irritants. A nuisance in general, but a baffling, aggravating one. One of them bought a place in Madison County and broke most of the code of the hills and all of one man's personal code. "Well, why don't you just go ahead and kill him?" a neighbor said.

"I would but I don't know him that well," said the exasperated mountaineer.

For many decades, that was all the time and effort the mountaineers considered the stranger to be worth. Now their value has ballooned into what the mountaineer perceives to be tyranny. Again consider the huge tracts of hunting ground posted, the many miles of native trout streams either silted past use or posted.

The mountain man, like his ancestors, maintains a keen interest in the law, especially in those property matters—and matters of violence—rooted in the old common law. He sees the strangers as oblivious to the law or the invisible code, "except the sons-of-bitches know how to nail a no-trespassing sign on every tree in five hundred square miles."

The record of development has been almost uniformly bad in the western part of North Carolina. Roads are built haphazardly and maintained with even less concern. The strangers care no more for the mountain than they do for the feelings of the people who have lived there for generations.

Hard freezes come, the earth heaves, the thaw and the rain and the road washes and the trout stream is again silted, the fish beds ruined, the insects gone. The developer often says tough shit, the hillbillies can buy food cheaper at the market anyway.

The mountaineer despairs, lightly rattles the matches in his pocket.

If there were stronger laws, if they had to be tried for offenses against the land, then some of these bastards would be punished, but some of the guiltiest bastards are our very own—filling places of political, civic and business leadership.

The old line mountaineers watch the coming and staying and posting. Representatives and other elected officials pander to the strangers, giving various tax breaks and other special considerations, offering the weak rationale that it is helping to improve the economy. But in the case of bigger developments such as motels, resorts, etc., all that one can see for the little man is maintenance and custodial jobs. Maids and waitresses. At the end the season, the big money goes to Florida—to return later to buy up some more old homeplaces.

Dignity in tatters, the mountaineer rattles his matches.

In politics someone sometime must come to grips with those things of the land and also those things of the spirit. Yes, the local and state governments at times seem to pander to the tackiest and most uninspired of urban tastes.

The air is stale and the spirit coughs feebly.

Will the people of the mountain culture go the way of the southern blacks, whose traditions and hallmarks were either appropriated or shamed out of use?

The blacks. All the power and prejudice whitey brought to bear could not keep them from being what they were. Yet in the end, whitey took it all. Negroes got land after the Civil War, but The Man got hold of it by means dastardly and foul, yet eminently legal. They had good women, tried and true, yet The Man took them and spewed mulatto. They had jobs but only those whitey wouldn't work at. They finally raised hell, true enough. Not for the preservation of anything, but to get the same things whitey had. And they got it and they lost their agrarian clothing to the child of The Man—status and prestige now accrue to faded denim. At last they lost their distinct speech. "Say man, be cool now," belongs to those pampered children of the late 1960s and early 1970s.

Now guess who sits about in faded overalls playing bluegrass and trying to talk the natural mountain brogue?

The children of The Man.

Several years ago a girl VISTA worker was murdered in Madison County, apparently by being hogtied so that she strangled herself. The publisher of the Asheville paper, Robert Bunnelle—a Yankee transplant—said to a reporter: "That has to be an outsider. Our people don't kill like that, do they?"

The reporter was a native mountaineer. He smiled, shrugged, walked away.

Our people? Who the hell are our people? The question asked is answered: a mountaineer will kill any way he has to—rifle, pistol, pocketknife, ax, chainsaw, rock, stick—even by hogtied strangulation. It all depends on how angry or psychopathic he or she is.

But the publisher raised a question. The outlanders are afraid, even with their wealth. They buy up places deep in the mountains where the nights are profound and silent. Then they put up sodium lights, fences, and place attack dogs here and there. Except for the lack of machine-gun nests, it is like a combat zone.

There is a low cough in the night. Fingers fondle the matches.

One hastily-built development near Asheville was touted as an exclusive, expensive layout. Yet it was as tacky and poorly conceived as any other. They silted up a trout stream and ruined a mountain ideal for wildlife. Then a bad thing happened to one respected mountaineer living on an adjacent tract. Some of the outlanders threatened to kill his coondogs. He went directly to one of those threatening the dogs and told him to pray day and night that nothing happened to those dogs, because someone would get shot.

"I've heard that somebody might burn off their leaves for them, too, but not me. Just somebody. I've heard that," the mountain man said.

In a county further west, several unnecessary things were said by some well-to-do outlanders—sleek brusque Floridians. It was on a Saturday that one mountaineer said: "Well, we'll see how pretty it looks to the sons-of-bitches charred black."

Monday, an outbreak of fires, and in Macon County, the grotesque tourist attraction, Gold Mountain, for God's sake, with its conquistador actors and chairlifts, was struck by arson. Then a sawmill and several patches of woods. Later this comment; "The posted signs burned off right early. They didn't last no time."

Yes, outlanders. They can gain a mountain by a tax deed or some such. They can fight it and wound it with bulldozers and backhoes, they can draw up its waters with strong pumps, and they can sneer at the people and their primitive churches and small income.

But they can lose too. The same court that gave up a tax deed will also fore-close on a mortgage. The ski resorts, so out of character for the place (but not the time), can close.

The winds can bring limbs down across power lines, and it will bring rain which will then draw itself and gather force and run swift and red and wash the road and silt also the wells. Again the pumps will break and the ground water will deepen ag ain.

It is not so much that they screwed up the land. The land will recover. They screwed up the spirit, because the old weary spirit does not believe the land can return.

Yes the outlanders lose along with the mountaineer. The properties will go into the hands of other out-of-staters. And the mountaineer, he of broken spirit, will go once again toe the woods with a pocket full of matches.

And for a little while longer the ones who carry the weakened, tattered genes of colonial anger and rebellion will last, then they will be gone, filed away in the old dust bins of time.

Buck Lyda, In Memory Of...

A short piece on Buck. This former Sheriff and retired U.S. Secret Service Agent rates a book by himself. He had many friends and admirers, but found that hard to believe at his end. He knew he was dying of cancer and had grown bitter. Near the end he hinted that he didn't want anyone to come to his funeral. This memorial has to do mostly with my own experiences and relationship with a man I knew as a friend, but whom I did not trust too far, either in politics or law enforcement. (But then, that was applied to me and others who operated in our environments.)

I first knew him as a rookie cop with the Asheville Police Department. But he was good at it and had political connections and made it into the Secret Service. From there he was able to open many doors for his friends. Many years ago he pressed me into service doing some undercover work in north Georgia and east Tennessee on a counterfeiting and drug ring. It was tricky and dangerous, but the agents I met then also inspired a lot of ribald laughter.

I lost track of Buck for long periods of time, although he would call from time to time to talk politics. His immediate family was heavily involved in the old Laurence Brown faction of the Democratic Party and he was raised up in that. Brown was Sheriff in Buncombe for about 32 years, and he and the late J. Weldon Weir shared most of the Democratic Party power. Buck's father was one of Brown's deputies, and all this is to place Buck in the inner circle.

In 1972, shortly after I founded The Native Stone, N.C. Congressman Nick Galifinakis filed for the U.S. Senate race. He was appearing at every political event in the state. Local Dems were looking out for him. It was announced that a Billy Graham birthday party would be held in Charlotte, attended by President Nixon. A Democratic friend, the late Herb Wallace, asked me to attend and get coverage of Nick. I told him I didn't have enough money for gas at that time. He assured me he would take care of it. But the day before the event, Buck called me from the White House to tell me he would be in charge of security for President Richard Nixon, who was going to star in the Graham affair. He asked if I would be interested in covering it, and if so, he would arrange for credentials. Yes. Buck told me that when I reached the outer ring of Secret Service security at the Charlotte airport I was to mention his name.

I drove there and did that. The first agent stopped me and I asked him to get Buck Lyda on the radio. That agent asked "Are you Lewis?" That let me through, and I was given a small "E" badge for my lapel, which indicated I had complete access to the President's group. The national press was roped off. They saw me wandering about freely and finally a woman reporter asked me who I represented. I told her The Native Stone. "What is The Native Stone?" she asked.

"It's a building material, lady," I told her. Another reporter told her that it was obvious I was a Secret Service operative. Another agent whom I knew grinned and said "Hell, he fits the profile of an assassin."

I made about three rolls of film up close with the President and Billy Graham. I never did see Nick and so I had to later run a two-page layout of him to get Herb Wallace settled down. He was mollified and said he didn't want Nick in the same edition with Nixon anyway.

Later on, closer to retirement, Buck was named Secret Service laison to Congressional budget appropriations and rode out his career there. He knew how to use that to his advantage later.

The many incidents. Jerry Vehaun, Head of Emergency Management, whose friendship with me had gone back as far as that with Buck, had told me he was going to run for Sheriff that year and I assured him of my support. But Buck retired and came back to Buncombe. At a meeting at the Governor's western residence Buck, the old-line Democrat, shocked many of us. He told me he intended to run for Sheriff on the Republican ticket and asked for my support. I checked with Vehaun who said if Buck would run he would not. Buck began to mobilize his resources, which were considerable. Some important Washington figures with whom he had worked set up a fund-raiser for him in D.C.

Two van loads of his partisans drove up to attend. We were all properly impressed with how it was coming down.

The campaign began. An aside—I ran a letter on the front page of The Independent Torch that the chief photographer at the Citizen-Times had written to management there resigning because of the bias and incompetence of the newspaper. Waiting for a Lyda press conference to begin at Gatsby's, C-T editor Jay Hensley came to me and demanded to know where I got that letter. I was only mildly surprised that someone of Hensley's general incompetence and insensitivity would ask for a source to be identified. At the time I was at a table with Peggy Gosselin, editor of The Canton Enterprise. We got up and moved. Hensley obsessively persisted. (Buck was in the men's room during this exchange.) Finally

I told Hensley that a member of his staff had given me the letter. "That's a lie, Green," he said.

I suggested he come outside with me and I'd beat his ass. "You won't do nothing," he spat. I had waited a long time for this shot so I knocked him on his ass. He leaped up and screamed "Call the Chief of Police. I've been assaulted."

"You've not been assaulted," I said. "You've just had the shit slapped out of you. Come on outside and I'll assault you."

At that time, Buck walked out of the men's room and saw the stir. The rest of this story can best be told in another format, but one of Buck's advisor's later told him the incident hadn't hurt him, but had probably helped it because the newspaper was not held in high esteem.

Buck won the election. He called me in a couple of days and said he wanted me on his narcotics squad. I told him he didn't owe me anything. He said he was going to form a "Dirty Dozen" drug squad and wanted me on it. Both of us were familiar with the military's use of "Dirty Dozen" units. How could I refuse? It was after my trial for assaulting Hensley that the newspaper tried to have me fired. Citizen-Times executive editor, Larry Pope (Pope Larry the Tird, now gone from the scene) tried to get him to fire me. Buck did not bend, so I stayed on with the Dirty Dozen for about a year.

Someone inside the department was leaking information. I had been working with a lady in AA. She called me one night, saying she knew she had to get honest, but the only employment she could find was cutting cocaine two and three nights a week for a dealer. But she wanted me to know that the cocaine was coming in to the airport those nights, and it was being dropped on the runway before they landed.

I told Buck. He told me to get up on the runway those nights. I got an air-to-ground radio with the right frequency. They transmitted in a prearranged landing code, but I never found dope. I called the woman several times. She said she knew it had been dropped because she had been up late cutting it. I told Buck they may be dropping it in the cornfield on the runway approach. He insisted I stay on the runway. (Some months after I resigned I saw a report where a man fishing in Lake Julian had found a taped up cooler filled with cocaine floating around. He had taken it to the SBI instead of the Sheriff's Department. Make what you will of that.

But this is in memory of some of the decent things in my experience with him. Buck and I were initiated into Blue Lodge freemasonry together, and for a time he did well in it. He left for a stay in Honolulu and neglected his work in the lodge. I remained on and rose to master mason. Later Buck returned and I was privileged to participate in the ceremony raising him to the third degree.

There were some politically questionable things to his career here. He began losing Republican support and switched his registration back to Democrat. That may have sealed his subsequent defeat. But in some law enforcement circles, he left behind a legend. I will remember him as a friend.

The Sheriff and Barbara

I was entering the outer office of the Sheriff's Department just as two ambulance attendants were going out the back door with a moaning, bleeding patient on a stretcher. I turned to the blank-faced Chief Deputy. "Willis, who is that?"

He fixed me with the usual ironic tilt to his brow.

"Oh, that's just the high sheriff of Buncombe County."

"What's happened?"

"His secretary stabbed him"

"What for?"

"She says she don't know. They've both been holed up in there drunk for two days."

The Wop At The Top

Since The Independent Torch went on the internet, we received a number of e-mail and other requests for explanation as to the background of what we're writing about concerning the All Souls Cathedral. The new readers seem amused, bemused, alarmed, outraged, etc.

We reproduced a letter sent out to thousands of Episcopalians from a group which calls itself **Concerned Clergy and Laity of the Episcopal Church** in Atlanta.

A couple of years ago I was invited to address that group concerning what has gone on at All Souls since the homosexual takeover, and the tactics I have used to combat the devious but largely amateurish tactics of the gay-liberal clergy and council here. I have since included some of the leaders in my mailing.

CCLEC has slowly and patiently put together an agenda. A news release last week revealed that a major fight is brewing among the Bishops to jolt the church back from its extreme leftist position. CCLEC and other groups forming will be joining in that fray. We will run that news release soon.

I once more began reiterating past events at Oral Souls Lesbyterian Church and the efforts to dislodge me there. (You can forget that shit, brothers and sisters in Christ. I'm there, all ears and eyes.)

The dean is Todd Donatelli, who was brought here a couple of years ago to replace a decrepit old polack priest, Neil Zabriskie, who once had aspirations for a bishop's seat, and who had held the church in a liberal political position for many years. I now treat Oral Souls as a liberal Democratic precinct with appropriate insult and slur. Such scorn is invited because of the stupidity involved in trying to set up this editor for humiliation and embarrassment.

Donatelli, from a struggling but pretentious Italian family in Chicago, came here from a church in Jackson, Miss. He makes his hints of an elitist background, but it's transparent.

Some of his former parishioners came for the ordination. They said he was known there as The Italian Stallion and Father Yum Yum. Well, he can fit in with this off-the-wall bunch, thinks I at the time. He retained the Zabriskie political emphasis.

Last Sunday's service saw an admitted dyke Noreen Hill-Duffy (of 510 Wind-swept Dr. Asheville, N.C. 28801, phone no. 254-3635) blurt out, during prayer time, that she was thankful to God that she was allowed to attend this church. I include her address and phone number in case any of you homophobes on the internet from the Charlotte-Gastonia area want to express yourselves.

But how gauche of her, to inject religion into the precinct meeting. That may not be constitutional. But Yum Yum graciously overlooked it for the moment. Maybe he warned here afterward. She admitted to me some time ago that she was one of the lesbians who had tried to mount an economic boycott against The Torch and tried to get certain businesses to quit selling The Torch. More on such violations of Constitut-ional rights later.

To offer some brief explanation as to my approach to these matters, we will go back several years. I had not included All Souls in my political commentary until one of the Diocesan priests got caught up in a lawsuit concerning his sexual devi-ancy, more particularly the molestation of some young boys. The settlement cost the diocese heavily, and in a headline I mentioned the "queer" priest.

It was that word, interestingly enough, that seemed to upset Zabriskie. Why? Even the faggots themselves were parading about all over the country chanting "We're here and we're queer". Later I noted in print that "I'm Green and I'm mean."

Then one of the church ladies appeared at a news conference for Maggie Lau-terer, a liberal candidate for Congress here, where her Magness came out against guns. I covered that. Shortly that woman, Betty Parks, and her husband began fanning out lies about me at coffee hour and I jumped them. That uncovered the gossip circle. Ms Parks has since died and gone on to whatever corner awaits lie-ing church biddies.

Then one of her cronies, Bobbie Underwood, coyly told me at church one day that I'd be surprised to know what they're saying about me. There, you see, another gaucherie. I later had to tell Underwood, when she tried to start a con-versation with me, that I didn't want any further conversation with her.

I was fast becoming the resident demon laureate. Thinks I to myself, this ought to be good. These idiots don't really know how to play with the fire of the spirit.

I wrote something referring to the Rev. Mason Wilson, one of the adjunct priests, as Pudge. He threatened to sue. I said truth is the best defense. You are a pudge. Susan Stevenson took it upon herself to approach me and ask what I was even coming there for. Good God at the gaucherie. She also said I had hurt poor Mason's feelings. I told her I had certainly meant to and I wasn't half through.

These poor people protected from the realities. They can't handle this kind of shit.

I always sit in the same pew. One day one of the ladies who had apparently had her assertive training to better deal with Male Chauvinist Pigs, notified me that "we don't have reserved seats here". You see, these supposedly sophisticated and worldly people practice the most blatant form of gaucherie. That always unmasks them.

I ask her, who the hell is we? Is she the Father or the Son or the Holy Spirit. That's who the church belongs to.

An aside here. I had a couple of bad auto accidents, one of which broke my jaw in five places and required a five hour operation. No one came to visit except one friendly church lady.

That was before I started my stuff. So it became obvious that what we have here is an exclusive social club with its attendant snobbery.

In last Sunday's sermon, Yum Yum predictably talked about the Martin Luther King incident at the bridge in Selma, Ala., of how the man fought such evil things as the violation of constitutional rights and worked to institute justice and all that. How very gauche!

First, let us note that All Souls, with all the emphasis on "diversity" has no blacks attending, nor would they be welcome, me thinks.

As I have written previously with some relish, we got buggers but we got no niggers, we got dykes but we got no kikes. However, we do have that one token Wop, who is now referred to as "The Wop At The Top".

That is also not including the demonic hillbilly writer/editor whom Yum Yum suspects of ties with the Klan, the Militia, the KGB, the CIA, the devil and other shadowy right wing groups. We'll write about the bomb threat rattling around in his head later, and the police surveillance, though my attorney has suggested not at this time.

There is the obvious—and expected—hypocrisy among the priests (and con-greg-ation). But as one contemplated Yum Yum's sermon, there came into view the tint of schizophrenia and delusion. Need we say paranoia?

He condemned the police for violating those rights of Martin Luther King, and yet it has only been a few weeks ago that Yum Yum hired an off-duty Asheville detective to come and surveil the editor during services, and to arrest me if need be.

(That was on the heels of the latex glove incident, during which I gave the one-finger salute to one of the dung-beetles serving communion. We will reiterate that later also. On the secondary employment form he filled out he indicated fear of terrorism or some-such. That one will cost the Diocese and the cops.

As to further violations, we find these liberals doing the very things they condemned in the 1960s. At one point some dykes were going to my advertisers and sellers in an effort to boycott The Torch. What about my constitutional rights?

Hell, even that idiot David Fortney, a teacher at Asheville Country Day School, called the attorney who advertises with me to try to get him to quit running his ad. The attorney asked him his name and Fortney did his idiot number, he told him who he was. Not out of moral courage, but out of stupidity. We will subpoena him.

The Wop at The Top, apparently feeling his authority slipping, began several other unethical, cowardly, hidden and unconstitutional moves against The Torch.

That included some denunciation from the pulpit, flattering enough in this case, f rom both he and one of the female priestettes, who also apparently does not have all her candles lit. Then there were other incidents in which Donatelli pulled some dumb dupes into his cause. So far we have caught most of them.

One other matter before we close this account. It seems that some in the congregation are boycotting the church. The Wop has announced in the weekly leaflet that they are going to have to cut it back to twice a month due to financial shortages.

Perhaps he spent the printing money on the detective's fee. Ironic indeed. The week the Wop at The Top With the Cop conspired to surveill me, I got there too late to be watched.

Surveillance of The Editor
At All Souls

Asheville Mayor Leni Sitnick was notified that Police Chief Will Annarino had okayed secret surveillance of this editor at services the last two Sundays at All Souls Episcopal Cathedral by two undercover detectives, apparently at the request of Donatelli, cathedral dean, under the thin pretext that he might "create a scene".

This is the latest in a long-running series of efforts by Donatelli and others at the Cathedral to demonize the editor because of a similiarly long-running series of articles here exposing the efforts of homosexuals to dominate the cathedral by whatever means.

Several police officers tipped me over a week ago that Annarino had apparently agreed to Donatelli's request. The information at that time was that the two detectives would be "moonlighting" and that Donatelli would pay them each $50 an hour or $50 a service.

Annarino is universally detested by the men in his own department and is looked upon mostly by them as a pimp for political forces.

"He's got no business being a police chief," one said to the nods of others. "He's pretty damned stupid and plays silly favoritism games."

Another said "Hell, you think you've got a lot of queers at that church. We've got a bunch of them—and lesbians—in the police department."

That opened up a plausible reason for Annarino and Donatelli to hatch the scheme to put me under probably illegal surveillance.

Some of the volunteers at All Souls also gave me part of the scenario and said they had overheard talk about paying the officers some fees for watching me.

We have more information from both All Souls people and police officers on this matter, but it is in the hands of attorneys at this time.

Donatelli's rationale for what seems to be a violation of my rights, that he feared I would "create a scene" springs from a small incident a couple of weeks ago when I saw that the homosexual Ron Currant was going to serve the communion chalice. So I put on a latex glove and went to the rail. (What the hell? If anyone is dangerous at All Souls it is those people. There have been instances of these bastards biting people and giving them AIDS.)

Anyway, I'll leave it to the readers. On page 4 is Curran's photo with his wife (or husband or fiance or whichever they are) David Henderson (they are also known as Adam and Steve) and they live in domestic bliss, one supposes, at 108 (for God's sake) Weeping Cherry Forest Road in Fairview, 28730 home phone no. 628—0005 work phone 509-0077.

As a result of my salute of an upraised latexed middle finger, Donatelli informs me that he is placing me on "pastoral discipline" until I apologize to the pansy, apologize in writing to the congregation, read some verses in the Bible and confer with him. (See his letter, also on page 4.)

He telephoned me with this shit, taping it, I assume, and my attitude is that shooting a bird to a fairy serving communion is not in violation of any of God's ordinances. Also Donatelli is sadly mistaken if he thinks the entire congregation needs apologizing to. I had a couple of callers after that who were laughing.

So much for the "congregation". I am going to mail most of them a copy of this edition, and for those who are in agreement with his sentiments you must know by now that I don't give a shit.

Nine Gays In Group Orgy In Public Park

Nine queers engaged in a group homosexual orgy in a public park were arrested on felony crime against nature charges in a joint raid by officers from three different law enforcement agencies, according to a magistrate's report.

Officers said those charged were engaged in group oral sex activities and at first did not realize they were being busted. They were in Hominy Creek Park off Brevard Road, and citizen complaint had been constant before the raid, according to the magistrate's report.

Participating in the arrests were members of the Buncombe County Sheriff's Department, N.C. Wildlife Resources Commission and Biltmore Estate Company Police.

A spokesman from The Buncombe County Sheriff's Department noted that Hominy Creek Park is county owned and open to the public. The spokesman said additional such efforts are planned and being organized. Public recreational areas will be the primary target of these operations.

An officer said the scene at the surprise raid was so gross that one deputy noted for his religion was so traumatized that he had to be sent for therapy.

Descriptions of the scene were so fantastic that officers both giggled and gagged.

The scene was along a park trail and as the officers stepped in, one sodomite who was doing oral sex on another (who was also doing oral sex on another) raised his head, his lips leaking semen onto his chin and arm and smiled in welcome as if he thought the strangers wanted to join the party.

At the same instant, a white faggot was down on a black queer, who was down on another white and on and on. When the first white's head was pulled up, he lost his dentures and officers had to wait until he found them and got them reloaded.

(As they were being booked, that one who lost his teeth was thoroughly chastised by an outraged fellow queer who told him he should remove his teeth before he gives a blow job. "You can hurt somebody that way," officers said he whimpered and promised to remember who.

Several other hilarious scenes transpired and perhaps next week when we run their photos we shall have time for them. We are also checking to see how many of the suspects are members of All Souls Cathedral (Oral Souls Lesbyterian Church), that notorious den of sexual deviates.

The Piss-ant Factor At Oral Souls Lesbyterian Cathedral

Enough time has passed now since the flurry of excitement about my excommunication from All Souls Cathedral (Oral Souls Lesbyterian Church) to begin assessing the impact locally.

There are wider implications which have spread not only nationally but internationally throughout the Anglican Communion. Those will be taken up in these pages as more clippings and Email comes in.

But for these purposes presently, we will consider the piss-ant factor. One is reminded of a saying by former Chicago Mayor Richard Daley. They have ostracized me, they have crucified me and yes, they have even criticized me.

In reaction to the initial story which The Citizen-Times apparently moved on the Associated Press wire, there were some columns in smaller newspapers in outlying areas and there were surprisingly few "outraged" letters to their editor, and of these, most were identifiable as people with vested interests or close ties to All Souls or sympathetic to the queer movement here.(That response has been miniscule compared to the mail, Email and phone calls I have received from all over the United States.

Most seemed to have been influenced by the news coverage and spun around some misunderstanding of what brought the excommunication on. That information was handed up to the press by the Wop-at-the-Top, the extremely-limitless-very Rev. Todd Donatelli, who has either low cunning or schizophrenia. Most of this evaluation will come in a later article or articles.

What the letter writers seemed to be responding to was my "behavior" over the years.

The only misbehavior they can cite with truth was the fact that finally I put on a (one) latex glove, went to the communion rail and gave a FU signal with my middle finger to that simpering little queer Ron Curran, who was serving the wine.(Letting the perverts serve is demonic in itself. Later we shall take up the cult factor and similiarity to devil worship at All Souls. I feel Curran had been

211

placed there by arrangement numerous times by the priests for some kind of reaction from me. They got it.

Now for the record, I did not offer the finger to the congregation (most of whom had not even seen the gesture), and even the Wop didn't know about it until later. Nor did I spit in the cup. Also for the record, in dispute of what Donatelli has spread about, I did not scream at children, I did not talk rude to the elderly (except I said no to one overpainted dyke when she tried to get me to shake her hand) and I did tell Bobbie Underwood, who admittedly is getting to be elderly, that I didn't care to talk to her; and that was in the wake of a history of her spreading gossip about me.

My motive was simple. I only asked that the perverts stay away from me, not the church. More later on that too.

Space and time requires that I now go to the pissants, whose motives I now inspect.

Bill Mebane (now dead) wrote a column for C-T, which in light of facts, was distortion and left out some vital parts. He was essentially a dullard whom I have known for years. We both worked for the daily newspaper here in the 1960s. A true piss-ant, he exhibited much grandiosity about his place in the church, community and thereby, one supposes, the universe.

But what of motive, outside of trying to brownnose the priests? He approached me several times at the coffee hour and I finally had to tell him I just didn't feel right about him—there was something suspicious—and I wanted him to stay away from me. That went on for numerous Sundays. Finally one Sunday he took it upon himself to sit beside me in the pew. As usual, the two dung-beetles, Curran and his sweetie Henderson seated themselves immediately in front of me. So! Once again a stage was set.

On this occasion I decided to talk to Mebane. I said loud enough for the dung-beetles to hear that it seemed most of the queers had quit coming. In keeping with his arch grandiosity, Mebane grinned and said "Oh, I don't know. I may be one myself."

Oh really? That explains everything. Get your hand off my leg, says I. Then I wrote about that, to his chagrin. That will suffice for Mebane's motive. I did wonder if his wife, Pat, knew about his possible predeliction???

Another piss-ant? David Hopes, the queer professor at UNC-A who puts himself in for a Pulitzer Prize and whose criminal record I have published several times, and intend to do so again soon to make a major political point. He was arrested for writing anonymous letters, one threatening the life of President Reagan. He signed the name of a police officer who had arrested him for DWI.

Other letters went to the superiors of the officers claiming he was the officer's gay lover and had given him AIDS. He also wrote to the officer's bosses in part-time jobs with the same lies, and then swore in an affadavit that the officer had pulled him from his car by "engaging him in digital anal intercourse". (Sticking his finger up his ass.) God. Surely there is a Pulitzer in that. Over a period of time, I have received anonymous letters and voice mail. Since Hopes has a history of that, I may safely assume…

Professor Hopes is a prime example of the queers at All Souls. He teaches your kids at UNCA.

Another strange and/or queer professor at UNCA is Robert Yeager, the Senior Warden at Oral Souls, who weighed in with some quotes in The Church Times. He is quoted as saying I carried a gun and disturbed the elderly and they were relieved to see me banned.(Yeager was later convicted of embezzling more than $34,000 from a small UNC-A publishing shop, given jail time and was last heard of working in Japan.)

Yeager has a low credibility index. When he taught at Warren Wilson College years ago, he was known as an "A for a lay" professor among various coeds, who were also contemptuous of his immature sexual efforts.;

There was a letter from the non-descript Max Langley, a queer All Souls parishioner who lives in Hendersonville with his lover. That letter smacked of the Donatelli writing style. I ran Langley's photo once. (He sent me a lengthy list of male couples he identified as homosexual saints and martyrs down through the centuries.)

Another letter came from a Henry Hansen, who apparently is a neighbor to Jed Bierhaus, one of the adjunct priests at All Souls, and former English professor at Warren Wilson College, so we may assume some bias and influence.

Then there is a letter from a John Fragale, which headline states that *A Saddened Church Gave Up On Green.*

Fragale admits he does not know me, and says "if actions cited in various columns of The Citizen-Times are true, Mr. Lewis disturbance of a service…"

Listen Fragale, the actions cited are not true and there was no disturbance of a service. No one saw me give that queer the bird. Other than that, I had more than a decade of faithful attendance with no disturbance, other than writing in The Independent Torch about the outrageous behavior of those parishioners and clergy. And if you think they were saddened, a newspaper here, The Tribune, reported that they applauded and cheered when the Wop "sadly" told them of his decision to excommunicated me.

By the way, the Bishop himself has said that there was no excommunication. That enraged me. The only laymen ever excommunicated from the Anglican Communion were King Richard VIII a couple of centuries ago, and Lewis W. Green. Now they are trying to rob me of my place in history by denying that I was excommunicated.

Another letter writer, working off the same misinformation provided by Donatelli, was parishioner Charles E. England of Asheville, who apparently mistook the latex glove as a fear of AIDS from the dung-beetle. No Charles, it was merely a gesture of contempt and defiance. It was worth getting kicked out to see the look on the face of the queer and that priestette Jan Walker. (What is she doing in the ministry? I got more spiritual uplift out of the Citizen-Times horoscopes than I ever did those women, and I admit that is hitting low.)

Then there was a letter from Barbara Allison Goldstein of Sylva, who was critical of both sides in this uproar.

And the pathetic voice of Rosalie Witbeck of Arden, whose son is queer. She noted that both columnist Will Haynie and I had the right to be as intolerant as we like as long as the intolerance doesn't hurt others. First off, I am not intolerant—worse, I am indifferent to all this push for queers, and further, I have generally a compassionate contempt for them. I just want them to stay away from me.

Briefly let us listen to the voices of a small-town columnists writing for one of those "free" newspapers which crop up from time to time, the recently founded Smoky Mountain News out of Waynesville. That editor, Scott McLeod, couldn't make it at The Mountaineer and that is revealing.

Those papers have a marginal existence and usually use wannabe columnists and writers as little more than filler. One of those bottom-feeders checked in on the All Souls story, seeking his place in the glare created by this editor.

First, Jeff Minnick, whose wandering commentary remains unremembered except he did call this editor the quintessential eccentric. Here is a man who either got kicked out or dropped out of the US Military Academy, wandered through small and undramatic experiences for years, came to Waynesville and opened a bed-and-breakfast (A certain tipoff as to being eccentric) and bookstore. Apparently remaining confused, he entered an alcoholic treatment program, drifted then to Grace Episcopal Church in Waynesville, foundered there and now has moved on to St. John's Catholic Church. He turned his bookstore into a Catholic oriented place called Saints and Scholars, perhaps to exploit his new-found Catholicism, and turned to home-schooling for his children.

Hardly a mainstream existence, and yet not smacking of a compensatory intellectual new-time avant garde elitism. He tries for a sincere ultra-sensitivity but falls into a clumsy imitation of it. In the All Souls matter, Minnick brought his own axe to grind, disregarding the basic causes which were explained to him over a period of years.

Yes what about that bottom-feeder from Sylva, Gary Carden, a purported storyteller who generally avoided that simple crux of the matter in a commentary in the Smoky Mountain News.

Carden, who for years has played the role of a "gifted" local character and sage, eternally ailing, who gets by on handouts much like the old minstrels—sings for his supper, don't you know?—brought a certain condescending stance to his piece. It was also filled with error. I do not mind being their legend, but I do have to laugh at some of what they include.

Carden sees a drop in my "literary legacy" (I do not see myself leaving a legacy of Appalachian, nor do I see myself as having a literary career. I do other things.)

Anyway, Carden notes that I have become more strident in recent years and much the reading public has turned from me. Christ! I never knew they were with me. He noted that many mountain area "journalists" and editors would not cooperate with some institution's efforts to publicize some affair having to do with me. Good. They did get the message I've been sending for years that they are not to be believed. Too many mistakes.

An example came from Carden's own efforts.

He mentions some "notorious brawl" I started at a carnival in Hazelwood. That never happened. He wrote of going into a Raleigh bookstore to get a signed copy of one of my books, and found the "owner" nursing a new black eye inflicted by me. True, true, God I enjoyed that one. But Carden thought it was over a discussion on air pollution. Here, for Carden's sake, to straighten out his files on the legend:

A young man working there opined I would get a parking ticket if I remained where I parked. I shrugged. He asked impatiently what I would do about that. I told him I would try to get it fixed, and picked up the phone to call a friend at the News &Observer. Just as I got an answer this idiot tried to jerk the phone from my hand so I popped him one.

He did not own the store, as Carden reported. He called the owner, who then apologized to me and said such dismal help was all he could hire.

Carden further got the name of the Cathedral wrong. It is not All Saints, but All Souls.

Away from this. Carden is not alone in missing the significance of the gay movement not only in Asheville but nationwide, if not worldwide. It is perhaps the biggest story of this era and I was enabled to see its encroachment and invasion of a venable old church. All Souls has been described among many of the disenchanted as a church now under a devil's curse with a bad future.

Carden's concern about my legacy seems shortsighted. I can see one or more books from my experiences there. Bill Fishburne and I have talked of the possibility of teaming up on a book on what happened at All Souls, how it happened, the tactics used to swing the old-timers who did not leave and reaction to the resistance I offered. It could become a textbook on resisting such encroachment if this battle takes shape throughout established churches as it is now predicted.

Literary Comments & Reviews Of The Books By Lewis W. Green

In this section will be found scholarly reviews of some of my books which were published in The Appalachian Review under the auspices of The Appalachian Consortium at Appalachian State University at Boone, N.C. The leading article in this section, however, is not a review of this author's work, but begins as a <u>review by this author</u> of a book by another author, and at the suggestion of the editors of The Appalachian Journal became a treatise on creative writing directed at the regional writer working in the Southern Appalachians.

Following that, the first review will be a lengthy one entitled The High-Pitched Laugh of A Sainted Crazy (a take-off on the title of a collection of short stories by this author entitled The High Pitched Laugh of A Painted Lady), and reviewed by Dr. Donald Seacrest.. This review is an exhaustive one on all three of the Lewis W. Green books set in the mountains of Western North Carolina (the first novel And Scatter The Proud; the collection of short stories The High Pitched Laugh of A Painted Lady; and the novel The Silence of Snakes.

Dr. Seacrest's review encompasses the sociological aspects of those works, in addition to examining the spiritual and mystic explorations which begin to search for and find outlet in these works. All were published by the late publisher John Fries Blair of Winston-Salem in the 1960s and 1970s.

The second review of The Silence of Snakes appeared unsigned in The Appalachian Journal and also makes a scholarly examination.

The third review is by North Carolina poet laureate Fred Chappell, and is taken up with a scholarly look at the short stories, The High Pitched Laugh of A Painted Lady.

There is review of my novel, The Kabbalah Pillars by Patrick Killough, a U.S. State Department Foreign Service officer who retired to the mountains of Western North Carolina. He is also a literary scholar and takes a long, deep look at The Kabbalah Pillars.

The folder with reviews of the Korean War novel, Spirit Bells, has been misplaced and so no review of that will appear. But there is also included a review/commentary of my career by Gary Carden entitled *Straying From The Path,* which appeared in A Country Rag Review in Jonesboro, Tennessee. Following that review (which can be termed damning with faint praise or praising with faint damns), we shall briefly comment and straighten out some of his factual errors.

Copies of these books are available from:
Indian Rock Publishers
99 Rocky Fork Road
Fairview, N.C. 28730
Telephone (828) 628-1840
EMAIL lgreen@brinet.com

Ghosts By The Wind Grieved

By Lewis W. Green

A book review morphing into an essay on regional writing from The Appalachian Journal.

The book entitled Mountain Ghost Stories (and curious Tales of Western North Carolina) has appeared in bookstores in the state. The book itself is not an important addition, but for the purposes of speculation or grist for the mill, it poses important questions (and sometimes the writers of the region are sadly lacking in important questions). But before moving to those considerations, some criticism of Mountain Ghost Stories.

Published by John F. Blair, Publisher, of Winston-Salem, Mountain Ghost Stories was written by Randy Russell. His new wife, Janet Barnett, acted as research assistant. From Kansas City, the couple became enchanted by the mountains while here on their honeymoon. According to the dust-jacket information, Russell has published poetry in The Paris Review and the Kansas Quarterly, and has two mystery novels ready for publication by Bantam Books this year.

The book is chatty with brisk narrative and sudden but brief shifts in mood. It is not without tight images of death, carts, white owls, fairy crosses, and—more bizarre—peacock coats and slant-eyed giants. One gets the sense of an outlander grasping for the strange essence of the land and people and turning away time and again baffled.

The Blair firm is noted for young, inexperienced editors. While they are competent at spelling, syntax and sometimes understanding context, one is left with the sense that they cannot understand some of the forces brought to play in forming a story or book—the ebb and flow, the indication of unconscious factors at work. Developing that requires time, quality time. The creative spirit is a genius, is a genie, is a djin, is a daimon, is a demon. It is not always agreeable and pleasant. It robs the social amenities for its energy. One must be careful then in placing blame. The writer may have done, or could have done, a better job than we are allowed to see.

In this book the writing is generally tight enough but seems somewhat discon-nected from the time and the land—matters to be taken up later here. There is the feel of haste, and thereby lies a caveat for writers. Those who pick regional fields in which to work should not hurry. Readership may be small on a national scale, but it is discriminating and picky. In such cases—and this is such a case—we must heed Maxwell Perkins' admonition to a commercial writer who submitted an idea for a literary novel, but whose work habits had congealed. He created and executed hurriedly. "Much material is dropped in and awkwardly handled," Perkins wrote, and that applies here.

The book does not seem, overall, to rise to the dust-jacket puff. Some may say the book is what it says it is, but it is no more. Books like this, touted as a work about ghosts and haunts, of necessity ought to be ghostly and haunting. And the title raises expectation. Those few ghosts in the book are too pale. There are some curiosities also—none too interesting from the standpoint of lore.

Now to the possibilities in the subject itself, the opening of new avenues and far strange vistas from off the road, for the regional (read Appalachian, especially) writer. One who tries by artistic starts and fits, out of some inner suppression, to break free of the regional boundary and begin development in psychology, phys-ics, or the profounder poetry of art, might find a clear path here. (If one stays within the traditional structure, he or she soon mines ore already smelted and thrown back. Nettlesome comparisons begin in early career. Those reviewers and capable critics, caught in the same trap, are justified in such lame comparisons because regionalism almost dictates conformity.)

But for the nonce, let us try some soft comparisons. The same publisher brought out a much more realized book in 1968, if memory keeps. It was *Ghost Tales of the Uwharries* by Fred T. Morgan. (The Uwharries are some small moun-tains in central North Carolina.) There were twenty of the stories, unhurried and more poetic.

The state's noted playwright, Paul Green, writing in the N.C. Folklore Series (Vol. 16, No. 4, Cape Fear Valley Folklore, also in 1968), touched upon folk medicine, the sixth sense, premonition, prescience, and ghosts. None of it was compelling but informative and well-blended with other anecdotes and lore.

Nearly to the point (not quite but worth mentioning), Manley Wade Well-man published Dead and Gone—Classic Crimes of North Carolina (UNC Press, 1954), entered here solely to make the point that excepting the Uwharrie ghost stories, most of the ghost-occult-etc. work done in the state is dryasdust, pedan-tic, and that fact makes them lifeless, devoid of wonder, and incomplete as ghost stories.

Others? If John Ehle has touched upon the subject I'm unaware of it. Fred Chappell has written some weirded-out stuff and though he makes hints, he too refrains from open exploration of occult matters. Thomas Wolfe did, in a brief but major use of a ghost.

True enough, regional writers seem to be afraid to break away from tradition. Repressed, do we shade the alter egos? Do we fear some inner critic, some monitor which tries to keep us within those oppressive bounds of regional respectability or literary conformity. Occult figures may seem to come and go in our work, but fleetingly and at a distance. Yet the field seems to offer ideal opportunity for stretching ones talents to the widest.

Ghosts, boogers, h'ants, spirits—cliched nomenclature taking the imagination nowhere. Yet there is an eager willingness to suspend disbelief for this. Every house has its noises; every dark road its lorn, puzzling stretches; every mind its faint whispers and footfall in the night, dim faces out beyond the lilac at dusk. Or the old, stirred air of winter, or that strange atavism—old death coming—as autumn proceeds. Enough to jangle the senses and set the faint, troublesome, fey vision to work. Stories told at old midnight. The pulse quickens.

Not horror. Ghosts. Haunting. It requires poetry and poetry of a sort. (The best is in Poe.) The set tone of something strange and out of phase must be there. The gypsy mind must have a poetic feel for matters like these: other lands, other skies, dark woods, and the cold breath of the grave from which the ghost emerges.

The opportunities for expanding this fiction are many and heavy. In the last issue of The Appalachian Journal, Alessandro Portelli explores possibilities in an essay entitled "Appalachia as Science Fiction" Portelli presents the ghost as "contemporary ancestor". (Does the psyche really need a concrete pretense?)

But!

The imagination is set free once this file is opened. While the regional writer may insist doggedly that his prime metier is the land he is working with, he now has options to go with the land: science, psychology, metaphysics, all to be developed in the ghost-fey-occult mix. Who should shrink from that in this strange time?

There are ghosts, of course, if we say there are. We have license to invent them or fashion them out of some shadow or "summon them from the vasty deep" (though they may not come, as the bard Shakespeare points out). Do we need to know where they come from? How? When? What are they? The fevered by-product of some guilt on the conscience? No, well where? It is not enough to say there was a strange sad child on the dusky empty road or a voice in the night just outside the house. (Or is it? Perhaps that is just enough. But it must be explored and fashioned)

Try General Semantics then, that dreary science of the Polish engineer Count Alfred Korzybski, the author of *Science and Sanity* and founder of the discipline of General Semantics. He uses language for time-binding, also hints at the graphic shadows of the deeper mind which do seem to be thrown down from the past to bind today's mentations from yesterday's: all in keeping with Dr. C.G.Jung's suggestion on the projecting mode of the psyche. Room here, indeed, for playful experimenting.

How about the great question raised by the doppleganger (or double-ghost, one's own ghost)? Goethe himself—as have many other writers, artists, musicians and assorted cranks, including this one—had some encounters with himself. Goethe wrote that he passed a man on the road one evening, one whom he was certain he recognized. Then years later, coming down the road from the opposite direction at the same place, he met a man he immediately recognized as himself ten years younger.

So! Ghosts. Time? Can we now look at our surroundings and imagine them a hundred years hence and thrust ourselves out into that future land from the onward rushing cage of the present. Are we then, by mere effort of will, ghosts of that time? No? Are we sure?

Or are we hinting at a yet undiscovered dimension for time itself to travel in—not us traveling time but time the traveler with us? More. What can grow out of the time-warp concept, where it buckles and passes itself in a bend where its wall has grown thin? There then, on a drear road through soughing wood and scudding cloud in iron sky, we see through the thin, worn wall to the sad man looking at us as if to say something or to answer some question he heard us think. Time? Does the ghost now slip back to us from the future, a contemporary descendant?

This then: add the incredibly stimulating concept of parallel reality, best advanced as fiction by Borges in his cabalistic "*The Garden of Forking Paths*," but better as physics, by Adrian Berry in *The Iron Sun—Crossing the Universe Through Black Holes (Warner Books, 1977)*. In a simple/profound examination of the theory of relativity, he came upon the doctoral thesis of the Princeton physicist Hugh Everett :

Everett proposed that from the birth of the universe, reality has been branching into different states. There is no basic state of reality, as everyday experience would indicate, but instead an infinite number of "relative states". We live today in a relative state in which the Allied powers won the

Second World War. But according to Everett's Metatheory, there exists another parallel reality in which the Nazis won. It is futile to assert that one of these states is true and the other false. Both are equally true…and it depends simply on which one you happen to live in. And you might be quite a different personality in the relative state, assuming that "you" were alive at all. But the matter does not end here, since the Metatheory predicts that reality branches in a different direction at every microinstant of time. (p. 63)

Another angle? The phenomena of miraged fantasms might fit into speculation on apparitions, etc., and in ways not yet pondered or discovered. There is also something to be gained in time-warp speculations by a perusal of the four books compiled by that strange Brooklyn writer and collector of odd facts Charles Fort *(The Book of The Damned: New Lands; Lo; and Wild Talents)*. Only a small sample, then, for this illustration from *New Lands* (Boni & Liveright, Inc. 1923)

It may be that witnesses have seen human beings dragged from our own existence either into the objectionable fourth dimension, perhaps then sifting into the fifth, or up to sky by some exploring thing. I have data, but they are from records of psychic research. For instance, a man has been seen walking along a road— sudden disappearance. Explanation? That he was not a living human being, but an apparition that had disappeared…(p. 148)

Many routes are available now. Why not some studies of the more "popular" scientific journalism of the past decade? Some kind of affirmation can be found in the work of Drs. Raymond Moody and Elizabeth Kubler-Ross on life-after-death experience.

Now back to the needs of the craft (and art) of writing. How to break free? Why not use ghosts (and other occult or aberrant figures) as more than images.? Why not keys and symbols, symbols replete with the tone of both the regions "feel" or "occultness" and of the universe? These references to the occult have far-reaching implications for the creative writer. From old they have been recognized as veiled openings at the gateway to a creative unconscious and may be used by sensitive enough artists as both keys and symbols.

Such handy tools, once learned, such freedom to work. The great poet T.S. Eliot used the Tarot, and more creative people than can be imagined have used the I Ching, the ancient Chinese magical and philosophical text.

If writing is to be part of spiritual development—and used rightly it is, a development which must be shared if it is to be valid—then the figures in it must be both hidden and open, guarded and free, and it must be recognized anew that symbols are individual, the potency of varying duration, depending on the artist's readiness to develop.

Combinations can fork into endless paths using ghosts, spirits and various concepts of time. A writer working in various forms must additionally be a playwright and director and make assignments of role to his characters, shift the stage to suit his needs and focus the illumination. As mentioned, in our regional literature, ghosts are now useful except for a small chill factor, are usually done awkwardly and are inevitably deus ex machina, raising more problems than they solve by their appearance. If they come, they also go and do not linger to say very much.

Ghosts can be used as effective oracular spokesmen, (as can madmen and drunks). Though ghosts are from the other side, we do not let them say interesting things about that side or even about this side. Ghosts may be used to say things not acceptable from other tongues (Shakespeare did not flinch from this), just as drunks and madmen are used to speak or misspeak higher truth in elevated rhetoric (which might seem pretentious or ridiculous from ordinary human mouths). Take for instance the high cant of a drunken W.O. Gant in Wolfe's *Look Homeward, Angel* or the curious ranting of the slightly touched Bacchus Pentland about Gettysburg's rout.

Which is now to see Wolf's use of an oracular ghost in what is without argument his finest, most memorable chapter, the final scene in *Look Homeward, Angel,* where on a haunting, moonlit Pack Square he sees and converses enigmatically with the ghost of his brother Ben. Several stone angels in his father's stone shop begin a ponderous stroll about also. If Eugene is dreaming, Wolfe does not let us know. Nor is he drinking or under the influence of anything. In this finale and crescendo, we unquestioningly accept the conversation from the cynical ghost and the blank-faced angels in motion. (Wolfe also refers to this or some private ghost in a recurring theme set apart from this chapter: "O lost, and by the wind grieved, ghost, come back again." This small part of the work adds inescapably to its overall impact.)

Ghosts as symbol, being also vague and ambiguous, can work to release many other symbols (veiled by the ghost) from the creative unconscious, which unveil personal mysteries, paradoxes and contradictions, freeing the mind to question imbedded concepts. For instance, the spirits can serve devious, i.e. double purposes. Even the Bible remarks on the God of ancient Israel's use of a lying spirit to deceive a prophet used by Ahab, so that he might destroy himself (one of the more subtle insinuations in Melville's use of Ahab's name and task in Moby Dick.)

Death and ghosts have taken on a renewed, major mystical significance in New Age awareness, which actually feeds on ancientry. The death card of the Tarot is interpreted as a sign of rebirth and/or renewal. Ghosts, to the initiate, become another interesting, if ambivalent, symbol used to detect, snare and express things often betrayed and lost by the treachery of words.

Taking what should be loosely described as the Jungian view, creative works may—or should—be treated as the same substance as dreams. The same development of symbols applies. Granting this, one can then go to the classic Evans-Wentz translation of the old work on Tibetan yoga, where one is instructed to first give eleven interpretations to a dream, then as skill develops, nineteen interpretations. (Of course this is work, but if such work is not stimulating and exciting to a writer, why bother? It is one of the more profound and satisfying reasons for the craft.)

In this technique one also finds hints of cabalistic "equilibrium" or the need to see all things from all angles (Borges again, The Library of Babel"), shifting the attitude or identification until one day, in theory, one may see all things and all aspects of all things from all angles and attitudes simultaneously.

We may diminish now for these purposes, the importance of such voices in local writing. But there is yet a use. Since some writers might shrink from assigning a ghost an oracular role, perhaps they could subtly weave such figures into bare sentences as simile, metaphor, allusion—never allowing such images to stand on their own (the potency either too weak or too great), but adding radiance to drab exposition—glitter and shadow, fire and ice, etc.

Yet, for all of this, when we reach for spiritual dimension (as if the subject itself were not entirely of spiritual substance), and for the soul's poetic explanations, we must take into account the land itself. The British occult writer Colin Wilson has said that while the American continents are well explored, the occultness of the land, its own spirit, has been barely considered. Even if there were no magical or magnetic "leys", would not the very shape of the mountains themselves evoke subconscious forces and throw format across the imagination? The Southern mountains, brooding, ancient, too warm to be empty (yet desolate enough in mist) have always raised supernatural specters strange to the ordered mind.

If the form is cast across the imagination, then the mind would try to explain those impulses, first in graphic symbols, then converting them to verbal symbols—a metaphoric or parabolic structure, naturally. For writer (and reader), that verbal rendering ought to be ghostly (not horrible), brooding, haunting...the strange cold breath of the land beyond the grave.

The High-Pitched Laugh Of A Sainted Crazy

◆

Reviewed in *The Appalachian Journal* by Dr. Donald Seacrest

In the climax of Lewis W. Green's novel, *The Silence of Snakes,* Earl Skiller lures five deputies into what they think is his hideout—a shack surrounded by a high wall of dry brush. After a brief gun battle, the deputies rush the shack only to find it empty. Prior to disappearing into a tunnel beneath the shack's floor, Earl sets the brush on fire. All the deputies die: some burn to death, some are shot as they try to escape through Earl's tunnel.

Earl had been building his trap for over three years, even before he was sent to prison a third term for making moonshine. What brings the deputies this time, though, is not his illegal whiskey. Earl has chopped off the head of a deputy sheriff, "…dehorned that young deputy Sanger, starting right about at his adam's apple" (p.242), as one town drunk describes it.

The carnage continues, somewhat abated but no less inventive. One deputy gets his throat cut after trying to track Earl in the snow. When the other officers find his body, they find no footprints around it. For a few minutes they are convinced that Earl is a ghost or a demon. Then higher up the mountain slope, they find the bloody spot of ground where Earl killed his man then used a sapling to catapult him down the hill, knowing the deputies would be puzzled by the lack of clues.

Not content to simply hunt Earl, the sheriff tries to set his own trap. Earl, who is as methodical a trapper as he is a moonshiner, makes his way to the very center of the sheriff's trap, cuts a deputy's thigh, and holds a gun on him until he bleeds to death. The dead man sits in full view of the other men the entire day. Earl is long gone.

As an author, Lewis W. Green is a great deal like Earl Skiller. He doesn't build plots so much as he constructs traps. In fact, I wouldn't be surprised to find out that all four of Lewis Green's books are part of some long-term, diabolic, literary trap which will be sprung ten or fifteen years from now. If he isn't building a trap for the entire outlander world, he is at least moving toward some extraordinary vision of what man must become is he is to fathom the mystery of his own existence. Of course, many writers have visions of what man must become, but very few of these writers are as original and forceful as Lewis Green.

As far back as his second book, *And Scatter The Proud*, Green was looking for a way to show how the mountains are able to season a man and prepare him for the dark truths of life. All the important truths are dark even when they seem to come from God, like when the lightning bounces off a tree and kills the young boy's mother in "The Beauty of Embers" section of And Scatter The Proud. People must suffer. That's one of the dark truths that Green reveals in the six novellas that make up And Scatter The Proud.

The land must suffer as well. And time is simply one form that suffering can assume. Obviously the older the land, the more it suffers. Because the Appalachian region is one of the oldest on the planet, the degree of suffering experienced here has grown intense enough to warp or crack the frail crust which is both the product and process of human perception. Civilization works against truth because it tries to convince man that the reality he perceives is stable, constant, immutable. Green writes as though bent on reversing most of the basic assumptions that modern men are raised on.

For example, in *And Scatter The Proud*, seeing should not be believing. In the first two-thirds of this book—"The Trauma" section—eight characters travel to the top of Big Lonesome Mountain. All of them are troubled people, desperate, despicable, and at the most critical moment of their lives, they come face to face with a tall figure dressed in black, leading a dark horse. Behind the dark horse floats a white casket. One of the characters loses her mind, four die, two are redeemed, and one is amazed.

The last third of the book—"The Beauty of Embers" section—is an explanation of what these people have seen. "The Beauty of Embers" is the brief biography of Clemmons Jenkins, the young boy who sees his mother struck down by lightning. What these eight people have seen is Clemmons Jenkins on his way to a special piece of land where he is going to bury his wife. As the quintessential mountain man, he is a vision sent from the mountain to each of these people either to help them or punish them.

The structure of *And Scatter The Proud* is fairly simple. Green creates tension in the first five sections by presenting the sprectral appearance of a dark man and a casket. In each section, the horse provides appropriate sound effects. All action in "The Trauma" is self-contained and resolved with the exception of telling us who the dark man is. That is a loose thread which binds all these sections together. That dark man, it turns out, is the bait for Green's trap, a simple trick which leads us to the second section of the book.

As in all his writing, Green takes chances when he tried to lead us into his trap. In the first section of *And Scatter The Proud*, he is more concerned with outlining spiritual types than with developing real characters. A hasty or unsympathetic critic might accuse Green of using stereotypes. Such a criticism misses the point of "The Trauma". It is there to soften our defenses, lower our expectations, encourage us to believe that the world can be divided neatly into psychological categories. "The Trauma" appears to be a thinly disguised collection of case studies—frustrated and frightened people who have one grim hallucination in common.

The dark man and his white casket become an obsession. Green uses this obsession to focus our attention on the single mystery in all these characters' lives. Just as we are beginning to feel pretty smug, superior to the shallowness of Green's characters, he drops us into "The Beauty of Embers". The caricature disappears. Clemmons Jenkins, the spectre, is absolutely real, probably the best man who ever lived, even though he does spend nine years in prison for beating a man to death.

Essentially, Clemmons draws his strength and purity of spirit from Big Lonesome. Green shows us that people who do not receive their identity from some force larger than themselves will become caricatures. Just how deeply irritated we are by the mysterious figure in "The Trauma" is an indication of how far removed we are from the kind of person Green thinks we should be. Just how much we think part two dissolves that mystery also indicates how far below Green's expectations we fall. Green's trap reveals to us that the explanation of a mystery is often harder to accept than the mystery itself.

If anyone had any doubts about Green's ability to create real people, mountaineer or outlander, all he'd have to do is read Green's third book, *The High-Pitched Laugh of A Painted Lady*, and he'd be forced to admit that Green has earned himself enough suspension of disbelief to get him elected Governor. These eight stories—mixtures of Gothicism, regionalism, and myticism—are as lyrical as Barry Lopez's best pieces and as significantly detailed as any Flannery O'Connor story. His stories are meticulous, traditionally structured, but at the end of each we are left in a place, abandoned: a blindfold has been removed, and now we must find our way back to what used to be familiar.

Such generalities do not do justice to this great collection of stories, but I am on my way to making a point. Lewis Green's books continue to get better. His vision grows more penetrating. In *The Silence of Snakes*, Green constructs an eerie metaphysics and succeeds in keeping it within a wonderfully dramatic framework. All of the mental energy found in his first three books merges in *The Silence of Snakes*. On the surface it is still a book about the mountains and people of Western North Carolina, but the novel pushes us far beyond the realm of any familiar region either on earth or in heaven.

I think Lewis W. Green must be practicing to become a prophet. This is why I suspect him of building some huge trap in his writing. His landscape, his characters, his action all work perfectly on a fictional level, but this latest novel is also a story deeply concerned with spirituality. In this sense, the literary elements work as lures which draw us into a dark and violent dimension.

In the Silence of Snakes Green distorts the bucolic. The mountains are the ally of a dangerous man like Earl Skiller. They are a place to hide—old and secret. The villages of Hollytown and Wadenton are dominated by a few factories and a tannery. Even the collection of saloons, called the Western Front, which make up a no-man's land between the two villages, offers little in the way of recreation except drunkenness and fighting. About the only reason that families stay together is because blood ties offer a weak defense against the crushing pressure of the landscape. Yet Green makes misery so compelling that the pain itself becomes an inducement to keep reading.

Nothing is as it should be in this novel. It begins with the birth of Logan Guffey, March 21, 1932 (the same day and month when Earl Skiller was born years earlier). As the novel progresses, Logan grows closer and closer to Earl. Earl and his mother Clementine are present when Logan is born. Clementine, a witch, has come to read the signs accompanying Logan's birth. Because a wild thunderstorm breaks just as Logan is delivered, Clementine has plenty of signs to read. She runs out into the storm when the thunder first begins. The rest of the visitors are terrified by her behavior, but she returns soon enough, certain that she has been given signs which will help her predict the child's future:...

> **I went into the storm to see if I'd live or die at this young'un's birth, and as ye can see, I live. The storm wuz all around me, and out of h'it I heard a child with a loud scream. The storm brought it, you see, and h'it howled back at the storm like the storm was h'its mama and she wuz a-aleavin' h'it stranded here. (P 17)**

During this scene, Earl Skiller is little more than an observer. At first, it is easy to discount him as nothing more than an extra, someone who helps round out Mrs. Skiller's fictional reality.

But Earl is transparent because he wants to be. Many chapters later, we learn that Earl is a master of camouflage. When Earl makes his second appearance in chapter four, he is traveling to his still at night. He notices "…there were troublesome promises about the moon and its dimension" (P. 53) He stops to rest for a moment, to think about those troublesome promises, but he never stops being cautious, easy enough to understand. He is after all, a convicted moonshiner, and it is quite possible that he is being watched. But Green forces another opinion on us:

> **Earl walked among people seeing and was thought blind. With seeing came revelations, surprises, disappointments. Yet he made no labels in his brain, used no words in his hidden heart. There was a creature in him that moved in all directions, and it watched, watched, watched—a free and wild spirit, fearful of its own destruction, yet aware of its own permanence, watching, waiting, watching, waiting. For destiny. (P 59)**

Green further burdens him with an obsession: "The thought of graves flitted often through Earl's mind" (p 61). Plenty of literary characters have been obsessed with death, but Earl's obsession is more than a fixation. It isn't simply part of his personality. It is the very substance out of which his personality is constructed.

During World War I, Earl distinguished himself as a guerrilla fighter. He was called the Silent Sergeant because he was able, time and time again, to slip behind the German lines and create chaos. Most people who knew of Earl's heroics misunderstood his motive. They had Earl associate the Germans with rattlesnakes, and they mistakenly assumed that Earl regarded the enemy as snakes. As it turns out, Earl was really saying that he was able to kill the way he did because he himself could become a snake.

One important key to Earl Skiller's existence—which is the basis of the whole book—lies in chapter twenty-seven. In several earlier chapters, Green has mentioned Earl's dominant memory of WW1. The fullest description of the memory occurs in chapter eighteen:

—Back in France, he had lost his gas mask. The enemy had spread clouds of poison gas, and it came across the field and wood toward him. In it he sensed something inexorable, a destiny he had somehow missed. He seemed to be above it then realized it was his destiny and descended to it. He headed

into the gas and took it, and smiled, and nodded his head, and no longer wondered. (p.226)

Why do we keep getting references to Earl's experience with that poison gas. He was another Sergeant York. We'd expect him to remember sneaking behind enemy lines and stealthily killing Germans. Then in chapter twenty-seven, as we watch Earl die in the gas chamber, we realize that Green has been preparing us for this execution. Just as Earl is about to die from cyanide gas, he slips into a final memory:

> **Then the fields of France, and him alone facing the angels of death, and suddenly he saw truth—a cloud of luminous gas arising from the German lines. He went to it rather than letting it come to him. without a gas mask he entered it breathing deeply and then floated above it, realizing with a happy, numb jerk to his lips that he had died in early 1918, and that everything he had experienced after that was merely a death dream. (p. 332)**

The Silence of Snakes, then, is a sort of ghost story. Earl Skiller is not so much a man as he is a spirit. One reason the landscape is so foreboding is because we see much of it through the eyes of this spirit, as part of the death dream. Green is arguing that the spiritual landscape is every bit as real as the physical landscape, especially in the Appalachian mountains.

Other ghosts also appear in *The Silence of Snakes.* For example, when Logan Guffey is dying from worms, he is visited by the ghost of a woman who died in his house:

> **Logan roused and saw an ancient woman sitting beside him.**
> **She spoke and he strained to hear.**
> **"I'm here to see about you," she said, or seemed to say. He stared.**
> **"Do you want to go with me?" she asked.**
> **His small face pouted. He was too tired to be frightened.**
> **Then he realized that she was not so old, and he not so young.**
> **"Don't be afraid to go," she said. "It is not a strange place. It is as familiar as the old homeplace. You will hardly notice you've gone. We come and go there all through time."**
> **Her face was weary yet alive with currents of tidal energy, sometimes coming, sometimes flowing off.**
> **"Are you hurting?" Logan asked.**
> **"No, I left my pain in this very room. You can see it if you will."**
> **He looked, almost saw something, saw nothing at all. He heard the steps of his aunts in the hall, heard his father snoring and his mother moaning**

**in their room across the hallway. He saw that he and some old woman
had been riding on a sea of light. She rose from beside him with an easy
movement.
"You can come with me," she said. "Do you want to come now?
Sooner or later..." (p. 176)**

This incident stands out as a clear signal that reality in this novel actually takes
its existence from a spiritual rather than a physical source. Green is very careful to
show us that Logan is awake. He can hear the noises of his family coming from
other parts of the house. They are part of his perception, not part of an hallucination.

Perhaps the most difficult aspect of Green's reality is his insistence that we
must accept events rather than explanations for events. For most educated people, an event is usually less important than what it means. Psychology has limited
the number of realities and blinded us us to life's richer dimensions. Every super-
stition, every spell, every conjuration represents a world, but psychology has
taught us that all those different worlds are invalid, insubstantial, inconsequential. *The Silence of Snakes* demolishes the arrogance of rationality and establishes
the ascendancy of spirituality over materialism. As Green makes clear in his other
books, spirit is all that can survive suffering. Spirit is what defines the world. At
best, psychology is a minor cult with a very shabby doctrine.

Although Green forces us to wait until chapter twenty-seven before he tells us
the full truth about Earl Skiller and the nature of the reality surrounding Earl, he
uses visions, dreams and hallucinations to flavor the action of his novel. One of
the times that Earl mentions his dream of dying in France he also mentions his
mother's death.

**"Yes, I dreamed I was breathing poison gas in, and I had to face it to beat
it, and I knew than that I had death to dream about. I saw my mama
there on the wall, and she was froze to death at Wild Cat, and that nearly
killed me because I know she could have been saved with just a little heat
out of a little fire..." (p. 296)**

In the last chapter, we find out that Mrs. Skiller does freeze to death sitting in
front of her fireplace. In this story the only difference between dream reality and
physical reality is time. But Green also wants to show us that the reality in which
most of us are trapped is only one swerve in a serpentine undulation of events.
What happens in physical reality might sometimes be an extension of a more

spiritual movement. Shortly after Earl talks of dreaming about his mother's death, he tells about being visited by the deputies he would kill a few years later:

> "Sometimes I used to think I could get in other people's minds, but I found out it was the other way around. They get in my mind. Then I saw that young Deputy Sanger was going to use me to kill hisself with. That boy really wanted to die, and he told me just how to do it. Then there was the others. They took a gamble and come to see what I was like and they come to my mind and told me how they wanted to go." (p.297)

One startling implication made in this confession and throughout the novel is that we are all simply the continuation of one spirit. This is a spirit of place rather than person. Such a spirit does not enter us—we enter it as we would a shadow or a patch of fog or a cloud of poison gas. In this sense of the word, spirit is synonymous with landscape. Time and suffering have shaped the spirit of Wild Cat settlement, and that spirit is named Earl Skiller.

In this novel, the main purpose of a spirit is to shock and trouble the physical world. In its mildest moments, spirit forces us to break old habits of seeing and thinking. In its fiercest moments, spirit destroys us. Earl Skiller is the central spirit of *The Silence of Snakes,* just as Clemmons Jenkins is the central spirit of *And Scatter The Proud.* All action radiates from these two men—one a spirit mistaken for a man, the other a man mistaken for a spirit. Neither man, however, intentionally begins the disruptive movement. Jenkins is forced to action by his wife's death. Earl, a more complex creation, is motivated by his wife's death and more significantly, by his baby's death.

> "Late one evening she was cooking and holding our baby boy. She took him to his crib so she could set the table. It was dark in that room. She heard the baby crying and went back in there. She had set him in the crib on top of a big rattlesnake, and it bit him in the face and neck." (p. 297)

The outer boundary for the novel is the boy Logan. In the physical world, he was Earl's student, learning about the mountains and the woods. On the spiritual plane, Logan is an extension of Earl's son and of Earl himself. In Logan's short life, he witnessed the beheading of Deputy Sanger, discovered the corpse of Clementine Skiller, talked to Earl's dead wife, and dreamed of Earl's death and transformation. Logan is already being purified by suffering. He is on his way to becoming the new spirit of the mountains. He is able to see

"…the fusion of time with light, both fading into death" (p.341)

Green uses the same simple structure in *The Silence of Snakes* that he uses in *And Scatter The Proud.* He presents a series of events, leading us to believe that we are watching the development for the cause of some climactic action, but in both novels our expectations are reversed. What we have assumed to be causes are merely effects. Green moves us backward but convinces us it's all forward motion.

In *And Scatter The Proud,* we are delighted to find out that the ghost which haunts the mountain is really a man but in *The Silence of Snakes,* we are astonished to discover that a man has been a ghost. Green's trap closes more dramatically in this novel—it has sharper teeth and a stronger spring. Green's phantoms are creatures of pure suffering and pure vision, their reality, silence and time—the blood and bone of the mountains.

Fred Chappell, Novelist and Poet Laureate of North Carolina, Here reviews Green's Collection of Short Stories, The High Pitched Laugh of A Painted Lady

It ain't the sound of the "high-pitched laugh of a painted lady" that first strikes the reader in Lewis W. Green's collection of stories given that title. Rather it is the sound of strong voices, voices of courageous, enduring humanity that sounds through these pages, voices directed throughout by the sure, forceful voice of the author. Behind the author's voice and enriching his eight stories are the voices of the tradition in which he works—T.B. Thorpe, Mark Twain, John Fox Jr., Anderson, Hemingway, Faulkner—and over those once cacophonous, now harmonious voices, the reader hears a bit of the dissonance of a Tom Wolfe. The result of the mixture is a book that is pleasing and haunting, worth several readings.

All of the eight stories set in Green's "little postage stamp" of North Carolina are populated with mountain people who, through Green's handling, become heroes as they struggle to achieve a communion of sorts while deciphering time and facing death. For the most part, the characters are not handsome as one might wish heroes to be: Balky Guffin in "Chaingang Preacher" finds communion with the twisted, cowed Woodrow in a prison camp; in the title story Trapline in his final understanding of time translates the shrill laughter of a whore into the siren call of life; Lon and Landon, two hardy old backwoodsmen, mountain men in "The Burial of Big Blue", find communion over Big Blue's grave—and a bottle of Landon's brandy; the Cherokee Sam Welch (Sam Welch Is Not The Name of A Whit e Man) communes with time and through that communion understands nature and wins respect even as he murders; and Shelton, the legendary old man of Big Laurel Cove in "The Breakaways", achieves communion with his kidnappers, controlling them by strength of his indomitable will.

The fourth story, "The Moonbather", the only story peopled with handsome people, is a lyric love story of Sore Paws and Slow Tracker as they endure time and face death. Although it pictures the ugliness of disease and the harshness of nature, "The Moon Bather" is the most romanticized of the stories.

In "Larse's Place", the "hero" never really appears; the struggle occurs between a reprobate shopkeeper and three cocky Indian youths. While the story is well told and funny, it lacks the appeal to the "old verities" that the first six stories have. The same is true of the last story, "The Blue Glint of A Queen's Last Jewel"; the main characters, Parker and the Counselor, are artificial people out of tune with nature, and as such, become artificial characters.

Even with disappointment with the trickery of plot in the last two stories does not diminish the reader's involvement with the courage of humanity in the collection as a whole. Green is a storyteller, one who respects his characters, who knows the cadence of ordinary or ceremonial speech, and who knows that laughter is one of the forces that keeps humanity sane in the struggle with isolation, time and death.

Unsigned review

The Silence of Snakes is a jewel of a novel by an author previously unknown to me. That Green's sprawling novel is better than McCarthy's is about the best you can say of it.. His story wanders all over the western North Carolina Mountains for a hundred pages or more in search of its own center, but the material is inherently interesting and the characters are well drawn. The novel is one more document to add to the evidence in a case that I thought was closed: the destruction of community and tradition by the encroachment of the modern world.

The main character of *The Silence of Snakes*, and one of the most splendid creations I have encountered in a long time, is Earl Skiller, but you will have to read a while to find this out. First there are the Guffeys, an extended family of mountain people, and Paul Fortune, a drunk journalist from the North who has decided to stop off in the town of Wadenton for no better reasons than loneliness and despair. There are the local doctor and the sheriff, several tramps, and people who work in the tannery. There are the mountains and the golf club, where rich people from Florida play in the summer, and the Western Front, a collection of bars and flophouses, where almost all of the characters sooner or later and with more or less frequency come to drink and perhaps spend a dollar or two on the whores.

The Skiller brothers—how many there are is not made clear in the novel—show up here sometimes for pleasure, sometimes to sell the whisky that Earl runs. Earl is no ordinary moonshiner. He is the Shakespeare, the Rembrandt, of his trade, an artist who works for the love of his art. He knows how to build a still and how to hide it, how to sprout the grain—except on rare occasions he eschews the use of sugar, how to tend the fires to get a constant and exact heat,and how to be cautious. More than any farmer or woodsman Earl knows the ways of nature: his concern is not only with weather and land and cultivated plants but with the all the wilderness as well. He is an accomplished hunter and trapper, a connoisseur of herb and grass and weed, and scholar who knows the properties of trees. Killer of snakes in one mode of his existence, he can sit in the midst of them when they come out warm themselves on rocks, and pick them up, not in religious fervor but in the calm patience which he has learned from nature.

He can move or he can wait for as long as waiting is necessary because he is at one with himself and with creation.

Earl sells only enough whiskey to support his family, but the federal authorities think a little is too much and from time to time he is caught. During his last term in the penitentiary he has fearful dreams that he cannot fathom and begins to feel alienated from himself. After Earl's release, a deputy sheriff, his vanity flattered by cagy federal agents,

2/unsigned review

devotes his professional life to catching Earl again. The close scrutiny of Earl by the deputy is a violation of the rules by which the community lives. The sheriff knows that Earl makes whiskey just as he knows that loose women work their beats on the Western Front. But as long as this catering to illicit appetites is pursued with restraint and prudence, the sheriff is willing to look the other way. When Earl decides he has suffered harassment enough, he cuts off the deputy's head with an ax. This scene, though not as vividly portrayed as the decapitation in Blood Meridian, is vivid enough, and it marks the beginning of a splendid sequence in which Earl, using his skill as a mountaineer keeps the rest of the world at bay.

There are plenty of moonshiners in southern fiction and plenty of alienated characters who take to the woods to engage in an uneven struggle with the forces of civilization, but I know of none so fully realized as Earl. One of the problems a novelist faces in making a hero of an outlaw is that of finding the proper empathetic pitch. How does the writer induce his readers to have sympathy for a murderer without resorting to the sort of Jesse James romanticism that renders the narrative false? Through the early parts of the novel Green develops Earl Skiller as a man of courage and a particular kind of honor. During the first war he was a sniper of such competence that he devised his own plans and carried out his own program, working frequently behind enemy lines. As a runner of whiskey he went armed and ready to kill anyone who attempted to highjack or cheat him, but he gave his brothers strict orders not to shoot at officers of the law. Having lost his infant son and wife before the book opens, he becomes a kind of godfather to young Logan Guffey, to whom he imports his knowledge of nature, and when he learns that Logan has seen him kill the deputy, he turns himself in.

But there is even more to Earl than this. The visions that obsess and torment Earl are dimly perceived in this world, but they are to be understood in the next. His sense of right and wrong, of honor and duty and manhood, is validated by his increasing comprehension of what the events in his life have signified and finally by the mystical vision with which the author endows him at his death. Earl

Skiller is a major creation: the power of his personality, his life as a fictional being, brings order to what is otherwise a disorderly book. And though we can see the impending end of the mountain community in the foundering of marriages and the removal of Walton and Loretta Guffey to Boston, the sacrifice of Earl's life gives the community a reprieve.

After his execution everyone meets the train on which Earl's body comes home: the Skillers, of course; the sheriff; the doctor; the drunk, Paul Fortune (the reporter); and the girls from the Western Front. The storekeeper offers his truck to take the casket to the country cemetery, and Mrs. Skiller rides in the doctor's car. The example of Earl, who was brave and enduring, who lived by his own code and met his own responsibilities and died with fortitude, seems to enhance the humanity of all who knew him. All those who go to watch his last arrival somehow feel better about themselves and more charitable toward one another. They have seen an extraordinary man plumb the depths of his own evil and rise to the limits of his own good. They see themselves in him and see their own possibilities for redemption in his end.

You will have noticed that *The Silence of Snakes* was published by John F. Blair in Winston-Salem. I know nothing about where this novel might have been submitted. Blair may have been Green's publisher of choice, but I doubt it, and this fine book is probably one more bit of evidence that shows the disarray of the publishing business in New York. It is a shame that The Silence of Snakes has not had wider distribution but perhaps if a bigger house had done it, an editor there might have worked the life out of the book before it saw the light of day. In any event, *The Silence of Snakes* should make all who cherish literature thankful for publishers such as Blair, for programs in fiction such as the one Leslie Phillabaum and Martha Hall run at the LSU Press, and for new companies such as Algonquin Books of Chapel Hill, which Louis Rubin founded for the main purpose of publishing good fiction. Remember these and similar workers in the vineyard in your prayers.

A Country Rag Rural Review

❖

Straying from the Path

LEWIS W. GREEN AND THE WAYWARD GATE

The excommunication by a local parish
of this Smoky Mountain poet, novelist
and journalist has stirred debate and
controversy over issues of personal
and public behavior.

Review by Gary Carden

Gary Carden is a dramatist, author, lecturer and storyteller living and traveling
from Sylva, N.C. and a journalist for regional publications.

After reading "Excommunication…American Style", a somewhat breathless
and eager account of Lewis Green's latest controversy in a recent Jackson Tribune, I remembered a line from Hamlet, "Lord, we know what we are but know
not what we may be." The line is spoken by poor deranged Ophelia, and while
there is no resemblance between Asheville's literary curmudgeon and Hamlet's
girlfriend, the quote seems apt.

Some thirty years ago I discovered Lewis' novel, **And Scatter The Proud.**
Then came other works, including **The Silence of Snakes,** and like many others
in this region I suspected that a major Appalachian writer was on his way. However, in conjunction with a series of novels and short stories that depicted mountain culture with authenticity, Lewis became embroiled in controversy. Lewis
denounced political corruption, chicanery and incompetence throughout the
region. Allthough there are those who would disagree, I think that most would
concede that initially, Lewis spoke out with courage and honesty. He also did so

to his own detriment. Little by little, the literary Lewis Green gave way to the uncompromising journalist. Some of the articles in Lewis' newspaper *The Native Stone* were memorable for their in-depth research and objecdtivity.

But there is an old edict about literary figures that espouse social and political causes: their art seems t. to invariably suffer. I don't think that the actual quality of Lewis' literary writing changed, but the public reaction did. More and more, people associated Lewis with abrasive journalism, name-calling and denunciation. He made enemies. Several years ago, when an institution in the region attempted to get a bit of promotion regarding a program honoring his accomplishments as an Appalachian writer, many (in the media) were reluctant to cooperate. They still remembered altercations, rudeness and insults.

There is little doubt that Lewis enjoys his reputation for brashness and occasional violence. Some of his confrontations have ended in court, and with each new incident, the legend has grown. There was the famous carnival brawl in Hazelwood; then the columnist from The Asheville Citizen who was attacked by the short-tempered crusader, etc. I once entered a Raleigh bookstore to acquire a signed copy of The High-Pitched Laugh of A Painted Lady, only to find the owner with a swollen eye, and a stack of signed books but no "guest author". The owner told me he had a disagreement with Lewis about air pollution. In recent years, the voice has become more strident and the barbs more poisonous.

Excommunication. The word is fraught with significance. However, the issue here may be: has the action taken by the Dean of All Souls church branded Lewis a pariah? Or is this episode a form of apotheosis, the crowning achievement for a man who seems to delight in provoking the ire of "the establishment"? Has the imp of the perverse gone too far at last?

By coincidence I have been doing research on another outspoken (and gifted) writer/journalist, William Dudley Pelley. Beginning as a script writer in Hollywood in the 20s Pelley wrote award-winning scripts for Lon Chaney, published hundreds of magazine articles, won prestigious awards for short stories, Broadway plays and in-depth reportage. When Pelley moved to Asheville and established his own publishing company in the 30s, his life s eemed predestined for success. Then he began to publish articles that were anti-Semitic, and words like "the Jewish conspiracy" began to appear in his publications. When other writers expressed dismay, Pelley became more strident and beg an to talk openly about his admiration for Hitler, the concept of the supremacy of the Aryan race and the need to purge America of "certain racial types." Finally, he established the Silver Shirts, an organization that openly endorsed "extreme measures" in removing

"racial cancers" that threatened to destroy the economic and spiritual institutions in this country.

In a sense, Pelly too was excommunicated. Branded "un-American," he was charged with sedition, his publications confiscated and his printing company closed. His constant baiting of President Roosevelt, and his charges against the government in regard to Pearl Harbor and its aftermath brought him before t he Un-American Activities Committee. Sentenced to prison, Pelley became a shameful memory in Asheville…and yet, before he lost his way, before he wandered down the dark path of the hatemonger and muckraker, he was a man of infinite promise…a man that friends and other writers remembered as a brilliant stylist. His books are out of print and the novels forgotten. Pelley has been reduced to a footnote in history books that deal with pro-Nazi sentiment in pre-WWII America.

Certainly Lewis Green is not anti-Semitic, nor is he likely to be deemed a threat to national security. No, Lewis merely believes that homosexuals and lesbians should not be allowed to attend his church. Lewis "worries" about AIDS and the communion service, and the possible corruption of Christian youth through association. He hints at dark and devious doings on church property—activities that would hopelessly compromise the church's spiritual purity. Certainly, any comparison between Pelley, the anti-Semitic, and Lewis Green, the homophobe and lesbian-baiter is spurious…Well, isn't it?

Lewis could recant but he probably won't. He could say, "Hey, I'm an old newspaperman with the tenacity of a bulldog, and I just got carried away." He could say "Mea culpa", apologize and be welcomed back into All Saints (All Souls). But I can't imagine it. I can't see a contrite Lewis Green, a man admitting a mistake.

I'll still read passages from **_The Silence of Snakes_** to my classes, and recommend his books to anyone who wants to read works that treat the mountains with authenticity and integrity. But there is a duality in this man. Like Forest Carter, the man who wrote The Education of Little Tree and also wrote racial speeches for George Wallace, Lewis Green is at odds with himself. Perhaps he is merely a "conduit"—something that spirits can speak through. Sometimes angels speak, sometimes, a perverse imp.

(Here Carden adds a quote from *The Song of Samuel*, a chapter in *And Scatter The Proud*, perhaps to make some point.)

"To each man a song, born into his blood and vision—the working force, the fire of spirit. To each his gift, the song that he is committed to sing in his time on earth. Yet a man must hear it forming and feel the composition of it

along the strings of his soul. In the quiet and secret places of his heart the music waits. Voices he does not know sing it to him when he does not watch, and those bells that rang in other lands, in other times, ring yet to reach each soul.

"But he must take along his soul into the riven, quarrelsome streets and into the furious arenas where he meets with life. And there is no place to hide.

"And music, so gossamer and tender, born of innocence and frail substance, is thrust into the forge and laid upon the anvil and struck there with hammers and beaten upon from diverse directions.

"If he cannot protect his song and slip away from the destruction of his soul, if he cannot hide from the clamor and the weight and the heat, then he is lost.

"If the calloused hand of circumstance reaches inside him and scrambles the notes, scattering them to the lost reaches of his soul as the planets are flung through the heavens, then he is doomed and lost.

"And if the searing finger of despair reaches in to cauterize, to seal up his soul, and the cold wash of fear descends upon him and his metal has no temper, then he will not live.

"For of what use is life if a man cannot find the lost knowledge of himself, or put together again a song that has been broken and scattered, or restore his soul."

A note of correction on Carden's "facts", of which many are needed but only these few will suffice.

Not only do I not deny a hell-raising past, but mostly I gleefully admit most of it. However, the incident at the Raleigh booksigning was this: I arrived early. A young hippie clerk was alone there—he was not the store owner. An old friend worked at the News & Observer so I borrowed the phone to call him. While I waited on the call to go through, the clerk asked where I parked, then said I would get a ticket there. I shrugged. He asked what I did when I got a ticket in Asheville. I told him I generally got it fixed. That incensed him so he jerked the phone out of my hand. I then decked him. After I finished the call, the callow young man then called the store owner, a Raleigh attorney, and told him what had happened, then handed the phone to me. The first thing the owner did was apologize to me and stated he had had similar incidents out of this young man and good help was hard to find.

As far as I know, while I did participate in many brawls in earlier days, there were no carnivals in Hazelwood. These examples are to show how creative small town journalists can get as they try to add shit to the legend. His sympathy for the homosexual agenda reveals itself. He may be one himself. He hints that I may become another Pelley, and calls me a homophobe and lesbian-baiter. Wrong. While I do not fear homosexuals or homosexuality, I do detest most of them because they mostly engage in this very example of spurious criticism of someone who don't take their side.

The Professional Background of Editor-publisher Lewis W. Green

He is a novelist, author, award winning reporter, editor and teacher whose career spans more than four decades.

A native of Haywood County, he began his career in journalism in 1961 as a staff writer for The Asheville Citizen-Times. During his ten years there he won five feature exchange press awards from the Associated Press, including two first place awards.

The first award came for a personality profile on Mamie Spears Raynolds, who lived then in Biltmore Forest. She was a daughter of the late U.S. Senator Bob Reynolds and the late Evelyn Walsh McLean, heiress to a silver fortune and the Hope Diamond.

Another first place AP award came as a result of interviews with people who had personally known the author, Thomas Wolfe. Both those stories, and others by Green, were used by researchers at colleges and universities in several states.

There were three other lesser Associated Press awards before Green resigned from the daily and founded a weekly newspaper in 1971 entitled The Native Stone. Under his editorship that publication won three awards from the N.C.

Press Association, including one for an investigative series on the devious fina-
gling on the local city political machine on a controversial third referendum on
Asheville's Civic Center.

The North Carolina Press Association also awarded Green for a series on the
Asheville Area Chamber of Commerce's receipt of tax funds from city and county
governments without accounting for the disbursements. As a result, State Senate
committee hearing were held here, which resulted in a law requiring that the
Chamber account for those funds.

Green has also served as a correspondent for United Press International, The
Charlotte Observer and other North and South Carolina newspapers.

He founded a monthly political journal, Overtones, and operated that in
Asheville for three years. In 1985 he founded The Independent Torch (A Journal
For The Outraged and The Outrageous) and operated it for 16 years.

He taught the first courses ever in journalism, creative writing and an independent studies course in wilderness survival at Warren Wilson College in 1977;
served as faculty adjunct in the Political Science department at The University of
North Carolina at Asheville; and taught creative writing at Haywood Technical
College; taught a course entitled "A Jungian Approach to Creative Writing" at
the prestigious Intentional Growth Center at Lake Junaluska; a course in novel
writing and also a course in the Kabbalah at Montreat-Anderson College at Mon-
treat.

He is the author of four novels and one collection of short stories, a book of
poetry entitled *Voices From The Native Stone,* and an Oriental fable with woodcuts entitled *The Year of The Swan.* Two of the novels are set in the mountains of
Western North Carolina, *And Scatter The Proud* (1969), which was called "The
best novel in a decade by The Seattle Times and received high praise from the late
Dr. Carlos Baker of Princeton University, the preeminent Hemingway biogra-
pher) and The *Silence of Snakes* (1984) as is the collection of short stories, *The
High-Pitched Laugh of A Painted Lady,* (1980). All those were published by John
F. Blair. A novel on the Korean War, *Spirit Bells,* was published in 1995 by
Indian Rock Publishers, which also published a metaphysical novel *The Kabbalah
Pillars* in 2002, and the book of poetry.

The Oriental fable was published in 1966 with woodcuts by Professor Eugene
Bunker, head of the art department at Asheville Biltmore College (which later
became UNC-A).

In 1961 Green was editor of Bluets, A-B College's literary magazine, and
under his editorship Bluets became the only small college literary magazine to
win All-Columbian Honors from Columbia University.

Green has also published poetry, short-stories, articles and scholarly reviews in other magazines and university journals. One of his short stories, *Sam Welch Is Not The Name of A White Man,* was included in and exclusive research library anthology of American Indian stories at the University of New Mexico.

He has been a guest lecturer at The University of Virginia, The University of Miami and Western Carolina University.

He is a 1950 veteran of the Korean War, where he received five battle stars, and is a member of The VFW, The American Legion, and The Chosin Few. He was the first chairman of the scholarship committee of the North Caroliina Outward Bound School at Table Rock in Linville Gorge. He is a member of The Civitan Club. He is a Master Mason and a 32d degree Mason in Scottish Rite Masonry.

0-595-30544-X